AN
ANONYMOUS
GIRL

Greer Hendricks spent over two decades as an editor.
Prior to her tenure in book publishing, she worked at
Allure Magazine and earned her Masters in Journalism from
Columbia University. Her writing has been published in the
New York Times and *Publishers Weekly*. Greer lives in Manhattan
with her husband, two children and very needy dog, Rocky.
The Wife Between Us is her first novel.

Sarah Pekkanen is the internationally and *USA Today*
bestselling author of several novels including *Skipping a Beat*.
A former investigative journalist and feature writer, her work
has been published in *The Washington Post*, *USA Today* and
many others. She is the mother of three sons and lives
just outside Washington, D.C.

By Greer Hendricks and Sarah Pekkanen

The Wife Between Us
An Anonymous Girl

AN
ANONYMOUS
GIRL

GREER HENDRICKS

AND

SARAH PEKKANEN

MACMILLAN

First published in the United States 2019 by St. Martin's Press, New York

First published in the UK 2019 by Macmillan
an imprint of Pan Macmillan
20 New Wharf Road, London N1 9RR
Associated companies throughout the world
www.panmacmillan.com

ISBN 978-1-5290-1072-5

1 3 5 7 9 8 6 4 2

A CIP catalogue record for this book is available from the British Library.

Printed and bound by CPI Group (UK) Ltd, Croydon, CR0 4YY

Visit **www.panmacmillan.com** to read more about all our books
and to buy them. You will also find features, author interviews and
news of any author events, and you can sign up for e-newsletters
so that you're always first to hear about our new releases.

From Greer:
For my parents, Elaine and Mark Kessel

From Sarah:
For Roger

PART
ONE

You're Invited: Seeking women aged 18 to 32 to participate in a study on ethics and morality conducted by a preeminent NYC psychiatrist. Generous compensation. Anonymity guaranteed. Call for more details.

It's easy to judge other people's choices. The mother with a grocery cart full of Froot Loops and Double Stuf Oreos who yells at her child. The driver of an expensive convertible who cuts off a slower vehicle. The woman in the quiet coffee shop who yaks on her cell phone. The husband who cheats on his wife.

But what if you knew the mother had lost her job that day?

What if the driver had promised his son he'd make it to his school play, but his boss had insisted he attend a last-minute meeting?

What if the woman in the coffee shop had just received a phone call from the love of her life, a man who'd broken her heart?

And what if the cheater's wife habitually turned her back on his touch?

Perhaps you would also make a snap judgment about a woman who decides to reveal her innermost secrets to a stranger for money. But suspend your assumptions, at least for now.

We all have reasons for our actions. Even if we hide the reason from those who think they know us best. Even if the reasons are so deeply buried we can't recognize them ourselves.

CHAPTER
ONE

Friday, November 16

A LOT OF WOMEN want the world to see them a certain way. It's my job to create those transformations, one forty-five-minute session at a time.

My clients seem different when I've finished helping them. They grow more confident, radiant. Happier, even.

But I can only offer a temporary fix. People invariably revert to their former selves.

True change requires more than the tools I wield.

It's twenty to six on a Friday evening. Rush hour. It's also when someone often wants to look like the best version of themselves, so I consistently block this time out of my personal schedule.

When the subway doors open at Astor Place, I'm the first one out, my right arm aching from the weight of my black makeup case as it always does by the end of a long day.

I swing my case directly behind me so it'll fit through the narrow passageway—it's my fifth trip through the turnstiles today alone, and my routine is automatic—then I hurry up the stairs.

When I reach the street, I dig into the pocket of my leather jacket and pull out my phone. I tap it to open my schedule, which is continually updated by BeautyBuzz. I provide the hours I can work, and my appointments are texted to me.

My final booking today is near Eighth Street and University Place. It's for two clients, which means it's a double—ninety minutes. I have the address, names, and a contact phone number. But I have no idea who will be waiting for me when I knock on a door.

I don't fear strangers, though. I've learned more harm can come from familiar faces.

I memorize the exact location, then stride down the street, skirting the garbage that has spilled from a toppled bin. A shopkeeper pulls a security-grate over his storefront, the loud metal rattling into place. A trio of college students, backpacks slung over their shoulders, jostle one another playfully as I pass them.

I'm two blocks from my destination when my phone rings. Caller ID shows it's my mom.

I let it ring once as I stare at the little circular photo of my smiling mother.

I'll see her in five days, when I go home for Thanksgiving, I tell myself.

But I can't let it go.

Guilt is always the heaviest thing I carry.

"Hey, Mom. Everything okay?" I ask.

"Everything's fine, honey. Just checking in."

I can picture her in the kitchen in the suburban Philadelphia home where I grew up. She's stirring gravy on the stove—they eat early, and Friday's menu is always pot roast and mashed potatoes—then unscrewing the top on a bottle of Zinfandel in preparation for the single glass she indulges in on weekend nights.

There are yellow curtains dressing the small window above the sink, and a dish towel looped through the stove handle with the words *Just roll with it* superimposed over an image of a rolling pin. The flowered wallpaper is peeling at the seams and a dent marks the bottom of the fridge from where my father kicked it after the Eagles lost in the playoffs.

Dinner will be ready when my dad walks through the door from his job as an insurance salesman. My mother will greet him with a quick kiss. They will call my sister, Becky, to the table, and help her cut her meat.

"Becky zipped up her jacket this morning," my mother says. "Without any help."

Becky is twenty-two, six years younger than me.

"That's fantastic," I say.

Sometimes I wish I lived closer so I could help my parents. Other times, I'm ashamed at how grateful I am that I don't.

"Hey, can I call you back?" I continue. "I'm just running in to work."

"Oh, did you get hired for another show?"

I hesitate. Mom's voice is more animated now.

I can't tell her the truth, so I blurt out the words: "Yeah, it's just a little production. There probably won't even be much press about it. But the makeup is super elaborate, really unconventional."

"I'm really proud of you," my mom says. "I can't wait to hear all about it next week."

I feel like she wants to add something more, but even though I haven't quite reached my destination—a student housing complex at NYU—I end the call.

"Give Becky a kiss. I love you."

My rules for any job kick in even before I arrive.

I evaluate my clients the moment I see them—I notice eyebrows that would look better darkened, or a nose that needs shading to appear slimmer—but I know my customers are sizing me up, too.

The first rule: my unofficial uniform. I wear all black, which eliminates the need to coordinate a new outfit every morning. It also sends a message of subtle authority. I choose comfortable, machine-washable layers that will look as fresh at seven P.M. as they do at seven A.M.

Since personal space vanishes when you're doing someone's makeup, my nails are short and buffed, my breath is minty, and my curls are swept up in a low twist. I never deviate from this standard.

I rub Germ-X on my hands and pop an Altoid in my mouth before I ring the buzzer for Apartment 6D. I'm five minutes early. Another rule.

I take the elevator to the sixth floor, then follow the sound of loud music—Katy Perry's "Roar"—down the hallway and meet my clients. One is in a bathrobe, and the other wears a T-shirt and boxers. I can smell the evidence of their last beauty treatment—the chemicals used to highlight blond streaks into the hair of the girl named Mandy, and the nail varnish drying on the hands Taylor is waving through the air.

"Where are you going tonight?" I ask. A party will likely have stronger lighting than a club; a dinner date will require a subtle touch.

"Lit," Taylor says.

At my blank look, she adds: "It's in the Meatpacking District. Drake was just there last night."

"Cool," I say.

I wind through the items scattered across the floor—an umbrella, a crumpled gray sweater, a backpack—then move aside the SkinnyPop popcorn and half-empty cans of Red Bull on the low coffee table so I can set down my case. I unlatch it and the sides fold out like an accordion to reveal tray upon tray of makeup and brushes.

"What kind of look are we going for?"

Some makeup artists dive in, trying to cram as many clients as possible into a day. I take the extra time I've built into my schedule to ask a few questions. Just because one woman wants a smokey eye and a naked mouth doesn't mean another isn't envisioning a bold red lip and only a swipe of mascara. Investing in those early minutes saves me time on the back end.

But I also trust my instincts and observations. When these girls say they want a sexy, beachy look, I know they really want to resemble Gigi Hadid, who is on the cover of the magazine splayed across the love seat.

"So what are you majoring in?" I ask.

"Communications. We both want to go into PR." Mandy sounds bored, like I'm an annoying adult asking her what she wants to be when she grows up.

"Sounds interesting," I say as I pull a straight-back chair into the strongest light, directly under the ceiling fixture.

I start with Taylor. I have forty-five minutes to create the vision she wants to see in the mirror.

"You have amazing skin," I say. Another rule: Find a feature to compliment on every client. In Taylor's case, this isn't difficult.

"Thanks," she says, not lifting her gaze from her phone. She begins a running commentary on her Instagram feed: "Does anyone really want to see another picture of cupcakes?" "Jules and Brian are so in love, it's gross." "Inspirational sunset, got it . . . glad you're having a rocking Friday night on your balcony."

As I work, the girls' chatter fades into background noise, like the drone of a hair dryer or city traffic. I lose myself in the strokes of different foundations I've applied to Taylor's jawline so I can match her skin tone flawlessly, and in the swirl of copper and sandy hues I blend on my hand to bring out the gold flecks in her eyes.

I'm brushing bronzer onto her cheeks when her cell phone rings.

Taylor stops tapping hearts and holds up her phone: "Private number. Should I get it?"

"Yes!" Mandy says. "It could be Justin."

Taylor wrinkles her nose. "Who answers their phone on a Friday night, though? He can leave a message."

A few moments later, she touches the speakerphone button and a man's voice fills the room:

"This is Ben Quick, Dr. Shields's assistant. I'm confirming your appointments this weekend, for tomorrow and Sunday from eight to ten A.M. The location again is Hunter Hall, Room 214. I'll meet you in the lobby and take you up."

Taylor rolls her eyes and I pull back my mascara wand.

"Can you keep your face still, please?" I ask.

"Sorry. Was I out of my mind, Mandy? I'm going to be way too hungover to get up early tomorrow."

"Just blow it off."

"Yeah. But it's five hundred bucks. That's, like, a couple sweaters from rag & bone."

These words break my concentration; five hundred is what I make for ten jobs.

"Gah. Forget it. I'm not going to set an alarm to go to some dumb questionnaire," Taylor says.

Must be nice, I think, looking at the sweater crumpled in the corner. Then I can't help myself: "A questionnaire?"

Taylor shrugs. "Some psych professor needs students for a survey."

I wonder what sort of questions are on the survey. Maybe it's like a Myers-Briggs personality test.

I step back and study Taylor's face. She's classically pretty, with an enviable bone structure. She didn't need the full forty-five-minute treatment.

"Since you're going to be out late, I'll line your lips before I apply gloss," I say. "That way the color will last."

I pull out my favorite lip gloss with the BeautyBuzz logo on the tube and smooth it along Taylor's full lips. After I finish, Taylor gets up to go look in the bathroom mirror, trailed by Mandy. "Wow," I hear Taylor say. "She's really good. Let's take a selfie."

"I need my makeup first!"

I begin to put away the cosmetics I used for Taylor and consider what I will need for Mandy when I notice Taylor has left her phone on the chair.

My rocking Friday night will consist of walking my little mixed terrier, Leo, and washing the makeup out of my brushes—after I take the bus across town to my tiny studio on the Lower East Side. I'm so wiped out that I'll probably be in bed before Taylor and Mandy order their first cocktails at the club.

I look down at the phone again.

Then I glance at the bathroom door. It's partly closed.

I bet Taylor won't even bother to return the call to cancel her appointment.

"I need to buy the highlighter she used," Taylor is saying.

Five hundred dollars would help a lot with my rent this month.

I already know my schedule for tomorrow. My first job doesn't begin until noon.

"I'm going to have her do my eyes kind of dramatic," Mandy says. "I wonder if she has false lashes with her."

Hunter Hall from eight to ten A.M.—I remember that part. But what was the name of the doctor and his assistant?

It's not even like I make a decision to do it; one second I'm staring at the phone and the next, it's in my hand. Less than a minute has passed; it hasn't locked out yet. Still, I need to look down to navigate to the voice mail screen, but that means taking my eyes off the bathroom door.

I jab at the screen to play the most recent message, then press the phone tightly to my ear.

The bathroom door moves and Mandy starts to walk out. I spin around, feeling my heartbeat erupt. I won't be able to replace the phone without her seeing me.

Ben Quick.

I can pretend it fell off the chair, I think wildly. I'll tell Taylor I just picked it up.

"Wait, Mand!"

Dr. Shields's assistant . . . eight to ten A.M. . . .

"Should I make her try a darker lip color?"

Come on, I think, willing the message to play faster.

Hunter Hall, Room 214.

"Maybe," Mandy says.

I'll meet you in the lob—

I hang up and drop the phone back onto the chair just as Taylor takes her first step into the room.

Did she leave it faceup or facedown? But before there's time to try and remember, Taylor is beside me.

She stares down at her phone and my stomach clenches. I've messed up. Now I recall that she left it with the screen facing down on the chair. I put it back the wrong way.

I swallow hard, trying to think of an excuse.

"Hey," she says.

I drag my eyes up to meet hers.

"Love it. But can you try a darker lip gloss?"

She flops back onto the chair and I slowly exhale.

I redo her lips twice—first making them berry, then reverting to the original shade, all the while steadying my right elbow with my left palm so my shaking fingers don't ruin the lines—and by the time I'm finished, my pulse has returned to normal.

When I leave the apartment with a distracted "Thank you" from the girls instead of a tip, my decision is confirmed.

I set the alarm on my phone for 7:15 A.M.

Saturday, November 17

The next morning, I review my plan carefully.

Sometimes an impulsive decision can change the course of your life.

I don't want that to happen again.

I wait outside Hunter Hall, peering in the direction of Taylor's apartment. It's cloudy and the air is thick and gray, so for a moment I mistake another young woman rushing in my direction for her. But it's just someone out for a jog. When it's five minutes past eight and it appears that Taylor is still asleep, I enter the lobby, where a guy in khakis and a blue button-down shirt is checking his watch.

"Sorry I'm late!" I call.

"Taylor?" he says. "I'm Ben Quick."

I'd correctly gambled on the assumption that Taylor wouldn't phone to cancel.

"Taylor is sick, so she asked me to come and do the questionnaire instead. I'm Jessica. Jessica Farris."

"Oh." Ben blinks. He looks me up and down, examining me more carefully.

I've traded my ankle boots for Converse high-tops and slung a black nylon backpack over one shoulder. I figure it won't hurt if I look like a student.

"Can you hang on a second?" he finally says. "I need to check with Dr. Shields."

"Sure." I aim for the slightly bored tone Taylor used last night.

The worst thing that'll happen is he'll tell me I can't participate, I remind myself. No big deal; I'll just grab a bagel and take Leo for a long walk.

Ben steps aside and pulls out his cell phone. I want to listen to his side of the conversation, but his voice is muted.

Then he walks over to me. "How old are you?"

"Twenty-eight," I respond truthfully.

I sneak a glance at the entrance to make sure Taylor isn't going to saunter in at the last minute.

"You currently reside in New York?" Ben asks.

I nod.

Ben has two more questions for me: "Where else have you lived? Anywhere outside the United States?"

I shake my head. "Just Pennsylvania. That's where I grew up."

"Okay," Ben says, putting his phone away. "Dr. Shields says you can participate in the study. First, I need to get your full name and address. Can I see some ID?"

I shift my backpack into my hand and dig through it until I find my wallet, then I hand him my driver's license.

He snaps a picture, then takes down the rest of my information. "I can Venmo you the payment tomorrow at the conclusion of your session if you have an account."

"I do," I say. "Taylor told me it's five hundred dollars, right?"

He nods. "I'm going to text all this to Dr. Shields, then I'll take you upstairs to the room."

Could it possibly be this simple?

CHAPTER
TWO

Saturday, November 17

YOU AREN'T THE SUBJECT who was expected to show up this morning.

Still, you meet the demographic criteria of the study and the slot would otherwise be wasted, so my assistant Ben escorts you to Room 214. The testing space is large and rectangular, filled with windows along the eastern-facing side. Three rows of desks and chairs line the shiny linoleum floor. At the front of the room is a SMART Board, its screen blank. High on the back wall is an old-fashioned round clock. It could be any classroom in any college campus in any city.

Except for one thing: You are the only person here.

This venue has been selected because there is little to distract you, facilitating your ability to concentrate on the task ahead.

Ben explains that your instructions will appear on the computer that is being provided for your use. Then he closes the door.

The room is silent.

A laptop waits on a desk in the first row. It is already open. Your footsteps echo across the expanse of the floor as you walk toward it.

You ease into the seat, pulling it up to the desk. The metal leg of your chair grates against the linoleum.

A message is visible on the screen:

Subject 52: Thank you for your participation in Dr. Shields's morality and ethics research project. By entering this study, you agree to be bound by confidentiality. You are expressly prohibited from discussing the study or its contents with anyone.

There are no right or wrong answers. It is essential that you are honest and give your first, instinctive response. Your explanations should be thorough. You will not be permitted to move on to the next question until the prior one is completed.

A five-minute warning will be issued before the conclusion of your two hours.

Press the *Return* key when you are ready to begin.

Do you have any idea of what to expect?

You bring your finger to the *Return* key, but instead of touching it, your hand hovers over the keyboard. You are not alone in your hesitation. Some of the fifty-one subjects before you exhibited varying degrees of uncertainty, too.

It can be frightening to become acquainted with parts of yourself that you don't like to admit exist.

Finally, you press the key.

You wait, watching the blinking cursor. Your hazel eyes are wide.

When the first question blooms on the screen, you flinch.

Perhaps it feels strange to have someone probing intimate parts of your psyche in such a sterile setting, without disclosing why the information is so valuable. It is natural to shy away from feelings of vulnerability, but you will need to surrender to this process if it is to be successful.

Remember the rules: Be open and truthful, and avoid pivoting away from any embarrassment or pain these questions provoke.

If this initial query, which is relatively mild, unsettles you, then you might be one of the women who wash out of the study. Some subjects don't return. This test isn't for everyone.

You continue to stare at the question.

Maybe your instincts are telling you to leave without even starting. You wouldn't be the first.

But you lift your hands to the keyboard again, and you begin to type.

CHAPTER
THREE

Saturday, November 17

AS I STARE AT THE LAPTOP in the unnaturally quiet classroom, I feel kind of anxious. The instructions say there are no wrong answers, but won't my responses to a morality test reveal a lot about my character?

The room is cold, and I wonder if that is deliberate, to keep me alert. I can almost hear phantom noises—the rustle of papers, the thud of feet against the hard floors, the jostling and joking of students.

I touch the *Return* key with my index finger and wait for the first question.

Could you tell a lie without feeling guilt?

I jerk back.

This wasn't what I expected when Taylor mentioned the study with a dismissive flip of her hand. I guess I didn't anticipate being asked to write about myself; for some reason, I assumed this would be a multiple choice or yes/no survey. To be confronted with a question that feels so personal, as if Dr. Shields already knows too much about me, as if he knows I lied about Taylor . . . well, it rattles me more than a little.

I give myself a mental shake and lift my fingers to the keyboard.

There are many types of lies. I could write about lies of omission or huge, life-changing ones—the kind I know too well—but I choose a safer course.

Sure, I type. *I'm a makeup artist, but not one of the ones you've read about. I don't work on models or movie stars. I get Upper East Side teenagers ready for prom, and their moms ready for fancy benefits. I do weddings and bat mitzvahs, too. So yeah, I could tell a high-strung mother that she could still be carded, or convince an insecure sixteen-year-old that I didn't even notice her pimple. Especially because they're more likely to give me a nice tip if I flatter them.*

I hit *Enter,* not knowing if this is the kind of response the professor wants. But I guess I'm doing it right, because the second question appears quickly.

Describe a time in your life when you cheated.

Whoa. That feels like a presumption.

But maybe everybody has cheated, even if just at a game of Monopoly when they were little. I think about it a bit, then type: *In the fourth grade, I cheated on a test. Sally Jenkins was the best speller in the class, and when I looked up and chewed on the pink rubbery eraser of my pencil, trying to remember if "tomorrow" had one r or two, I caught sight of her paper.*

Turns out it was two r's. I wrote the word and mentally thanked Sally when I got an A.

I press *Enter.*

Funny how those details came back to me, even though I haven't thought about Sally in years. We graduated from high school together, but I missed our last few reunions, so I have no idea how she turned out. Probably two or three kids, a part-time job, a house near her parents. That's what happened to most of the girls I grew up with.

The next question hasn't materialized yet. I tap the *Enter* key again. Nothing.

I wonder if there's a glitch in the program. I'm about to go poke my head out the door to see if Ben is nearby, but then letters begin to appear on my screen, one by one.

Like someone is typing them in real time.

Subject 52, you need to dig deeper.

My body gives a sudden start. I can't help looking around. The flimsy plastic blinds on the windows are pulled up, but there isn't anyone outside on this drab, gloomy day. The lawn and sidewalk are deserted. There's another building across the way, but it's impossible to tell if anyone is in it.

Logically, I know I'm alone. It just feels like someone close to me is whispering.

I look back at the laptop. There's another message:

Was that really your first, instinctual answer?

I almost gasp. How does Dr. Shields know?

I abruptly push back my chair and start to stand up. Then I get how he figured it out; it must have been my hesitation before I started typing. Dr. Shields realized I rejected my initial thought and chose a safer response. I pull my chair back toward the computer and exhale slowly.

Another instruction creeps across the page:

Go beyond the superficial.

It was crazy to think Dr. Shields could know what I'm thinking, I tell myself. Being in this room is obviously playing with my mind. It wouldn't feel as weird if other people were around.

After a brief pause, the second question reappears on the screen.

Describe a time in your life when you cheated.

Okay, I think. You want the messy truth about my life? I can dig a little deeper.

Is it cheating if you are just an accessory in the act? I write.

I wait for a response. But the only movement on my screen is the blinking cursor. I continue typing.

Sometimes I hook up with guys I don't know all that well. Or maybe it's more like I don't want to know them all that well.

Nothing. I keep going.

My job has taught me to carefully evaluate people when I first meet them. But in my personal life, especially after a drink or two, I can deliberately dial back the focus.

There was a bass player I met a few months ago. I went back to his place. It was obvious a woman lived there but I didn't ask him about it. I told myself she was just a roommate. Is it wrong that I put on blinders?

I press *Return* and wonder how my confession will land. My best friend, Lizzie, knows about some of my one-night stands, but I never told her about seeing the bottles of perfume and the pink razor in the bathroom that night. She also doesn't know about their frequency. I guess I don't want her to judge me.

Letter by letter, a single word forms on my computer screen:

Better.

For a second, I'm glad I'm getting the hang of the test.

Then I realize a complete stranger is reading my confessions about my sex life. Ben seemed professional, with his crisp oxford shirt and horn-rimmed glasses, but what do I really know about this psychiatrist and his study?

Maybe it's just being *called* a morality and ethics survey. It could be anything.

How do I know the guy is even a professor at NYU? Taylor doesn't seem like the type to verify details. She's a beautiful young woman, and maybe that's why she was invited to participate.

Before I can decide what to do, the next question appears:

Would you cancel plans with a friend for a better offer?

My shoulders untense. This query seems completely innocuous, like something Lizzie might ask me if she were seeking advice.

If Dr. Shields were planning something creepy, he wouldn't have set this whole thing up in a university classroom. Plus, he didn't ask about my sex life, I remind myself. I'm the one who offered it up.

I answer the question: *Of course, because my jobs aren't regular. I have weeks when I'm swamped. I sometimes do seven or eight clients a day, ricocheting around Manhattan. But then I can go a few days when I only get a couple of call times. Turning away work isn't an option for me.*

I'm about to hit the *Return* key when I realize Dr. Shields won't be satisfied by what I wrote. I follow his instructions and dig deeper.

I got my first job in a sandwich shop when I was fifteen. I left college after two years because I couldn't take it. Even with financial aid, I had to waitress three nights a week and get student loans. I hated being in debt. The constant worry about whether my ATM receipt would show a negative balance, the way I'd have to sneak a sandwich to take home when I left work . . .

I'm doing a little better now. But I don't have a cushion like my best friend, Lizzie. Her parents send her a check every month. Mine are pretty broke, and my sister has special needs. So sometimes, yeah, I might need to cancel plans with a friend. I have to take care of myself financially. Because when it comes down to it, I've only got myself to rely on.

I stare at my final line.

I wonder if I sound whiny. I hope Dr. Shields gets what I'm trying to say: My life isn't perfect, but whose is? The hand I've been dealt could be worse.

I'm not used to expressing myself like this. Writing about hidden thoughts is like washing off makeup and seeing a bare face.

I answer a few more, including: *Would you ever read a spouse's/significant other's text messages?*

If I thought he was cheating, I would, I type. *I've never been married, though, or lived with anyone. I've only had a couple of sort-of serious boyfriends, and I never had reason to doubt them.*

By the time I've finished the sixth question, I feel different than I have in a while. I'm keyed up, like I've had an extra cup of coffee, but I'm not jittery or anxious anymore. I'm super-focused. I've completely lost track of time, too. I could have been in this classroom for forty-five minutes, or for twice that length.

I've just finished writing about something I would never be able to tell my parents—how I secretly pay some of Becky's medical bills—when letters begin to surface on my screen again.

That must be difficult for you.

I read the message a second time, more slowly. I'm surprised by the comfort Dr. Shields's kind words give me.

I lean back in my chair, feeling the hard metal press into the space between my shoulder blades, and try to imagine what Dr. Shields looks like. I picture him as a heavyset man with a gray beard. He's thoughtful and compassionate. He's probably heard it all. He isn't judging me.

It *is* difficult, I think. I blink rapidly a few times.

I find myself typing, *Thank you.*

No one has ever wanted to know so much about me before; most people are satisfied with the sort of superficial chatter that Dr. Shields doesn't like.

Maybe the secrets I've been holding are a bigger deal than I thought, because telling Dr. Shields about them makes me feel lighter.

I lean forward slightly and fiddle with the trio of silver rings on my index finger as I wait for the next question.

It seems to take a few moments longer than it did for the last ones to appear.

Then it does.

Have you ever deeply hurt someone you care about?

I almost gasp.

I read it twice. I can't help glancing at the door, even though I know no one is peering in through the glass pane at the top.

Five hundred dollars, I think. It doesn't seem like such easy money anymore.

I don't want to hesitate too long. Dr. Shields will know I'm evading something.

Unfortunately, yes, I type, trying to buy myself some time. I twist one of my curls around my finger, then type some more. *When I first came to New York, there was this guy I liked, and a friend of mine had a crush on him, too. He asked me out—*

I stop. Telling that story isn't a big deal. It isn't what Dr. Shields wants.

I slowly backspace over the letters.

I've been honest, like I agreed when I accepted the terms at the start of the study. But now I think about making something up.

Dr. Shields might know if I didn't tell the truth.

And I wonder . . . what would it feel like if I did?

Sometimes I think I've hurt everyone I've ever loved.

I want to type the words so badly. I imagine Dr. Shields nodding sympathetically, encouraging me to continue. Maybe if I told him what I did, he'd write something comforting again.

My throat tightens. I swipe my hand across my eyes.

If I had the courage, I'd start by explaining to Dr. Shields that I'd taken care of Becky all summer while my parents were at work; that I'd been pretty responsible even though I was only thirteen at the time. Becky could be annoying—she was always barging into my room when I had friends over, borrowing my stuff, and trying to follow me around— but I loved her.

Love her, I think. I still love her.

It just hurts to be around her.

I still haven't written a single word when Ben knocks on the door and tells me I have five minutes left.

I lift my hands and slowly type, *Yes, and I'd give anything to undo it.*

Before I can rethink the words, I hit the *Enter* key.

I stare at the computer screen, but Dr. Shields doesn't write anything in return.

The cursor seems to throb like a heartbeat; it's mesmerizing. My eyes begin to burn.

If Dr. Shields typed something to me right now, if he asked me to continue, and said it was okay for me to go over my allotted time, I'd do it. I'd let it all out; I'd tell him everything.

My breathing grows shallow.

I feel like I'm standing on the edge of a cliff, waiting for someone to tell me to jump.

I keep staring at the screen, knowing I've only got a minute or so left.

The screen is still blank except for the blinking cursor. But words suddenly begin to pulse in my mind, in time with the cursor: *Tell me. Tell me.*

When Ben opens the door, I have trouble dragging my gaze away from the screen to nod at him.

I twist around and slowly pull my coat off the back of my chair and pick up my backpack. I look at the computer one last time, but it's still blank.

The minute I stand up, a wave of exhaustion envelops me. I'm completely depleted. My limbs feel heavy and fog invades my brain. All I want to do is go home and crawl under the covers with Leo.

Ben stands just outside the doorway, looking down at an iPad. I catch a glimpse of Taylor's name at the top, followed by three female names below it. Everyone has secrets. I wonder if they'll reveal theirs.

"I'll see you tomorrow at eight," Ben says as we begin to descend the stairs to the lobby. It's an effort to keep up with him.

"Okay," I say. I grip the rail and focus on the steps so I don't miss one.

When we reach the bottom, I pause. "Um, I have a question. Exactly what kind of survey is this?"

Ben looks a little irritated. He's kind of fussy, with his shiny loafers and fancy stylus. "It's a comprehensive study on morality and ethics in the twenty-first century. Dr. Shields is evaluating hundreds of subjects in preparation for a major academic paper."

Then he looks past me, toward the next woman waiting in the lobby: "Jeannine?"

I walk outside, zipping my leather jacket. I pause, needing to get my bearings, then I turn and begin to head toward my apartment.

All the people around me seem to be engaged in ordinary activities: A few women with brightly colored yoga mats enter the studio on the corner. Two guys holding hands stroll past me. A kid zipping by on a scooter is chased by his father, who shouts, "Slow down, buddy!"

Two hours ago, I wouldn't have looked twice at any of them. But now it's disorienting to be back in the noisy, bustling world.

I head to my apartment, pausing at a stoplight when I reach the corner. It's cold, and I reach into my pockets for my gloves. As I put them on, I notice the clear polish I'd applied to my fingernails only yesterday is chipped and peeling.

I must've been scraping at it while thinking about whether I should answer that last question.

I shiver and cross my arms over my chest. I feel like I'm coming down with a bug. I have four clients today, and I have no idea how I'm going to summon the energy to haul my case around the city and make small talk.

I wonder if the survey will continue where it left off when I return to the classroom tomorrow. Or maybe Dr. Shields will let me skip that last question and give me a new one.

I turn the final corner and my apartment building comes into view. I unlock the main door, tugging it hard behind me until I hear the latch click into place. I drag myself up the four flights of stairs and unlock my door, then collapse onto my futon. Leo jumps up and curls next to me; sometimes he seems to sense when I need comfort. I adopted him almost on a whim a couple of years ago when I stopped in to an animal shelter to look at the cats. He wasn't barking or whining. He was just sitting in his cage, looking at me, like he'd been waiting for me to show up.

I set the alarm on my phone to ring in an hour, then rest my hand on his small, warm body.

As I lie there, I begin to wonder if it was worth it. I wasn't prepared for how intense the experience would be, or how many different emotions would engulf me.

I roll onto my side and close my heavy eyes, telling myself that I'll feel better once I've rested.

I don't know what could happen tomorrow, what new things Dr. Shields will ask. No one is forcing me to do this, I remind myself. I could pretend I overslept. Or I could pull a Taylor and simply not show up.

I don't have to go back, I think right before I sink into oblivion.

But I know I'm only lying to myself.

CHAPTER
FOUR

Saturday, November 17

You TOLD A LIE, which is an ironic entrance into a study on morality and ethics. Quite entrepreneurial, too.

You were not a substitute for the eight A.M. appointment.

The original participant called to cancel at 8:40 A.M., explaining she had overslept, long after you were escorted into the testing room. Still, you were allowed to continue, because by then you had proven to be an intriguing subject.

First impressions: You are young; your license confirmed that you are twenty-eight. Your chestnut-brown curls are long and a tad unruly, and you are clad in a leather jacket and jeans. You don't wear a wedding ring, but a trio of slim silver bands is stacked on your index finger.

Despite your casual appearance, there's a professionalism about your manner. You did not carry a to-go coffee cup and yawn and rub your eyes, like some of the other early morning subjects. You sat up straight, and you did not sneak glances at your phone between questions.

What you revealed during your initial session, and what you didn't intentionally reveal, were equally valuable.

A subtle theme began to emerge from your very first answer that set you apart from the fifty-one other young women evaluated thus far.

First you described how you could tell a lie to appease a client and secure a better tip.

Then you wrote about canceling a night out with a friend, not for last-minute concert tickets or a promising date, as most of the others did. Your mind returned to the prospect of work instead.

Money is vitally important to you. It appears to be an underpinning of your ethical code.

When money and morality intersect, the results can illuminate intriguing truths about human character.

People are motivated to break their moral compasses for a variety of primal reasons: survival, hate, love, envy, passion. And money.

More observations: You put your loved ones first, as evidenced by the information you withhold from your parents to protect them. Yet you describe yourself as an accessory in an act that could destroy another relationship.

It was the question you didn't answer, though, the one you struggled with as you scraped at your nails, that holds the most intrigue.

This test can free you, Subject 52.

Surrender to it.

CHAPTER
FIVE

Saturday, November 17

MY POWER NAP pushes away thoughts about Dr. Shields and his strange test. A cup of strong coffee helps me turn my focus onto my clients, and by the time I arrive back at my apartment after work, I almost feel like myself again. The idea of another session tomorrow doesn't seem daunting anymore.

I even have the energy to tidy up, which mostly consists of gathering the clothes that are heaped on the back of a chair and hanging them in my closet. My studio is so small there isn't a single wall that's not blocked by a piece of furniture. I could afford a bigger place if I moved in with a roommate, but years ago I made the decision to live alone. My privacy is worth the trade-off.

A sliver of fading late-afternoon light peeks through the single window as I sit down on the edge of my futon. I reach for my checkbook, thinking that I won't dread paying my bills as much as usual with an extra five hundred dollars coming in this month.

As I begin writing a check to Antonia Sullivan, it's as if Dr. Shields is in my head again:

Have you ever kept a secret from someone you loved to avoid upsetting them?

My pen freezes.

Antonia is a private speech and occupational therapist, one of the best in Philly.

The state-funded specialist who works with Becky on Tuesdays and Thursdays makes a little progress. But on the days Antonia comes, small miracles occur: An attempt to braid hair or write a sentence. A question about the book Antonia has read to her. The resurfacing of a lost memory.

Antonia charges $125 an hour, but my parents think she bills them on a sliding scale and they pay a fraction of that. I cover the rest.

Today I acknowledge the truth: If my parents knew I paid most of the bill, my father would be embarrassed, and my mother would worry. They might refuse my help.

It's better that they don't have a choice.

I've been paying Antonia for the past eighteen months. My mother always calls to fill me in after her visits.

I didn't realize how hard it was to engage in that charade until I wrote about it in this morning's session. When Dr. Shields responded that it must be difficult, it's like he gave me permission to finally admit my true feelings.

I finish writing the check and stick it inside an envelope, then I jump up and head to my refrigerator and grab a beer.

I don't want to analyze the choices I make any more tonight; I'm going to have to be back in that world soon enough.

I reach for my phone and text Lizzie: *Can we meet a little earlier?*

I walk into the Lounge and scan the room, but Lizzie isn't there yet. I'm not surprised; I'm ten minutes early. I see a pair of empty barstools and snag them.

Sanjay, the bartender, nods at me. "Hey, Jess." I come here often; it's three blocks away from my apartment, and happy-hour beers cost only three dollars.

"Sam Adams?" he asks.

I shake my head. "Vodka-cran-soda, please." Happy-hour prices ended nearly an hour ago.

I'm halfway through my drink when Lizzie arrives, peeling off her scarf and jacket as she approaches. I pull my bag off the stool next to me.

"I had the weirdest thing happen today," Lizzie says as she plops down and gives me a quick, hard hug. She looks like a Midwestern farm girl, all pink cheeks and tumbling blond hair, which is exactly what she was before she came to New York to try to break into theatrical costume design.

"To you? No way," I say. The last time I talked to Lizzie, she told me she'd tried to buy a homeless guy a turkey sandwich and he'd expressed annoyance that she didn't know he was a vegan. A few weeks earlier, she'd asked someone to help her find the aisle with bath towels at Target. It turned out to be Oscar-nominated actress Michelle Williams, not an employee. "She knew where they were, though," Lizzie said when she'd recounted the story.

"I was in Washington Square Park— Wait, are you drinking a vodka-cran-soda? I'll have one too, Sanjay, and how's that hot boyfriend of yours? Anyway, Jess, where was I? Oh, the bunny. It was just right there in the middle of the path, blinking up at me."

"A bunny? Like Thumper?"

Lizzie nods. "He's precious! He's got these long ears and the tiniest pink nose. I think someone must have lost him. He's totally tame."

"He's in your apartment right now, isn't he?"

"Only because it's so cold out!" Lizzie says. "I'm going to call around to all the local schools on Monday to see if any of them wants a classroom pet."

Sanjay slides Lizzie's drink over and she takes a sip. "What about you? Anything interesting?"

For once, I had a day that could rival hers, but when I start to speak, the words on the laptop screen float before my eyes: *By entering this study, you are agreeing to be bound by confidentiality.*

"Just the usual," I say, looking down as I stir my drink. Then I dig into my bag for a few quarters and jump up. "I'm going to pick out some tunes. Any requests?"

"Rolling Stones," she says.

I punch in "Honky Tonk Women" for Lizzie, then I lean against the jukebox, flipping through the choices.

Lizzie and I met shortly after I moved here, when we both worked backstage at the same off-off-Broadway play, me as a makeup artist and her as part of the costume crew. The production closed after two nights, but by then we'd become friends. I'm closer to her than just about anyone. I went home with her for a long weekend and met her family, and she hung out with my parents and Becky when they visited New York a few years ago. She always gives me the pickle from her plate when we eat at our favorite deli because she knows how much I love them, just as I know that when a new Karin Slaughter book comes out she won't leave her apartment until she's finished it.

Although she certainly doesn't know everything about me, it still feels strange to not be able to share today's experience with her.

A guy approaches and stands next to me, looking down at the song titles.

Lizzie's song begins to play.

"Stones fan, huh?"

I turn to look at him. He's a B-school grad for sure, I think. I see his type every day on the subway. He's got the Wall Street vibe, with his crewneck sweater and jeans that are a bit too crisp. His dark hair is short, and his stubble looks more like genuine five o'clock shadow than some sort of facial hair artistic expression. His watch is a giveaway, too. It's a Rolex, but not an antique that would signal old family money. It's a newer model that he probably bought himself, maybe with his first end-of-year bonus.

Too preppy for me.

"They're my boyfriend's favorite," I say.

"Lucky guy."

I smile at him to soften my rejection. "Thanks." I select "Purple Rain," then walk back to my stool.

"You have Flopsy in your bathroom?" Sanjay is asking.

"I put down newspapers," Lizzie explains. "My roommate's not that happy about it, though."

Sanjay winks at me. "Another round?"

Lizzie pulls out her phone and holds it up to show me and Sanjay. "You guys want to see a picture of him?"

"Adorable," I say.

"Ooh, I just got a text," Lizzie says, staring down at her phone. "Remember Katrina? She's having people over for drinks. Wanna go?"

Katrina is an actress who is working with Lizzie on the new production. I haven't seen Katrina in a while, since she and I worked on a play together just before I left theater. She reached out to me over the summer, saying she wanted to get together and talk. But I never responded.

"Tonight?" I ask, stalling.

"Yeah," Lizzie says. "I think Annabelle's going, and maybe Cathleen."

I like Annabelle and Cathleen. But other theater people will probably be invited. And there's one I'd prefer not to see ever again.

"Gene won't be there, don't worry," Lizzie says, like she can read my mind.

I can tell Lizzie wants to join them. These are still her friends. Plus, she's building her résumé. New York theater is a tight-knit community, and the best way to get hired is to network. She'll feel badly about going without me, though.

It's like I can hear Dr. Shields's deep, soothing voice in my head again: *Could you tell a lie without feeling guilt?*

Yes, I answer him.

I say to Lizzie: "Oh, it's not that, I'm just really tired. And I have to get up early tomorrow."

Then I signal to Sanjay. "Let's have one more quick drink and then I need to get to bed. But you should go, Lizzie."

Twenty minutes later, Lizzie and I walk out the door. We're heading in opposite directions, so we hug good-bye on the sidewalk. She smells like orange blossoms; I remember helping her pick out the scent.

I watch as she turns the corner, heading toward the party.

Lizzie had said Gene French wouldn't be there, but it's not just him I'm avoiding. I'm not eager to reconnect with anyone from that phase of my life, even though it consumed me for the first seven years after I moved to New York.

Theater was what drew me to this city. My dream caught hold early, when I was a young girl and my mother took me to see a local production of *The Wizard of Oz*. Afterward, the actors came to the lobby and I realized that all of them—Tin Man, the Cowardly Lion, the Wicked Witch—were just ordinary people. They'd been transformed by chalky face powder and freckles drawn on with an eyebrow pencil and green-tinted foundation.

After I left college and moved to New York, I started at the Bobbi Brown counter at Bloomingdale's while I auditioned as a makeup artist for every play I could find on Backstage.com. That's when I learned the pros carry their contour wheels, foundations, and false eyelashes in black accordian-style cases instead of duffel bags. At first I worked sporadically on small shows, where I was sometimes paid in comp tickets, but after a couple of years, the jobs came easier and the audiences got bigger and I was able to quit the department store. I began to get referrals, and I even signed with an agent, albeit one who also represented a magician who performed at trade shows.

That period of my life was pure exhilaration—the intense camaraderie with actors and other crew members, the triumph when the audience rose to their feet and applauded our creation—but I earn a lot more now doing freelance makeup. And I realized long ago that not everyone's dreams are meant to come true.

Still, I can't help thinking back to that time and wondering if Gene is the same.

When we were introduced, he took my hand in his. His voice was deep and robust, as befitting someone who worked in the theater. He was already on his way to making it big, even though he was only in his late thirties. He got there even faster than I anticipated.

The first thing he ever said to me, as I tried to keep from blushing: *You've got a great smile.*

The memories always come back in this order: Me bringing him a cup of coffee and nudging him awake from his catnap in a seat in the darkened auditorium. Him showing me a *Playbill*, fresh from the printer, and pointing out my name in the credits. The two of us alone in his office, him holding my gaze as he slowly unzipped his pants.

And the last thing he ever said to me, as I tried to hold back tears: *Get home safe, okay?* Then he hailed a cab and gave the driver a twenty.

Does he ever think of me? I wonder.

Enough, I tell myself. I need to move on.

But if I go home, I know I won't be able to sleep. I'll be replaying scenes from our final night together and what I could have done differently again, or thinking about Dr. Shields's study.

I look back at the bar. Then I pull open the door and stride in. I see the dark-haired banker playing darts with his friends.

I walk directly up to him. He's only an inch or two taller than I am in my low boots. "Hi again," I say.

"Hi." He draws out the word, turning it into a question.

"I don't really have a boyfriend. Can I buy you a beer?"

"That was a quick relationship," he says, and I laugh.

"Let me get the first round," he says. He hands his darts to one of his friends.

"How about a Fireball shot?" I suggest.

As he approaches the bar, I see Sanjay look over at me and I avert my gaze. I hope he didn't hear me when I told Lizzie I was going home.

When the banker comes back with our shots, he clinks his glass to mine. "I'm Noah."

I take a sip, feeling cinnamon burn my lips. I know I'll have no interest in seeing Noah again after tonight. So I say the first name that pops into my head: "I'm Taylor."

I lift up the blanket and slowly ease out from under it, looking around. It takes me a second to remember I'm on the couch in Noah's apartment. We ended up here after a few more shots at another bar. When we realized we'd both skipped dinner and were starving, Noah ran out to the deli at the corner.

"Don't move," he'd ordered, pouring me a glass of wine. "I'll be back in two minutes. I need eggs to make French toast."

I must have fallen asleep almost immediately. I guess he took off my boots and covered me with a blanket instead of waking me. He also left me a note propped on the coffee table: *Hey, sleepyhead, I'll cook that French toast for you in the morning.*

I'm still in my jeans and top; all we did was kiss. I grab my boots and coat and tiptoe to the door. It creaks when I open it and I flinch, but I don't hear any signs of Noah stirring in his bedroom. I ease it shut slowly, then slip on my boots and hurry down his hallway. I take the elevator to the lobby, smoothing my hair and rubbing beneath my eyes to remove any smudged mascara while I descend the nineteen flights.

The doorman looks up from his cell phone. "Good night, miss."

I give him a little salute and try to orient myself once I'm outside. The nearest subway stop is four blocks away. It's almost midnight, and a few people are milling around. I head for the station, digging my MetroCard out of my wallet as I walk.

My face stings in the cold air and I reach up to touch a tender patch on my chin from where Noah's stubble rubbed against it when we kissed.

The discomfort is somehow comforting.

CHAPTER
SIX

Sunday, November 18

YOUR NEXT SESSION BEGINS as your first one did: Ben meets you in the lobby and escorts you to Room 214. As you climb the stairs, you ask if the format will be the same as yesterday's. He responds affirmatively, but can't provide you with much more information. He isn't permitted to share what little he knows; he has also signed a nondisclosure agreement.

As before, the slim, silver laptop is set up in the first row. Your instructions are visible on the screen, along with a greeting: *Welcome Back, Subject 52.*

You take off your coat and ease into the chair. Many of the other young women who have occupied this seat are almost indistinguishable, with their long, straightened hair, nervous giggles, and coltish frames. You stand out, and not only because of your unconventional beauty.

Your posture is almost rigid. You remain immobile for approximately five seconds. Your pupils are slightly dilated and your lips are pressed firmly together; classic symptoms of anxiety. You take a deep breath as you press the *Enter* key.

The first question appears on the screen. You read it, then your body relaxes and your mouth softens. You lift your eyes to the ceiling. You give a brisk nod, bend your head, and begin to type quickly.

You are relieved the final query from yesterday, the one you struggled with, is not on the screen.

By the third question, any remaining tension has evaporated from your body. Your guard is down. Your answers, as during the last session, do not disappoint. They are fresh, unfiltered.

I didn't even leave him a note when I snuck out, you write in response to the fourth question, the one that asks: **When was the last time you treated someone unfairly, and why?**

The survey questions are deliberately open-ended so subjects can steer them in the direction of their choosing. Most female subjects shy away from the topic of sex, at least this early in the process. But this is the second time you've explored a subject that makes many people self-conscious. You elaborate: *I figured we'd sleep together and then I'd leave. That's what usually happens on nights like this. But on the way to his place, we passed a pretzel vendor and I started to buy one because I hadn't eaten since lunch. "No way," he said, pulling me away. "I make the best French toast in the city."*

But I fell asleep on his couch when he ran out to get eggs.

You are frowning now. Is this due to regret?

You continue to type: *I woke up around midnight. But I wasn't going to stay, and it's not just because of my dog. I guess I could have left my number, but I'm not looking for a relationship.*

You don't want a man to get too close to you right now. It will be interesting if you elaborate on this, and for a moment, it seems as if you will.

Your fingers remain poised above the keyboard. Then you give a little shake of your head and you touch *Enter* to submit your answer.

What else was it that you were tempted to write?

When the next question appears, your fingers fly back to the computer. But you don't respond to it. Instead, you pose a query of your own to your questioner.

I hope it's okay if I break the rules, but I just thought of something, you type. *I didn't feel guilty when I left that guy's place. I went home, walked Leo, and slept in my own bed. When I woke up this morning, I'd almost forgotten about him. But now I wonder if I was rude. Is it possible that this morality survey is making me more moral?*

The more you disclose about yourself, Subject 52, the more compelling the picture of you becomes.

Out of all the subjects who have participated in this study, only one has ever directly addressed the questioner before: Subject 5. She was different from the rest in many other ways, too.

Subject 5 became . . . special. And disappointing. And ultimately, heartbreaking.

CHAPTER
SEVEN

Wednesday, November 21

MORAL QUESTIONS lurk everywhere.

As I buy a banana and water for the bus ride home, the weary-looking cashier in the terminal kiosk gives me change for a ten instead of a five. A woman with pockmarked skin and crooked teeth holds a flimsy piece of cardboard that reads: *Need $$$ for ticket home to see sick mother. God Bless.* The bus is crowded, as it always is right before the holidays, but the thin, longhaired man sitting across from me puts his backpack down on the empty seat beside him, claiming the territory.

I pick a seat and immediately regret my choice. The lady next to me spreads out her elbows as she reads on her Kindle, edging into my space. I pretend to stretch, then bump her arm and say, "Excuse me."

As the bus driver turns on the engine and pulls out of the terminal, I think about my Sunday session with Dr. Shields again. The question I dreaded never resurfaced, but I still dug into some pretty serious stuff.

I wrote about how a lot of my friends call their dads when they need to borrow money, or to get advice on how to handle a difficult boss. They dial their moms when they come down with the flu, or for comfort during a breakup. If things had been different, that's the kind of relationship I might've had with my parents.

But my parents have enough stress; they don't need to worry about me. So I carry the burden of needing to construct a great life not just for one daughter, but for two.

Now I rest my head against the seat back and think about Dr. Shields's response: *That's a lot of pressure to endure.*

Knowing that someone else gets it makes me feel a little less alone.

I wonder if Dr. Shields is still conducting his study, or if I was one of his last subjects. I was addressed as Subject 52, but I have no idea how many other anonymous girls sat in the same uncomfortable metal chair, pecking away at the same keyboard, on other days. Maybe he's talking to another one right now.

My seatmate shifts, crossing the invisible boundary into my space again. It's not worth battling. I edge closer to the aisle, then reach for my phone. I scroll through some old texts looking for one from a high school classmate who was organizing an informal reunion at a local bar the night after Thanksgiving. But I scroll down too far, and instead pull up the text that came in from Katrina over the summer, the one I never responded to: *Hey Jess. Can we meet for a cup of coffee or something? I was hoping we could talk.*

I'm pretty sure I know what she wants to talk about.

I slide my finger over the screen so I don't have to see her message any longer. Then I reach for my earbuds and pull up *Game of Thrones*.

My dad is waiting at the bus station in his beloved Eagles jacket, a green knit cap pulled down over his ears. I can see his exhalations make white puffs, like cotton balls, in the cold air.

It has been only four months since I last visited, but when I glimpse him through my window, my first thought is that he appears older. The hair peeking out from beneath his cap is more salt than pepper, and his posture sags a little, like he's weary.

He looks up and catches me watching him. His hand flicks away the cigarette he is sneaking. He officially quit twelve years ago, which means he no longer smokes in the house.

A smile breaks across his face as I step off the bus.

"Jessie," he says as he hugs me. He is the only one who calls me that. My father is big and solid, and his embrace is almost too firm. He lets go and bends down to peer in the carrier I'm holding. "Hey, little guy," he says to Leo.

The driver is pulling suitcases out from the belly of the bus. I reach for mine, but my father's hand gets there first.

"You hungry?" he asks, like he always does.

"Starving," I say, like I always do. My mom would be disappointed if I came home with a full stomach.

"The Eagles are playing the Bears tomorrow," my dad says as we walk to the parking lot.

"That game last week was really something." I hope my remark is flexible enough to cover a win or a loss. I forgot to check the score on the bus ride down.

When we reach his old Chevy Impala, he lifts my bag into the trunk. I see him wince; his knee bothers him more on cold days.

"Should I drive?" I offer.

He looks almost offended, so I quickly add: "I never get to do it in the city and I worry I'm getting rusty."

"Oh, sure," he says. He flips me the keys, and I snatch them out of the air with my right hand.

I know my parents' routines almost as well as I know my own. And within an hour of being at home, I realize something is wrong.

As soon as we pull up in front of the house, my father lifts Leo out of his carrier and offers to walk him around the block. I'm eager to get inside and see my mom and Becky, so I agree. When my dad returns, he has trouble unfastening Leo's leash. I go to help him. The smell of tobacco is so powerful I know he has snuck another cigarette.

Even when he was an official smoker, he never went through two cigarettes in such a short time.

Then, while Becky and I sit at stools in the kitchen, tearing up lettuce for a salad, my mother pours herself a glass of wine and offers me one.

"Sure," I say.

At first I don't think twice about this. It's the night before Thanksgiving, so it feels like a weekend.

But then she pours herself a second glass while the pasta is still cooking.

I watch as she stirs the tomato sauce. She's only fifty-one, not much older than the bat mitzvah mothers, the ones who want to look young enough to get carded. She colors her hair a chestnut brown and wears a Fitbit to monitor her ten thousand daily steps, yet she appears a little deflated, like a day-old balloon that has lost some helium.

As we sit at the round oak table, my mother peppers me with questions about work while my father sprinkles the grated Kraft Parmesan over the pasta.

For once, I don't lie to her. I say I'm taking a little break from theater to do freelance makeup.

"What happened to the show you told me about last week, honey?" my mother asks. Her second glass of wine is almost drained by now.

I can barely remember what I said. I take a bite of rigatoni before answering. "It closed. But this is better. I can control my own hours. Plus, I get to meet a ton of interesting people."

"Oh, that's good." The creases in her forehead soften.

Mom turns to Becky. "Maybe someday you'll move to New York and live in an apartment and get to meet interesting people!"

Now I'm the one who frowns. The traumatic brain injury Becky suffered as a child didn't just affect her physically. Both her short- and long-term memory are so damaged that she can never live alone.

My mother has always held on to false hope, and she has encouraged Becky to do the same.

It bothered me a little bit in the past. But today it seems kind of . . . unethical.

I imagine how Dr. Shields would pose the question: *Is offering someone unrealistic dreams unfair, or is it a kindness?*

I think about how I'd explain my thoughts on the situation to him. *It's not exactly wrong,* I'd type. *And maybe this faith is less for Becky and more for my mother.*

I take a sip of wine, then deliberately change the subject.

"Are you guys getting excited for Florida?"

They go every year, the three of them, driving down two days after

Christmas and returning on January 2. They stay in the same inexpensive motel a block away from the water. The ocean is Becky's favorite place, even though she doesn't swim well enough to go in past her waist.

My parents give each other a look.

"What?" I ask.

"The ocean's too cold this year," Becky says.

I catch my father's eye and he shakes his head. "We'll talk about it later."

My mom stands up abruptly and clears the plates.

"Let me," I say.

She waves her hand. "Why don't you and your father take Leo out for his walk? I'll help Becky get ready for bed."

The metal bar in the middle of the pull-out couch digs into my lower back. I flip over on the thin mattress again, trying to find a position that will coax sleep.

It's nearly one A.M., and the house is quiet. But my mind is whirling like a washing machine, spinning around images and snatches of conversation.

As soon as we'd stepped outside, my father had pulled a box of Winstons and a matchbook out of his coat pocket. He struck a match against the strip, shielding the spark from the wind with his cupped hand. It took him three tries to get a flame.

It took me almost that long to process the news he'd just told me.

"A buyout?" I'd finally echoed.

He'd exhaled. "We were strongly encouraged to take them. Those were the words on the memo."

It was dark, and although we'd only walked to the corner, my hands were already tingling from the cold. I couldn't see my father's expression.

"Are you going to look for another job?" I'd asked.

"I've been looking, Jessie."

"You'll find something soon."

The words had escaped before I'd realized I was doing exactly what my mother does to Becky.

I flip over on the mattress again and tuck my arm over Leo.

Becky and I used to share a room, but once I moved out, Becky deserved to have the extra space. There's a mini-trampoline with a safety bar and an arts-and-crafts table where my twin bed once stood. It's the only home she has ever known.

My parents have lived in this house for nearly thirty years. It would be paid off, but they needed to refinance it to cover Becky's medical bills.

I know how much they spend every month; I've gone through the bills my mother keeps in a drawer in their sideboard.

My head is filled with questions again. This is the one that matters most: What's going to happen to them when the buyout money is gone?

Thursday, November 22

Aunt Helen and Uncle Jerry host Thanksgiving every year. Their house is a lot bigger than my parents', with a dining room table that can easily seat the ten of us. My mother always makes green bean casserole with fried onions around the edges, and Becky and I prepare the stuffing. Before we leave, Becky asks me to do her makeup.

"I'd love to," I tell her. She was the one I first practiced on, back when we were kids.

I don't have my case with me, but Becky's coloring is so much like my own—fair skin with a scattering of freckles, light hazel eyes, straight brows—that I dig into my personal makeup bag and set to work.

"What kind of look are we going for?" I ask.

"Selena Gomez," Becky says. She's been a fan since Selena was on the Disney Channel.

"You love to challenge me, don't you?" I say, and she giggles.

I smooth a tinted moisturizer onto Becky's skin, thinking of what my mother had said at dinner. I stopped going to Florida with them once I moved to New York, but my mother always sends me photos of Becky collecting seashells in a bucket, or laughing as the spray hits her stomach. Becky loves the nonalcoholic Pink Panther drinks with a little umbrella and extra maraschino cherries that the server brings her at my parent's favorite seafood place. My dad takes Becky to play miniature golf while my mother walks on the beach, and they all go crabbing at the end of the pier. They rarely catch any crabs and when they do, they always throw them back.

It's the one time of year when they seem to truly relax.

"Why don't you come visit me in New York after Christmas?" I suggest. "I could take you to see the giant tree. We could watch the Rockettes kick and sing, and get hot chocolate at Serendipity."

"Sounds good," Becky says, but I can tell she's a little nervous about the idea. She has come to see me in the city before, but the noises and crowds unsettle her.

I add some blush to try to bring out her cheekbones, then dab a soft pink gloss on her lips. I tell her to look up as I gently apply a coat of mascara.

"Close your eyes," I say, and Becky smiles. She likes this part best.

I reach out and take her hand, then guide her to the bathroom mirror.

"I look pretty!" Becky says.

I give her a big hug so she doesn't see my eyes fill. "You are," I whisper.

After my aunt Helen has served the pumpkin and pecan pies, the guys head to the living room to watch the game, and the women decamp to the kitchen for cleanup. It's another ritual.

"Ugh, I'm so full I'm going to barf," my cousin Shelly moans as she untucks her blouse.

"Shelly!" Aunt Helen admonishes.

"It's your fault, Mom. The food was great." Shelly winks at me.

I reach for a dish towel as Becky brings in the plates, carefully setting them down in a row on the counter. Aunt Helen redid her kitchen a few years ago, replacing the Formica with granite.

My mom starts to scrub the platters that Aunt Helen carries in from the dining room. My cousin Gail, Shelly's sister, is eight months pregnant. She plops down on a chair at the kitchen table with a theatrical sigh, then drags over another chair so she can put her feet up. Somehow Gail always manages to avoid cleanup, but for once she has a reasonable excuse.

"Sooo . . . tomorrow night everyone's getting together at the Brewster," Shelly says as she scoops leftover stuffing into a Tupperware container. By *everyone*, she means our high school classmates who are having an informal reunion.

"Guess who's going to be there?" She pauses.

Does she really want me to start guessing?

"Who?" I finally ask.

"Keith. He's separated."

I can barely remember which football player he was.

Shelly isn't interested in him for herself; she got married a year and a half ago. I'd bet twenty bucks that by next year, she'll be the one with her feet up.

Shelly and Gail look at me expectantly. Gail is rubbing slow circles on her stomach.

My phone vibrates in the pocket of my skirt.

"Sounds fun," I say. "You're going to be our designated driver, right, Gail?"

"Like hell," Gail says. "I'm going to be in a tub reading *Us Weekly*."

"Are you dating anyone in New York?" Shelly asks.

My phone vibrates a second time, which it always does when I don't immediately open a text.

"No one serious," I say.

Her tone is sugary: "It must be tough to compete with all those beautiful models."

Gail inherited her blond hair and passive-aggressiveness from Aunt Helen, who chimes in quickly.

"Don't put off having kids for too long," she says. "I bet someone is eager for grandchildren!"

Usually my mother lets Aunt Helen's digs slide, but now I can almost feel her bristle. Maybe it's because she was drinking again at dinner.

"Jess is so busy with all those Broadway shows," my mom says. "She's enjoying having a career before she settles down."

Whether my mom is defending me or herself with the exaggeration isn't clear.

Our conversation is interrupted when Gail's husband, Phil, wanders in. "Just going to grab a few beers," he says, opening the refrigerator.

"Nice," Shelly says. "Aren't you lucky, getting to sit around and watch the game and drink while we women clean up."

"You really want to be watching the football game, Shel?" he says.

She bats her hand at him. "Get out of here, you."

I'm trying to feign interest in the discussion of whether yellow is the right color palette for Gail's nursery when I give up and excuse myself. I go to the bathroom and slip my phone out of my pocket.

The overly sweet aroma of the gingerbread-scented candle burning on the sink counter almost makes me gag.

Across the screen is a new text from an unfamiliar number:

Excuse me if I am intruding on your holiday. This is Dr. Shields. Are you in town this weekend? If so, I would like to schedule another session with you. Let me know your availability

I read the text twice.

I can't believe Dr. Shields has reached out to me directly.

I thought the study was only a two-part thing, but maybe I misunderstood. If Dr. Shields wants me for more sessions, it could mean a lot more money.

I wonder if Dr. Shields texted because Ben has the day off. It is Thanksgiving after all. Maybe Dr. Shields is in his home office, getting in a bit of work while his wife bastes the turkey and his grandkids set the table. He could be so committed to his job that he finds it hard to turn off, kind of like the way I'm beginning to find it difficult to stop thinking about moral issues.

A lot of the young women doing this survey would probably love the chance to go back for more sessions. I wonder why Dr. Shields chose me.

My bus ticket back to the city is for Sunday morning. My parents would be disappointed if I left early, even if I told them it was for a big job.

I don't reply yet. Instead, I tuck the phone back in my pocket and open the bathroom door.

Phil is standing there.

"Sorry," I say, and try to squeeze past him in the narrow hallway. I can smell the beer on his breath when he leans closer to me. Phil went to high school with us, too. He and Gail have been together since he was in twelfth grade and she was in tenth.

"I heard Shelly wants to set you up with Keith," he says.

I give a little laugh, wishing he'd move aside and stop blocking my path.

"I'm not really interested in Keith," I say.

"Yeah?" He leans closer. "You're too good for him."

"Uh, thanks," I say.

"You know, I always had a thing for you."

I freeze. His eyes lock on to mine.

His wife is eight months pregnant. What is he doing?

"Phil!" Gail calls from the kitchen. Her words shatter the silence. "I'm tired. We need to get going."

He finally steps aside and I hurry past him, hugging the wall.

"See you tomorrow, Jess," he says, just before he shuts the bathroom door.

I pause at the end of the hallway.

My wool sweater suddenly feels itchy and I can't get enough air into my lungs. I don't know if it's from the pungent candle or Phil's flirtation. The feeling isn't unfamiliar; it's why I left home years ago.

I make my way to the back porch.

As I stand outside and gulp in the cold air, my fingers reach into my pocket and feel for the smooth plastic encasing my phone.

My parents are going to run out of money eventually. I should stockpile as much of it as I can now. And if I turn Dr. Shields down, maybe he'll find another subject, one with more flexibility.

Even I recognize that I'm coming up with too many rationalizations.

I pull out my phone and respond to Dr. Shields: *Anytime Sat or Sun works great for me.*

Almost immediately, I see the three dots that mean he is writing a response. A moment later, I read it: *Wonderful. You are confirmed for noon on Saturday. Same location.*

CHAPTER
EIGHT

Saturday, November 24

YOU HAVE NO IDEA how eagerly your third session has been anticipated, Subject 52.

You look as lovely as ever, but your manner is subdued. After you enter Room 214, you slowly slip out of your coat and place it on the back of your chair. It hangs unevenly, but you don't adjust it. You sit down heavily and hesitate before you touch the *Enter* key to begin.

Were you lonely on Thanksgiving, too?

Once the first query appears and you open your thoughts, your true nature asserts itself and you grow more animated.

You are learning to enjoy the process, aren't you?

When the fourth question emerges, your fingers move across the keyboard swiftly. Your posture is excellent. You do not fidget. This all indicates that you have especially strong and clear feelings on this particular subject.

You see your friend's fiancé kiss another woman a week before the wedding. Do you tell her?

What I'd do is this, you type. *I'd confront him and say that he has 24 hours to confess, or I'll tell her myself. It would be one thing if he were with his buddies at a bachelor party at a strip club and he put a twenty in a G-string. A lot of guys do that sort of stuff for show. But outside of a situation like that, there isn't any excuse. I couldn't look the other way and pretend I didn't see it. Because if a guy cheats once, you know he's going to do it again.*

After you write those words, you stop typing, hit *Enter*, and wait for the next question.

It doesn't immediately appear.

A minute passes.

Is everything okay? You type.

Another minute passes.

A response is crafted: *Just a moment, please.*

You look puzzled, but you nod.

Your answer is absolute: It seems you believe humans are incapable of reshaping their innate natures, even when their urges lead to pain and destruction.

Your furrowed brow and slightly narrowed eyes illustrate the depth of your convictions.

Because if a guy cheats once, you know he's going to do it again.

You are waiting for the next question. But it isn't forthcoming.

Your responses have formed an unexpected connection; when linked together, they create an epiphany.

The vital lines in your previous answers are reviewed:

I'm not looking for a serious relationship. You typed this in your second session.

You twist around and peer at the clock on the wall behind you, then you look toward the door. From every angle, you are enchanting.

I hope it's okay if I break the rules. You wrote these words before you confided that this study is reshaping your relationship with your own morality.

You fiddle with the silver stacking rings on your index finger as you frown at the computer screen. This is one of your habits when you are being thoughtful, or experiencing anxiety.

I really need money, you wrote in your first session.

Something extraordinary is occurring.

It is as though you are now guiding the study into a different realm. You, the young woman who wasn't supposed to be a part of it at all.

You are presented with two more questions. They are out of sequence, but you won't know this.

You reply to them both confidently. Flawlessly.

The final query you will receive today is one no other subject will ever see.

It has been developed expressly for you.

When it appears, your eyes widen as they fly across the screen.

Answer it one way, and you will walk out of this room and you won't return.

But if you answer it another way, the possibilities are endless; you could become a pioneer in the field of psychological research.

It is a gamble, posing this query.

You are worth the risk.

You don't reply immediately. You push back your chair and stand up.

Then you disappear.

Your footsteps rap against the linoleum floor. You briefly come into view, then you vanish again.

You are pacing.

Now the roles have been upended: You are the one causing a delay. You are also the one who will decide whether this study will undergo a metamorphosis.

You return to your seat and lean forward. Your eyes flit across the screen as you read the question once more.

Would you consider expanding your participation in this study? The compensation would be significantly higher, but significantly more would be asked of you.

Slowly, you lift your hands and begin to type.

I'll do it.

CHAPTER
NINE

Saturday, November 24

EVERYTHING STARTED OFF the same for my third session: Ben waiting in the lobby in a navy V-neck sweater. The empty classroom. A laptop on a desk in the first row, the words *Welcome Back, Subject 52* floating on the screen.

I was almost looking forward to answering Dr. Shields's questions this afternoon; maybe it was the possibility of unloading my tangled feelings after my visit home.

But toward the end of the session, things got weird.

Right after I answered the question about a guy cheating on his fiancée, there was this long pause, and the tone of the queries changed. I can't say exactly how, the next two just felt different. I'd come to expect writing about things I could relate to or experiences I'd had. Those final questions seemed like the big, philosophical type you'd get on a civics exam. They required some thought to answer, but I didn't have to dig deep into painful memories, like Dr. Shields often wants me to.

Should a punishment always fit the crime?

And then:

Do victims have the right to take retribution into their own hands?

Right before I left, I had to wrestle with the decision of whether to

take the study to the next level. *Significantly more would be asked of you,*
Dr. Shields wrote. It sounded kind of ominous.

What did Dr. Shields mean? I tried to ask him. His reply appeared
on my computer screen, just like his questions always do. He simply
wrote that he'd explain next Wednesday if I could meet him in person.

I finally decided the extra money was too tempting to turn down.

Still, as I head home, I can't stop wondering what he has planned.

I'm not going to be stupid about all of this, I tell myself as I fasten
Leo's leash and head toward the 6BC Botanical Garden. It's one of my
favorite neighborhood walks in Alphabet City, and a good place to
think.

Dr. Shields wants to meet me in person. He gave me a different address than the NYU classroom, though. He told me to come to a place
on East Sixty-second Street.

I don't know if it's his office, or his apartment. Or something else
entirely.

Leo pulls sharply on his leash, jerking me toward his favorite tree. I
realize I've just been standing there.

I see a neighbor approach with her toy poodle. I quickly lift my phone
to my ear and pretend to be involved in a conversation as she passes. I
can't engage in a casual conversation with her now.

There are always stories about young women in the city who get
lured into dangerous situations. I pass their faces on the cover of the
New York Post, and receive alerts on my phone when there's a violent
crime in my borough.

It's not like I don't take calculated risks; I walk into unfamiliar homes
and locations every day for my job, and I've gone home with guys I've
barely met.

But this feels different.

I haven't told anyone about this study; Dr. Shields designed it that
way. He knows an awful lot about me, yet I know virtually nothing
about him.

Maybe, though, there's a way I can find out.

We've just made it to the garden, but I give Leo a gentle tug and we
head back to the apartment, my stride quicker than it was at the beginning of the walk.

It's time to turn the tables. Now I'm going to do some probing of my own.

I pop the cap off a Sam Adams, reach for my MacBook, and sit down on my futon. Although I don't know his first name, it should be easy enough to narrow down the various Dr. Shieldses in New York City by adding "research" and "psychiatry" as Google search terms.

Immediately, dozens of hits appear. The first one that comes up is a professional article about ethical ambiguity in familial relationships. So that part of his story fits.

I move my mouse toward the images link.

I need to see a picture of the man who knows everything from where I live to the details of my last sexual encounter.

I hesitate before clicking on it.

I've imagined Dr. Shields as I want him to be, wise and grandfatherly, with kind eyes. That image is so concrete it's hard to envision him any other way.

But the truth is, I was projecting onto a blank canvas.

He could be anyone.

I click the mouse.

Then I recoil and suck in my breath.

My immediate thought is that I've made a mistake.

Images bloom across my screen, filling it like a mosaic.

My eyes barely alight on one before another photograph pulls my gaze away, then another.

I read the captions to double-check, then I gape at the biggest image on the screen.

Dr. Shields is nothing like the portly professor I've imagined.

Dr. Shields, Dr. *Lydia* Shields, is one of the most strikingly beautiful women I've ever seen.

I lean forward, drinking in her long, strawberry-blond hair and creamy skin. She's maybe in her late thirties. There's a cool elegance to her chiseled features.

It's difficult to look away from her light blue eyes. They're mesmerizing.

Even through a picture, it feels like they see me.

I don't know why I assumed she was male. Thinking back, I realize Ben only called her "Dr. Shields." The way I incorrectly pictured her probably says something about me.

I finally click on an image, a full-length one. She stands on a stage, holding a microphone with her left hand. She appears to be wearing a diamond wedding band. Her silky blouse is paired with a fitted skirt and heels so high I can't imagine standing in them even for the duration of a walk to the stage, let alone for a speech. Her neck is long and graceful, and no amount of contouring can create the kind of cheekbones she possesses.

She looks like the type of woman who lives in a very different world from the one I inhabit, scrambling for jobs and flattering customers to get a bigger tip.

I believed I knew the person I was writing to: a thoughtful, compassionate man. But learning Dr. Shields is a woman causes me to rethink all of the questions.

And all of my answers.

What does this flawless-looking woman think about my messy life?

My cheeks grow warm as I remember casually describing lap dances and G-strings at a bachelor party when I answered the question about what I'd do if I saw a friend's fiancé kiss another woman. My grammar wasn't always perfect when I wrote my answers, and I didn't phrase things carefully.

Yet she was kind to me. She pushed me to reveal things I never talk about, and she comforted me.

She wasn't repelled by anything I confessed; she invited me back. She wants to meet me, I remind myself.

I zoom in on the photograph, noticing for the first time that Dr. Shields is smiling slightly as she holds the microphone to her lips.

I'm still a little nervous about Wednesday's appointment, but for different reasons now. I guess I don't want to disappoint her when we meet.

I start to close my laptop. Then I move my mouse back to click on the news link of my Google search. I grab my phone and begin typing notes. I write down her office address, which matches the location where she suggested we meet on Wednesday; the title of a book she wrote and her alma mater, Yale University.

I can't let the fact that Dr. Shields is a woman change my original plan. She is paying me an awful lot of money and I still have no idea why, or what for.

And sometimes the people who seem the most accomplished and together are the ones who can hurt you the deepest.

Monday, November 26

Her photos didn't lie, which is fitting, given her research study rules about telling the truth.

It was easy to find Dr. Shields's NYU class schedule online; it was one of the first things that popped up in my search. She teaches a single seminar a week, on Mondays from five to seven P.M. Her classroom is just down the hallway from Room 214. It's so different here today, with the hallways filled with noise and activity.

Dr. Shields adjusts her taupe wrap around her shoulders, untucking her glossy hair from beneath the folds as she walks down the corridor. I'm in a baseball cap and jeans, like a lot of the students milling around.

I hold my breath as she draws closer. I've positioned myself behind two girls chatting animatedly, but Dr. Shields is about to stride past them. Right before she does, I duck into a bathroom.

I poke my head out a few seconds later. She is continuing down the hallway toward the stairwell.

I let her get a dozen steps ahead of me, then I trail her out the door. I catch the faintest scent of something clean and spicy.

It's impossible to take my eyes off her.

It's as if she is gliding through the streets in a protective bubble, where the elements can't tousle her hair or snag her stockings or scuff her heels. A few men turn around to get a second look at her, and a UPS guy steering a heavy-looking cart twists it out of her path. The sidewalk is crowded with commuters and shoppers, but she never needs to slow her pace.

She turns onto Prince Street and proceeds past a row of designer boutiques that sell three-hundred-dollar cashmere hoodies and cosmetics in cases that look like jewels.

She doesn't glance in any of the windows. Unlike the people around her, she isn't on a cell phone or listening to music or distracted by her surroundings.

She continues to a little French restaurant farther down the block, then pulls open the door and disappears inside.

I stand there, unsure of what to do.

I want to get another glimpse of her, since I only saw her face fleetingly. But it would be too weird to wait outside the whole time she eats dinner.

I'm about to leave when I see the maître d' has led her to a seat by the window. She is only a dozen feet away from me. If she turns her head slightly and looks up, our eyes will meet.

I quickly shift to my left, pretending to read the menu displayed behind glass to one side of the entrance.

I can still see her out of the corner of my eye.

The waiter approaches Dr. Shields and hands her a menu. I glance back at the one in front of me. If I could afford this kind of place, I'd choose the filet mignon with béarnaise sauce and frites. But I bet Dr. Shields orders the broiled swordfish au Nicoise.

She chats briefly with the waiter, then hands him her menu. Her skin is so pale that in the candlelight her profile appears celestial. I'm reminded of the gorgeous items in the procession of storefront windows we passed earlier. It seems right that she should also be displayed here for others to admire.

It's growing darker outside now, and my fingertips are beginning to feel numb, but I'm not ready to go just yet.

She has asked me all these questions, but now I am the one brimming with queries for her. The most pressing one: Why do you care so much about the choices people like me make?

The waiter returns with a glass of wine. Dr. Shields takes a sip and I notice the burgundy color is almost a perfect match for the nail polish that adorns her long, tapered fingers.

She smiles and nods at the waiter, but after he leaves, she touches a fingertip to the corner of her eye. She could have an itch, or be brushing away a tiny fiber from her wrap. It is also the gesture someone makes to wipe away a tear.

She lifts her wineglass again, this time taking a much deeper drink.

I definitely saw a wedding band in the photo when she was holding a microphone. But her left hand is tucked in her lap and I can't tell if she's still wearing a ring.

I'd intended to stick around to see if I'd guessed right about what Dr. Shields ordered. But now I put in my earbuds and begin to walk east, toward my apartment.

Even though I've given a lot of intimate information about myself to Dr. Shields, it was voluntary. She has no idea I've been watching her in such a vulnerable moment. I feel like I've gone too far, like I've crossed a line.

The seat opposite her will remain empty tonight; the waiter removed the extra silverware and plate right after Dr. Shields handed him her menu.

At a table for two in a romantic restaurant, Dr. Shields is completely alone.

CHAPTER
TEN

Wednesday, November 28

YOU ENTER THE white-brick building on East Sixty-second Street and take the elevator to the third floor, as instructed. You press a buzzer to be admitted into the office, and you are welcomed inside.

You introduce yourself and offer your hand. Your grip is firm, and your palm feels cool.

Most people are intrigued by someone they've communicated with but have never met. They take a little time to reconcile the vision they may have created with the one standing before them.

Yet you make only perfunctory eye contact before you scan the room. Have you undertaken some research of your own?

Well done, Subject 52.

You are taller than presumed, perhaps five foot six, but otherwise there are no surprises. You unwrap the fringed blue scarf looped around your neck and smooth your hair, which is heavy with loose brown curls. Then you remove your coat, revealing a gray V-neck sweater and green cargo pants.

You've added subtle touches to your outfit: Your pants are rolled up to mid-calf length, just above your leather ankle boots. Your sweater is tucked in at the front to display a red woven belt. The ensemble should be a disaster, with the commingling of clashing colors and assorted fabrics. Yet it looks like something that could be featured on a fashion blog.

You are invited to sit down.

Where you choose to position yourself will be informative.

The seating area contains two leather wingback chairs and a love seat. Most people select the love seat.

Those who don't are typically men because, subconsciously, it allows them to feel authoritative in a vulnerable environment. The general rule is that clients who select a wingback are uncomfortable about being here.

You bypass the love seat and settle yourself in a chair, even though you exhibit no discomfort.

This is pleasing, and not completely unexpected.

The chair places you opposite the psychiatrist, directly at eye level. You look around again, taking an unhurried moment to orient yourself. The practitioner's office must make clients feel welcome, protected, and safe. If the environment is not harmonious, a client may find it more difficult to achieve a sense of ease, and therapeutic goals will prove more challenging.

Your eyes skim across the painting of steel-blue ocean waves, then past the fresh-cut camellias with crisp green stems wrapped inside an oval vase. Your gaze lingers on the books lining the shelves behind the desk. You are sharp; you take in details.

Perhaps you have even noticed the first rule of therapy: The clinician must remain somewhat of a blank slate. The items in the office that have drawn your eye cannot be identifiably personal. There are no family photographs; nothing controversial, such as an item that identifies political leanings or social causes; and nothing ostentatious, such as an Hermès logo on a couch pillow.

A second rule of therapy: Do not judge your clients. The clinician's role is to listen, to guide, to excavate the hidden truths of a patient's life.

The third rule is to allow the client to direct the initial course of the conversation, so the session is generally opened with a variation of, "What brings you here today?" But this is not a therapy session, so this particular rule is broken. Instead, you are thanked for your participation.

"Dr. Shields," you say, "before we begin, can I ask a few questions?"

Some people stumble, not knowing what form of address to use. You seem to understand the protocol instinctively: Despite the intimate revelations you have shared, boundaries need to be maintained . . . for now. Eventually the other two professional rules, as well as many more, will be broken for you.

You continue: "You said you'd explain about expanding my participation in your study. What does that mean?"

The project you have become engaged in is about to evolve from an academic exercise into a real-life exploration on morality and ethics, you are told.

Your eyes widen. With apprehension?

The scenarios will be perfectly safe, you are assured. You will be in complete control, and can back out at any time.

This appears to placate you.

You are reminded that the compensation is significantly higher.

This accomplishes the goal of further enticing you.

"How much higher?" you ask.

You are trying to move ahead too quickly. But this trial cannot be rushed. Trust must first be secured.

It is explained to you that a baseline must be established as the next step. You will be asked foundational questions.

If you agree to proceed, they will begin immediately.

"Sure," you say. "Fire away."

Your tone is nonchalant, but your hands slowly begin twisting together.

In response to the prompts, you describe your childhood in suburban Philadelphia, your younger sister with the traumatic brain injury and resulting cognitive and physical challenges, and your hardworking parents. You segue into your move to New York. Your eyes soften as you mention the little shelter dog you adopted, then you talk about selling cosmetics at Bloomingdale's.

You break eye contact and hesitate.

"I like your nail polish."

Deflection. This is a tactic you've not exhibited before.

"I could never wear burgundy, but it looks great on you."

Flattery. Common in therapy, when a client is trying to be evasive. Clinicians are trained to avoid making judgments about their patients. They simply listen for clues that will reveal what the client already knows, even if only subconsciously.

However, you are not in this office to explore your feelings, or to delve into unresolved issues with your mother.

You will not pay for this session, even though others who sit in your chair are charged $425 per hour. Instead, you will be compensated very generously.

Everyone has a price. Yours has yet to be determined.

You are staring at the therapist. The carefully constructed facade is working. It is all you see. It's all you will ever see.

However, you will be stripped bare. You will need to summon skills and strength you may not have known you possessed in the coming weeks.

But you appear up to the challenge.

You are here against all odds. You snuck into the study without being issued an invitation. You didn't share the same profile as the other women who were being evaluated.

The original study has been indefinitely suspended.

You, Subject 52, are now my sole focus.

CHAPTER
ELEVEN

Friday, November 30

DR. LYDIA SHIELDS'S SILVERY VOICE is a perfect match for her sleek exterior.

I perch on the love seat in her office during my second in-person session. Like the first one a few days ago, all I've done is talk about myself.

As I lean against the armrest, I continue peeling back the layers of lies I've told my parents: "If they knew I gave up on my dream of working in theater, it would be like they'd have to give up on theirs."

I've never been to see a psychiatrist before, but this seems like a traditional therapy session. A part of me can't help but wonder: Why is *she* the one who is paying *me*?

But after a few minutes, I'm not aware of anything other than the woman across from me and the secrets I'm sharing with her.

Dr. Shields looks at me so carefully when I speak. She waits a few moments before responding, as if she is rolling my words over in her mind, absorbing them thoroughly before choosing how to reply. Beside her, on a small end table, is the legal pad she occasionally reaches for to jot down notes. She uses her left hand to write, and she isn't wearing a wedding ring.

I wonder if she is divorced or maybe a widow.

I try to imagine what she is jotting down. On her desk rests a single manila folder with typed letters on the tab. I'm too far away to read the words. It could be my name, though.

Sometimes after I answer one of her questions, she pushes me to tell more; other times she offers insights so kind I'm almost brought to tears.

In such a short period, I already feel understood by her in a way I never have by anyone before.

"Do you think I'm wrong to deceive my parents?" I ask now.

Dr. Shields uncrosses her legs and rises from her cream-colored chair. She takes two steps toward me and I feel my body tense.

For a brief moment, I wonder if she plans to sit beside me, but she merely walks past. I twist my head and watch her lean down and grasp a handle at the bottom of one of her white wood bookshelves.

She pulls it open and reaches into a built-in mini refrigerator. She takes out two small bottles of Perrier and offers me one.

"Sure," I say. "Thanks."

I didn't think I was thirsty, but when I watch Dr. Shields tilt back her head and take a sip, I find my arm rising and I do the same. The glass bottle is comfortably substantial, and I'm surprised by how good the crisp, bubbly liquid tastes.

She crosses one leg over the other and I straighten up a bit, realizing I'm slumping.

"Your parents want you to be happy," Dr. Shields says. "All loving parents do."

I nod, and suddenly wonder if she has a child of her own. Unlike a wedding ring, there's no physical symbol you can wear to show the world that you're a mother.

"I know they love me," I say. "It's just . . ."

"They are accomplices in your fabrications," Dr. Shields says.

As soon as Dr. Shields speaks those words, I recognize the truth. Dr. Shields is right: My parents have practically encouraged me to lie.

She seems to realize I need a beat to take in the revelation. She keeps her eyes on me, and it feels almost protective, like she's trying to assess how her proclamation has landed. The silence between us doesn't feel awkward or heavy.

"I never thought of it that way," I finally say. "But you're right."

I take my last sip of Perrier, then carefully set the bottle down on the coffee table.

"I think I have all I need for today," Dr. Shields says.

She stands and I do the same. She walks over to her glass-topped desk, which holds a small clock, a slim laptop, and the manila folder.

As Dr. Shields slides open her desk's single drawer, she asks, "Any special plans for the weekend?"

"Not much. I'm taking my friend Lizzie out for her birthday tonight," I say.

Dr. Shields removes her checkbook and a pen. We've had two ninety-minute sessions this week, but I don't know how much I'll be getting.

"Oh, is she the one whose parents still give her an allowance?" Dr. Shields asks.

The term "allowance" takes me by surprise. I can't see Dr. Shields's expression, since her head is bent as she fills out the check, but her tone is mild; it doesn't seem like a criticism. Besides, it's the truth.

"I guess that's one way to describe her," I say as Dr. Shields tears off the check and hands it to me.

At the exact same moment, we both say, "Thank you." Then we laugh in unison, too.

"Are you available Tuesday, same time?" Dr. Shields asks.

I nod.

I'm dying to look at the amount on the check, but I feel like that would be tacky. I fold it and slip it into my bag.

"And I have a little something extra for you," Dr. Shields says. She reaches for her leather Prada purse and extracts a tiny package wrapped in silver paper.

"Why don't you open it?"

Usually I tear into gifts. But today I pull an edge of the little ribbon to unravel the bow, then slip my index finger under the tape, trying to be as neat as possible.

The Chanel box looks sleek and glossy.

Inside is a bottle of burgundy nail polish.

My head jerks up and I look into Dr. Shields's eyes. Then I glance at her fingertips.

"Try it, Jessica," she says. "I think it will look nice on you."

The second I'm in the elevator, I reach for the check. *Six hundred dollars,* she has written in graceful cursive.

She's paying me two hundred dollars an hour, even more than she did for the computer surveys.

I wonder if Dr. Shields will need me enough in the next month that I'll be able to surprise my family with a trip to Florida. Or maybe it'll be better to save the money in case my father can't land a decent job before they use up the buyout fund.

I tuck the check into my wallet and see the Chanel box in my bag. I know from my stint at the Bloomingdale's makeup counter that the nail polish costs close to thirty bucks.

I was planning to just take Lizzie out for drinks for her birthday, but she'd probably love this polish.

Try it, Dr. Shields had said.

I run my fingers over the elegant letters on the ebony box.

My best friend's parents are well-off enough to send her a monthly stipend. Lizzie is so unassuming I didn't realize until I went home with her for a weekend that her family's "little farm" is composed of a couple hundred acres. She can afford her own nail polish, even the fancy brands, I think to myself. I deserve this.

I walk into the Lounge a few hours later to meet Lizzie. Sanjay looks up from slicing lemons and beckons me over.

"That guy you left with the other night came in looking for you," he says. "Well, he actually was looking for a girl named Taylor, but I knew he meant you."

He rummages through a big beer mug next to the cash register that's stuffed with pens and business cards and a pack of Camel Lights. He pulls out a business card.

BREAKFAST ALL DAY it says across the top. Underneath is an illustration of a smiley face: Two sunny-side-up eggs serve as the eyes and a strip of bacon as the mouth. At the bottom is Noah's name and number.

I frown. "Is he a cook?"

Sanjay gives me a mock-stern look. "Did you talk at all?"

"Not about his profession," I shoot back.

"He seemed cool," Sanjay says. "He's opening a little restaurant a few blocks away."

I flip over the card and see the message: *Taylor, Good For One Free French Toast. Call To Redeem.*

Lizzie comes through the door just then. I jump off my stool and give her a hug.

"Happy Birthday," I say, palming the card so she doesn't see it.

She pulls off her jacket and I catch a whiff of the new leather smell. It looks a lot like the one I wear, which Lizzie has always admired, but I got mine at a thrift store. When I go to touch the fur collar, I see the label: BARNEYS NEW YORK.

"It's faux fur," Lizzie assures me, and I wonder what she read in my expression. "My parents gave it to me for my birthday."

"It's gorgeous," I say.

Lizzie lays it across her lap as she settles onto the stool next to me. I order us vodka-cran-sodas and she asks, "How was your Thanksgiving?"

The holiday seems like a lifetime ago.

"Oh, the usual. Too much pie and football. Tell me about yours."

"It was awesome," she says. "Everyone flew in and we played a giant game of charades. The little kids were hilarious. Can you believe I've got five nieces and nephews now? My dad—"

Lizzie cuts herself off as Sanjay slides the drinks over and I reach for mine.

"You never wear nail polish!" Lizzie exclaims. "Pretty color!"

I look down at my fingers. My skin is darker than Dr. Shields's, and my fingers are shorter. Instead of elegant, the color looks edgy on me. But she is right; it is flattering.

"Thanks. I wasn't sure if I could pull it off."

We chat through another two drinks, then Lizzie touches my arm. "Hey, can I borrow you Tuesday afternoon to do my makeup? I need an updated headshot."

"Ooh, I've got a sess—" I cut myself off. "A job way uptown."

During our first in-person meeting, Dr. Shields had me sign another, more detailed confidentiality agreement. I can't even mention her name to Lizzie.

"No prob, I'll figure it out," Lizzie says cheerfully. "Hey, should we get nachos?"

I nod and give the order to Sanjay. I feel bad that I can't help Lizzie.

And it feels strange to hide things from her, because she's the person who knows me best.

But maybe she doesn't any longer.

CHAPTER
TWELVE

Tuesday, December 4

YOU WERE UNSURE of the burgundy nail polish, but you wear it today.

This is evidence of your growing trust.

You also select the love seat again.

At first you lean back and fold your arms behind your head; your body language signals your increasing openness.

You don't believe you are ready for what will happen next. But you are.

You have been groomed for this; your emotional stamina stretched, similar to how a methodically planned increase in endurance prepares a runner for a marathon.

A few perfunctory warm-up questions about your weekend are asked.

And then: *In order for us to move forward, we need to go back.*

When those words are spoken, you abruptly adjust your position, pulling your arms down and crossing them over your body. Classic protective posturing.

You must already sense what lies ahead.

It is time for this final barrier to come down.

The question you shied away from during your very first computer session in Room 214 is presented once more, this time verbally, with a gentle but firm inflection:

Jessica, have you ever deeply hurt someone you care about?

You curl into yourself and look down at your feet, shielding your face.

The silence is permitted to linger.

Then:

Tell me.

Your head jerks up. Your eyes are wide. You suddenly look much younger than twenty-eight; it is as if a glimpse of your thirteen-year-old self briefly emerges.

That is the age when everything changed for you.

Every lifetime contains pivot points—sometimes flukes of destiny, sometimes seemingly preordained—that shape and eventually cement one's path.

These moments, as unique to each individual as strands of DNA, can at their best cause the sensation of a catapult into the shimmer of stars. At the opposite extreme, they can feel like a descent into quicksand.

The day you were watching your younger sister, the day she fell from a second-story window, was perhaps the most elemental demarcation for you thus far.

As you describe running toward her limp figure on the asphalt driveway, tears stream down your face. You begin to hyperventilate, gulping air between your words. Your body is retreating with your mind into this emotional chasm. You release one more anguished sentence, *It was all my fault,* before you succumb to violent trembling.

When the warm cashmere wrap is gently tucked around you and smoothed over your shoulders, it has the desired calming effect.

You take in a shuddering breath.

You are told what you need to hear:

It was not your fault.

There is more for you to share, but this is enough for today. You are nearing exhaustion.

You are rewarded through words of praise. Not everyone is brave enough to face their demons.

You absently stroke the taupe-colored wool draped across your shoulders as you listen. This is self-soothing, a signal that you are now in the recovery phase. A new, gentler conversational rhythm eases you into safer terrain.

When your breathing has steadied and your cheeks are no longer flushed, you are given subtle clues that the session will soon end.

Thank you, you are told.

Then a small reward:

It's so chilly out. Why don't you keep the wrap?

You are walked to the door, and when you leave, you feel the brief pressure of a hand squeezing your shoulder. The gesture is one that conveys comfort. It is also used to express approval.

As you exit the building, you are visible from three stories above. You hesitate on the sidewalk, then you reach for the wrap and loop it so that it hangs like a scarf, flipping one end over your shoulder.

Though you have physically departed, you linger in the office for the rest of the day, through the final client scheduled for twenty minutes after your departure. Maintaining focus to assist him on reining in a gambling addiction is more of a challenge than usual.

You are still there as the taxi weaves through congested Midtown traffic, and in Dean & DeLuca while the cashier rings up a single medallion of beef tenderloin and seven spears of white asparagus.

You don't award confidences easily, yet you yearn for the relief that comes with the release of a secret.

Presenting an unremarkable facade to the outside world is the norm; superficial conversations comprise the majority of social encounters. When an individual trusts another sufficiently to expose the true self—the deepest fears, the hidden desires—a powerful intimacy is born.

You invited me in today, Jessica.

Your secret will be kept in confidence . . . if all goes well.

The front door to the town house is unlocked and the bag from Dean & DeLuca deposited on the white marbled kitchen counter.

Then the new, ecru cashmere wrap that was purchased only hours before your session today is removed from its bag and placed on a side shelf in the coat closet.

It is identical to the one you are now wearing.

CHAPTER
THIRTEEN

Tuesday, December 4

THE AIR IS SHARP AND GRAY; during the short time I've been in Dr. Shields's office, the sun has dropped beneath the skyline.

I should have worn my heavy peacoat rather than my thinner leather jacket, but Dr. Shields's wrap keeps my chest and neck cozy. The wool holds a faint scent of the clean and spicy fragrance I now associate with Dr. Shields. I inhale deeply and it prickles my nose.

I stand on the sidewalk, at a loss about what to do. I feel drained, but if I go home, I doubt I'll be able to relax. I don't want to be alone, yet calling Lizzie or another friend to meet for dinner or a drink has no appeal.

Even before I realize I've made a decision, my feet begin to move, taking me toward the subway. I ride the 6 train to Astor Place, then exit the station and turn west on Prince Street.

I pass by the shop windows displaying designer sunglasses and cosmetics in jewel-like cases. Then I arrive at the French restaurant.

This time, I go in.

It's still early, so it is fairly empty. Just one couple occupies a booth near the back.

The maître d' takes my jacket, but I hold on to the wrap. He then asks, "Table for one? Or would you prefer the bar?"

"Actually, how about that table near the window?"

When he leads me to it, I select the chair Dr. Shields used when I followed her last week.

The wine list is a thick, heavy document. There are nearly a dozen options for glasses of red wine alone.

"This one, please," I tell the waiter, pointing to the second-cheapest. It's twenty-one dollars a glass, which means dinner tonight will be a peanut-butter sandwich at home.

I never would have found this restaurant if it hadn't been for Dr. Shields, but it is exactly what I need. It's hushed and elegant without being stuffy; the dark-wood walls and velvet-topped chairs are comfortingly substantial.

It's a safe place to be anonymous but not alone.

The waiter approaches. He's wearing a dark suit and balancing my glass of wine on a tray.

"Your Volnay, miss," he says, setting it down before me.

I realize he's waiting for me to approve of it. I take a small sip and nod, like Dr. Shields did. The burgundy liquid is a perfect match for my nail polish.

When he leaves, I glance out the window, watching people pass by. The wine warms my throat and isn't overly sweet, like the stuff my mom drinks; it tastes surprisingly good. My shoulders relax as I lean back into the soft leather of my seat.

Dr. Shields finally knows the story I haven't even shared with Lizzie: It was my deliberate negligence that ruined the lives of everyone in my family.

As I sat on Dr. Shields's love seat and stared at the soothing blue waves in the painting on her wall, I described how I was supposed to watch Becky that summer while my parents went to work.

It was late on that August afternoon when I decided to go to the corner market, the one that sold penny candy and *Seventeen* magazine. The new issue had recently come out. Julia Stiles was on the cover.

I was tired of Becky; I needed a break from my seven-year-old sister. It was a long, hot day toward the end of a long, hot month. In the past few hours alone, we'd run through the sprinklers and made ice pops by pouring lemonade into ice-cube trays and sticking in toothpicks. We'd caught bugs in the backyard and made homes for them in an old Tupperware container. And still, my parents weren't due back from work for a couple of hours.

"I'm bored," Becky had whined as I'd tweezed my eyebrows in the bathroom mirror. I was worried I had overplucked the right one and now wore an awkward quizzical expression.

"Go play with your dollhouse," I said as I turned my attention to my left brow. I was thirteen, and newly concerned about my appearance.

"I don't want to."

The house was warm, since we had only two window air-conditioning units. I couldn't believe I was looking forward to going back to school.

A few moments later Becky called out, "Who's Roger Franklin?"

"Becky!" I yelled as I dropped the tweezers and ran into my room. I snatched my diary out of her hands. "That's private!"

"I'm bored," she whined again.

"Fine," I told Becky. "Don't let Mom and Dad know, but you can watch some more TV in their room."

My parents had a one-hour-a-day rule, which we routinely exceeded.

On that long-ago afternoon, I put three Chips Ahoy! cookies on a paper plate and gave them to Becky as she lay sprawled on my parents' bed. "Be neat," I instructed. On the screen, Lizzie McGuire began telling a friend to stop mimicking her. I waited until a glazed look came into Becky's eyes. Then I crept outside and hopped on my bike. Becky didn't like being alone, but I knew she would never even notice I was gone.

I'd done this a few times before.

I'd also locked the bedroom door, so Becky couldn't get out. I thought it would keep her safe. But I didn't think to lock the second-floor window that was just a few feet away from where she lay watching her show.

I'd pulled my gaze away from the painting on Dr. Shields's wall when I got to this part. It was difficult to speak because I was crying so hard. I didn't know if I'd be able to continue.

I saw Dr. Shields looking at me. The compassion in her eyes seemed to give me strength. I choked out the awful words.

Then I felt a sudden warmth and softness cocoon me.

Dr. Shields had removed her wrap from around her shoulders and placed it over mine. It still seemed to hold the heat from her body.

I realize I'm absently stroking the wrap again now as I sit in the dim restaurant.

Dr. Shields's gesture felt protective, almost maternal. Immediately, the tension in my limbs had begun to ease. It was like she somehow pulled me out of that dark moment and back into the present.

It was not your fault, she'd said.

I take the last sip of wine, listening to the classical music playing over the speakers, thinking that of all the things she could have said, these seem like the only words that could have truly comforted me. If Dr. Shields—someone so wise and sophisticated, someone who has spent her career studying the moral choices people make—could absolve me, then maybe my parents could, too.

There's something they don't know about that day.

My parents never asked where I was when Becky fell. They just assumed I was home in another room.

I didn't tell a lie. But there was a small, still moment at the hospital when I could have spoken up. While a team of doctors tended to Becky, my parents and I waited in a small private area just outside the ER. "Oh, Becky. Why were you playing around with that window?" my mother wondered aloud.

I looked into my parents' red-rimmed, anguished eyes. And I let that moment pass.

I didn't know the omission would continue to swell and gain in strength with every passing year.

I didn't know that tiny bit of silence would deafen all of my relationships.

But now Dr. Shields knows.

I realize my fingers are playing with the stem of the empty glass and I pull them away as the server approaches. "Another glass of wine, miss?" he asks.

I shake my head.

My next session is in two days.

I wonder if Dr. Shields will want to talk more about that event, or whether I've told her enough.

My hand freezes as I reach into my bag to retrieve my wallet.

Enough for what?

The thought I had a moment ago, that now Dr. Shields has information I've hidden from my family for fifteen years, is no longer a comfort. Maybe Dr. Shields's accomplishments and beauty have blinded me and dulled my self-protective instincts.

I'd almost forgotten that I was Subject 52 in an academic study. That I was being paid to share my innermost secrets.

What is she planning to do with all the private information I've given her? I was the one who signed a confidentiality agreement; she didn't.

The waiter comes back to the table and I unzip my wallet. Then I see the bright blue business card tucked between the folds of my bills.

I look at it for a few seconds, and slowly ease it out.

Breakfast All Day it says on the front.

I remember waking up on Noah's couch, a blanket tucked around me.

I turn the card over, feeling a sharp corner gently scrape my palm.

Taylor, Noah wrote in his blocky penmanship.

I skim over his words offering to cook me French toast.

That's not why I'm staring at the card.

I suddenly know how I can learn more about Dr. Shields.

CHAPTER
FOURTEEN

Tuesday, December 4

THE CHERRY NOTES of the Pinot Noir melt away the icy rawness of the commute home.

The seared beef tenderloin and grilled asparagus are removed from the Dean & DeLuca containers and arranged on a china plate, flanked by heavy silverware. Chopin's piano chords fill the room. The single dish is carried to one end of the glossy oak rectangular table.

Dinners used to look different here. They were cooked on a six-burner Viking stove and adorned with sprigs of fresh rosemary or leaves of basil from the herb garden in the window box.

The table also held two place settings.

The psychology journal is laid down; it is impossible to concentrate on the dense words tonight.

Across the table, an empty chair remains where my husband Thomas once sat.

Everyone who met Thomas liked him.

He appeared on a night when the lights flickered, and then darkness swept in.

The last client of the day, a man named Hugh, had departed my office only a few minutes before. People come to therapy for different reasons, but his never became clear. Hugh was an odd one, with his sharp features and nomadic existence.

Despite his wanderings, he fixated on things, he divulged early on. Ending his sessions was difficult; he always wanted more.

Whenever he left, he lingered outside the door, his footsteps not beginning for a minute or two. His pungent scent could be detected in the waiting room even after he was gone, evidence of the time he'd spent there.

When the entire building went dark that night, even the lights outside the windows, it seemed natural to assume Hugh was involved.

The worst of humanity comes out in the shadows.

And Hugh had just been told that his therapy needed to be terminated.

Sirens began to wail in the distance. The noises and lack of illumination created a disorienting atmosphere.

To exit the building, it was necessary to take the stairs. It was seven P.M., late enough that all of the other offices appeared closed.

Although residents lived in the building, their apartments were only on floors five and six.

The sole light in the stairwell came from the screen of my phone, the only sound the tapping of my shoes against the steps.

Then a second pair of footsteps, much heavier ones, began to descend from somewhere above.

Symptoms of terror include a racing heart, light-headedness, and chest pain.

Breathing exercises can only help people through situations in which panic is not warranted.

Here, it was.

My presence would be announced by the glow of my phone. Running in complete darkness could lead to a fall. But these were necessary risks.

"Hello?" a man's deep voice called.

It did not belong to Hugh.

"What's going on? It must be a blackout," the man continued. "Are you okay?"

His manner was soothing and kind. He stayed by my side for the next hour, during the trek from Midtown to the West Village, until we reached my residence.

In every lifetime, there are pivot points that shape and eventually cement one's path.

Thomas Cooper's materialization was one of these seismic moments.

A week after the blackout, we went to dinner.

Six months later, we were married.

Everyone who met Thomas liked him.

But loving him was something reserved only for me.

CHAPTER
FIFTEEN

Tuesday, December 4

I HAVE LESS THAN forty-eight hours to locate Taylor.

She is my sole fragile link to Dr. Shields. If I can track her down before my next session on Thursday at five P.M., I won't be going into it blind.

After I leave the French restaurant, I find Taylor's contact info in my phone and text her: *Hi Taylor, It's Jess from BeautyBuzz. Can you call me asap?*

When I get home, I grab my laptop and try to glean more information about Dr. Shields. But my search yields only academic papers, reviews of the book she authored, her four-line NYU biography, and a website for her private practice. The website is sleek and elegant, like her office but, also like that space, it doesn't contain a single real clue about the woman it represents.

I finally fall asleep after midnight, my phone by my side.

Wednesday, December 5

When I wake up at six A.M., my eyes heavy from my restless night, Taylor still hasn't responded. I'm not really surprised; she probably thinks it's bizarre that some makeup artist is trying to reach her.

Thirty-five hours left, I think.

Even though I want to skip my back-to-back appointments and continue to try to get answers, I have to go to work. Not only do I need the money, but BeautyBuzz has a policy that makeup artists must give a full day's notice before canceling scheduled jobs. Three strikes in three months and you're eliminated from their roster. Since I called in sick a few weeks ago, I already have one.

I feel like I'm on autopilot as I smooth foundation, blend shadows, and line lips. I ask about clients' jobs, husbands, and kids, but I keep thinking about Dr. Shields. Especially about how little I know of her personally, and contrasting that with the deep secrets I've shared with her.

I'm persistently aware of my phone tucked inside my bag. The second I leave each appointment, I snatch it up and check the screen. But even though I leave Taylor another message, this one via voice mail at around noon, there is no response.

At seven P.M. I splurge on a taxi home, which burns through the tips from my last few jobs but gets me there faster. I drop my case just inside the door, hustle Leo up and down the street and throw him a few treats, then hurry back out.

I head directly to Taylor's apartment a couple dozen blocks away at a pace just short of a run. When I get there, it's nearly eight P.M. I lean a hand against the glass case containing the lobby directory, panting, and search the listed names.

I press the buzzer for T. Straub, then wait to hear her voice over the intercom. I try to slow my breathing, then smooth a hand over my hair.

I press my finger against the little black circle again, this time for a full five seconds.

Come on, I think.

I step back, looking up at the building, and wonder what I should do next. I can't just wait around, hoping Taylor will return. How long can I continue jabbing at her buzzer on the off chance she is napping or listening to music on her headphones?

Assistance arrives in the form of a sweaty guy dressed in an Adidas tracksuit, who taps in the front door code. He's busy staring at his phone and doesn't even notice me as I catch the door before it closes and sneak in behind him.

I take the stairs to the sixth floor. I find Taylor's apartment midway down the hall and rap my knuckles against the door so firmly they sting.

No answer.

I press my ear against the flimsy wood, listening for any sounds that would indicate she is inside—the blaring of a television or the drone of a hair dryer. But there is only silence.

Nausea grips my stomach. I fear Dr. Shields knows me so well that when I see her I won't be able to camouflage my worries. I'm desperate to ask her questions: *Why are you giving me all this money? What are you doing with the information I give you?*

But I can't. I've been telling myself it's so I don't risk losing the income. But the truth is, maybe it's more that I don't want to risk losing Dr. Shields.

I lift my fist and thump a few more times, until the next-door neighbor sticks out her head and glares at me.

"Sorry," I say meekly and she shuts her door again.

I try to think of what to do next. I've got twenty-one hours left. But tomorrow, like today, is full of clients; I won't be able to come back before my appointment with Dr. Shields. I dig into my bag and pull out the copy of *Vogue* I am carrying around and tear out a piece of the glossy paper. I locate a pen and scribble: *Taylor, It's Jess again, from Beauty-Buzz. Please call me. It's urgent.*

I'm about to stick it under her door when I think back to the messy apartment with the SkinnyPop popcorn and clothes lying about. Taylor might not even notice the scrap of paper. And even if she did, she probably still won't contact me. It's not like she has made any effort to return my call or text.

I turn to look at the door of the neighbor I just disturbed. I take a few steps to the side and hesitantly knock on it. The woman who answers is clutching a yellow highlighter. A smear of it bisects her chin. She is visibly unhappy.

"Sorry, I'm looking for Taylor or, uh . . ." I reach back in my memory for her roommate's name and find it. "Or Mandy."

The neighbor blinks at me. A strange premonition sweeps over me: She is going to say she doesn't know who they are, that no girls by those names have ever lived next door.

"Who?" she begins.

My heart stutters.

Then her frown clears.

"Oh, yeah . . . I don't know, finals are coming up, maybe they're at the library. Although with those two, it's more likely they're at some party."

She closes her door while I'm still standing there.

I wait until the feeling of light-headedness has passed, then head to the stairwell. I stand outside the building in the darkness, trying to think of my next move.

A girl with long straight hair passes me. Even though I instantly know she isn't Taylor, I still turn to look at her as she shrugs a blue backpack higher up onto her shoulders and continues down the sidewalk.

I stare at the heavy-looking bag. *Finals are coming up,* the neighbor had said. Her impression of Taylor and Mandy meshed with mine: that these two don't take school all that seriously.

It's hard to picture the jaded young woman with the enviable bone structure who was tapping away at her Instagram feed now bent over a stack of textbooks.

But aren't the most lackadaisical students sometimes the ones who have to cram the hardest before exams?

I spin around in a circle to orient myself, then head toward the NYU library.

The stacks are like a maze laid out for a laboratory rat. I begin at one corner, winding my way through the narrow passageways, hoping at every turn that I'll stumble upon Taylor reaching for a book on a high shelf, or sitting at one of the desks near the outer walls. I finish scouring the first three floors, then I make my way to the fourth.

Frenetic energy propels me forward, even though it's almost nine P.M. and I haven't eaten anything since a turkey sandwich I gobbled between my early-afternoon clients. There are far fewer people on this floor, though the towers of books are just as high. Whispered conversations filtered through to me on the first three levels, but now the only sounds I hear are my own footsteps.

I'm deep into the center of the stacks when I abruptly turn a corner and almost walk into a guy and girl passionately kissing. They don't break apart as I step around them.

Then I hear a familiar voice, stretched out into a whine: "Tay, let's take a break. I need a chai latte."

Relief courses through me and I have to restrain myself from sprinting in the direction of Mandy's voice.

I find them in a corner of the room. Mandy is leaning against the edge of a desk piled high with books and a laptop, and Taylor is sitting in the chair. Both girls have their hair piled up in artfully messy buns and are wearing Juicy Couture sweats.

"Taylor!"

Her name comes out almost as a gasp.

She and Mandy both turn to look at me. Mandy's nose wrinkles. Taylor wears a blank expression.

"Can I help you?" Taylor asks.

She has no idea who I am.

I draw closer. "It's me, Jess."

"Jess?" Mandy echoes.

"The makeup artist," I say. "From BeautyBuzz."

Taylor looks me up and down. I'm still in my work outfit, but my shirt has become untucked and I can feel the errant strands that have escaped from my low twist sticking to my neck.

"What are you doing here?" Taylor asks.

"I need to talk to you."

Shhh! someone hushes us from a few desks away.

"Please, it's important," I whisper.

Maybe Taylor can sense my desperation, because she nods. She shoves her laptop into her bag but leaves her books. We take the elevator down to the lobby with Mandy trailing behind us. When we reach the main doors, Taylor pauses. "What is it?"

Now that I've finally found her, I don't know where to begin.

"So, remember when I was doing your makeup and you mentioned a questionnaire?"

She shrugs. "Sort of."

It's been weeks since I took Taylor's phone and listened to her voice mail. I try to recall what I knew back then.

"The one with the NYU professor about morality. It paid a lot of money. You were supposed to go the next morning . . ."

Taylor nods. "Yeah, that's right. I was too tired, so I canceled."

I take a deep breath.

"So . . . I ended up doing it."

Wariness fills Taylor's eyes. She takes a step back.

Mandy makes a little sound in her throat: "Well, that's weird," she says.

"Yeah, anyway . . . I'm trying to find out a bit more about the professor." I try to keep my voice steady as I look at Taylor.

"I don't know her; a friend who's a psych major took her class and told me about the study. C'mon, Mandy."

"Wait, please!" My voice is shrill. I soften my tone. "Could I talk to your friend?"

Taylor assesses me for a moment. I try to smile, but I know it probably looks unnatural.

"It's complicated, and I don't want to bore you with all the details," I say. "But if you like, I can tell you the whole story—"

Taylor holds up a hand: "Just call Amy."

I'm glad I remembered these girls hate to be bored. It was the right tack to take.

She looks down at her phone, then recites the number as I tap it onto my own screen.

"Would you mind repeating that?" I ask. I'm pretty sure Mandy rolls her eyes, but Taylor gives me the digits again, this time more slowly.

"Thank you!" I call as they walk away.

Before they even turn the corner, I've dialed Amy.

She answers on the second ring.

"She was a great teacher," Amy says. "I had her last spring. A tough grader, but not unfair . . . She really worked you. I think only two people in the class got A's and I wasn't one of them." She gives a little laugh. "What more can I tell you? She has an amazing wardrobe. I'd kill for her shoes."

Amy is in a taxi, on her way to LaGuardia Airport to fly home for her grandmother's ninetieth birthday celebration.

"Did you know about her study?" I ask.

"Sure," Amy says. "I was in it."

She isn't suspicious about my questions, probably because I implied Taylor and I are friends, too. "It's a little weird, because she must have realized who I was when I signed up, but she didn't call me by my name. It was something strange . . . what was it again?"

She hesitates.

My breath catches in my lungs.

"Subject 16," Amy finally says. My skin tingles.

"I remember the number because that's my younger brother's age," she continues.

"What did she ask you?" I interject.

"Hang on a sec." I hear her say something to the taxi driver, then the sound of rustling and a trunk slamming.

"Um, there was one about whether I'd ever lied on a medical form— you know, like, how much I drink, or my weight, or how many sexual partners I've had. I remember that one because I'd just had a physical and I'd lied about all those things!"

She's laughing again, but I frown.

"I'm at the airport. I gotta go," Amy says.

"Did you ever meet with her in person for the study?" I blurt.

"Huh? No, it was just a bunch of questions on a computer," Amy says. The ambient noises are so loud—people calling and chattering, a loudspeaker blaring an announcement about unattended bags—that I have trouble hearing her clearly. "Anyway, I need to check in; it's total chaos here."

I press on: "You never went to her office on Sixty-second Street? Did any of the subjects go there?"

"I don't know, maybe some people did," she says. "How cool would that be? I bet it's totally chic."

I have more questions, but I know I'm about to lose Amy.

"Could you do me a favor?" I say. "Could you think about it a little more and call me if you remember anything unusual?"

"Sure," Amy says, but her voice is distracted and I wonder if she has even registered my request.

I hang up and feel something in my chest unclench.

My most important question has been answered, at least. Dr. Shields is a pro; she's not only a professor, she's a well-respected one. She wouldn't have this position if she were doing anything shady.

I'm not sure why I got so worked up. I'm hungry and tired, plus the stress I've been feeling about my family might be affecting me. My father's final day of work was November 30; his buyout is four months' salary. They'll run out of money by the time the Phillies have their first at bat of the season.

I'm exhausted by the time I turn the corner onto my street. My mind is whirling and my body feels simultaneously weighty and restless.

As I pass the Lounge, I look through the big glass windows. I can hear the faint strain of the music, and I see a group of guys playing pool.

I find myself looking for Noah.

I reach for Noah's card and pull it out. Before I think about it too much, I text him: *Hey, just walked by the Lounge and thought of you. Has that offer for breakfast expired?*

He doesn't respond immediately, so I keep walking.

I think about stopping by another bar. The Atlas is close by and it's usually packed around this time, even on weeknights. I could go in alone, sit at the bar, order a drink, and see what happens, like I've done before when the pressure gets to be too much and I need an escape.

Since I can't afford a spa day and I don't do drugs, this is the way I find a release. I don't do it all that often, although the last time I had to tell my doctor how many sexual partners I've had, I lied about it, just as Amy did.

I draw closer to the Atlas. I can hear the pulse of music; I can see the crush of bodies near the bar.

But then I picture sitting on the love seat in Dr. Shields's office, describing my night to her. She knows I do this sometimes; I wrote about it on the computer questionnaire. But having to look at her and reveal the details about a hookup would be mortifying. I bet even before she was married, she never had a one-night stand; I can just tell.

Dr. Shields seems to see something special in me, even though I don't often feel that way about myself.

So I keep walking.

I don't want to disappoint her.

CHAPTER
SIXTEEN

Wednesday, December 5

IT'S EASY TO JUDGE other people's choices. The mother with a grocery cart full of Froot Loops and Double Stuf Oreos who yells at her child. The driver of an expensive convertible who cuts off a slower vehicle. The husband who cheats on his wife . . . and the wife who is considering taking him back.

But what if you knew the husband was making every effort to reconcile? What if he swore it was a onetime lapse and that he would never be unfaithful again?

And what if you were the wife, and could not imagine a life without him?

The intellect does not reign supreme in matters of the heart.

Thomas captured mine in a hundred different ways. The inscription we chose for our wedding bands, the one that referenced our first meeting during the blackout, came close to describing a feeling that is impossible to put into words: *You are my true light.*

Since he moved out, his absence is everywhere in the town house: In the living room, where he splayed across the couch with the sports section scattered on the floor beside him. In the kitchen, where he always programmed the coffeemaker the night before so it would be ready in the morning. In the bedroom, where his warm body took away the chill at night.

When a marriage is shattered by the ultimate betrayal, physical reactions result: Insomnia. Loss of appetite. The constant worry, as relentless as a pulsing heartbeat: *What drew him to her?*

If the man you loved gave you reason to doubt him, could you ever trust him again?

This evening, Thomas blamed a work emergency for the cancellation of dinner plans.

He is also a therapist, so it's entirely possible a client could be suffering an acute panic attack or a recovering alcoholic could be having an uncontrollable urge to indulge in self-destructive behavior.

He cares deeply about his patients. Most even have access to his cell phone number.

But was his voice excessively flustered?

Doubt surrounds even the most banal of explanations.

This is the legacy of infidelity.

Many women might choose to take their worry to a friend for discussion. Others might accuse; provoke a confrontation. Neither of those courses is inappropriate.

But they may not unearth the truth.

Judgments might also be made about a wife who remained suspicious enough to spy on her husband despite his assurances.

But only clinical evidence can determine if insecurity or instinct is driving the suspicion.

In this case, facts can be easily enough obtained. All that is required is a twenty-five-minute taxi ride uptown, to the office space he shares with three other clinicians on Riverside Drive.

It is now 6:07 P.M.

If his Ducati is not parked out front, the facts will not support the excuse.

The symptoms of anxiety typically include perspiration, a spike in blood pressure, and physical restlessness.

But not for everyone. A rare few present the opposite symptoms: There is a physical quieting, an enhanced mental focus, and a chilling of the extremities.

The cabdriver is asked to increase the temperature by a few degrees.

From a block away, it is impossible to determine if the motorcycle is present. A FreshDirect truck clogs the narrow street, impeding the taxi's progress.

It is swifter to exit the taxi and proceed on foot.

A flood of relief accompanies the realization that the office is occupied: Light blazes through the slats of the blinds on the ground floor. His motorcycle is parked outside in its usual spot.

Thomas is exactly where he said he would be.

Doubt is banished, for now.

It is unnecessary to proceed any further. He is busy. And it is better if he doesn't know about this visit.

From a block away in the other direction, a woman approaches. She wears a long, swinging camel-colored coat and jeans.

She stops in front of Thomas's building. During business hours, a security guard requires guests to sign in. But the guard leaves at six P.M. At this time of night, visitors must press a buzzer to be admitted.

The woman is perhaps in her early thirties. Objectively attractive, even from a distance. She does not display any outward symptoms of a crisis; to the contrary, her affect is carefree.

She is not the same woman who tempted Thomas to stray from our marriage; that woman will never be a threat again.

The woman in the swinging coat disappears inside Thomas's building. A few moments later the blinds that were slightly ajar snap shut.

Perhaps the glare of the street lamp was in her eyes.

Or perhaps there is another reason.

If a guy cheats once, he's probably going to do it again.

You were the one who issued that warning, Jessica.

Some wives would push through the door to get a closer look. Others might choose to wait to see how long the woman remained inside, and if the parties in question emerged from the building together. A few might assume defeat and walk away.

Those are typical responses.

There are other, far more subtle courses of action.

Watching and waiting for the right moment is an essential component of a long-term strategy. It would be impulsive to swoop in and engage in a conflict before certainty is obtained.

And sometimes a warning shot, a decisive show of strength, can circumvent the need for a battle at all.

CHAPTER
SEVENTEEN

MY CLIENTS' SKIN often reveals something about their lives.

When the sixty-something woman opens her door, I notice the clues: Many smile lines; far fewer from frowning. Her pale complexion is dotted with freckles and sunspots, and her blue eyes are bright.

She introduces herself as Shirley Graham, then takes my coat and wrap, which I've brought so I can return it to Dr. Shields, and hangs them in her tiny hall closet.

I follow her into her galley kitchen, set down my makeup case, and gently flex and straighten my hand to ease the tightness. It's 3:55 P.M., and Mrs. Graham is my last appointment of the day. Right after I finish here, I'm going to see Dr. Shields.

I've vowed to finally ask her why she needs information about my personal life. It's such a reasonable question. I don't know why I haven't felt able to bring it up before.

Before we start, would you mind if I asked a question? That's how I'm going to phrase it, I've decided.

"Would you like some tea?" Mrs. Graham offers.

"Oh, no, I'm fine, but thanks," I say.

Mrs. Graham looks disappointed. "It's no trouble. I always have tea at four."

Dr. Shields's office is a half hour away, assuming there's no subway delay, and I'm due there at five-thirty. I hesitate. "You know what? Tea sounds great."

While Mrs. Graham pries the lid off a blue tin of Royal Dansk butter cookies and arranges them on a little china plate, I scout out the best lighting in the apartment.

"What's the big event tonight?" I ask as I step onto the living room's frayed rug and move aside a gauzy, lace-topped curtain covering the sole window. But the brick wall of a neighboring apartment blots out the sun.

"I'm going to dinner," she says. "It's my wedding anniversary—forty-two years."

"Forty-two years," I say. "That's wonderful."

I walk back to the small counter that separates the kitchen from the living area.

"I've never had my makeup done by a professional before, but I have this coupon, so I thought, *Why not?*" Mrs. Graham pulls the slip of paper off the refrigerator, where it was secured with a magnet shaped like a daisy, and hands it to me.

The coupon expired two months ago, but I pretend not to notice. Hopefully my boss will honor it; if not, I'll have to eat the cost.

The kettle shrieks and Mrs. Graham pours the steaming water into a china pot, then dips in two bags of Lipton tea.

"How about we work right here while we have tea," I suggest, gesturing to two high-back stools pulled up to the counter. The space is barely adequate for my supplies, but the overhead light is strong.

"Oh, are you in a rush?" Mrs. Graham asks as she covers the pot with a quilted cozy and sets it down on the counter.

"No, no, we've got plenty of time," I say reflexively.

I regret it when she goes to the refrigerator and takes out a pint of half-and-half, then retrieves a little china pitcher and transfers the cream into it. As she arranges the cups and teapot and cream and sugar on a tray, I steal a glance at the clock on the microwave: 4:12.

"Shall we get started?" I pull back Mrs. Graham's stool and pat the seat. Then I reach into my case and select a few bottles of oil-based foundation, which will be kinder to Mrs. Graham's skin. I begin to mix two together on the back of my hand, noticing my burgundy polish has a tiny chip.

Before I can begin to apply it, Mrs. Graham bends over and peers into my case. "Oh, look at all your little pots and potions!" She points to an egg-shaped sponge. "What's this for?"

"Blending foundation," I say. My fingers feel itchy with the need to continue. I fight the urge to turn around and glance at the kitchen clock. "Here, let me show you."

If I select a single shadow for her eyes rather than a trio—maybe an oatmeal hue to bring out the blue—I can finish on time. Her makeup will still look good; it won't betray the shortcut.

I'm smoothing the last bit of concealer under her eyes when a telephone rings a few inches away from my elbow.

Mrs. Graham eases off her stool. "Excuse me, dear. Let me tell them I'll call back."

What can I do but smile and nod?

Maybe I should grab a cab instead of taking the subway. But it's rush hour; a taxi could actually take longer.

I steal a glance at my phone: It's 4:28, and I've missed a couple of texts. One is from Noah: *Sorry I couldn't meet you last night. How about Saturday?*

"Oh, I'm doing just fine. I've got this nice young lady here and we're having tea," Mrs. Graham is saying into the receiver.

I quickly type a reply: *Sounds great.*

The second text is from Dr. Shields.

Could you please phone me before our appointment? Dr. Shields has written.

"Okay, sweetheart, I promise I'll call you back as soon as we're done," Mrs. Graham says. But her tone contains no indication that she's trying to wrap up the conversation.

The room is overly warm, and I can feel perspiration dampen my armpits. I fan myself with my open hand, thinking, *Wrap it up!*

"Yes, I visited earlier today," Mrs. Graham says. I wonder if I should just call Dr. Shields now. Or at least send her a quick text explaining I'm with a client.

Before I can make a decision, Mrs. Graham finally hangs up and returns to her stool.

"That was my daughter," she says. "She lives in Ohio. Cleveland. It's such a nice area; they moved two years ago because of her husband's job. My son—he's my firstborn—lives in New Jersey."

"How nice," I say, picking up a copper eyeliner.

Mrs. Graham reaches for her tea, blowing on it before she takes a sip, and I clench the eyeliner a little tighter in my hand.

"Try the cookies," she says, hunching her shoulders conspiratorially. "The ones with jelly in the middle are the best."

"I really need to finish your makeup," I say, my tone sharper than I intended. "I have a meeting right after this, and I can't be late. "

Mrs. Graham's expression dims and she sets down her teacup. "I'm sorry, dear. I don't want to hold you up."

I wonder if Dr. Shields would know how I should have handled the quandary: *Be late for an important appointment, or hurt the feelings of a sweet older woman?*

I look at the butter cookies, the little pink-and-white china pitcher and matching sugar bowl, the quilted cozy over the freshly made tea. The most any other client has ever offered me before is a glass of water.

Kindness is the right answer; I chose wrong.

I try to regain our merry banter, asking about her grandchildren as I dab a rose-colored cream blush onto her cheeks, but she is subdued now. Despite my efforts, her eyes appear less bright than when I entered her apartment.

When I finish, I tell her she looks great.

"Go check yourself out in the mirror," I say, and she heads to the bathroom.

I pull out my phone, planning to try to quickly call Dr. Shields, and see she has sent me another text: *I hope you receive this before you come here. I need you to pick up a package on your way to my office. It's under my name.*

All she has provided is an address in Midtown. I have no idea if it's a store, an office, or a bank. It'll only add ten minutes to my journey, but I don't have them to spare.

No problem, I text.

"You did such a nice job," Mrs. Graham calls.

I begin to take our teacups to the sink, but she comes back into the room and waves her hand at me. "Oh, I'll take care of all that. You have to get to your meeting."

I still feel guilty that I was impatient with her, but she has a husband and a son and a daughter, I remind myself as I pack up my things, tossing my brushes and cases into my kit rather than taking the time to organize them.

Mrs. Graham's phone rings again.

"Feel free to get that," I say. "I'm all finished here."

"Oh, no, I'll see you out, dear."

She opens the closet door and hands me my jacket.

"Have fun tonight!" I say as I slip it on. "Happy Anniversary."

Before she can reply, a man's voice fills the room, coming from the old-fashioned answering machine next to her phone.

"Hey, Mom. Where are you? I was just calling to say Fiona and I are heading out now. We should be there in about an hour . . ."

Something in his tone makes me take a closer look at Mrs. Graham. She is staring down, though, as if she is trying to evade my eyes.

Her son's voice grows rougher. "I hope you're doing okay."

The closet door is still ajar. My gaze is pulled inside, even though I already know what will be missing. Her son's tone told me what I've misjudged.

Mrs. Graham isn't going to dinner with her husband tonight.

I visited earlier today, she'd told her daughter.

I suddenly know where she went. I can see her kneeling to set down a bouquet of flowers, lost in the memories of the almost forty-two years they had together.

On one side of the closet hang three coats—a raincoat, a light jacket, and a heavier wool one. They're all women's coats.

The other half of the closet is bare.

CHAPTER
EIGHTEEN

Thursday, December 6

YOU'RE FIGHTING the urge to peek inside, aren't you?

You picked up the package a few minutes ago. The wrapping reveals no clues about its contents. The sturdy, generic-looking white bag with the reinforced handle and no logo, is stuffed with tissue paper to protect the object within.

You retrieved it from a young man who lives in a small apartment building. You probably barely got a look at him as he handed it over; he's a taciturn individual. There was nothing for you to sign; the object had been paid for and the receipt e-mailed to the purchaser.

As you quickly stride down Sixth Avenue, you might be rationalizing that it really wouldn't be snooping. There is no seal to break, or tape to remove. The next time you pause at a street corner waiting for the light to turn, you could simply peel back a few layers of tissue and catch a glimpse. *No one will ever know,* you might be telling yourself.

The bag is heavy in your hand, but not uncomfortably so.

Your mind is curious by nature, and you alternately shy away from and embrace risks. Which side of you will win dominance today?

You will need to see the contents of this bag, but you should only view it on the terms dictated in this office.

You've been told these are our foundational sessions, but there is more than a single foundation being laid.

Sometimes a test is so small and quiet you don't even notice it's a test.

Sometimes a relationship that appears caring and supportive carries hidden danger.

Sometimes a therapist who coaxes out all of your secrets is holding the biggest one in the room.

You arrive at the office at four minutes past the appointed time. You are out of breath, though you try to conceal this by taking quick, shallow inhalations. A lock of hair has worked itself loose from your topknot, and you are wearing a simple black top and black jeans. It's surprisingly disappointing that your ensemble is uninspired today.

"Hi, Dr. Shields," you say. "Sorry I'm a little late. I was at work when you texted."

You set down your large makeup case and offer up the bag. Your expression does not convey guilt or evasiveness.

Your response to the unorthodox request thus far has been flawless.

You agreed immediately. You did not ask a single question. You were not given much advance notice, yet you rushed to complete the task.

Now for the final piece.

"Are you curious about what is inside?"

The question is asked lightly, without the slightest hint of accusation.

You give a little laugh and say, "Yeah, I was guessing maybe a couple of books?"

Your response is natural, unfiltered. You maintain eye contact. You don't fiddle with your silver rings. You don't exhibit a tell.

You suppressed your curiosity. You continue to prove your loyalty.

Now the question you've carried for the past twelve blocks can be satisfied.

A sculpture of a falcon—Murano glass containing gold leaf flecks—is carefully eased out of the bag. The crest of the falcon is cold and smooth.

"Wow," you say.

"It's a gift for my husband. Go ahead, you can touch it."

You hesitate. A frown creases your brow.

"It's not as fragile as it looks," you are assured.

You run your fingertips over the glass. The falcon appears poised to take flight with a beat of its wings; the piece embodies coiled, dynamic tension.

"It's his favorite bird. Their exceptional visual acuity enables them to identify the presence of prey through the slightest ripple of grass in a verdant landscape."

"I'm sure he'll love it," you say.

You hesitate. Then: "I didn't know you were married."

When a response is not immediately offered, your cheeks redden.

"I always watch you take notes with your left hand and I've never seen you wear a wedding ring before," you say.

"Ah. You're very observant. A stone was loose, so it needed to be fixed."

This is not the truth, but while you have vowed to be scrupulously honest, no similar promise has been made to you.

The ring was removed after Thomas confessed to his affair. For a variety of reasons it is back on.

The falcon is returned to the bag, the tissue paper nestled around it once again. It will be personally delivered to Thomas's new rental apartment, the one he moved into a few months ago, tonight.

It isn't a special occasion. At least not one that he knows about. He will experience surprise.

Sometimes an exquisite gift is actually a vessel utilized to issue a warning shot.

CHAPTER
NINETEEN

Thursday, December 6

I FREEZE UP when Dr. Shields tucks the sculpture back into the bag and says that is all she needs from me today.

I'm so thrown I can't remember the exact wording of my question, but I plunge ahead anyway.

"Oh, I was just wondering . . ." I begin. My voice comes out a little higher than normal. "All the stuff I've been telling you, is that going to be used in one of your papers? Or—"

Before I can continue she interrupts, something she has never done before.

"Everything you've shared with me will remain confidential, Jessica," she says. "I never release the files of my clients under any circumstances."

Then she tells me not to worry, that I'll still be paid the usual amount.

She bows her head to look at the package again and I feel dismissed.

I simply say, "Okay . . . thank you."

I walk across the carpet, my footsteps swallowed by the delicately patterned carpet, and take a last glance back at her before I close the door behind me.

She is backlit by the window, and the low sunlight turns her hair the color of fire. Her periwinkle turtleneck sweater and silk skirt skim her long, lithe body. She is completely motionless.

The vision almost makes my breath catch in my throat.

I exit the building and walk down the sidewalk toward the subway, thinking about how I put together a few clues—Dr. Shields's missing wedding band, the empty chair across from her in the French restaurant, and the possibility of her wiping away a tear—and formed an assumption. I thought that her husband might be dead, similarly to how I misread signals and inferred Mrs. Graham's husband was alive.

As I descend the subway steps and wait on the platform, I glance at the guys around me, trying to imagine the kind of man Dr. Shields would marry. I wonder if he is tall and fit, like her. Just a few years older, probably, with thick blondish hair and the kind of eyes that crinkle in the corners when he smiles. He's still boyishly handsome, but he doesn't inspire double takes the way she does.

I can see him having grown up on the East Coast, then attending an elite boarding school. Exeter, maybe, followed by Yale. That could be where they met. He's the type to know his way around a sailboat and a golf course, but he isn't a snob.

She would choose someone more gregarious than she is. He'd offset her reserved, quiet nature, and she'd rein him in if he had a few too many beers and got rowdy during a poker game with the guys.

I wonder if it's his birthday, or if they're just one of those romantic couples who like to surprise each other with thoughtful presents.

Of course, I could have gotten it all wrong again.

That thought grips my mind as the subway car screeches to a stop.

What if I got something much more important wrong than the details about Dr. Shields's husband?

In no universe does it make sense that Dr. Shields just paid me three hundred dollars to run a quick errand. Maybe it wasn't a simple errand after all.

The project you have become engaged in is about to evolve from an academic exercise into a real-life exploration on morality and ethics, Dr. Shields told me the first time I met her.

What if the errand was my first test? Maybe I was supposed to protest when Dr. Shields assured me I'd be paid as usual.

The crowd around me surges into the subway car and I'm swept up in the collective motion. I'm one of the last ones to board. The doors lightly brush my back as they close.

Suddenly I feel a tightening around my throat.

An edge of the wrap Dr. Shields gave me is caught between the doors.

My hand flies to my neck and I pull at the fabric, gagging.

Then the doors jerk back open and I wrench the wrap free.

"Are you okay?" the woman standing across from me asks.

I nod and gasp, feeling my heart thud.

I reach up to unfurl the wrap from around my neck. That's when I realize I forgot to return it.

The subway car gains speed and the faces on the platform blur as we hurtle into a dark tunnel.

Maybe the payment for today wasn't a test, maybe it was the wrap. She might have wanted to see if I'd keep it.

Or maybe the real-life morality tests go back further, to the nail polish. Maybe all of these gifts are carefully designed experiments to see how I'll react.

A realization hits me with a jolt: Dr. Shields didn't set a time for our next appointment.

I'm suddenly panicked I failed her tests, and now she won't want me back.

Dr. Shields seemed really interested in me; she even texted me on Thanksgiving Day. But maybe after today she thinks she's made a mistake.

I pull out my phone and begin to thumb a text: *Hi!*

I immediately backspace; that sounds too informal.

Dear Dr. Shields.

That's too formal.

I settle on a simple *Dr. Shields.*

I can't sound desperate; I need to be professional.

I'm sorry I forgot to give you back your wrap. I'll bring it next time. Also, don't worry about paying me for today; you've been so generous.

I hesitate, then add: *I just realized we don't have a time for our next appointment. My schedule is flexible, just let me know when you need me. Thanks, Jess.*

I hit *Send* before I lose my nerve. I stare at my phone, waiting to see if there's a quick response.

But there isn't.

I shouldn't have expected one. After all, I work for her. She's probably on her way to see her husband right now, preparing to present him with his gift.

Maybe Dr. Shields was expecting me to have a more sophisticated response to her sculpture. All I said was "Wow." I should've come up with something more intelligent.

I've been staring down at my phone, waiting for a text from Dr. Shields, but somehow I didn't immediately notice the phone icon signaling I have a new voice mail message. I snatch it up, certain Dr. Shields phoned when I didn't have a signal.

I press *Play* but the train plunges deeper underground and I lose the connection again. I hold my phone tightly in my hand until I reach my stop. I sprint through the turnstile and up the stairs, my case swinging by my side. It bangs painfully against my knee, but I don't even slow down.

I burst onto the sidewalk, then stop short and jab at the voice mail button again.

The bright young voice—so different from Dr. Shields's cultured, carefully enunciated words—is jarring.

"Hey, it's me, Amy. I thought of something on the plane. Meant to call you earlier but it's been crazy. Anyway, one of my friends told me Dr. Shields just took a leave of absence from teaching. Anyway, I have no idea why. Maybe she has the flu or something. Okay, hope that helps. Bye!"

I slowly pull the phone away from my ear and stare at it, then I touch the button to make the message play again.

CHAPTER
TWENTY

Thursday, December 6

ADULTERY IS COMMONPLACE; it does not discriminate among socioeconomic groups, race, or gender. Anecdotal evidence from counselors' offices across the country supports this contention. After all, infidelity is one of the foremost reasons that compel couples to seek help from a professional.

Therapists are often the first responders when an affair shatters a relationship, leaving the betrayed to grapple with feelings of rage and pain. Forgiveness is not always possible; forgetting is unrealistic. However, infidelity need not be a marital execution. Clinicians also understand that work can be done to rebuild trust through difficult conversations, accountability, and a reestablishing of priorities so the relationship is paramount. Indeed, a betrayal can be surmounted. This requires time as well as the unwavering commitment of both parties.

Even though it is tempting to assume the correct course for a client is obvious, it is not a therapist's job to offer such a blueprint.

It is easy to judge other people's choices. It is far more complex when the choices are your own.

Imagine that seven years ago, you married a man who infused your life with color and laughter, who upended your existence in the best possible way.

Imagine waking up every morning in the arms of the person who was your safe harbor, whose whispered words of love made you feel a swell of emotions you never knew existed.

Then imagine doubts began to creep in.

Early on in your marriage, your questions about his hushed, late-night phone conversations and abrupt cancelations of plans were met with reasonable explanations: Clients were permitted to call at all hours on his emergency number. And sometimes a client needed an unscheduled session during a crisis.

Trust is a necessary component of a committed relationship.

But there was no explaining away the romantic text that landed on my phone screen three months ago: *See you tonight, Gorgeous.*

Thomas had said he would be playing poker with a few male friends that evening, and that he would be home late.

When he realized he'd misdirected the text, he immediately confessed. He spoke of his guilt and sorrow.

He was asked to move out that same night. He stayed in a hotel for a week, then he sublet an apartment near his office.

But expunging him from my heart . . . well, that proved far more difficult.

Several weeks after Thomas moved out, a line of communication was reopened.

It would never happen again, Thomas swore. It was a singular indiscretion. She was the aggressor, he proclaimed.

When questioned, he supplied details. The narrative of their clandestine relationship was freely offered by Thomas, though it is typical for offenders to minimize their misdeeds. Her demographic information—first name, age, appearance, profession, marital status—was ascertained.

Thomas seemed to want to rebuild our relationship. With any other man, this would have been impossible. But Thomas is unlike any other man.

And so counseling sessions were scheduled. Difficult conversations were had. And eventually, date nights were reestablished. A rebuilding commenced.

There was only one problem. Certain aspects of his story did not add up.

Uncertainty is an excruciating state in which to exist.

A moral question that never appeared in my study continues to claim prominence in my mind: *Is it possible to look someone you love in the eye and tell a lie without experiencing remorse?*

A new perspective soon intruded, threatening the fragile peace we were painstakingly trying to rebuild: What if the other woman was merely the kindle?

What if Thomas was the flame?

Perhaps he burned through the one fling that has been verified.

But a fire is perpetually hungry.

One evening shortly after you snuck into the study, Jessica, my husband arrived home and dropped his keys and change in a small dish on our bureau, as was his habit. Mixed in with the coins was a tiny, folded piece of paper: a receipt for a restaurant lunch for two.

Over glasses of wine enjoyed on the couch, a husband tells his wife of the mundane details that comprised his day: the irritating subway delay, the receptionist who learned she was having twins, the lost glasses that were discovered in the pocket of a blazer.

Lost glasses were mentioned. Yet an expensive lunch for two at a Cuban restaurant was not.

Had you not cunningly inserted yourself into the morality study, Jessica, this question might never have been answered. This experiment might never have existed. It is you who is bringing it to life.

Recollections can be faulty; personal agendas can color one's words and actions. Only by conducting a scrupulously executed inquiry can the truth be independently verified.

You may have given up your dreams of theater, Jessica, but you have earned a starring role in the next act of this unfolding drama.

When your text appears inquiring about your next session, it is as if you are confirming this, urging us forward: *It's time.*

You, with that heavy makeup case you lug around and the wild hair you attempt to tame and the vulnerability you fail to hide.

You have proved your devotion today. Your text confirmed how much you need me.

What you don't know is how much we need each other.

It is time to prepare for the next phase. It begins with the setting. Outer order engenders an inner sense of calm. The desk in the study—just a dozen feet away from the bedroom where Thomas's pillowcase used to hold the sweet scent of his shampoo—holds a laptop. Excessive alcohol will further muddy the mind, but two inches of Montrachet are poured into a crystal glass and brought to the workspace. There are minimal distractions in the room, facilitating the ability to concentrate on the task ahead.

An unorthodox plan must be considered from every possible angle. Mistakes are born when methodology is ignored.

Conducting an empirical inquiry requires an established protocol: The collection and examination of data. Astute observations. Painstaking record-keeping. The interpretation of results and formation of a conclusion.

The title of the project is entered on the blank screen of the computer: *The Temptation of Infidelity: A Case Study.*

The hypothesis: Thomas is an unrepentant adulterer.

There is only one subject: My husband.

There is only one variable: You.

Jessica, please don't fail this test. It would be a pity to lose you.

PART
TWO

We began as strangers, you and I.

By now, we have become acquaintances. We are beginning to feel as if we know each other.

Familiarity often ushers in an enhanced appreciation and understanding.

It also shepherds in a new level of evaluations.

Maybe you have judged the choices of people you know: The neighbor who screams so loudly at his spouse that the harsh words carry through their thin apartment walls. The colleague who opts out of caring for aging parents. The client who becomes overly dependent on a therapist.

Even with the realization that these acquaintances have pressures of their own—an impending divorce, depression, a complicated family—your judgments still materialize with the surety and swiftness of a reflex.

These reactions might be immediate, but they are rarely simple or precise.

Pause for a moment and consider the subconscious factors that may be coloring your evaluations: Everything from whether you enjoyed eight hours of sleep, are experiencing an annoyance, such as a recently flooded bathroom, or are still absorbing the aftershocks of a domineering mother.

If there is a chemical formula that decrees whether a verbal or silent *condemnation is made during the course of everyday, mundane interactions, it contains an ever-changing variable.*

That unstable element is you.

We all have reasons for our judgments, even if those reasons are so deeply buried we don't recognize them ourselves.

CHAPTER
TWENTY-ONE

Friday, December 7

I WAS SO WORRIED I'd messed up the last time I saw Dr. Shields that when she finally phoned me back, I snatched up the phone before the first ring ended.

She asked if I'd be free tonight, like nothing was wrong. And maybe it wasn't. She didn't even mention my message about not expecting to be paid for bringing her the sculpture and forgetting to return her wrap.

The call lasted only a few minutes. Dr. Shields gave me a few instructions: *Wear your hair down, polished makeup, and a black dress suitable for an evening out. Be ready by 8 P.M.*

It's twenty past seven right now. I stand in front of my closet, staring at the clothes crammed inside. I push aside the charcoal suede mini-skirt that I usually pair with a blush-colored silky top, then I reach past my high-neck black dress that's way too short.

Unlike Lizzie, who often texts me a series of selfies before we meet up, I'm as confident putting together outfits as I am blending a color palette for a client. I know what styles flatter me, but an evening out probably means something very different for Dr. Shields than it does for me.

I consider the most elegant dress I own, a black jersey with a low V-neck.

Too low? I wonder as I hold it up against my body and look in the mirror. My closet doesn't contain a better option.

I wanted to ask Dr. Shields for more information—*Where am I going? What will I be doing? Is this one of those tests you mentioned?*—but her voice sounded so focused and professional when she inquired if I'd be free that I didn't have the nerve.

As I slip into the dress, I picture Dr. Shields in her refined skirts and sweaters, the lines so structured and classic that they could take her from her office to the ballet at Lincoln Center.

I tug up the neckline, yet I'm still showing too much cleavage. My hair is rogue, and the big hoop earrings I wore to work now look cheap.

I leave my hair down, as she instructed, and swap out the hoops for cubic zirconia studs. Then I find the double-sided fashion tape in my underwear drawer and seal up two inches from the bottom of the V.

Normally I go bare-legged or wear tights; tonight I pull out the pair of sheer black stockings that has been sitting in my dresser drawer for at least six months. They have a snag, but it's on my upper thigh, so the dress hides it. I dab a bit of clear nail polish on the tear to keep it from running, then dig out the basic black pumps I've had forever.

I grab a zebra-print belt from my closet and fasten it around my waist. I can always slip it in my purse if it seems like a miscalculation when I show up wherever it is that I'm going.

I think of the question I always ask my clients: *What kind of look are you going for?* It's difficult to answer when I have no idea who my audience will be. I follow Dr. Shields's directive and add a neutral eyeshadow and tone down my liner.

It's eight o'clock sharp, and still my phone is silent.

I check the signal, then walk around my apartment, mindlessly refolding sweaters and putting shoes back in my closet. At 8:17 I consider texting Dr. Shields, then decide against it. I don't want to seem like a bother.

Finally, at 8:35, after I've reapplied my lip gloss twice, plus ordered some glittery paint and thick paper online for one of Becky's Christmas presents, my phone chimes with a new text from Dr. Shields.

I look away from the T.J. Maxx website, where I've been checking out shirts for my mom:

An Uber will be outside your apartment in four minutes.

I take a final swig of the Sam Adams I've been sipping, then pop an Altoid into my mouth.

When I exit the building, I pull the door closed tightly until I hear the lock engage. A black Hyundai is idling by the curb. I locate the *U* sticker on the rear window before opening the back door.

"Hi, I'm Jess," I say as I slide into the backseat.

The driver simply nods and pulls away, heading west.

I pull my seat belt across my body and click it into place.

"Where exactly are we going?" I ask, trying to affect a casual tone.

All I can see are his brown eyes and heavy brows in the rearview mirror. "You don't know?"

He doesn't say it like a question, though. It's almost a statement.

As I watch the city begin to whirl by through the tinted back window, I suddenly realize how truly isolated I am. And how power-less.

I backpedal: "Oh, my friend arranged this ride for me," I say. "I'm meeting her. . . ."

My voice trails off. I slide my hand beneath the seat belt strap that feels too tight against my chest. There's no give in it.

The driver doesn't reply.

My heartbeat quickens. Why is he acting so strangely?

He makes a right turn and we begin to head uptown.

"Are we stopping at Sixty-second Street?" I ask. Perhaps Dr. Shields wants to meet me at her office. But then why all the specifics about how to dress?

The driver's gaze remains fixed straight ahead.

The realization slams into me: I'm trapped alone with a strange man. He could be taking me anywhere.

I've hailed countless cabs and ordered numerous Vias and Ubers. I've never felt unsafe before.

My eyes dart again to the windows in the back row of his car, my row. Nobody can see in.

I instinctively check the locks. I can't tell if they are engaged. There isn't a lot of traffic, so we're moving relatively quickly. We're bound to hit a traffic light. Should I try to open the door and jump out?

I slowly reach for the button on my seat belt and press it, wincing when my thumb gets pinched between the metal. I ease it off my shoulder carefully, so it doesn't snap back into the holder.

How do I even know he's an Uber driver? It's probably not all that hard to get one of those *U* stickers. Or he could have borrowed the car.

I look at him more carefully. He's a large man with a thick neck and beefy arms; his hands gripping the steering wheel are about twice the size of mine.

I'm fumbling for the button to roll down the window when the driver says, "Yeah, okay."

I seek out his eyes in the rearview mirror, but they are fixed on the road.

Then I hear the slightly tinny, distinct sound of another male voice.

The tightness in my chest releases as I realize the driver didn't respond to my questions because he's on a phone call. He's not being deliberately evasive, he simply didn't hear me.

I take a deep breath and sink back into the seat.

I'm being silly, I tell myself. We're traversing up Third Avenue, surrounded by cars and pedestrians.

Still, it takes a full minute for me to feel steadier.

I lean forward and repeat my query a third time, my voice louder.

He glances back over his shoulder, then says something that sounds like "Madison and Seventy-sixth."

Between the radio and the noise of the engine, though, I'm not sure, and the driver has resumed his phone conversation.

I pull out my phone and google the location. A bunch of businesses show up—the Sussex hotel, Vince and Rebecca Taylor clothing boutiques, a few residential apartments, and an Asian fusion restaurant.

Okay, I think. All innocuous places. Which one is my destination? The restaurant seems the most likely.

I reassure myself that Dr. Shields is probably seated there already, waiting for me. Perhaps she wants to give me more instructions about the real-life test.

Still, I can't help but wonder why she needs to see me outside the office for that. Maybe there's another reason.

For a brief moment, I imagine we're two friends, or maybe a younger sister going to meet her older, more sophisticated one, to share a sea-weed salad and some sashimi. Over a carafe of warm sake, we'd share confidences, too. This time, though, I would ask her all the questions that have been bubbling up in my mind.

In the side mirror, I see the bright headlights of an approaching car. At almost the same instant, my driver begins to swerve into that lane.

A horn blares and the Hyundai jerks back, brakes squealing. I'm flung against the door, then forward. My hands shoot out and I brace myself against the back of the passenger seat.

"Asshole!" my driver yells, even though the near-collision was his fault. He was so busy on his phone call, he didn't check his blind spot.

For the rest of the ride, I keep watch out my side window. I'm so busy looking out for pedestrians and other vehicles that it takes me a few seconds to notice that the Uber has pulled up behind a black Town Car. We're directly in front of the Sussex hotel.

"Here?" I ask the driver, pointing to the entrance.

He nods.

I step out onto the sidewalk and gaze up and down the block, un-sure of what to do next. Am I supposed to wait inside the lobby?

I turn back to look at the Uber, but it is already gone.

A group of people pass by and one of the men bumps against my arm. I'm so startled I almost drop my phone.

"Sorry!" the man calls.

I look around for Dr. Shields, but the only faces on the street are unfamiliar.

I am on one of the safest blocks in all of Manhattan, so why do I feel so uneasy?

A few seconds later, another text arrives: *Go directly to the bar on the lobby level. You'll see a group of men at a large circular table about halfway back. Choose a seat at the bar close to them.*

Clearly, I've guessed wrong. I have no idea what's in store for me this evening, but it's not going to be an intimate dinner with Dr. Shields.

I walk the nine steps to the entrance of the hotel and a bellman pulls open the door.

"Good evening, miss," he says.

"Hi," I say. My voice sounds timid, so I clear my throat. "Which way is the bar?"

"Past reception and all the way to the back," he says.

I feel his eyes linger on me as I proceed through the entrance. I realize my dress rode up a bit when I got out of the Uber and I tug down the hem.

The lobby is mostly empty except for an older couple sitting on the leather couch by the fireplace. Behind the reception desk, a woman wearing glasses smiles at me and says, "Good evening."

My heels sound too loud tapping against the ornate wood floor. I'm acutely conscious of my stride, and not just because I'm unaccustomed to wearing pumps.

I finally make it to the bar and pull open the heavy wooden door. It's a good-size space, filled with a few dozen people. I squint as my eyes adjust to the dim lighting. I look around, wondering if Dr. Shields is waiting to greet me. I don't see her, but I do spot a bunch of guys at a large table about halfway back.

Choose a seat at the bar close to them.

Are they working with Dr. Shields, too?

I check out the group as I draw closer. They appear to be in their late thirties. At first glance, they're almost indistinguishable with their short haircuts and dark suits and crisp, collared shirts. They've got an air about them I've seen before: They're a younger version of the dads who pay for the fancy bar mitzvahs and sweet-sixteen parties, the ones that cost as much as a nice wedding.

There are only a few empty high-back stools at the bar. I take one that's about six feet away from the men.

When I slide onto it, I feel the warmth of the wood against my thighs, as if someone has just vacated it. I loop the handle of my purse on the hook beneath the counter, then shrug off my coat and put it on the back of my seat.

"Be with you in just a minute," the bartender says as he muddles herbs for a craft cocktail.

Am I supposed to order a drink? Or is something else going to happen?

Even though I'm in a public place, anxiety swirls in my gut. I remind myself of what Dr. Shields said during my first visit to her office: *You will be in complete control and can back out at any time.*

I twist slightly in my seat, so I can glance around the room, searching for clues. But all I see are the monied customers drinking and talking, a stunning blonde leaning in across the table to point to an item on the bar menu to her date, a well-built guy with a slightly receding hairline in a blue shirt, typing away on his phone, and two smiling, middle-aged couples raising their glasses in a toast.

My phone vibrates in my hand, startling me.

Don't be nervous. You look perfect. Order a drink.

My eyes jerk back up.

Where is she?

She has to be in one of the back booths, but my line of vision is obscured by the dim lighting and the other occupants of the bar.

I've been fiddling with the rings on my index finger. I put my hands in my lap. Then I look at the table full of guys again, wondering why Dr. Shields wanted to position me near them. My eyes run over each of the five men in turn. One meets my gaze. He leans over and whispers something to his friend, who laughs and turns to check me out. I twist back around, feeling my cheeks grow warm.

The bartender tilts toward me over the counter. "What can I get you?"

Normally I'd have a beer or a shot, but not in a place like this. "Red wine, please."

He's still waiting for something. I realize he's expecting me to be more specific.

I cast back in my memory, then blurt, "Volnay," hoping I pronounced it the same way the waiter did in the French restaurant a few nights ago.

"I'm afraid we don't have that," he says. "Would you care for a Gevry?"

"That'll be fine," I say. "Thank you."

When the bartender delivers my glass, I grip it extra hard to disguise the fact that my hand is shaking.

Usually the warmth of alcohol relaxes me, but I still feel on edge as I scan the room again. I sense the presence of the man next to me before I see him out of the corner of my eye.

"Looks like you're waiting for someone," he says. It's the guy from the table, the one who was whispering to his friend. "Mind if I keep you company until they show up?"

I quickly glance at my phone's screen, but it's blank.

"Um, sure," I say.

He sets his drink down on the counter and takes the stool to my left. "I'm David."

"Jessica." My full name must have slipped out because I'm in Dr. Shields's world now.

He rests an arm on the bar.

"So, Jessica, where are you from?"

I tell him the truth, not only because I don't know what else to say, but because of Dr. Shields's rules about honesty.

It hardly matters, though, because he just replies, "That's cool," and then launches into a story about how he moved here from Boston for a big job four years ago. I'm in the midst of feigning interest when my phone vibrates.

"Excuse me." I grab it and see the text from Dr. Shields.

I tilt my phone so David can't read the message:

Not him.

I blink in surprise, wondering what I've done wrong.

I flash back to when I first entered Dr. Shields's study and she spoke to me through the computer.

I see three dots indicating Dr. Shields is still typing.

Her next instruction arrives:

Locate the man in the blue shirt sitting alone at a table to your right. Start up a conversation. Get him to flirt with you.

Dr. Shields must be close by. So why can't I spot her?

"Was that your friend?" David asks, gesturing to my phone.

I take a sip of my wine, trying to stall so I can think a step ahead. My heart is beating faster than usual, and my mouth feels dry. I nod and take another sip but avoid making eye contact with him. Then I signal for the bill and extract two twenties from my wallet.

I glance over my shoulder at the guy in the blue shirt. I can't bring myself to just walk over to him and use some cheesy pickup line. I try to remember some of the things men have said to me in bars, but my mind is blank.

I can't even catch his eye and smile; he's still looking down at his phone.

David touches my arm, stopping me from setting down the twenties. "Let me take care of that." He nods at the bartender: "Another gin and tonic, buddy," he says as he settles back in his seat.

"No, I've got it," I say, pushing the money forward on the counter.

"Actually, your bill has already been settled," the bartender tells me.

I search the room for Dr. Shields again, trying to peer into the shadowy booths. But most of them are blocked by the occupants of the tables between us.

I swear I can feel the heat of her gaze, though.

I don't know the time frame for Dr. Shields's instructions, so I force myself to stand up, lifting my glass and my phone. The wine swirls around in the goblet and I realize my hand is trembling again.

"Sorry," I say. "But I just realized I know that guy. I should go say hello."

Maybe this is the best strategy to use with the guy in the blue shirt, too. I'll pretend I recognize him. But from where?

David frowns. "Okay, but then come join me and my friends."

"Sure," I say.

The man is off his phone now. He's alone at a table for two against a wall. His empty plate has been pushed to the center of the table, his napkin crumpled beside it.

He looks up as I approach.

"Hi!" My voice is too bright.

He nods at me. "Hello," he says, but it comes out more like a question.

"Um, it's me, Jessica! What are you doing here?"

I've seen a lot of bad acting, and I know my performance isn't going to fool anyone.

He smiles, but his forehead wrinkles.

"Nice to see you . . . How do we know each other again?"

The couple at the next table is clearly eavesdropping. I'm terrible at this. I look down at the patterned rug with its floral design and notice a tiny threadbare patch. Then I make myself meet the man's gaze again. Here's the tricky part.

"Didn't we meet at, ah, Tanya's wedding a few months ago?" I say.

He shakes his head. "Nope, must have been some other good-looking guy." But he says it in a self-deprecating way.

I give a dry little laugh.

I can't just walk away, so I try again.

"Sorry," I say softly. "The truth is I was at the bar and this guy was bothering me and I just needed to get away." Maybe the desperation I'm feeling comes through in my eyes, because he stretches out his hand to shake mine.

"I'm Scott." I can't place his accent, but it sounds Southern. He gestures to the empty chair across from him. "Want to join me? I was about to get another drink."

I slide onto the chair and a few seconds later my phone buzzes. I glance down at it on my lap: *Well done. Keep going.*

I'm supposed to get this polite businessman to flirt with me. So I lean forward and put my elbows on the table, aware that the sticky tape only covers so much.

"Thanks for rescuing me," I say, looking directly into his eyes.

I can't sustain the eye contact for long; this feels so artificial. Flirting is fun when it's natural, and when I've chosen the guy, like with Noah the other night.

But this is like dancing without music. And even worse, there's an audience.

I echo the question David just asked me: "So where are you from?"

As Scott and I continue to talk, I puzzle over why Dr. Shields needs me to have a conversation with him instead of with David. They seem almost interchangeable. It's like those tests in the backs of magazines: Spot the difference in these two images. But I don't see any significant differences: late thirties, clean shaven, dark suits.

I can't relax, knowing Dr. Shields is watching me, but by the time I've finished most of my wine, the conversation is flowing surprisingly easily. Scott is a nice guy; he's from Nashville and he owns a black lab that he clearly adores.

Scott lifts up his glass tumbler and takes the last sip of amber Scotch.

That's when I realize the difference between the two men, the tiny detail in the pictures that doesn't match up.

David's ring finger was bare.

Scott is wearing a thick platinum wedding band.

CHAPTER
TWENTY-TWO

Friday, December 7

SHE LEANS FORWARD in her black dress and touches his hand. Her dark hair tumbles forward, nearly obscuring her profile.

A smile spreads across his face.

At what moment does a flirtation become a betrayal?

Is the demarcation line drawn when physical contact occurs? Or is it something more ephemeral, such as when possibilities begin to infuse the air?

Tonight's setting, the bar at the Sussex Hotel, is where it all began.

But the cast was different.

Thomas stopped by for a drink during that evening, back when our marriage was still pure. He met an old friend from college who was in town for the night and staying at this very hotel. After a few cocktails, the friend explained that he was suffering from jet lag. Thomas insisted he go up to his room while Thomas paid the check. My husband's generosity has always been one of his many appealing qualities.

The bar was busy, and the service was slow. But Thomas was seated at a comfortable table for two, and he was in no rush. He knew that even though it was barely ten o'clock, the blackout shades would be down in our bedroom and the temperature set to a cool sixty-four degrees.

It was not always this way. In the beginning of our marriage, Thomas's arrival home was met with a kiss and a glass of wine, followed by engaging conversation on the couch about a recent class lecture, an intriguing client, a weekend getaway we were considering.

But something had shifted during the course of our marriage. It happens in every relationship, when the first heady months yield to a more serene cohabitation. As work exerted more and more demands, the pull of a silk nightgown and crisp, 1,000-thread count Egyptian cotton sheets proved more irresistible than Thomas on some nights. Perhaps this rendered him . . . vulnerable.

The dark-haired woman reached my husband before the server delivered the check. She claimed the empty seat across from him. Their encounter did not end when they left the restaurant; instead, they went to her apartment.

Thomas never said a word about his indiscretion.

Then the errant text landed on my phone: *See you tonight, Gorgeous.*

Freud postulated that there are no accidents. Indeed, the argument could be made that Thomas wanted to get caught.

I didn't go looking for this. But she threw herself at me. What guy in my situation could resist? Thomas pleaded during one of our therapy sessions.

It would be so comforting to believe this, that his response wasn't a referendum on our marriage, but rather a yielding to the hardwired fragility of males.

Tonight the booth in a far corner provides a satisfactory vantage point. The man with the platinum wedding band appears to be falling under your spell, Jessica; his body language has grown more alert since your arrival.

He is not nearly as alluring as Thomas, but he fits the basic profile. In his late thirties, alone, and married.

Was this how Thomas first responded?

The temptation to move closer to the scene now unfolding just two dozen yards away is almost unendurable, but this deviation could invalidate the results.

Although you know that you are being observed, the true subject, the man in the blue shirt, must remain unaware that he is being scrutinized.

Subjects typically modify their behavior when they recognize that they are part of an experiment. This is known as the Hawthorne effect, named after the place where this result was first encountered, the Western Electric's Hawthorne Works. A basic study to determine how the level of light in their building affected the productivity of laborers revealed that the amount of luminosity made no difference in the employees' productivity. The workers increased output whenever the light was manipulated, whether from low to high or vice versa. In fact, a change in productivity occurred when *any* variable was manipulated, which made the researchers postulate that the staff altered their behavior simply because they were aware that they were under observation.

Since subjects have this predisposition, all researchers can do is attempt to factor this effect into the research design.

Your flirtations appear convincing, Jessica. It seems impossible that the target would know he is part of an experiment.

The test must proceed to the next stage.

It is difficult to type the instruction—a wave of nausea briefly delays its transmission—but it is a vitally necessary one.

Touch his arm, Jessica.

The scene with Thomas also followed this progression: a brief caressing of the arm, another round of drinks, an invitation to continue the conversation at the woman's apartment.

An abrupt movement from the table by the wall and the memory of Thomas's duplicity glitches. The man in the blue shirt stands up. You rise as well. Then you head toward the lobby with him trailing a few feet behind you.

It took less than forty minutes from the time you entered the bar for you to seduce him.

Thomas's defense was sound; it appears that men are incapable of steeling themselves against blatant offers of temptation. Even married ones.

The flood of relief that accompanies this realization is so profound it has a weakening effect on the body.

It was all *her* fault. Not his.

Bits of shredded cocktail napkin, evidence of the contained anxiety, litter the table. They are scooped into a pile. The untouched glass of sparkling water on the table is finally tasted.

Several moments later, the bell of an incoming text peals.

It is reviewed.

And immediately, it is as though the busy, welcoming bar is plunged into ice and silence.

There is nothing save for the three lines from you.

They are read once.

Then again.

Dr. Shields, I flirted but he rejected me. He said he was happily married. He went up to his room and I'm in the hotel lobby.

CHAPTER
TWENTY-THREE

Friday, December 7

BEING TOLD TO HOOK UP with a man, and being paid for it, is the same as being a prostitute.

I'm trembling again as I stand in the lobby, waiting for Dr. Shields to respond to my text. But this time it's with anger.

Did she really expect me to go up to Scott's room? She probably assumed I would because of my confessions about my one-night stands on her stupid questionnaire.

My pumps pinch my feet and I alternate easing up my left heel, then my right one.

She still hasn't responded, even though I sent the message several minutes ago. Now the front desk clerk is staring at me, and I feel even more out of place than I did when I walked in.

I can't believe Dr. Shields put me in this position. It wasn't about being in danger. It was about the humiliation. I saw the way David and his friends eyed me when I walked out with Scott. And I saw the way Scott looked at me right before he stood up from the table.

"Is there something I can help you with?"

The front-desk clerk has come from behind her post to stand next to me. She's smiling, but I see in her eyes what I already know: I don't belong in a place like this, with my sixty-dollar dress from a sample sale and my fake diamond earrings.

"I'm just— I'm waiting for someone," I say.

Her eyebrows lift.

I fold my arms across my chest. "Is that a problem?" I ask.

"Of course not," she says. "Would you like to take a seat?" She gestures to the couch over by the fireplace.

We both know what her hospitality is thinly disguising. She probably thinks I'm a hooker, too.

I hear the rapid clicking of heels against the wood floor. I turn to see Dr. Shields striding toward us, and even though I'm upset by what she has just done to me, I can't help but marvel at her beauty: Her hair is pulled into a sleek chignon and her legs are slim and impossibly long beneath the hemline of her black silk dress. She is everything I tried to be tonight.

"Hello, there," Dr. Shields calls. When she reaches us, she puts her hand on my arm, like she is claiming me. I see her glance at the woman's name tag. "Is everything all right here, Sandra?"

The clerk's manner transforms. "Oh, I was just offering your friend a seat by the fireplace, where it's more comfortable."

"How thoughtful," Dr. Shields says. But her tone is a subtle rebuke, and the clerk retreats.

"Shall we?" Dr. Shields asks, and for a moment I think she wants to leave. But then she leads the way to the couch.

Instead of taking a seat, though, I remain standing. I keep my voice low, but it's thick with emotion: "What was that all about?"

If Dr. Shields is surprised, she doesn't show it. She pats the cushion next to her. "Jessica, please sit down."

I tell myself it's because I want to hear Dr. Shields's explanation. But the truth is, I feel a gravitational pull toward her.

As soon as I am beside her, I smell her clean, spicy perfume.

Dr. Shields crosses her legs and folds her hands in her lap. "You seem very agitated. Can you tell me what that experience was like for you?"

"It was awful!" My voice cracks unexpectedly and I swallow hard. "That guy Scott, who was he?"

Dr. Shields lifts her shoulders once. "I have no idea."

"He wasn't part of this?"

"He could have been anyone," Dr. Shields says. Her voice is airy and distant. It's almost as if she is reciting from a script. "I needed a man with a wedding ring to test as part of my study on morality and ethics. I selected him at random."

"You were using me as bait? To trick some guy?" My words come out too loudly for this hushed, serene lobby.

"It was an academic exercise. I did let you know there would be real-life scenarios involved with this phase of my research."

I can't believe I'd ever thought we might be eating dinner together. Who was I kidding? I am her employee.

The tightness in my throat eases, but I can't let go of my anger. Nor do I want to, because it's what is finally giving me the courage to ask questions.

"Did you really expect me to go up to his room, though?" I blurt.

Dr. Shields's eyes widen; I don't think anyone could fake that kind of surprise.

"Of course not, Jessica. I merely told you to flirt with him. Why would you ever consider that?"

The minute she says it, I feel foolish. I look down at my feet. I can't meet her gaze; it was such an extreme assumption.

But Dr. Shields's voice contains no judgment; it holds nothing but kindness. "I promised that you would always be in complete control. I would never put you in danger."

I feel her hand briefly touch mine. Despite the warmth of the fire, it is so delicate and cold.

I take in a few deep breaths, but my eyes remain fixed on the herringbone pattern on the wood floor.

"Something else is troubling you," she says.

I hesitate and look into her cool blue eyes. I hadn't planned on telling her this part. Finally, I blurt out: "Right before he left the table . . . he called me 'Sugar.'"

Dr. Shields doesn't reply, but I know she is listening to me in the way no one else ever has before.

My eyes fill with tears. I blink them back before continuing.

"There was this guy . . ." I hesitate, inhale deeply, and then continue. "I met him a few years ago and at first I thought he was amazing. You may have heard of him, he's a well-known theater director now. Gene French."

She nods almost imperceptibly.

"I was hired to do makeup for one of his shows. It was a huge deal for me. He was always really nice, even though I was a nobody. When we got the *Playbill* printed, he showed me my name in the credits and said I should celebrate it, that life had so many hardships and we should honor the triumphs."

Dr. Shields is utterly still.

"He did . . . something to me," I say.

The images I can't ever seem to erase seep into my mind again: Me slowly lifting up my shirt, up over my bra, while Gene stands a few feet away, staring. Me saying, *I really should go now.* Gene positioning himself between me and the door to his office, which is closed. His hand moving toward his belt buckle. His answer: *Not yet, Sugar.*

"He didn't touch me, but . . ." I swallow hard and continue. "He told me a prop was missing from the show, an expensive necklace. He said I had to lift up my shirt to prove I wasn't wearing it." A shudder runs through my body as I recall standing there in that claustrophobic, darkened room, trying to look anywhere but at him and what he was doing to himself, until he finished and dismissed me.

"I should have told him no, but he was my boss. And he said it so matter-of-factly, like it was no big deal." I look into Dr. Shields's light blue eyes and I manage to shake off the image. "That guy Scott reminded me of him for a minute. Just the way he said 'Sugar.'"

Dr. Shields doesn't respond immediately. Then she says softly, "I'm so sorry this happened to you."

I feel her hand graze mine again, light as a butterfly.

"Is this why you aren't interested in a serious boyfriend?" she asks. "It isn't uncommon, when a woman endures an assault like you did, for her to withdraw, or to change her relationship patterns."

Assault. I'd never thought of it like that. But she's right.

I suddenly feel depleted, like I did after our first session. I reach up and massage my temples with my fingertips.

"You must be exhausted," Dr. Shields says, like she can see inside me. "I have a car waiting. Why don't you take it home? I'd prefer to walk anyway. Text or call if you want to talk over the weekend."

She stands up and I do the same. I feel oddly disappointed. A few minutes ago, I was furious with her; now I don't want her to leave me.

We head together toward the exit, and I see the black Town Car idling by the curb. The driver comes around to open the back door and Dr. Shields tells him to take me anywhere I want to go.

I sink onto the seat and tilt my head back against the soft leather as the driver walks back around to the front of the car. Then I hear a gentle tap on my window, so I roll it down.

Dr. Shields smiles at me. Her silhouette is backlit by the bright city lights. Her hair is a halo of fire, but her eyes are in the shadows. I can't see their expression.

"I nearly forgot, Jessica," she says, pressing a folded slip of paper into my hand. "Thank you."

I look down at the check, feeling oddly reluctant to open it.

Maybe this is all just a business transaction to Dr. Shields. But what exactly am I being paid for now? My time, the flirtation, my confidences? Or something else I don't know about?

All I know is that it feels unclean.

When the driver pulls away, I slowly unfold the check.

I stare at it for a long moment as the car's wheels spin almost soundlessly against the asphalt.

It's for $750.

CHAPTER
TWENTY-FOUR

Saturday, December 8

SATURDAY EVENING. Most couples call it date night.

Traditionally, it has been for us, too: dinners at Michelin-star restaurants, nights at the Philharmonic, a leisurely stroll through the Whitney Museum. However, after Thomas's missent text, he moved out and these encounters were terminated. Gradually, after the counseling, apologies, and promises, they were reinstated, but with a new focus: An emphasis was placed on connection and rebuilding.

At first the atmosphere was infused with strain. If you were watching us from the outside, Jessica, you might assume a new relationship was unfolding, which, in a sense, it was. Physical contact was kept to a minimum. Thomas was solicitous, verging on overly so: He arrived with flowers, rushed to open doors, and filled his unwavering gaze with admiration.

His pursuit was more ardent than even during our initial courtship. At times it had a desperate, almost fear-laced quality. As if he were terrified of losing our relationship.

Over time, a softening reshaped the interactions. Conversations grew less stilted. Hands found each other across the table once the plates had been cleared.

Tonight, a mere twenty-four hours after the experiment at the hotel, progress has been reversed. It is clear that not all men are susceptible to the attention of a beautiful young woman. The man in the blue shirt resisted you, Jessica, yet Thomas was not immune when the opportunity was offered.

As a result, an invisible agenda has been superimposed over this Saturday evening's encounter with Thomas.

An intimate location, the town house we once shared, is selected to eliminate outside distractions, such as an overbearing waiter or a boisterous party of six at the next table. The menu is carefully curated: A bottle of Dom Pérignon, the same vintage served at our engagement party; Malpeques oysters; a rack of lamb; creamed spinach; oven-roasted baby potatoes with rosemary. For dessert, a variation of Thomas's preferred sweet: chocolate torte.

Traditionally, the torte is purchased at a patisserie on West Tenth Street. For tonight's meal, however, ingredients have been procured from two separate gourmet markets.

My appearance tonight is also a departure. Jessica, you were the one who illustrated how seductive a smokey shadow and sable liner can be, when applied correctly.

The makeup rests atop the dressing room vanity. Beside it is my phone. The device sparks a reminder: a solicitous text or call is the appropriate course of action following an incident in which an acquaintance or friend is unnerved.

Jessica, I wanted to check in and make sure you are feeling better after last night's assignment. I'll be in touch soon.

One more line is needed.

A moment of thought. Then it is typed and sent.

CHAPTER
TWENTY-FIVE

Saturday, December 8

IF YOU NEED ME, *I'm always here.*

Dr. Shields's text arrived just as I was entering Noah's building for his famous French toast. I began to type out a response, but then I deleted it and shoved the phone back in my purse. As I rode the elevator, I ran a hand over my hair, feeling the dampness of freshly fallen snowflakes.

Now, as I sit perched on a stool in Noah's kitchen and watch him uncork a bottle of Prosecco, I realize it's the first time I haven't replied to her immediately. I don't want to think about Dr. Shields and her experiments tonight.

I don't realize I'm frowning until Noah asks, "Taylor? You okay?"

I nod and try to hide my discomfort. My first encounter with Noah at the Lounge, when I introduced myself with a fake name and fell asleep on his couch, feels like a lifetime ago.

I wish I could undo that decision. It feels immature; worse than that, it seems mean.

"So . . ." I begin. "I have to tell you something. It's sort of a funny story."

Noah raises an eyebrow.

"My name isn't really Taylor . . . It's Jess." I give a nervous laugh.

He doesn't look amused. "You gave me a fake name?"

"I didn't know if you were a crazy person," I explain.

"Seriously? You came home with me."

"Yeah," I say. I inhale deeply. With his bare feet and the dish towel he's tucking into the waistband of his faded jeans, he looks cuter than I remembered. "It was a really weird day and I guess I wasn't thinking straight."

A weird day. If only he knew how much of an understatement that was. I can hardly believe I met Noah the same weekend I snuck into the study. That too-quiet classroom, the questions creeping across the computer screen, the sense that Dr. Shields could know my private thoughts . . . And yet things have only gotten stranger since then.

"I'm sorry," I say.

"Jess," Noah finally responds.

He hands me a glass of Prosecco.

"I don't like to play games." He holds my gaze, then he gives an almost imperceptible nod.

Before I can block it, the notion flutters into my mind that I've just passed a test. I wouldn't have had this thought a few weeks ago.

I take a sip of Prosecco. The tangy, sweet bubbles feel welcome against my throat.

"I'm glad you're being honest now," Noah finally says.

You must be honest . . . that was one of the instructions waiting for me on the computer screen when I first entered the survey. Even when I'm consciously trying to dislodge Dr. Shields from my mind, she finds a way to sneak back in.

Noah starts to lay ingredients neatly on the counter and I take another sip of Prosecco. I still feel like I owe him a bigger apology, but I don't know what else there is to say.

I look around his small, gleaming kitchen, noting the heavy cast-iron pan on the stove next to the green stone mortar and pestle and a stainless-steel upright mixer. "So, is Breakfast All Day your restaurant?" I ask.

"Yep. Or it will be if my funding comes through," he says. "I've got the space picked out, just waiting on the paperwork."

"Oh, that's really cool."

He cracks eggs with one hand, then whisks them in a bowl while he pours in a drizzle of milk. He pauses to swirl foaming butter around in a griddle pan, then adds cinnamon and salt to the eggs.

"My secret ingredient," he says, holding up a bottle of almond extract. "Not allergic to nuts, are you?"

"Nope," I say.

He stirs in a teaspoonful, then sinks a thick slice of challah bread into the mixture.

When the bread meets the pan with a gentle sizzle, a mouthwatering smell fills the room. There's nothing better than fresh bread, warm butter, and cinnamon cooking together, I realize. My stomach growls.

Noah's a tidy cook, cleaning as he goes: The eggshells are dropped into the wastebasket, his dish towel dabs at a few drops of spilled milk, the spices are immediately returned to their drawer.

As I watch him, it's as if a buffer forms between me and the tension I've been carrying around. It isn't gone, but at least I'm getting a reprieve.

Maybe this is the kind of Saturday night date a lot of women my age experience; a quiet evening in with a nice guy. It shouldn't be that remarkable. It's just that we've already kissed, yet tonight seems more intimate than a physical act. Even though we randomly met in a bar, Noah seems to want to get to know the real me.

He pulls place mats and real cloth napkins out of another drawer, then reaches into a cabinet for a couple of plates. He slides two pieces of golden-brown French toast onto the center of each plate, then sprinkles fresh blackberries on top. I didn't even realize he was warming the syrup in a saucepan until he ladles generous spoonfuls atop it all.

I stare down at the food he serves me, feeling a wash of emotions I can't easily identify. Other than my mother when I go to visit, no one has cooked for me in years.

I take my first bite and groan. "I swear, this is the best thing I've ever eaten."

An hour later, the bottle of Prosecco is empty and we're still talking. We've moved to the living room sofa.

"I'm going to Westchester to see my family for Hanukkah later this week," he says. "But maybe we can do something Sunday night when I get back."

I lean over to give him a kiss and taste sweet syrup on his lips. As I rest my head on his solid chest and his arms wrap around me, I feel something I haven't in months, or maybe years. It takes me a moment to define it: contentment.

CHAPTER
TWENTY-SIX

Saturday, December 8

THOMAS ARRIVES five minutes prior to the appointed time. Punctuality is one of the new habits he seems motivated to adopt.

His broad shoulders fill the doorway as a smile spreads across his face. The first snow of the season has just begun to fall, and sparkly crystals cling to his sandy hair. It's a bit longer than he usually wears it.

Thomas offers a bouquet of red ballerina tulips and is thanked with a lingering kiss. His lips are cold, and he tastes like mint. His hands move to deepen the embrace as he prolongs the intimacy.

"That's all for now," he is told as he is playfully pushed away.

He wipes his damp shoes on the mat and steps into the town house.

"It smells delicious," he says. He looks down briefly. "I've missed your cooking."

His coat is hung in the closet next to the lighter jackets he wears in the warmer weather. He was never asked to remove those particular items from the town house, and not only because he moved out so abruptly. Springtime symbolizes hope, renewal. The presence of his belongings served the same purpose.

He is wearing the sweater that brings out the gold flecks in his green eyes; he knows it's a favorite.

"You look beautiful," he says. He reaches out and runs his fingers so gently through a long, loose wave of my hair that his touch is barely discernible.

My taupe and lavender fabrics have been replaced by black suede jeans and a cobalt-blue silk camisole, but only a hint of color is visible beneath a thigh-length black cardigan made of fine merino wool.

Thomas takes a stool at the granite island with the built-in cooktop. The oysters are on ice; the bottle of champagne is retrieved from the refrigerator.

"Would you?"

He sees the label and smiles. "A great year."

The cork gives a gentle *pop*; then Thomas fills two slim flutes.

A toast is offered: "To second chances."

Surprise and pleasure collide on Thomas's face.

"You have no idea how happy that makes me." His voice is a shade huskier than usual.

A slate-gray shell is lifted from the ice and tilted toward him. "Hungry?"

He nods as he accepts it. "Starving."

The lamb is removed from the oven to rest on the counter. The potatoes just need a few more minutes; Thomas prefers them on the crispier side.

As champagne and oysters are savored, conversation flows easily. Then, just as Thomas is carrying the platter of lamb to the dining room table, a loud chime sounds. He sets down the tray and reaches into his pocket for his phone.

"Do you need to get that?" It is vital that the question carries no hint of reproach.

Thomas merely returns to the kitchen and places his phone facedown on the island. Inches away from the torte.

"The only person I want to give attention to now is you," he says.

He moves away from the phone to bring the decanted red wine to the table and is awarded with a sincere smile.

Thomas's flowers are placed in the vase in the center of the table. Candles are lit. Nina Simone's sultry voice fills the air.

Thomas's wineglass is refilled twice. His cheeks grow slightly flushed; his gestures more expansive.

Thomas offers up a bite of his lamb: "This is the best piece."

Our eyes lock.

"You seem different tonight," he says, stretching out his hand.

"Maybe it's us being together back in the house."

He is awarded another brief kiss, then contact is broken.

"Sweetheart? Have you heard anything more from that private investigator?"

His question seemingly comes out of nowhere; it feels discordant on this romantic evening. But then, Thomas has always been protective. He knows how unsettling it was for me to receive the e-mail from the investigator hired by Subject 5's family.

This is not the first time he has asked whether the private investigator has instigated more contact.

"Nothing since I responded that I would not violate confidentiality by relinquishing my notes on her," he is told.

Thomas nods approvingly. "You're doing the right thing. A client's privacy is sacred."

"Thank you."

The unpleasant memory is skirted past; tonight's agenda is already complex enough.

It is time to bring the glass cake pedestal to the table.

He is served a generous three-inch slice.

The edge of his fork slices through the rich, thick mousse. He raises the chocolate confection to his lips.

He closes his eyes. Savors it. "Mmm. Is this from Dominique?"

"No, La Patisserie," he is told.

"Delicious. I'm almost too full to eat it."

A pause.

"You'll work it off tomorrow at the gym."

He nods and takes another bite. "Aren't you having any?"

"Of course."

The torte melts on the tongue. No one would know it was not purchased at a specialty bakery, just as no one would be able to detect the taste of the two hazelnuts that were ground up and included in the batter.

When Thomas's plate is clean, he leans back in his chair.

But he cannot settle here. A hand is offered to him: "Come."

He is led to a small love seat in the library and given a glass of Dalva port. The space is cozy, with its Steinway piano and gas fireplace. His eyes flit around the room, alighting on original paintings by Wyeth and Sargent, and then a whimsical bronze sculpture of a motorcycle, before landing on the silver-framed photograph of me as a teenager, astride Folly, the chestnut mare, on our Connecticut grounds, my red hair peeking out from beneath my riding helmet. Angled beside that picture is one of our wedding day.

Thomas wore black tie; the tuxedo was purchased especially for the wedding, since he hadn't worn one since his high school prom. The bridal gown, with its lace top and tulle skirt, was custom-made; my father had to ask a business associate to call in a favor at Vera Wang because the engagement was so short.

My father did not approve of the low dip in the dress that reached nearly to the small of my back, but it was too late to have it altered. As a compromise, a long veil was worn during the ceremony at St. Luke's, the church my mother and father still attend.

Our parents flank us in the photo. Thomas's family had flown in from a small town outside San Jose, California, two days before the wedding. We'd only met once before; Thomas dutifully called his mother and father every week, but he wasn't particularly close to them or to his older brother, Kevin, who worked as a construction foreman.

My father is unsmiling in the photograph.

Prior to proposing, Thomas had driven to my parents' Connecticut estate to ask for my hand in marriage. He'd concealed this from me; Thomas was skilled at keeping a secret.

My father appreciated the nod to tradition. He clapped Thomas on the back and they celebrated with brandy and Arturo Fuente cigars. However, the following morning, my father requested my presence at lunch.

He asked only one question. It was direct, as befitting his nature. It came even before we placed our orders: "Are you certain?"

"I am."

Love is an emotional state, but my symptoms were highly physical: A smile formed at the mere mention of Thomas's name, my step felt lighter, even my core temperature—which since my childhood had been consistently recorded at 96.2, well below the average of 98.6—rose by a degree.

The music now switches to John Legend's "Tonight."

"Let's dance."

Thomas's eyes follow the path of my cardigan as it slips from my shoulders down onto the love seat. As he rises, he reaches with his free hand to massage the back of his neck.

The gesture is a familiar one.

He appears a shade paler than normal.

Our bodies fit together seamlessly, just as they did on our wedding night. It's as though the memory has always been stored in our muscles.

The song ends. Thomas removes his glasses, then presses his thumb and index finger to his temples. He grimaces.

"Are you feeling unwell?"

He nods. "Do you think there were nuts in the torte?"

He isn't in danger; his allergy is not life-threatening. However, it is triggered by even the tiniest taste of tree nuts.

The sole side effect is a severe headache. Alcohol worsens this sensation.

"I did ask at the patisserie . . ." My voice trails off. "I'll get you some water."

Five steps toward the kitchen, where his cell phone stills rests on the counter.

Now Thomas is positioned closer to the staircase.

This is important; he will be more inclined to think his next movements are of his own accord, rather than the result of a subtle manipulation.

"Would you like some Tylenol? It's just in the medicine cabinet upstairs."

"Thanks, I'll be right back," he says.

His heavy footsteps ascend the stairs, then sound directly overhead as he moves toward the master bathroom.

The path has already been traced and timed with a stopwatch. He will likely be occupied for sixty to ninety seconds. Hopefully, it will be enough time to gather the desired information.

One of the first questions in the morality survey: *Would you ever read your spouse's/significant other's text messages?*

Thomas's passcode has traditionally been the month and day of his birth.

It is unchanged.

"Lydia? The Tylenol isn't in the medicine cabinet." His voice carries from the top of the stairs.

My footsteps are swift, but when my tone comes from the bottom landing, it remains steady and unhurried.

"Are you certain? I just bought some."

The Tylenol *is* in the medicine cabinet, but tucked behind a box containing a new skin-care cream. More than a cursory glance will be necessary to locate it.

A creak in the floorboard indicates he is moving toward the master bathroom again.

His glass of water is procured. Then the green phone icon is touched. Recent texts and phone calls are surveyed.

My phone's camera function is already engaged.

Quickly, but meticulously, the record of Thomas's many recent calls is captured. His texts appear completely unremarkable and so are disregarded.

Every photograph is assessed to make sure the digital evidence is clear; quality cannot be sacrificed to speed.

The house is utterly quiet. Too quiet?

"Thomas? Are you okay?"

"Yep," he calls.

Perhaps he is applying a cold washcloth to his pulse points.

More photographs are amassed, documenting perhaps thirty-five phone calls. Some numbers are assigned to contacts with recognizable names: Thomas's dentist, squash partner, and parents. Others, eight in total, are unfamiliar. They all have New York City area codes.

The deleted call record log is similarly documented, which turns up one additional unfamiliar number, this one with a 301 area code.

It will be a simple matter to determine whether these numbers are completely innocuous. If a man answers, or if it belongs to a place of business, the phone number will be considered irrelevant and the call will be immediately terminated.

If a woman answers, the call will also be quickly aborted.

But that number will be saved for further scrutiny.

His phone is replaced on the counter. His glass of water is brought to the library.

He should have returned by now.

"Thomas?" He does not respond.

He is met at the top of the staircase just as he emerges from the bedroom.

"Were you able to find it?"

He looks distinctly unwell now. He will require three aspirin followed by a long rest in a darkened room.

The evening's encounter will come to a necessary, abrupt end.

The hope in Thomas's eyes that further intimacies would progress has been extinguished.

"No," he says. His distress is evident.

"I'll get it," he is told.

In the bathroom, he squints against the bright light. The medicine cabinet is surveyed. The luxury moisturizer is moved aside.

"It's right here."

Back downstairs, he swallows three pills and is offered a respite on the couch.

He shakes his head, then winces at the movement.

"I think I'd better go," he says.

His coat is retrieved and offered to him.

"Your phone." He nearly left it on the counter.

As it is picked up, a quick glance at the screen confirms it has automatically re-locked.

He tucks it into the pocket of his coat.

"I'm so sorry I had to cut this night short," he says.

"I'll make a call to the bakery first thing in the morning." A pause. "The woman who waited on me needs to know her mistake."

Phone calls concerning a mistake will be made tomorrow. That much is true.

But not to anyone Thomas expects.

CHAPTER
TWENTY-SEVEN

Monday, December 10

NOTHING ABOUT Dr. Shields's home comes as a surprise to me.

I get invited into many people's residences on Monday mornings to do makeup, and evidence of their weekend's activities is usually on display: the Sunday *New York Times* splayed out on a coffee table, wineglasses from a party drying upside down on a dish rack, kids' soccer cleats and shin guards scattered by the entryway.

But when I arrived at Dr. Shields's town house in the West Village, I figured it would look like a spread in *Architectural Digest*—all muted colors and elegant pieces of furniture, chosen for aesthetics rather than comfort or function. And I'm right, it's like an extension of her meticulous office.

After Dr. Shields greets me at the door and takes my coat, she leads me into the open, sunny kitchen. She's wearing a creamy turtleneck sweater and dark-rinse fitted jeans, and her hair is in a low ponytail.

"You just missed my husband," she says, clearing away two matching coffee mugs from the counter and depositing them in the sink. "I was hoping to introduce you, but unfortunately he had to head into his office."

Before I can ask more—I'm so curious about the man—Dr. Shields gestures to a small platter of fresh berries and scones.

"I didn't know if you'd had the chance to eat breakfast," she says. "Do you prefer coffee or tea?"

"Coffee would be great," I say. "Thanks."

When I finally texted Dr. Shields back on Sunday afternoon, she again asked how I was feeling before she invited me here. I truthfully replied that I was a lot better than when I left the hotel bar on Friday night. I slept in until Leo licked my face demanding a walk, worked a few jobs, and went out with Noah. I did one other thing, too. As soon as the bank opened on Saturday morning, I deposited the check for seven hundred fifty dollars. I still feel like the money could float away; until I see the balance on my statement, it doesn't seem real that I could be earning so much.

Dr. Shields pours the coffee from a waiting carafe into two china cups with matching saucers. The curve of the handle is so delicate I'm a little worried I might break it.

"I thought we could work in the dining room," Dr. Shields says.

She places the coffee and the platter on a tray, along with two small china plates in the same pattern as the cups. I follow her into the adjoining room, passing by a small table that holds a single silver-framed photograph. It's of Dr. Shields with a man. His arm is around her shoulders and she is gazing at him.

Dr. Shields looks back at me.

"Your husband?" I ask, gesturing to the picture.

She smiles as she arranges the teacups in front of two adjacent chairs. I take a closer look at the man, because this is the first thing about Dr. Shield's house that doesn't fit.

He's maybe ten years older than she, with slightly bushy dark hair and a beard. They appear to be almost the same height, about five foot seven.

They don't seem like a match. But they both look very happy in the photo, and she always lights up when she mentions him.

I move away from the picture and Dr. Shields motions to a chair at the head of the glossy oak table, beneath a crystal chandelier. The table is bare save for a yellow legal pad and, beside it, a pen and a black phone. It isn't the silver iPhone I've noticed on Dr. Shields's desk before.

"You said I'd just be making some calls today?" I ask. I don't know how this fits into a morality test. Is she going to ask me to set someone up again?

Dr. Shields places the tray on the table, and I can't help noticing that every single blueberry and raspberry is perfect, like the same designer who chose the graceful pieces of furniture for this room also selected the fruit.

"I know Friday evening was unsettling for you," she says. "Today will be more straightforward. Plus I'll be right here in the room with you."

"Okay," I say, sitting down.

I center the legal pad in front of me and that's when I see the first page isn't blank. Listed in what I now recognize as Dr. Shields's handwriting are the names of five women and, beside the names, phone numbers. All have New York City area codes: 212, 646, or 917.

"I need some data concerning how money and morality intersect," Dr. Shields says. She places my cup and saucer in front of me, then reaches for her own. I notice she takes her coffee black. "It occurred to me that I can use your profession to help with this fieldwork."

"My profession?" I echo. I pick up the pen and press the bottom with my thumb. It makes a loud clicking noise. I put it back down and take a sip of coffee.

"When given a hypothetical scenario, say, winning the lottery, most subjects claim they would donate a portion of the money to charity," Dr. Shields says. "But in reality studies show winners are often less giving than their own predictions would indicate. I would like to delve into a variation of this."

Dr. Shields freshens my coffee from the carafe she has brought to the table, then takes the seat next to me.

"I want the people who answer your call to believe someone has gifted them a free makeup session with BeautyBuzz," Dr. Shields says.

Something about her energy seems especially intense today, even though she is practically motionless. But her expression is serene; her ice-blue eyes are clear. So maybe I'm just projecting my own feelings. Because while I know this all makes perfect sense to her, I'm having trouble understanding why it would be important to her research.

"So I just call and say they've been given a free makeup session?"

"Yes. And it's the truth," Dr. Shields says. "I will pay you for the sessions—"

"Wait," I interrupt. "I'll really be doing these women's makeup?"

"Well, yes, Jessica. Like you do every day. That shouldn't be a problem, right?"

She makes everything sound so logical; she sweeps away my question like it's a tiny crumb on the table.

But the reprieve I found when I was with Noah is already vanishing. Every time I'm with Dr. Shields I feel like I understand what she's doing less and less.

She continues, "What I'm curious about is whether the recipients will tip you more generously since they received the service for free."

I nod, even though I still don't get it.

"Why these numbers, though?" I ask. "Who am I calling?"

Dr. Shields takes an unhurried sip of coffee. "They were all original subjects in an earlier morality survey I conducted. They signed a waiver agreeing to a broad range of possible follow-up trials."

So they know something might be coming, but they don't know what it is. I can relate.

Intellectually, I can't see how this could hurt anyone. Who wouldn't want a free makeup session? Still, my stomach tightens.

Dr. Shields slides a piece of paper over to me. On it appears to be a typewritten script. I stare down at it.

If BeautyBuzz finds out I'm doing this, I could be in trouble. I signed a noncompete clause when they hired me. And even though, technically, I'm not freelancing off their name, I doubt they'd see it that way.

I kind of hope none of these five women accept the free gift.

I wonder if there's another way I could help with this experiment without using the name of my company.

I'm about to voice my concerns when Dr. Shields puts her hand over mine.

Her voice is low and soft. "Jessica, I'm so sorry. I got so wrapped up with my research and I didn't even think to ask about your family. Has your father begun a new job search?"

I exhale. My family's impending crisis is like a dull, chronic pain; it's always lurking in the back of my mind. "Not yet. He's waiting for the new year. Nobody hires in December."

Her hand is still over mine. It's so light. The slim white gold-and-diamond band looks to be the tiniest bit too big for her finger, as if she's lost some weight since it was first placed there.

"I wonder if I could be of help . . ." Her voice trails off, as if she is in the throes of an idea.

My head jerks up. I stare at her.

"I mean, that would be amazing. But how? He's in Pennsylvania, and the only job he's ever had is selling term life insurance."

She withdraws her hand. Even though hers was cold, its removal feels like a loss. Suddenly I'm aware that my own fingers are icy, almost as if she has transferred a bit of herself to me.

She plucks a single raspberry from the platter and lifts it to her mouth. Her expression is thoughtful.

"I don't usually share personal details with subjects," she finally says. "But I feel as though you are becoming more than that."

Her words send a thrill through me. I haven't been imagining it; we really do have a connection.

"My father is an investor," Dr. Shields continues. "He has a stake in a number of companies on the East Coast. He's an influential man. Perhaps I could put in a call to him. I don't want to overstep, though . . ."

"No! I mean, you wouldn't be overstepping, not at all." But I know my father would feel like a charity case; his pride would be destroyed if he found out about this.

As usual, Dr. Shields seems to sense what I'm thinking. "Don't worry, Jessica. We'll keep this just between us."

This is so much more than just a generous check. This could save my family. If my father got a job, my parents could stay in their house; Becky would be okay.

Dr. Shields doesn't seem like someone who makes promises lightly. Her life is so together; she's totally different from anyone I know. I have the feeling she could truly make this happen.

I'm almost dizzy with relief.

She smiles at me.

She reaches for the phone and places it in front of me.

"Shall we do a run-through first?"

CHAPTER
TWENTY-EIGHT

Tuesday, December 11

EVERY FAMILY GENERATES its own particular dysfunction.

Many people believe that once they cross the threshold into adulthood, this legacy can be shed. But the maladjusted dynamics that have been imprinted upon us, often since childhood, are tenacious.

You have provided me with crucial information that engenders an understanding of the tangled interactions resulting from your familial patterns, Jessica.

Have you wondered about mine? Clients do typically speculate about their therapist's lives, superimposing images onto a blank canvas.

You have experience in theater. How close have you come to accurately envisioning the cast? Paul, the powerful father. Cynthia, the former beauty-queen mother. And Lydia, the high-achieving older daughter.

These character sketches will provide context for the following scene.

It is lunchtime on a Tuesday, the day after you visited my home. The occasion is festive: the mother's sixty-first birthday, although she proclaims it to be her fifty-sixth.

Here is what can be observed:

The mother, father, and daughter are led to a corner table for four at the Princeton Club on West Forty-third Street.

For many years, the fourth chair was occupied by the younger sister in the family. It has remained empty since the terrible accident during that daughter's junior year in high school.

Her name was Danielle.

The surviving daughter settles into her brown quilted leather chair and shifts ever so subtly so that she is equidistant between her mother and her father. The waiter does not need to take an order to know their preferred drinks; he quickly brings a tumbler of Scotch and two glasses of crisp white wine to the table and greets each member of the trio by name. The father shakes his hand and inquires how the waiter's son performed in his last high-school wrestling match. The mother immediately takes a long drink of wine, then pulls a gold compact from her purse and examines her reflection. Her coloring and features are similar to the daughter's, but the passage of time has robbed them of their luster. The mother frowns slightly and touches a fingertip to the edge of her lipstick. Orders are placed, and the waiter withdraws.

Here is what can be overheard:

"It's a pity Thomas couldn't join us," the mother says as she closes her compact with a snap and replaces it in her quilted purse with a clasp composed of gold interlocking C's.

"Haven't seen much of him lately," the father states.

"He has been so overworked," the daughter responds. "The holidays are always the busiest time for therapists."

The statement is elastic, allowing its recipients to infuse it with a meaning of their own choosing: It could be the stress of shopping and travel and elaborate meal preparations that prompts patients to seek extra help; or shorter, darker days could serve as the culprit, causing a worsening in depression or the onset of seasonal affective disorder. But as any therapist can tell you, the driving force behind an increase in both scheduled and emergency appointments during December is the very familial relationships that are supposed to conjure peace and joy.

"Lydia?"

The daughter lifts her head and casts an apologetic smile at her father; she has been lost in contemplation.

Here is what remains invisible:

The daughter has been reflecting on the information gleaned from yesterday's round of phone calls. It is impossible to dislodge this train of thought from her mind.

Based on the demographics you obtained, Jessica, two of the women appear to be improbabilities for Thomas. One volunteered that she would be taking care of her grandchildren this week but could schedule an appointment on Saturday; the other turned out to belong to a house-keeping service, which sparked a remembrance that Thomas had recently mentioned needing to switch his current service.

Three prospects, however, remain question marks.

Two accepted the offer of the free makeup session, and their appointments have been scheduled for this Friday evening.

The third number had been disconnected. This is not yet a cause for concern.

Thomas's single betrayal might be surmountable. But confirmation of even one more act of infidelity would do more than establish a pattern of cheating. It would reveal systemic fraud, a doubling down of deception.

Still, results are not guaranteed in this line of inquiry; too many variables remain in play. Therefore, a parallel avenue of research must be simultaneously set in place.

It is time for you to meet my husband, Jessica.

The luncheon progresses.

"You've barely touched your sole," the father says. "Is it overdone?"

The daughter shakes her head and takes a bite. "It's perfect. I'm just not very hungry."

The mother puts down her fork. It clinks gently against the plate containing a half-finished grilled chicken paillard and vegetables. "I don't have much of an appetite, either."

The father keeps his gaze on his daughter. "Are you sure there isn't something you'd rather order?"

The mother drains her wine. The waiter approaches and discreetly refills it. It is the second time he has done so. The daughter has abstained save for a single sip; the father has waved away an offer of a second Scotch.

"Perhaps I am a bit preoccupied," the daughter confesses. She hesitates. "There's a young research assistant I've been working with. Her father's job is being phased out, and there is a disabled sister. I'm wondering if there is any way we can help the family."

"What did you have in mind?" The father leans back in his seat.

The mother has taken a breadstick from the basket on the table and snapped off the end.

"He lives in Allentown. Do you know any companies there?"

The father frowns. "Line of work?"

"He sells life insurance. They're not fancy. I'm sure he'd be open to doing something else."

"You never cease to amaze me," the father says. "You're so busy doing such important work, but you still take the time to get involved."

The mother has finished consuming the breadstick. She says, "You're not still feeling badly about that other girl." It is more a statement than a question.

The daughter does not outwardly exhibit any signs of distress or agitation.

"There is no connection between the two," she says. Her tone remains even.

An observer would have no indication of the effort this requires.

The father pats the daughter on the hand. "I'll see what I can do," he says.

The waiter delivers a birthday cake to the table. The mother blows out the single candle.

"Take a big piece home for Thomas," the mother says.

Her eyes linger on the daughter.

Then they sharpen. "We look forward to seeing both of you on Christmas Eve."

CHAPTER

TWENTY-NINE

Thursday, December 13

THERE IS NO CAR SERVICE or wardrobe directions or written script for today's assignment.

All I have is a destination and a time: the Dylan Alexander photography exhibit at the Met Breuer. I'm supposed to be there from eleven to eleven-thirty, then head directly to Dr. Shields's office.

When Dr. Shields called me on Tuesday afternoon with the instructions, I asked: "What exactly do you need me to do?"

"I realize these assignments are a bit disconcerting," she'd replied. "But it's essential that you go into the scenarios blind so that your knowledge doesn't affect the outcomes."

She'd said only one more thing:

"Just be yourself, Jessica."

That threw me.

I know how to play the various roles in my life: the hardworking professional makeup artist; the girl at the bar laughing with her friends; the dutiful daughter and big sister.

But the person Dr. Shields sees isn't any of them. She knows the woman on the couch who reveals secrets and vulnerabilities. But surely that isn't who I am supposed to be today.

I try to remember the compliments Dr. Shields has given me, the things that might have led her to say she felt as though I was more than just a subject to her. Maybe that's the part of me I'm to reveal today. But I can't recall a lot of specific praise, just that she likes my fashion sense and my forthrightness.

As I get dressed, I am aware my outfit is more for her than it is for the assignment. At the last minute I retrieve Dr. Shields's taupe wrap. I tell myself it's to ward off the December cold, but the truth is I'm nervous, and the scarf feels comforting. I inhale and imagine I can detect the faint smell of her spicy perfume, even though it surely must have worn off the fabric by now.

Before I make my way to the museum, I head to a diner to meet Lizzie for breakfast. I'd told her I had an important makeup appointment and needed to leave at ten o'clock sharp. I wanted to give myself an extra cushion, because even though midday in the city isn't usually a busy travel time, you can never predict a subway delay or traffic jam or broken heel.

At breakfast, Lizzie talks about her adored youngest brother, Timmy, who is a sophomore in high school. I met him when I went home with her for a weekend last summer; he's a sweet, good-looking kid. Apparently, he decided against trying out for the basketball team, something he has always loved. Now the whole family is in a tizzy; he is the first of the four brothers to not letter in the sport.

"So what does he want to do?" I ask.

"The robotics club," Lizzie said.

"There's probably more of a future for him in that than in basketball," I say.

"Especially since he's five five," she agrees.

I tell her a little bit about Noah. I don't get into the details of how we met, but I reveal we had a second date on Saturday night.

"A guy who offers to cook for you?" Lizzie asks. "Sounds sweet."

"Yeah. I think he is." I look down at my burgundy nails. It feels strange to be keeping so much from her. "I need to run. Talk soon?"

I reach the museum ten minutes early.

I'm walking toward the entrance when I hear tires screech and someone shouting, "Holy crap!"

I spin around. Just a dozen yards away, a white-haired woman is sprawled on the street in front of a taxi cab. The driver is getting out, and a few people are rushing toward the accident scene.

I hurry over in time to hear the driver say, "She walked right in front of me."

By now there are five or six of us clustered around the woman, who is conscious but looks dazed.

A thirty-something couple standing next to me immediately takes charge; they have an air of calm competence around them.

"What's your name?" the man asks, taking off his blue overcoat and laying it on top of the white-haired woman. She's small and frail-looking underneath his large jacket.

"Marilyn." Even that single word seems to rob her of her strength. She closes her eyes and grimaces.

"Someone call an ambulance," the woman says, arranging the coat more securely around Marilyn.

"I've got it," I say as I dial 911.

I give the dispatcher the address, then I sneak a quick glance at my watch. It's 10:56.

A thought strikes me: Maybe this accident was staged. At the hotel bar, Dr. Shields used me to assess a stranger.

Today I could be the one being evaluated.

Perhaps *this* is the test.

The couple bent over Marilyn are both attractive and wear business clothes and glasses. Could they be a part of this?

I glance around, half expecting to glimpse Dr. Shields's red hair and piercing blue eyes, as if she's going to be standing just offstage in the wings, directing this scene.

I shake off the suspicion; it's crazy to think she could have set this all up.

I bend down and say to Marilyn, "Is there anyone we can call for you?"

"My daughter," she whispers.

She recites the phone number; it seems encouraging that she can remember it.

The man who gave her his coat quickly speaks into his cell.

"Your daughter is on her way," he says as he hangs up. He looks at me. From behind his glasses, his eyes are concerned. "Good idea."

I check my watch: 11:02 A.M.

If I head into the museum right now, I'll only be a minute or two late for my assignment.

But what kind of person could walk away?

In the distance, I hear the wail of an ambulance. Help is coming.

Is it ethical for me to leave now?

If I wait any longer, I'll have violated Dr. Shields's explicit instructions. I feel perspiration prickle my back.

"I'm so sorry," I say to the man who is shivering slightly now without his coat. "I have an assignment for work. I really need to go."

"It's okay, I've got this," he says kindly, and the knot in my chest loosens a bit.

"You sure?"

He nods.

I look down at Marilyn. She's wearing pink frosted lipstick that looks like the same CoverGirl brand my mom has worn for years, even though I used to give her expensive Bobbi Brown shades when I worked at that counter.

"Can you do me a favor?" I ask the man. I take out one of my Beauty-Buzz business cards and scribble my cell number on it. I hand it to him. "Will you just let me know when you hear how she is?"

"Sure," he says.

I really do want to make sure Marilyn is okay. Plus, now when I tell Dr. Shields about the accident, she won't judge me for callously leaving the scene of the accident.

It's six minutes after eleven by the time I rush through the doorway of the museum.

I take a final look back and see that the guy still holding my card isn't looking toward the approaching ambulance. He's watching me.

I give the woman at the ticket counter ten dollars, and she points me in the direction of the Dylan Alexander exhibit: up the narrow staircase to the second level, then left down the hallway.

As I hurry up the steps, I look at my phone to see if Dr. Shields has texted, like she did at the bar. A message has come in, but not from her:

Just checking in again. Coffee? Katrina, my old friend from the theater, wrote.

I shove my phone back into my pocket.

The Dylan Alexander exhibit is at the end of the hall, and I'm nearly gasping by the time I reach it.

I googled the artist right after Dr. Shields gave me the assignment, so the subject of his work doesn't come as a surprise.

It's a series of black-and-white photographs of motorcycles, unframed, on giant pieces of stretched canvas.

I look around for any clues to orient me.

Several people are lingering before the images—a docent leading a trio of tourists, a French-speaking couple holding hands, and a guy in a black bomber jacket. None of them seems to notice me.

By now the ambulance should be here, I think. Marilyn is probably being lifted up on a stretcher. She must be scared. I hope her daughter gets there fast.

I peer at the pictures, remembering again how I'd given an un-inspired response when Dr. Shields had shown me the glass falcon. I now wonder if my assignment has to do with these images. I need something more profound to say about this exhibit in case she asks.

I know a little about motorcycles, but I know even less about art.

I stare at a photo of a Harley-Davidson, tilted so far to the side that the rider is almost parallel to the ground. It's a powerful shot, life-size like the others, and practically bursting out of its frame. I am struggling to find the hidden meaning that artwork is supposed to contain, which, in turn, could give me a hint about Dr. Shields's hidden meaning in sending me here. All I see is a big, hulking machine and a rider who seemed like he was risking his life unnecessarily.

If the real-life morality test isn't in these photos, where could it be?

I can hardly concentrate on the photographs as I begin to wonder if the test already happened. The Met has a suggested fee of twenty-five dollars, but you don't have to give anything. When I'd first arrived at the museum, there was a ticket counter with a sign that read THE AMOUNT YOU PAY IS UP TO YOU. PLEASE BE AS GENEROUS AS YOU CAN.

I was in a rush, and I was only going to be there for thirty minutes,

I'd thought as I'd opened my wallet. I had a twenty and a ten. So I'd pulled out the ten, folding it in half before sliding it under the glass to the ticket agent.

Dr. Shields was probably planning on reimbursing me for the entrance fee. Maybe she'd assume I'd paid the full amount. I'd have to tell her the truth. I hope she didn't think I was cheap.

I decide that when I go back down I'll get change and donate another fifteen dollars.

I try to refocus on the art. Next to me, the couple is having an animated discussion in French as they point to one of the images.

Farther down, toward the beginning of the exhibit, the tall man in the black bomber jacket stares at a photograph.

I wait until he moves on to the next picture, then I approach him.

"Excuse me," I say. "This is a dumb question, but I can't figure out what it is about these photos that makes them so special."

He turns and smiles. He is younger than I'd thought at first. Better looking, too, with his juxtaposition of classically handsome features and edgy clothes.

He pauses. "It seems to me the artist chose to use black-and-white because he wants the viewer to focus on the beautiful form. The lack of color really enables you to notice every detail. And see how he has carefully chosen the light here to enhance the handlebars and speedometer."

I turn to look at the image from his perspective.

The motorcycles all appeared alike to me at first, a blur of metal and chrome, but now I realize they are quite distinct.

"I get what you mean," I say. I still can't figure out what this exhibit has to do with morality and ethics, though.

I move to the next photograph. This motorcycle isn't in motion. It is shining and new and stands atop a mountain. Then, the man in the bomber jacket walks over to it, too.

"See the person reflected in the side mirror?" he asks. I hadn't, but I nod anyway as I peer closer at the image.

The buzzer on my phone sounds, startling me. I give the man an apologetic smile in case the noise has broken his concentration, then I reach into my pocket to silence it.

I'd set the alarm on my way to the museum, wanting to make sure I followed Dr. Shields's directions to leave at eleven-thirty sharp. I need to go.

"Thanks," I tell the man, then I take the stairs down to the main level. Rather than waste more time getting change, I tuck the twenty into the donation box and hurry out the door.

As I exit the door, I see that Marilyn, the cabdriver, and the guy with the tortoiseshell glasses are all gone.

Cars are driving over the spot where she had lain; people are milling around the sidewalk, talking on their cell phones and eating hot dogs from a nearby vendor.

It's like the accident never happened.

CHAPTER
THIRTY

Thursday, December 13

To you, this is simply a thirty-minute assignment.

You have no idea that it may spark the unraveling of my entire life.

Since this plan was set into motion, measures were required to counterbalance my resulting physical reactions: sleeplessness, lack of appetite, a plummeting core temperature. It is essential that these base distractions be offset to avoid wreaking havoc with the clarity of the thought process.

A warm bath infused with lavender oil coaxes sleep. In the morning, two hard-boiled eggs are consumed. An increase in the thermostat from seventy-two degrees to seventy-four degrees compensates for my physiological alteration.

It begins with a call to Thomas's cell phone right before we are supposed to meet.

"Lydia," he says, pleasure lacing his voice. What would it be like to live the rest of my life without hearing it in all of its incarnations, slightly scratchy when he wakes up in the morning, soft and tender during intimate moments, and masculine and passionate when he cheers for the Giants?

Thomas confirms that he is at the Met Breuer, waiting for my arrival.

However, the pleasure in his tone disappears when he learns a work emergency will require cancelation of our plans to view one of his favorite photographer's exhibits.

But he can hardly complain. He called off a date just over a week ago.

The exhibit will only be there through the weekend; Thomas won't want to miss it.

"You can tell me about it at dinner on Saturday," Thomas is told.

Now you are both in place, set on a collision course.

All that remains is the waiting.

The condition of waiting is universal: We wait for traffic lights to change from red to green, for the grocery store line to advance, for the results of a medical test.

But the wait for you to arrive and relay what happened at the museum, Jessica, isn't measurable by any standard unit of time.

Often the most effective psychological studies are rooted in deception. For example, a subject can be led to believe he or she is being evaluated for one behavior when, in fact, the psychologist has engineered this decoy to measure something else entirely.

Take the Asch Conformity Study: College students thought they were participating in a simple perceptual task with other students when, in actuality, they were placed one at a time in a group along with actors. The students were shown a card with a vertical line on it, then another card with three more lines. When asked to say out loud which lines matched in length, the students consistently provided the same answer as the actors, even when the actors picked one of the clearly incorrect lines. The student subjects believed they were being tested on perception, but what was actually being assessed was adherence to conformity.

You assume you are visiting the Met Breuer to look at photographs. But your opinion of the exhibit is of no concern.

It is 11:17 A.M.

That particular exhibit will be uncrowded at this time of day; only a few people should be viewing the artwork.

You will have seen Thomas by now. And he, you.

Sitting down is an impossibility.

A hand is run along the row of books filling the white wood built-in shelf, even though the spines are already perfectly aligned.

The single legal-size folder on the desk is moved slightly to the right, centering it more precisely.

The tissues on the table beside the couch are replenished.

The clock is checked again and again.

Finally, 11:30. It is over.

The length of the office is sixteen steps, back and forth.

11:39.

The far window affords a view over the entranceway; it is checked with every pass by that corner.

11:43.

You should be here by now.

A check in the mirror, a reapplication of lipstick. The edges of the sink are cold and hard. The reflection in the mirror confirms the facade is in place. You will suspect nothing.

11:47.

The buzzer sounds.

You are finally here.

A slow, measured breath. Then another.

You smile as the inner door to the office is opened. Your cheeks are flushed from the cold, and your hair is windblown. You radiate the full bloom of youth. Your presence serves as a reminder of time's inexorable cruelty. Someday you, too, will be pulled toward its cusp.

What did he think when he encountered you instead of me?

"It's like we're twins," you say.

You touch your cashmere wrap by way of explanation.

My laugh is forced. "I see . . . it's perfect for such a blustery day."

You settle into the love seat, now your preferred spot.

"Jessica, tell me about your experience at the museum."

The prompt is delivered matter-of-factly. There can be no research bias. Your report needs to be unpolluted.

You begin: "Well, I have to tell you I was a few minutes late."

You glance down, avoiding my eyes. "There was a woman who was hit by a cab and I stopped to help her. But I called an ambulance and these other people took over and I rushed to the exhibit. For a second I wondered if she was part of the test." You give an awkward little laugh, then blunder on: "It was hard to tell where I was supposed to start, so I just went to the first picture that caught my eye."

You are speaking too quickly; you are summarizing.

"Take it more slowly, Jessica."

Your posture slumps.

"I'm sorry, it just threw me. I didn't see the accident, but I saw her lying on the street right after . . ."

Your anxiety must be indulged. "How upsetting," you are told. "It was good of you to help."

You nod; some of the tension eases from your rigid posture.

"Why don't you just take a deep breath, then we can proceed."

You unwind the wrap and place it on the seat next to you.

"I'm okay," you say. Your tone is tempered now.

"Describe what happened in chronological order after you entered the exhibit. Don't leave out any detail, no matter how inconsequential it may seem," you are told.

You speak of the French couple, the docent and her tourists, and your impression of Alexander's decision to photograph in black-and-white to emphasize the form of the vehicles.

You pause.

"To be honest, I really didn't understand what made the photographs special. So I asked this guy who seemed really into them why he liked them."

A hitch in the pulse. An almost uncontrollable surge of queries.

"I see. And what did he say?"

You recount the exchange.

It is as though Thomas's deep voice is reverberating through the office, mingling with your higher tones. When you spoke, did he notice the rounded cupid's bow on your upper lip? The smoky sweep of your eyelashes?

A slight ache forms in my hand. My grasp on the pen is eased.

The next question must be chosen with exquisite care.

"And then did your conversation with him continue?"

"Yeah, he was nice."

A brief, involuntary smile alights on your face. The memory now gripping you is a pleasurable one.

"He came up to me a minute later when I was looking at the next photograph."

There were only two possible outcomes in this scenario. The first was that Thomas would pay no attention to you. The second, that he would.

Although the latter was repeatedly envisioned, its power is nevertheless devastating.

Thomas, with his sandy hair and the smile that starts in his eyes, the one that promises everything will be okay, could not resist you.

Our marriage dwelled within a lie; it was built on a foundation of quicksand.

The swelling rage and deep disappointment do not reveal themselves. Not yet.

You continue to describe the conversation about the reflection of the rider in the motorcycle mirror. You are stopped when you begin to detail how the alarm on your phone sounded.

You are jumping ahead to your exit from the museum. You must be led backward, to the room where you and Thomas met.

The question has to be asked, even though it seems a foregone conclusion that Thomas found you attractive, that he sought a way to prolong your contact.

You have been trained to be honest in this space. Your foundational sessions have led us to this pivotal moment.

"The sandy-haired man . . . Would you—"

You are shaking your head.

"Huh?" you interject. "You mean the man I was talking to about the photographs?"

It is imperative that any confusion be eliminated.

"Yes," you are told. "The one in the bomber jacket."

Your expression grows perplexed. You shake your head again.

Your next words send the room spinning.

Something has gone deeply wrong.

"His hair wasn't light," you say. "It was dark brown. Almost black, really."

You never met Thomas at the museum. The man you encountered was someone else entirely.

CHAPTER
THIRTY-ONE

Friday, December 14

ON THE SURFACE, it's business as usual: the Germ-X, the Altoids, my arrival five minutes before the appointed time.

It's Friday night, and I have two clients left before I wrap up work. But neither of these appointments was scheduled by BeautyBuzz.

These are women Dr. Shields has selected, as part of her study.

When I went to her office yesterday after the museum, Dr. Shields seemed a little confused about my conversation with the guy in the bomber jacket. Then she excused herself to go the ladies' room. When she came back a few minutes later, I tried to tell her about the rest of my visit, how I put more money in the collection box and saw no sign of the accident when I left the exhibit.

But Dr. Shields cut me off; she only wanted to focus on this new experiment.

She explained again that these women had been subjects in an earlier morality survey and had signed a waiver agreeing to a broad range of possible follow-up trials. But they don't know why I'm really going to show up at their homes.

At least I do, or I think I do. This is the first time I've been told what is being evaluated before I go into an experiment.

I'm relieved I'm not going in blind, but it still feels strange. Maybe that's because the stakes seem so small. Dr. Shields wants to know if these clients will tip me more generously since the service is free. I'm to collect some basic demographic data on them—their ages, their marital status, their occupations—for her to include when she writes a paper on her research, or whatever it is she's using the information for.

I wonder why she needs me to confirm these details. Wouldn't she or her assistant, Ben, have gotten it prior to letting them into the study, like they did with me?

Before I enter the Chelsea apartment building and take the elevator to the twelfth floor, I reach into my pocket for my phone.

Dr. Shields has stressed the importance of one more instruction.

I press the button to dial her number.

The call is connected.

"Hi, I'm about to go in," I say.

"I'm going to mute myself now, Jessica," she says.

A moment later I don't hear anything, not even her breathing.

I press *Speaker.*

When Reyna opens the door to her apartment, my first thought is that she is pretty much what I expected when I envisioned the other women in Dr. Shields's study: early thirties, with shiny dark hair in a blunt cut at her collarbone. Her apartment is furnished with an artistic flair—a giant, swirling stack of books serves as an end table, the walls are a rich maroon, and a funky menorah that looks like an antique rests on the windowsill.

For the next forty-five minutes, I try to weave all the questions Dr. Shields needs me to ask. I learn Reyna is thirty-four, originally from Austin, and that she's a jewelry designer. She points to a few of the pieces she is wearing as I select a dove-gray eyeshadow, including the eternity ring she designed for her wedding to her partner.

"Eleanor and I have matching ones," she says. She'd already told me that they're attending a friend's thirty-fifth birthday party tonight.

Reyna is so easy to talk to I almost forget this isn't one of my usual jobs.

We chat a little more, then she goes to check her reflection in a mirror.

When she comes back, she hands me two twenties. "I can't believe I won this," she says. "Which company do you work for again?"

I hesitate. "One of the big ones, but I've been thinking about going freelance."

"I'll definitely call you again," Reyna says. "I still have your number."

But that number is to the phone Dr. Shields had me use. I just smile and pack up quickly. When I'm back on the sidewalk, I immediately take Dr. Shields off speakerphone and put my cell phone to my ear.

"She gave me forty dollars," I say. "Most clients only tip ten."

"Wonderful," Dr. Shields says. "How long until you're at the next appointment?"

I check the address. It's just a quick cab ride up the West Side Highway.

"It's in Hell's Kitchen," I say. I'm shivering; the temperature has plummeted in the past hour. "So I should be there by around seven-thirty."

"Perfect," she says. "Call me when you arrive."

The second woman is unlike any other client I've worked on. It's hard to imagine how she would have gotten into Dr. Shields's study.

Tiffani has bleached blond hair and is rail thin, but not like the fancy Upper East Side moms.

She starts chattering the minute I wheel my case into her tiny entryway. It's a studio with a minuscule kitchen and a couch pulled out into a bed. Bottles of liquor line the kitchen cabinet and the sink is full of dirty dishes. The television is blaring. I glance over and see Jimmy Stewart on the screen in *It's a Wonderful Life*. It's the only sign of the holidays in this dark, dreary apartment.

"I've never won anything!" Tiffani says. Her voice is high and almost shrill. "Not even a stuffed animal at the fair!"

I'm about to ask about her plans for the night when another voice comes from the rumpled covers on the sofa bed: "I fucking love this movie!"

I start, then look over to see a guy lounging against the cushions.

Tiffani follows my gaze: "My boyfriend," she says, but she doesn't introduce me. The guy doesn't even look over, and the blue light from the screen that washes over his face blurs his features.

"Going anywhere special tonight?" I ask.

"I'm not sure, maybe a bar," Tiffani says.

I open my case on the floor; there's nowhere to spread out. Already I know I don't want to spend any longer here than I need to.

"Can we turn on a light?" I ask Tiffani.

She reaches for a switch and her boyfriend reacts instantly, throwing a hand over his eyes. I catch a glimpse of sharp limbs and a tattoo sleeve. "Can't you guys do that in the bathroom?"

"There's no space," Tiffani says.

He exhales. "Fine."

I set my phone on the top shelf of my case, making sure the screen is facedown. I wonder how much of this Dr. Shields can hear.

Tiffani drags over a brown packing box and sits on it. I notice a couple others stacked against the wall.

As I examine her skin I realize Tiffani is older than she first appeared: Her complexion is sallow, and her teeth have a grayish tint.

"We just moved here," she says. Her sentences tip up like questions at the end. "From Detroit."

I begin to blend an ivory foundation on my hand. She's so pale I need to use my lightest shade.

"What brought you to New York?" I ask. I know her marital status, now I just need to get her occupation and age.

Tiffani glances at her boyfriend. He still seems immersed in the movie. "Just some work stuff for Ricky," she says.

But clearly he's been listening to us because he calls out: "You girls sure are chatty."

"Sorry," Tiffani says. Then, more quietly, she continues: "Your job seems really fun. How did you get it?"

I lean over and begin to dab foundation onto her skin. That's when I see the faint purple bruise on her temple. It was hidden by her hair when she answered the door.

My hand pauses.

"Ouch, what happened here?" I ask.

She stiffens. "I hit it on a cabinet door when I was unpacking." For the first time, her tone is flat.

Ricky mutes the television, then peels himself from the sofa and saunters to the refrigerator. His feet are bare and he's wearing saggy jeans and a faded T-shirt.

He pulls out a Pabst and pops the top.

"How'd she win this, anyway?" he asks. He's only three feet away, directly under the fluorescent light. I can now see him clearly: His choppy, dirty-blond hair and sallow skin nearly match Tiffani's, but her eyes are light blue and his are nearly black.

Then I realize his pupils are so dilated they've crowded out the irises.

I instinctively look toward my phone, then drag my gaze back to him. "My boss arranged it," I say. "I think it's a free promotion to spread the word about her company."

I grab an eye pencil, not caring if it's the right shade.

"Close, please," I instruct Tiffani.

Three loud cracks erupt to the right of me.

I whip my head around. Ricky is rolling his neck from side to side. But his eyes stay fixed on me as he does it.

"So you just go around giving people free makeup?" he says. "What's the catch?"

Tiffani pipes up: "Ricky, she's almost done. I didn't give her a credit card or anything. Just watch your movie and then we can go out."

But Ricky doesn't move. He keeps staring at me.

I need to get one more piece of information, then I'm going to finish as fast as I can and leave.

"For women like you, who are under twenty-five, I prefer a creamy blush," I say, reaching into my case. The blush is on the top shelf, next to my phone.

I begin to blend it on Tiffani's cheek. My fingers are unsteady but still I try to make sure my touch is gentle in case the area by her bruise is tender.

Ricky moves a step closer. "How do you know she's under twenty-five?"

I look at my phone again. "Just guessing," I say. He smells like old sweat and cigarette smoke and something else I can't identify.

"What, you're trying to sell her this stuff?" he says.

"No, of course not," I say.

"Seems weird you picked her. We just moved here two weeks ago. How'd you get her number?"

My hand slips, smudging the blush down Tiffani's cheek.

"I don't— I mean, my boss just gave it to me," I say.

Two weeks, I think. And they moved all the way from Detroit.

There's no way Tiffani could be part of Dr. Shields's study.

I don't even realize that I've stopped working on Tiffani and am staring at my phone until I see a sudden movement out of the corner of my eye.

Ricky lunges forward. I twist out of the way, a scream rising in my throat.

Tiffani is frozen. "Ricky, don't!"

Instinctively I cower down on the floor. But it isn't me he's trying to grab.

It's my phone.

He snatches it up and flips it to see the screen.

"It's just my boss—" I start to blurt.

Ricky looks at me. "Are you a fucking narc?"

"What?"

"Nothing's ever free in life," he says.

I wait to hear Dr. Shields's voice come over the speakerphone. Beauty-Buzz has safeguards in place to protect us workers; they require a credit card and say we are authorized to leave immediately if something doesn't seem right.

All I have is Dr. Shields. She'll fix this; she'll explain everything.

I crane my neck up to look at the phone, but Ricky pulls it out of my line of vision.

"Why do you keep staring at this?" Ricky asks. Then he slowly turns around the phone, holding it up.

The screen shows nothing but my home screen photo of Leo.

Dr. Shields has hung up.

I'm on my own.

I'm crouched on the floor, with no way to protect myself.

"My boyfriend is picking me up, so I wanted to make sure to see his call come in," I lie, my voice high and frantic. "He should be here any second now."

Slowly I stand up, as if I'm trying to avoid antagonizing a wild animal.

Ricky doesn't move, but I feel as though he could explode at any second.

"I'm sorry I upset you," I say. "I can wait outside."

Ricky's eyes lock onto mine. His hand closes like a fist over my phone.

"There's something off about you," he says.

I shake my head. "I promise, I'm just a makeup artist."

He stares at me for another long moment.

Then he tosses my phone into the air and I scramble to catch it.

"Take your fucking phone," he says. "I'm going back to my movie."

I don't exhale until he's back on the sofa.

"I'm sorry," Tiffani whispers.

I want to reach into my case and extract one of my cards and give it to her. I want to tell her to call me if she ever needs help.

But Ricky is too close. His awareness of me is like a force in the room.

I grab a few lip glosses out of my case and hand them to Tiffani. "Keep these," I say.

I shove my things back into my case and shut it, then I stand up. My legs feel weak. I hurry to the door, imagining Ricky's eyes searing into my back. By the time I reach the stairwell, I'm running, my arm straining with the effort of holding up my heavy case.

After I'm in the back of an Uber, I check my phone log.

I can't believe it. Dr. Shields hung up after only six minutes.

CHAPTER
THIRTY-TWO

Friday, December 14

YOUR VOICE IS SURPRISINGLY agitated when you telephone following your encounter with the second woman: "How could you have hung up on me? That guy was bad news!"

Therapists are trained to set aside their own turbulent emotions and focus on their clients. This can be quite challenging, especially when unspoken questions vie with yours, Jessica: *What is Thomas doing tonight? Is he alone?*

But you must be appeased swiftly.

There could be any number of reasons why these two women called my husband—therapy, for example. In any case, they have been eliminated as potential paramours; Reyna is a married lesbian, and Tiffani relocated here only weeks ago.

The other possible avenues leading to information are closing up. This heightens the urgency of your participation.

Everything depends upon you now.

You must be managed.

"Jessica, I am so sorry. The call cut off and obviously you could not be phoned back. What happened? Are you safe?"

"Oh." You exhale. "Yeah, I guess. But that woman you sent me to? Her boyfriend was clearly on drugs."

A tinge of something—resentment? anger?—lingers.

This must be extinguished.

"Do you need me to send a car to pick you up?"

The offer is declined, as expected.

Still, the solicitous attention to your well-being has the desired effect. Your voice modulates. Your words come more slowly as you describe your interactions. Cursory questions are asked about the two women. You are complimented on your ability to draw out their basic demographic details.

"I left Tiffani too soon to get a tip," you say.

You are assured that you handled the situation perfectly, that your safety comes first.

Then a seed is carefully planted: "Is it possible that your prior experience with the theater director, the one you described to me in the hotel lobby, has left you feeling more vulnerable with men than you would otherwise?"

The question is delivered with compassion, naturally.

You fumble with an answer.

"I don't— I hadn't really thought about that," you say.

The hint of self-doubt in your voice reveals that the query has landed effectively.

The buzz of an incoming call interrupts you. You stop speaking briefly. The number is quickly checked, but it belongs to my father. Not Thomas.

"Continue, please," you are instructed.

Thomas has not responded to a message left for him more than an hour ago. This is atypical.

Where is he?

Your tone has remained deferential since the introduction of the possibility that your past is tainting your perceptions of your encounters with men. Perhaps you also remember how you jumped to conclusions with Scott in the hotel bar.

"The second woman, Tiffani . . . she mentioned she just moved here from Detroit." Your sentence is halting. You are probing for information without wanting to appear accusatory.

"I was just wondering . . . you said she was a part of your study?"

It was hoped that you would overlook this detail.

You were underestimated.

A quick recovery is necessary.

"My assistant, Ben, must have transposed two digits when he took down her phone number," you are told.

Effusive apologies are offered, and you accept them.

You must be drawn back in quickly; you will be needed again in just a few days for your most important assignment yet. A distraction is required.

Inspiration arrived serendipitously just moments ago, when my phone vibrated to signal the incoming call. The words that will entice you are selected:

"My father called today. He has a lead on a job that might be of interest."

Your relief is obvious and immediate. A gasp, followed by a cry of delight. "Really?"

This exchange is followed by a promise that a check for your evening's work will be ready for you the next time you come to the office.

You are brimming with questions, but you do not allow yourself to release them.

Excellent, Jessica.

You are eased off the phone.

Supplies are gathered: A laptop. A pen and a fresh legal pad. A cup of peppermint tea, to engender alertness and warm the hands and throat.

The blueprint for your encounter with Thomas must be quickly drawn. Not a single detail can be left to chance.

There can be no missed connection this time.

CHAPTER
THIRTY-THREE

Friday, December 14

LEO JUMPS ON ME as soon as I unlock my door, his little paws barely reaching my knees. He hasn't been out since I left to do makeup on Reyna and Tiffani. I set down my case and grab my wool scarf, then clip on his leash.

I need this walk as much as he does right now.

Leo tugs me down the three flights of stairs and through the building's front door. Even though I'm only going to be gone for a few minutes, I yank it hard to make sure the sometimes-sticky lock engages.

While Leo relieves himself on a fire hydrant, I wrap the scarf around my neck and check my phone. Two missed texts. The first is from my theater friend Annabelle: *Miss you girl, call me!*

The second is from an unfamiliar number: *Hey, just wanted you to know Marilyn is doing okay. Her daughter said she was released from the hospital a few hours ago. Hope you got to your work assignment on time.* At the end, he added a smiling emoji.

Thanks for the update, that's good news! I type back.

As I continue to walk, I reach my free hand around to rub the back of my neck, trying to ease the knots. Even the promise of a possible new job for my dad doesn't offset the agitation I'm feeling.

I want to talk to someone about everything that is going on. But I can't unburden myself to my father and mother, and not just because of Dr. Shields's rule of secrecy.

I look at my phone again.

It's not quite nine P.M.

Noah is out of town until Sunday. I could call Annabelle or Lizzie and try to meet up with them. Their happy banter would be a diversion, but right now it doesn't feel like a welcome one.

I turn a corner and pass a restaurant with a string of white holiday lights dangling around windows. On the doorway of the shop next door is a wreath.

My stomach rumbles and I realize I haven't eaten since lunch.

A group comes toward me, led by a guy in a floppy Santa hat. He's walking backward, singing "Rudolph the Red-Nosed Reindeer" loudly and mixing up the lyrics while his friends laugh.

I step to one side to let them pass, feeling as if I'm disappearing into the shadows in my all-black work outfit.

A year ago, I was also part of a happy, loud group. We sat around after rehearsals on Friday nights, and Gene ordered in Chinese food for everyone. Sometimes Gene's wife would stop by with homemade brownies or cookies. In a way, it felt like a family.

I didn't realize how much I miss it.

I'm alone tonight, but I'm used to that. It's just that I don't often feel lonely.

The last time I googled Gene, I saw his wife had just had a baby girl. My search turned up a picture of the three of them together at the opening of one of his shows, the wife smiling down at the infant in her arms. They looked happy.

I think about the two texts from Katrina, the ones I haven't answered.

A question has been forming in my mind, despite my efforts to move on from that period in my life. As I think about Gene's innocent wife, it's like I can hear Dr. Shields asking it:

Is it ethical to destroy one blameless woman's life if it means there's a chance of protecting other women from future harm?

I need an escape from my thoughts. If I did drugs, now is when I'd be reaching for a joint. But I don't lose control that way. There's another outlet I crave when the pressure gets to be too much.

Noah thinks I'm the kind of girl you cook for and only kiss on the first date. But that's not who I am anymore, ever since that evening with Gene French. Maybe because I trusted him so much, now it's hard to be emotionally vulnerable with men. Even if Noah were in town, he's not what I'm looking for tonight.

I think instead about the guy who just texted, and how he stared after me when I walked toward the museum. With him, I can just be an anonymous girl.

So I text him again: *Any chance you're free for a drink now?*

I briefly think about Noah with the dishcloth tucked away in his jeans as he cooked for me.

He won't ever know, I think.

All I'm going to do is see this guy for a few hours. I'll never need to talk to him again.

CHAPTER
THIRTY-FOUR

Friday, December 14

AFTER YOU FILE YOUR REPORT on your encounters with Reyna and Tiffani, the phone remains silent for an agonizingly long stretch of time. When Thomas finally calls at 9:04 P.M., the cup of peppermint tea has been freshened three times. Nearly two pages of the legal pad are filled.

"I'm so sorry I didn't see your text earlier," he begins. "I was running around Christmas shopping and I didn't hear my ringer because the stores were so packed."

Thomas typically does leave holiday shopping until the last minute. And the rush of city noises can be heard in the background.

Still, suspicion swells. Would he truly have not felt the vibration of his phone?

But his excuse is readily accepted, because it is even more vital that he enters the experiment blind.

A bit of light chatting ensues. Thomas says he is worn out, and is heading home for an early night.

Then he utters one final sentence before hanging up.

"I'm looking forward to seeing you tomorrow, gorgeous."

The teacup clatters into the saucer, chipping the fine china. Fortunately, he terminated the call before the noise erupted.

During the course of our marriage, Thomas freely bestowed compliments: *You're beautiful. Stunning. Brilliant.*

But never gorgeous.

In the errant text that he addressed to me, though, it was the term he'd used for the woman he confessed to having an affair with.

Experiencing emotional phases of dark and light is universal. A healthy and loving partnership can provide a supportive infrastructure during a downward trajectory, but it can never erase the pain that infuses an individual during pivot points such as the death of a sister, or the infidelity of a husband.

Or the suicide of a young female subject.

This seismic tragedy occurred at the beginning of this past summer: June 8, to be exact. Our marriage suffered, Jessica. Whose wouldn't? It was difficult to summon the energy to wholly engage. Visions of my subject's earnest, brown eyes intruded at all hours. A retreat both emotionally and physically resulted, despite Thomas's reassuring words: "Some people are beyond help, my love. There's nothing you could have done."

Our marriage could have recovered from the estrangement formed during this time. Except for one thing.

A season later, in September, the text he said was intended for the boutique owner with whom he'd had a one-night stand landed on my phone. The bright, chiming noise seemed to reverberate throughout my quiet office. It was 3:51 P.M. on a Friday afternoon.

Thomas likely sent it at that particular time because his own office was empty, too; clients typically depart at ten minutes before the hour, leaving a small window for the therapist to attend to personal needs before the next patient is welcomed.

During that summer of internal darkness, my office hours were also maintained, Jessica. No patient was turned away. This was perhaps more vital than ever before.

Which meant the nine vacant minutes that followed the receipt of the text could be spent staring at Thomas's message: *See you tonight, Gorgeous.*

It was as though the words expanded until they blotted out all else.

As a therapist, one often witnesses a client's attempt to rationalize, to make excuses, as a defense mechanism to quash overwhelming emotions. However, those four words could not be ignored.

When just one minute remained before new clients would be ushered in to both of our offices, the trancelike state broke. A reply was transmitted to Thomas.

I do not think this was intended for me.

The phone was then silenced and my four P.M. appointment, a single mother struggling with anxiety that was exacerbated by her teenage son's belligerence, was utterly unaware that anything was amiss.

However, Thomas must have canceled his final appointment of the day, because fifty minutes later, after the agitated mother was escorted out, he sat slumped in my waiting room, leaning forward with his elbows on his knees, his face drawn and gray.

In the wake of Thomas's text, data was amassed.

Some information was offered by Thomas. Her first name: Lauren. Her place of employment: a small, upscale clothing boutique near Thomas's office.

Other information was independently collected.

A brief phone call to the boutique at noon on a Saturday was all that was required to verify Lauren's presence on the premises. It was a simple matter to wander inside and pretend to be absorbed in the colorful fabrics.

She was ringing up a customer with easy chatter. The boutique contained one other sales clerk and several other shoppers. But she was the one who drew the eye, and not just because of her history with my husband. You look a bit like her, Jessica. There's a similarity in your essence. And it was easy to see why even a happily married man would be susceptible to her overtures.

She completed the transaction and approached me with a warm smile. "Looking for anything special?" she asked.

"Just browsing," she was told. "Can you make a recommendation?

I'm going away for the weekend with my husband and I'd like a few new outfits."

She recommended several items, including the unstructured dresses she'd picked up on her recent buying trip to Indonesia.

A brief conversation ensued concerning her travels.

She was exuberant and brimming with joy; she wore her zest for life.

After Lauren was allowed to prattle on for several minutes, the encounter was abruptly terminated. Nothing was purchased, of course.

The meeting answered a few questions, but it raised others.

Lauren still has no idea of the true intention of my visit.

A drop of bright red blood stains the white china saucer.

A Band-Aid covers my tiny wound. The broken teacup remains on the table.

Thomas is not a tea drinker.

He prefers coffee.

The legal pad rests on the desk next to the teacup.

The question at the top of the yellow lined page, written in all capital letters, can finally be answered: *WHERE WILL THEY FINALLY MEET?*

Every Sunday, following his squash game, Thomas enjoys a simple routine: He reads *The New York Times* at a diner two doors down from his gym. He pretends this is because the location is convenient. The truth is that he craves their greasy bacon and fried eggs with a heavily buttered bagel. Despite a marriage filled with so many overlapping regimes, our Sunday-morning routines were always divergent.

In thirty-six hours, Thomas will indulge his weekly craving.

And you, Jessica, will arrive to provide a different sort of temptation.

CHAPTER
THIRTY-FIVE

Sunday, December 16

I SPOT DR. SHIELDS'S TARGET the instant I step into the diner that's filled with the clatter of dishes and the buzz of customers' conversations. He's alone in the third booth on the right, his face partially obscured by his newspaper.

Yesterday Dr. Shields called to tell me she had a check for a thousand dollars for my work on Friday night. Then she gave me this assignment: Find a certain man, at this particular coffee shop, and exchange phone numbers. It was uncomfortable enough to flirt with Scott at a hotel bar, but doing the same thing without the dim light and alcohol seems a hundred times worse.

The only way I can do it is by imagining my family's expressions when they learn they're going on vacation after all.

Sandy hair. Six foot two. Tortoiseshell glasses. New York Times. Gym bag. Dr. Shields's description runs through my mind again.

The man checks every box. I walk briskly toward him, poised to say my opening line. He looks up just as I reach his table.

I freeze.

I know my next line: *I'm sorry to bother you, but did you find a phone?* But I can't speak. I can't move.

The man in the booth isn't a stranger.

I first encountered him outside the Met Breuer four days ago, when we both stopped to help the woman who was hit by a taxi. We were two strangers bound together by serendipity—at least that's what I assumed.

I saw him again after he texted to tell me Marilyn was okay, and I suggested meeting for a drink.

He sets his newspaper on the table. He looks almost as surprised as I feel. "Jess? What are you doing here?"

My first instinct is to turn and walk out the door. My mouth is dry and it's hard to swallow.

"I just— I mean," I stutter. "I was just walking by and thought I'd grab a bite."

He blinks.

"What a coincidence." His eyes linger on my face and panic sweeps through me. "You don't live around here. What are you doing in the neighborhood?"

I shake my head and push away an image of him leaning forward in the darkened bar just two nights ago, his hand grazing my thigh. After three drinks, Thomas and I went back to my place.

"Um, a friend told me I should come because the food was good."

The waitress swings by with a carafe of steaming coffee: "Top you off, Thomas?"

"Sure," he says. He gestures to me. "Do you want to sit down?"

The restaurant feels stuffy and overly warm. I unwind the taupe wrap from around my neck, leaving both sides dangling down the front of my jacket. Thomas is still looking at me suspiciously.

I don't blame him.

I never learned what the morality test was in the museum. But in a city of eight million, what are the odds that I'd randomly run into the same person twice in four days, both times on assignment for Dr. Shields?

Everything feels so topsy-turvy that I can't gather my thoughts. Another image intrudes: him kissing his way down my bare stomach.

I can't say anything to Thomas that would explain my presence here. Who is he to Dr. Shields? Why did she pick him?

I feel sweat prickle my armpits.

The waitress returns. I'm still standing.

"Anything for you?" she asks me.

There's no way I can sit across from him and eat.

"You know, I'm not really hungry after all," I say.

I look at Thomas more closely—his green eyes behind his tortoise-shell glasses, his olive skin and his dirty-blond hair. It hits me that Dr. Shields assumed the guy I was talking to at the exhibit was Thomas, since she thought he had sandy hair. She lost interest as soon as she realized it wasn't him.

So this is a do-over.

But what is Dr. Shields going to say when she learns I've slept with the guy whose phone number I'm supposed to get?

I'm aware I'm fingering the edge of my wrap. I break eye contact with Thomas and pull it off, tucking it into my bag and anchoring it with the paperback book I'm carrying.

"I need to go," I say.

He raises his eyebrows. "Are you stalking me?" he asks.

I can't tell if he's kidding. I haven't talked to him since he left my place around one A.M. yesterday morning. Neither of us texted the other; it seemed pretty clear what our encounter was.

"No, no," I say. "It was just— I made a mistake."

I flee out the door.

I already completed my assignment days ago. I have Thomas's number stored in my phone. And he has mine.

When I'm a block away from the diner, I call Dr. Shields to tell her I'm en route to her town house. She answers midway through the first ring. Her silvery voice is edged with strain: "Did you find him?"

"Yes, he was right where you said he'd be."

I'm about to duck into a subway station when the beep of an incoming call interrupts her next question. All I can make out is: ". . . phone . . . plan?"

"Sorry," I say. "Yes, we have each other's numbers."

I hear the breezy sound of her exhalation.

"Wonderful, Jessica. I'll see you soon."

My heart is thudding.

I don't know how I'm going to manage to sit across from her and tell her I slept with the guy in the experiment. I could say that I would've told her about meeting Thomas, but she cut me off when I was talking about the taxi accident during our last session.

I have to do it. If I'm not honest, she'll find out.

I release a breath.

It's silly to think Dr. Shields will be upset with me, I tell myself. I made an innocent mistake. She can't hold it against me.

But I can't stop shivering.

I check my voice mail. One message.

I know who it's from even before I hear his voice.

"Hi, it's Thomas. We have to talk. I think I know the friend who sent you to the diner. She's . . . Look, just call me back as soon as you can."

He continues: "And please, don't tell her anything." There's a pause. "She's dangerous. Watch yourself."

CHAPTER
THIRTY-SIX

Sunday, December 16

You FINALLY MET my husband.

What did you think of him? And, more important, what did he think of you?

A vision of the two of you, leaning toward each other in a cozy booth at the diner, is pushed away.

When you arrive at the town house, the usual welcoming rituals are performed: Your coat and wrap are hung in the closet; your oversize purse placed on the floor beside them. You are offered a beverage but, for the first time, you refuse.

You are scrutinized. Your appearance is as compelling as ever. But you seem off today, Jessica.

You avoid sustained eye contact. You fidget relentlessly with your rings.

Why are you so distracted? Your encounter with Thomas proceeded flawlessly; you followed your directions. You describe it when prompted: You approached him and explained you thought you'd left your phone in his booth. After a cursory search, you asked him to use his own cell phone to dial your number. He did, and the ringing indicated you'd overlooked your phone in your purse. You apologized for bothering him and departed.

Now it is time to proceed to the next step.

But before you can receive your instructions, you stand up from the couch in the library. "I need to grab something from my bag," you say.

After a nod of acquiescence, you retreat to the hall closet. You return a moment later holding a small tube.

You are frowning. Perhaps you are worrying again about your family's finances, or maybe you're suppressing questions about your latest assignment, but your emotions are not going to be managed today. There are far more important matters at hand.

"My lips are so chapped," you say as you run the balm in the tube with the BeautyBuzz logo over your mouth.

No response is given. You reclaim your seat.

"I need you to text the man from the diner and invite him out."

You cast your eyes downward, to your phone. You begin to type.

"No!" you are told.

The directive is delivered with more urgency than intended. A smile softens my tone.

"I'd like you to write the following: 'Hi, it's Jessica from the diner. It was nice meeting you today. Would you like to get together for a drink sometime this week?'"

You frown again. Your fingers do not move.

"What is it, Jessica?"

"It's nothing. Just— Everyone calls me Jess. Except you. So I wouldn't refer to myself by my full name."

"Fine, make that edit," you are told.

You follow the directions. You lay the phone down in your lap and the waiting commences once more.

A chime sounds a few seconds later.

You raise your phone. "It's just BeautyBuzz," you say. "My next client is in an hour."

A powerful collision of relief and disappointment is experienced.

"I didn't realize you had booked other jobs today," you are told.

You appear flustered. You begin to scrape at your nail polish with a fingertip, then you catch yourself and still your hands.

"You said you only needed me for an hour or two, so . . ."

Your voice trails off.

"Are you sure your text went through?"

You glance at your phone again. "Yep, it says delivered."

Another three minutes tick by.

Surely Thomas must have seen the text. But what if he hasn't?

It is important that the following request contains authority rather than any hint of desperation.

"I'd like you to cancel your makeup session."

Your throat constricts as you visibly swallow.

"Dr. Shields, you know I'd do anything for your research. But this is a good client, and she's counting on me." You hesitate. "She's hosting a big holiday party this afternoon."

Such an inconsequential dilemma.

"Couldn't a substitute be sent in your place?"

You shake your head. Your eyes are pleading. "BeautyBuzz has this policy. You have to give a day's notice before you cancel."

This was a miscalculation on your part, Jessica. A good client can't be compared to the excessive generosity you've been shown. Your priorities are skewed.

A beat of silence fills the room following your explanation. When you have twisted long enough, you are dismissed.

"Well, Jessica, I wouldn't want you to disappoint a good client."

"I'm sorry," you say as you quickly rise from the couch. But words pull you back.

"I would like you to inform me as soon as Thomas replies to your text."

You look startled. "Of course," you say quickly.

Then you apologize again, and you are silently escorted to the door.

CHAPTER
THIRTY-SEVEN

Sunday, December 16

I MAKE MYSELF WALK two blocks away from Dr. Shields's town house before calling Thomas back, even though the whole time I was with her, all I could think about was his message.

She's dangerous. Watch yourself.

The question searing through my mind is: How does Thomas know Dr. Shields arranged my meeting with him?

He picks up on the first ring. Before I can ask, he says, "How do you know my wife?"

My legs buckle and I stagger, falling against a tree to balance myself. I flash to the picture of the dark-haired man with the beard in the photo in her library, the one who appeared to be about Dr. Shields's height. I'm certain she said she was married to him.

So how could Thomas be her husband? Yet Dr. Shields clearly knows him; she called him by name at the end of our meeting.

"Your wife?" I echo. Nausea roils my stomach and my head begins to spin. I stare down at the sidewalk to ground myself.

"Yes, Lydia Shields." I hear him take a deep breath, like he's trying to steady himself, too. "We've been married for seven years. Although we're separated now."

"I don't believe you," I blurt.

There's no way Dr. Shields, with her rules about honesty, would have created such an elaborate lie.

"Meet me and I'll tell you everything," he says. "That book sticking out of your bag . . . *The Morality of Marriage*. She wrote it a few years ago. I read the first draft in our living room. That's how I knew she was behind this."

I wrap my free arm around myself, bracing myself against the blustery wind.

One of them is lying. But who?

"I'm not meeting you until you prove you're really her husband," I tell Thomas.

"I'll get proof," he says. "In the meantime, promise me you won't say a word to her about seeing me."

But I can't agree. This interaction could be a test. Maybe Dr. Shields wants me to prove my loyalty.

I'm about to hang up on Thomas when he says one final thing.

"Please, Jess, just be careful. You're not the first."

His words land like a physical blow. I feel myself recoil.

"What do you mean?" I whisper.

"She preys on young women like you."

I'm frozen in place.

"Jess?" I hear him repeat my name. But I can't speak.

Finally, I disconnect the call. I slowly lower my phone and look up.

Dr. Shields is two feet away.

I gasp and instinctively shrink back.

She materialized out of nowhere, like an apparition. She isn't wearing a coat to protect her against the elements. She's standing there, motionless, except for her hair, which is whipping in the wind. How much of my conversation did she overhear?

Adrenaline floods my body.

"Dr. Shields!" I cry. "I didn't see you there!"

She looks me up and down, as if assessing me. Then she stretches out her clenched hand and slowly unfurls her fingers.

"You forgot your lip balm, Jessica."

I stare at her, trying to make sense of it. She followed me all this way just to return my lip balm?

I have an almost uncontrollable urge to blurt out everything Thomas has just said. If she set this all up, she knows anyway.

Prey.

The term Thomas used is chilling. I can almost see Dr. Shields's lips forming that exact word as she stroked the crown of the glass falcon in her office a few weeks ago. The falcon that she told me was a gift for her husband.

I take a step forward. Then another.

Now I'm so close I can glimpse the vertical furrow between her eyebrows, so faint and shallow it's almost like a crack in a piece of glass.

"Thank you," I whisper as I take the lip balm. My bare fingers are numb from the cold.

She looks down at the phone I'm still holding in my other hand.

My chest tightens. I can't breathe.

"I'm glad I caught you," she says, then she turns to go.

CHAPTER
THIRTY-EIGHT

Sunday, December 16

NINETY MINUTES AFTER your lip balm is returned, the doorbell rings.

A glance through the peephole reveals Thomas. He is so close to the small circle of glass that his face appears distorted.

This is a surprise.

His presence was unannounced.

The deadbolt is disengaged and the heavy front door swings open.

"Sweetheart, what brings you here?"

One arm is hidden behind his back.

He smiles and pulls it forward, revealing an enormous bouquet of paper-white narcissi.

"I was in the neighborhood," he says.

"How lovely!"

He is welcomed inside.

He must have read the text with your invitation by now; it was sent several hours ago. Why is he really here?

Perhaps he has come to prove his fidelity by revealing your invitation.

A hand is placed on his arm. He is offered a warm drink.

"No, thanks, I just had coffee," he says.

It is as though he is providing an entryway into the very topic that weighs heavily on both of our minds.

"Of course. You love the coffee at Ted's Diner." A light laugh. "And your fried eggs, buttered bagel, and extra bacon."

"Yup, the usual."

A pause.

Perhaps it is difficult for him to know where to begin.

A prompt could be helpful: "So, breakfast was good?"

His eyes dart around the living room. Evasion or unease?

"Uneventful," he responds.

This could be interpreted in two ways. One is that his encounter with you was inconsequential. The other is that he is actively concealing it.

"Shouldn't you place those in water?" Thomas is staring at the bouquet.

"Of course." We retreat to the kitchen. The green stems are snipped, and a porcelain vase is retrieved from a cabinet.

"Why don't I put the flowers in the library for you?"

Thomas's offer feels abrupt. He must realize it, too, because he quickly smiles.

But it isn't one of his wide, natural smiles that reaches to his eyes.

He picks up the vase and heads toward the library.

When he is followed, he hestiates.

"You know, coffee sounds really good after all," he says. "I'd love a cup if it isn't too much trouble."

"Wonderful. I just brewed a pot."

This is a good sign. Thomas wants to linger.

The coffee is fixed just the way he likes it, with a splash of real cream and brown sugar. A quick glance at my phone reveals you have not yet texted to report any response from Thomas.

When the tray is brought into the library, Thomas is still positioning the vase atop the Steinway.

He spins around, a surprised look on his face.

It's almost as though he forgot he requested the beverage.

What has startled him?

A reminder of the stakes is necessary.

"Thomas, I've been wondering, where did you ever decide to put that falcon sculpture?"

It takes him a moment to answer. But when he does, it is pleasing: "In my bedroom, on the dresser. I see it every night when I go to sleep, and every morning when I wake up."

"Perfect." Then: "Why don't we sit?"

He perches on the edge of the love seat and immediately reaches for his cup. He takes a quick sip, then jerks back, nearly spilling the hot liquid.

"You seem a bit unsettled. Is there anything you wanted to talk about?"

He hesitates. Then he seems to come to a decision.

"It's nothing for you to worry about. I just wanted to see you so I could tell you how much I love you."

This is better than any other outcome that was envisioned.

Until Thomas glances at his watch and abruptly rises to his feet.

"I have a lot of paperwork I need to get to," he says ruefully. His fingertips drum against his jeans-clad thigh. "I don't know my schedule yet for the week, but I'll call you after I figure it out."

He departs as quickly and unexpectedly as he arrived.

There are two strange things about Thomas's hasty exit.

He did not offer me a parting kiss.

And aside from that single sip, the coffee he seemed so eager for remained untouched.

CHAPTER
THIRTY-NINE

Sunday, December 16

I'M SITTING ON A BENCH right outside Central Park, holding a cup of coffee I can't drink. My stomach is too knotted to tolerate more than a sip of the bitter brew.

Their texts come in almost simultaneously.

From Dr. Shields: *Jessica, any response from Thomas yet?*

From Thomas: *I got the proof. Can you meet me tonight?*

I don't answer Dr. Shields, because there's not going to be any response from Thomas about a date. Although I typed the text asking him out for drinks while she sat watching me in her town house, I never actually sent it.

That was the first of two lies I told to Dr. Shields this morning. I also didn't have a BeautyBuzz client booked today, like I pretended. I just needed to get away from her.

I don't reply to Thomas, either. There's someone else I need to see first.

Ben Quick, Dr. Shields's research assistant, lives on West Sixty-sixth Street.

As soon as it hit me that he was the only person I'd met who might know the truth about her, he was surprisingly easy to find. At least the apartment his parents own was.

After the doorman called up to announce my arrival, a man who looked exactly like Ben would in thirty years emerged from the elevator.

"Ben's not here," he said. "If you want to leave your number, I'll tell him you stopped by."

The doorman gave me a piece of paper and a pen and I jotted down my information. Then I realized Ben might not remember me out of the procession of women in Dr. Shields's study.

I was Subject 52, I wrote, then folded the paper in half.

That was more than an hour ago, and I still haven't heard from him. I lift my arms over my head to stretch my back, listening as Mariah Carey's voice singing "All I Want for Christmas Is You" drifts over from Wollman Rink. I came here a lot when I first moved to New York, but I haven't skated yet this year.

Just as I stand up to throw my coffee cup in the trash can, my phone rings.

I snatch it up, then see Noah's name.

After everything that's happened this weekend, I almost forgot we were supposed to meet for dinner tonight.

"Italian or Mexican," he says when I answer. "Either of those sound good?"

I hesitate as another unwelcome image of Thomas in bed, tangled in the sheets, springs into my mind.

I shouldn't feel guilty; I've only seen Noah twice. And yet I do.

"I'd love to see you, but could we do something low-key?" I ask. "I've had a really stressful day."

He takes it in stride. "Why don't we just stay in, then? I can open a bottle of wine and order in Chinese. Or I could come to your place?"

I can't go on a date and make normal conversation right now. But I don't want to cancel on this guy.

A deep voice comes over the PA system for the ice rink: "We're going to take a ten-minute break to Zamboni the ice. Go grab some hot chocolate and we'll see you soon!"

"I have an idea," I say to Noah.

I grew up skating on the frozen lake near my parents' house, so I'm pretty good. But Noah unpacks his own skates from a backpack he'd brought to the rink and explains, "I still play club hockey on the weekends."

After we do a few laps, he spins around to skate backward. Then he reaches out to hold my hands.

"Keep up with me, slowpoke," he jokes, and I dig in to the ice, feeling my thigh muscles burn.

This was just what I needed, the lightly falling snow, the physical movement, the loud music, the pink-cheeked children all around us.

So is the silver flask full of peppermint schnapps that Noah offers me when we lean back against the boards to take a break.

I take a sip, then another quick one.

I hand it back to him, then push off the boards. "Try to catch me now," I say over my shoulder as I gain speed.

I whip toward the bend of the oval rink, feeling the cold burn my face and a laugh well up in my chest.

A solid form rams into me. The collision nearly knocks me down.

My feet stutter and I instinctively throw out my hands as I try to gain purchase on the ice.

"Watch yourself," a man's deep voice says in my ear.

I grab for the side rail and my fingers close around it just in time to break my fall.

I'm breathing hard when Noah swoops in a second later.

"Are you okay?" he asks.

I nod, but I don't look at him. I'm trying to pick the man who bumped me out of the crowd, but it's impossible to find him in the swirl of swinging scarves and heavy coats and feet kicking up silver blades.

"Yeah," I finally say to Noah, but I'm still breathing hard.

"Want to take a break?" he suggests. He reaches for my hand and leads me off the ice. My legs shake and my ankles feel like they might give way.

We find a bench away from the throngs of people and Noah offers to get us hot chocolate.

Although my phone is in my pocket and set to vibrate, I'm worried

I've missed a message from Ben. So I nod and thank him. The minute he's out of sight, I check it. But the screen is blank.

It had to have been an accident when the man knocked into me. It's just that he used the exact same words as Thomas: *Watch yourself.*

The happiness I experienced when I was on the ice, feeling Noah's hands close over mine, is gone.

I smile at Noah when he returns to the bench with two foam cups, but it's almost like he can feel the shift in my energy.

"That guy came out of nowhere," he says. "You didn't get hurt, right?"

I look into his warm brown eyes. His presence feels like the only solid thing around me right now. I wonder again how I could have slept with Thomas on Friday night.

I didn't realize then how much that impulsive dalliance could have cost me, and how much it could still.

It suddenly occurs to me that Noah is the only one in my universe that Dr. Shields doesn't know about. I described my first night with Noah during one of those early computer sessions, but I never mentioned his name. And I haven't revealed that we were still in touch.

Some part of me must have wanted to hold that back, to have one piece of my life be mine alone.

Dr. Shields has heard all about Becky, and my parents, and Lizzie. I've provided her with the name of my employer, home address, and birthday. She is privy to my deepest insecurities and my most intimate thoughts.

Whatever she is doing with all of this information, I know Noah isn't involved in it.

I make a split-second decision.

"I didn't get hurt, but I guess there's something on my mind," I begin. I take a sip of hot chocolate before I continue. "There's the situation at work, and it's complicated, but . . ."

I fumble for how to put it in words, but Noah sits there, not rushing me.

"How do you know if you can really trust someone?" I finally ask.

Noah raises his eyebrows and takes a sip of his drink.

Then he looks into my eyes again and the expression in his is so earnest I feel like he's answering from a deeply personal place.

"If you need to ask that question, then you probably already know the answer," he says.

Two hours later, after Noah and I grabbed slices of hot gooey pizza and he walked me back to my apartment, I'm curled up in bed. Just as I'm about to drift off to sleep, my phone buzzes.

My bedroom is dark and the thin blue light on my nightstand is all I can see.

I'm wide awake.

I reach for it.

Why haven't you replied? Thomas has written. *We need to meet.*

Beneath his text is a wedding photo. In it, Dr. Shields wears a lacy ivory gown and beams at the camera. I've never seen her look happy before now, I realize as I stare at the slightly grainy image. She appears to be about five or ten years younger than she is today, but I don't need that detail to confirm what Thomas has told me about them being wed seven years ago.

The groom beside her, his arm wrapped protectively around her, isn't the dark-haired man in the photograph in her dining room.

It's Thomas.

CHAPTER
FORTY

Monday, December 17

Are you being honest, Jessica?

You keep assuring me that Thomas has not responded to your invitation.

This strains credulity. Thomas has an almost Pavlovian response to the ding of an incoming message. He might have rebuffed your invitation. Or he might have accepted it. But it seems highly unlikely that he would simply ignore it.

It is now three P.M. on Monday. More than twenty-four hours have elapsed since you departed my town house. Three have elapsed since you last communicated.

Another phone call is required.

You do not answer.

"Jessica, is everything all right? I am . . . disappointed I haven't heard back from you."

You do not return the phone call. Instead, you send a text: *No word yet. I'm not feeling well, so I'm going to try to rest.*

It's impossible to accurately ascertain tone from a text message, yet yours carries the feel of impetuousness.

You are trying to slow down the rhythm of communication with your thinly veiled excuse. It's as though you think you are the one in control.

Why do you need to hit the pause button, Jessica? You've been so eager and accommodating until now.

You were carefully selected because of your anticipated appeal to Thomas.

Did he exert a similar pull on you?

Since his unexpected visit yesterday, Thomas has not followed up on his promise to review his forthcoming week's schedule.

Aside from a brief call to say good night, he has not been in touch at all.

It takes a deliberate, sustained effort to slow the raggedy inhalations of breath. Swallowing food is impossible.

There is a slightly loose floorboard in the area just outside the kitchen; it gently creaks with every step. The sound forms a mesmerizing rhythm, like the chirping of a cricket.

A hundred creaks.

Then two hundred.

Thomas's schedule remains murky, but he knows mine.

On Mondays from five to seven P.M., my presence has been reliably required in a classroom at NYU, just down from Room 214.

However, since a leave of absence was granted a few weeks ago, a substitute will conduct my seminar.

Doubting Thomas is an unfortunate but necessary side effect resulting from his actions.

But doubting you, Jessica . . . now, that is intolerable.

Impulsivity, or acting without forethought or reflection, can lead to disastrous consequences.

And yet at 3:54 P.M. a somewhat rash decision is made.

It is time to remind you who is in charge, Jessica.

You didn't say what ails you, but chicken soup is considered to be a universal remedy.

Nearly every deli in New York sells it, including one just down the block from your studio apartment.

A large container is selected, and several packets of saltine crackers are added to the plain brown paper bag. A plastic spoon and napkins are included.

Your apartment building, with its peeling yellow plaster facade and the metal fire escape snaking up the side, comes as a bit of a surprise. You always appear so chic and alluring, and it is difficult to imagine you emerging from such a discordant environment.

The buzzer is pressed for Apartment 4C.

You do not answer.

Judgment is suspended; perhaps you are resting, just as you indicated.

The buzzer is held for a longer stretch of time.

In your small studio, the noise must be reverberating loudly.

No response.

Even if you had fallen asleep, it seems extremely unlikely you would not have awakened by now.

Remaining on your stoop provides no answers, yet it proves difficult to depart.

Then, by chance, another glance at the main door to your building reveals it is ever so slightly ajar; the lock isn't engaged.

A push against it is all that is required to gain entry.

There's no elevator or doorman. The staircase is dim and bleak, with its steps covered in a frayed gray carpet. Still, residents of this building have brightened the hallways with amateur-looking pieces of art. Christmas wreaths adorn a few doors, and the aroma of something savory—a chili or stew, perhaps—fills the air.

Your apartment is toward the end of the hall. There's a welcome mat in front of the door.

A firm knock causes your dog, Leo, the little mixed breed you adopted from a shelter, to erupt in sharp, almost staccato barking.

But that is the only indication of sound or movement within.

Where are you, Jessica? Are you with my husband?

A crackling noise erupts as the paper bag is crumpled.

The parcel is left in front of your door, where you will see it the moment you arrive home.

Sometimes a simple gift is actually a vessel utilized to issue a warning shot.

But by the time you receive it, it may be too late.

Your loyalty has been methodically cultivated. You have been paid thousands of dollars for your services. You have received carefully curated gifts. Your emotional state has been attended to; you have received the equivalent of intensive therapy sessions for free.

You belong to me.

CHAPTER
FORTY-ONE

Monday, December 17

I SIT AT A TINY WOODEN TABLE wedged next to a holiday gift display, swirling the cardboard sleeve around my Starbucks cup and checking the door every time it swings open.

Ben was supposed to meet me here at five-thirty—his only availability today, he claimed. But he's already fifteen minutes late, and I'm worried he won't show up at all, given how reluctant he sounded on the phone.

I had to cancel my late-afternoon BeautyBuzz appointment to make it back to the Upper West Side. I didn't lie to Dr. Shields about my job's policy; the appointment coordinator let me know that if I missed another booking this month without the requisite notice, I'd be fired.

I glance at my phone in case Ben has tried to contact me, but all I see is another missed call from Thomas. It's his fifth attempt to reach me today, but I'm not going to talk to him until I hear what Ben has to say.

A blast of freezing air hits me as the door is pushed open again.

This time it's Ben.

His eyes find me immediately, even though the coffee shop is crowded.

He walks over, unwinding the tartan scarf from around his neck.

He leaves his overcoat on. Instead of saying hello, he slides into the chair across from me and looks around the room, his gaze skimming over the other customers.

"I've only got ten minutes," he says.

He looks the same as I remember: thin and preppy, with an air of fastidiousness. This comes as a relief; at least one thing in this whole study is consistent.

I pull out the list of questions I wrote down last night, after I saw the wedding photo Thomas sent and couldn't fall asleep.

"Okay," I begin. "Um, you know I am one of Dr. Shields's subjects. And I guess things are getting a little weird."

He just looks at me. He's not making this any easier.

"You're her research assistant, right?"

He folds his arms. "Not anymore. My position was eliminated when the study was terminated."

I jerk back in my chair, feeling the unyielding wood hit the middle of my spine.

"What do you mean, 'terminated'?" I cry. "I'm part of the study. It's still going on."

Ben frowns. "That's not the information I was given."

"But just the other night you looked up the phone numbers for some of Dr. Shields's former subjects. I had to do their makeup," I splutter.

He stares at me, confused: "What are you talking about?"

I try to collect myself, but my mind is swimming. A baby a few tables over begins to cry, a high, piercing sound. The barista flips on a giant electric grinder and it loudly chews through beans. I need to get Ben to help me, but I can't focus.

"Dr. Shields told me you transposed the numbers for one of the women who was involved in a past study, and then when I went to see her I wound up in the wrong place. I ended up in some drug addicts' apartment." My voice sounds high and rushed. The woman next to us turns to stare.

Ben leans in closer. "I haven't spoken to Dr. Shields in weeks," he says, his voice low. The way he's looking at me, I can't tell if he believes a word I've said.

I think back to the yellow legal pad with the five telephone numbers. They were all in Dr. Shields's neat cursive.

She did say Ben transposed the numbers, didn't she? Maybe she meant he made the error when he originally took down the information for the study.

But why would she let him go if she were still conducting her research with other young women?

Ben pointedly glances at his watch.

I scan my questions, but if Ben isn't aware of the ethical tests Dr. Shields is conducting on me, none of them can help.

"You don't know *anything* about what she's doing now?" I ask.

He shakes his head.

I suddenly feel chilled to the bone.

"I signed a nondisclosure agreement," he says. "I'm finishing up my master's and she could make trouble for me at the school. I shouldn't even be talking to you."

"So why are you?" I whisper.

He picks a piece of lint off his coat sleeve. His eyes survey the occupants of the coffee shop once more. Then he pushes back his chair.

"Please!" The word comes out sounding like a strangled cry.

Ben lowers his voice when he speaks again, and I can barely make out his words over the hum of conversation and the baby's crying.

"Find the file with your name on it," he says.

I gape at him. "What's in it?"

"She had me gather background information on all of her subjects. But she wanted more about you. Then she removed it from the cabinet that held all the other subjects' folders."

He turns to go.

"Wait!" I call. "You can't just leave."

He takes a step toward the door.

"Am I in danger?"

He hesitates, his body twisted away from me. Then he briefly turns back.

"I can't answer that, Jess," he says, just before he walks away.

———

The manilla folder sat on Dr. Shields's desk during our early sessions. What could be in it?

After Ben leaves, I sit there for a while, staring into space. Then I finally call Thomas.

He answers on the first ring: "Why haven't you been responding to my calls or texts? Did you see the picture I sent?"

"I saw it," I say.

I hear running water in the background, then a metallic clanking sound.

"I can't talk now," he says, sounding almost frantic. "I've got dinner plans. I'll call you first thing tomorrow. Don't tell her anything," he warns me again, just before he hangs up.

It's dark by the time I leave the coffee shop.

As I walk home, huddled against the cold bite of the wind, I try to imagine the contents of the folder Dr. Shields keeps on me. Don't most therapists take notes during their sessions? It probably contains a transcript of every conversation we've had, but why would Ben urge me to find that?

Then I realize I haven't seen that file in weeks.

I remember it in the center of Dr. Shields's meticulous desk, and attempt to visualize the typewritten letters on the tab. I never saw them clearly, but I'm now certain they spelled my name: Farris, Jessica.

Dr. Shields only ever called me Subject 52 and then, later, Jessica.

But the last thing Ben did in the coffee shop was call me "Jess."

When I finally reach my apartment building, I see the front door is ajar. I feel a flare of annoyance at the careless neighbor who failed to pull it closed tightly, and for the super who can't seem to permanently fix it.

I climb the frayed gray carpet on the stairs, passing Mrs. Klein's apartment one floor below mine and inhaling the aroma of curry.

I stop at the end of my hallway. There's something in front of my door.

When I draw closer, I see it's a plain brown paper bag.

I hesitate, then pick it up.

The smell is rich and familiar, but I can't identify it.

Inside is a container of chicken noodle soup. It's still warm.

There's no note in the bag.

But there's only one person who thinks I'm not feeling well.

CHAPTER
FORTY-TWO

Monday, December 17

A SHARP, SUDDEN NOISE alerts me to the presence of someone in the town house.

The cleaning lady does not come on Mondays.

The rooms are still, and bathed in shadows. The noise originated from the left.

A town house in New York City affords certain advantages: More space. Privacy. A backyard garden.

Of course, there is one significant disadvantage.

There is no doorman standing guard.

Another loud, clanking noise.

This one is recognizable: A pot has been placed on the six-burner Viking stove.

Thomas always has a heavy hand while cooking.

He is following our Monday-night routine, the one that was suspended when he moved out.

He does not immediately notice my appearance in the doorway to the kitchen; perhaps the sound of a Vivaldi concerto on the Sonos system covered the sound of my movements.

He is chopping zucchini for the whole-wheat pasta primavera; it is one of the few dishes in his repertoire. He knows it is my favorite.

Two white Citarella grocery bags rest on the counter, and a bottle of wine sits on ice in a silver bucket.

Calculations are swiftly performed: Thomas's last client of the day departs at 4:50 P.M. It is a twenty-five-minute journey from his office to the town house. An additional twenty minutes for grocery shopping. The preparation for this meal is well under way.

He could not have been with you earlier tonight, Jessica. Wherever you went when you pretended to be home sleeping, it was not to meet my husband.

The immediate, overwhelming rush of relief conjures the sensation of a physical weakening.

"Thomas!"

He spins around, holding out the knife as if to defend himself.

Then he releases a high, tight laugh.

"Lydia! You're home!"

Is this the only reason for his unease?

The relief begins to ebb.

Nevertheless, he is approached and greeted with a kiss.

"Class ended early," he is told. But no further explanation is given.

Sometimes silence is a more effective tool to loosen information than a direct question; members of the law enforcement community often employ this tactic when a suspect is in custody.

"I just— I know we didn't talk about it, but I thought you wouldn't mind if I came over and surprised you by making dinner," Thomas stammers.

It is his second unannounced visit in the past forty-eight hours.

This also violates the unspoken arrangement put into place following his indiscretion: Thomas has never before used the key he retained after he moved out.

Or has he?

By now, contradictory evidence is muddying the perception of the situation.

A new safeguard will be enacted tomorrow to detect his presence in the town house, should he enter without prior authorization in the future.

"How lovely," he is told in a tone a shade cooler than might be expected.

He pours a glass of wine. "Here, sweetheart."

"I'll just go put my coat away."

He nods and turns back to stir the pasta.

You have not yet reported any response to your text, Jessica.

If Thomas intends to decline your invitation, why has he not done so?

But perhaps you are the one who is concealing something.

You could believe that meeting Thomas is a necessary step for your continued participation in the study. Perhaps he withstood the temptation, but you are increasing the pressure. You could be stalling for time, hoping for an alternative outcome.

You, with your eagerness to please and your thinly veiled idolization, may not want to disappoint by providing the wrong result.

The instant Thomas leaves, you will be telephoned and summoned to a meeting tomorrow morning. No excuses will be tolerated: Not illness, not a social engagement, not a BeautyBuzz job.

You *will* be honest with me, Jessica.

By the time Thomas is rejoined in the kitchen, the pasta has been drained and tossed with the seasoned vegetables.

Conversation is kept light. Wine is sipped. Bright notes of the Vivaldi concerto fill the air. Both meals are picked at.

Perhaps Thomas is on edge, too.

Approximately fifteen minutes into the meal, the shrill peal of a cell phone cleaves through the room.

"It's yours," he says.

"Do you mind? I'm expecting a call from a client."

This is only a partial fabrication.

"Of course," he says.

The phone number on the screen is yours.

It is imperative that my tone remains steady and professional. "This is Dr. Shields."

"Hi, it's Jessica . . . I'm feeling better. Thanks so much for the chicken soup."

Thomas can't discern any clues from my end of this conversation.

"My pleasure."

You continue: "Also, I just wanted you to know that I heard back from that guy at the coffee shop. Thomas."

The instinctive reaction that follows: a quick intake of breath as my eyes fly to Thomas.

Thomas is staring. It's impossible to know what he is reading on my face.

"One moment, please," you are told.

Quickly, the distance away from Thomas is increased. The cell phone is carried into the next room.

"Continue," you are instructed.

Variations in tone, along with cadence, reliably provide information about the contents of a conversation. Bad news is often delayed, while good news bubbles forth.

But your voice remains neutral.

It's futile to attempt to prepare for what will follow.

"He said he'd like to meet. He's going to call me tomorrow to make a plan when he figures out his schedule."

CHAPTER
FORTY-THREE

Tuesday, December 18

I'VE LIVED IN NEW YORK for years, but I never knew this tucked-away garden existed.

The West Village Conservatory sounded like a place that would be filled with people. And maybe it is, in the summertime. But as I wait for Thomas on a raw, gray afternoon, feeling the damp wood of the bench seep through my jeans, I'm surrounded only by the husks of bushes and barren branches. They look like giant spiderwebs stretched across the bleak sky.

I thought I could trust Dr. Shields. But in the past forty-eight hours, I've learned she lied about so many things: Not only didn't Ben transpose those phone numbers, but there isn't even a study right now. Dr. Shields isn't married to the bushy-haired man in the photo in her dining room; she's married to Thomas. And I'm not anything special to her. I'm just useful, like a warm cashmere shawl or a shiny object to be dangled in front of her husband.

What I want to learn today is why.

Don't tell her anything, Thomas instructed me.

But I'm not going to let him call the shots.

I have to stall Dr. Shields until I figure out what's going on. So I told her Thomas replied to my text and wanted to get together. But I didn't say it would happen today; she thinks I'm still waiting to hear back from Thomas to confirm a time.

He appears on the path leading toward me at precisely four o'clock.

He looks much like he did when we first met at the museum and again at the bar: a tall, athletic-looking, thirty-something guy in a heavy blue overcoat and gray slacks. A knit cap covers his hair.

I glance behind me, suddenly fearful that Dr. Shields may appear again, just as she did outside her town house when I was talking to Thomas on the phone. But the area around me is empty.

As Thomas approaches, a pair of mourning doves burst into the air, loudly flapping their wings. I flinch and put a hand to my chest.

He sits down next to me, leaving a foot or so of space between us. It's still a little closer than I would like.

"Why did my wife send you to follow me?" he asks immediately.

"I didn't even know she was married to you," I say.

"Did you tell her we slept together?" He looks even more scared than I feel about the possibility of Dr. Shields finding out.

I shake my head. "She's been paying me to help her with her research."

"Paying you?" He frowns. "Are you in her study?"

I'm not sure I like the fact that Thomas is asking all the questions, but at least it's telling me how little he knows.

I exhale and watch my breath form a wisp of white. "That's how it started. But now . . ." I don't even know how to explain what I'm doing for Dr. Shields.

I switch gears: "That day at the museum, I didn't realize until I saw you at the diner that she must have wanted me to meet you. I never would have, uh, reached out to you had I known."

He grinds the knuckles of his right hand into his forehead.

"I can't get into Lydia's warped mind," he says. "I left her, you know. Or maybe you don't."

I think about the two coffee cups Dr. Shields cleared away the first time I went to her town house, and the lightweight men's jackets in her closet.

And there's one more thing.

"You were with her just last night!" I blurt.

I could hear clanking noises in the background when I'd phoned Thomas yesterday, the rattle of pots and pans and the running of water. It sounded like someone was cooking. And there was something else that at first didn't seem significant: classical music, but not the somber, almost tense kind. It was . . . cheerful.

I heard the same bright, energetic notes again later when I called Dr. Shields.

"It's not what it seems," he says. "Listen, you can't just leave some-one like Lydia. Not if she doesn't want you to."

His words send an electrical charge coursing through me.

"You said she preyed on young women like me," I say. I swallow hard. My next question is the hardest to ask, even though it's the one that has been consuming me. "What do you mean, exactly?"

He abruptly stands up and looks around. I realize Ben kept doing the same thing in the coffee shop.

Both men had strong ties to Dr. Shields, but now both claim to be adrift from her. More than that, they seem wary of her.

The Conservatory is nearly silent; there isn't even the rattle of leaves blowing in the wind, or the chatter of squirrels.

"Let's walk," Thomas suggests.

I start to head in the direction that will lead us out of the park, but he reaches for my arm and pulls it. I feel the hard pinch through the fabric of my coat: "This way."

I slip my arm out of his grasp before I follow him deeper into the gardens, toward a stone fountain with frozen water in its base.

A few yards past it, he stops and looks at the ground.

I'm so cold now that the tip of my nose is numb. I wrap my arms around myself, trying to contain a shiver.

"There was another girl," Thomas says. His voice is so low I have to strain to hear it. "She was young and lonely and Lydia took to her. They spent time together. Lydia gave her gifts and even had her over to the town house. It was like she became a little sister or something . . ."

Like a younger sister, I think. My heart begins to pound in my chest.

A sharp cracking noise sounds somewhere to my left. I whip my head around but I don't see anyone.

Just a branch falling, I tell myself.

"The girl . . . she had some issues." Thomas slides off his glasses and rubs the bridge of his nose. I can't see the expression in his eyes.

I struggle against the sudden, almost overpowering urge to turn and run. I know I need to hear what Thomas is saying.

"One night she came by to see Lydia. They talked for a while. I don't know what Lydia said to her; I wasn't home."

The sun has set and the temperature feels like it has plummeted ten degrees. I shiver again.

"What does this have to do with me?" I ask. My throat is so dry it's difficult to force out the words. And somewhere, deep inside, I don't even need an answer.

I already know how this story ends.

Thomas finally turns and looks me in the eye.

"This is where she killed herself," he says. "She was Subject 5."

CHAPTER
FORTY-FOUR

Tuesday, December 18

How dare you deceive me, Jessica?

At 8:07 p.m. tonight, you call to report that Thomas has just telephoned you.

"Did you make plans for a date?" you are asked.

"No, no, no," you immediately say.

Those extraneous "no's" are your undoing: Liars, like the chronically insecure, often overcompensate.

"He told me he couldn't meet this week after all, but that he'd be in touch," you continue.

Your voice sounds assured, and also hurried. You are trying to send a signal implying that you are too busy for a sustained conversation.

How naive you are, Jessica, to think that you could ever dictate the terms of our conversation. Or anything else, for that matter.

A lengthy pause is needed to remind you of this, even though this is not a lesson you should require.

"Did he imply that it was simply a function of his busy schedule?" you are asked. "Did you get the impression he would follow up again?"

Under this questioning, you make your second error.

"He really didn't give a reason," you reply. "That's all his text said."

It it possible you simply misspoke when you described the method of communication first as a phone call and then as a text?

Or was this a deliberate deception?

If you were within the confines of the therapy office, perched on the love seat, your nonverbal clues might emerge: a twirl of your hair, the fiddling of your stacked silver rings, or the scraping of one fingernail along another.

Over the telephone, however, your subtle tells are not apparent.

Your inconsistencies could be called out.

But if you are being duplicitous, such scrutiny might have the effect of causing you to more carefully cover your tracks.

And so you are allowed to exit the conversation.

What do you do when you hang up the phone?

Perhaps you continue your usual nightly routine, smug in the knowledge that you've evaded a potentially treacherous conversation. You walk your dog, then take a long shower and comb conditioner through your unruly curls. While you restock your beauty case, you dutifully call your parents. After you hang up, you hear the familiar noises through the thin walls of your apartment: footsteps overhead, the muted sound of a television sitcom, the honking of taxis on the street outside.

Or has the tenor of your evening shifted?

Perhaps the noises are not comforting tonight. The long, anemic wail of a police car. A heated argument in the apartment next door. The scrabble of mice in the baseboards. You may be thinking of the unreliable lock on your building's front door. It's so easy for a stranger, or even an acquaintance, to slip in.

You are intimately known to me, Jessica. You have consistently proved your devotion: You wore the burgundy nail polish. You quashed your instinctual hesitations and followed instructions. You didn't surreptitiously glimpse the sculpture before you delivered it. You surrendered your secrets.

But in the past forty-eight hours, you have begun to slip away: You did not prioritize our most recent meeting, instead leaving early to attend to a client. You evaded my calls and texts. You clearly lied to me. You are acting as though this relationship is merely transactional, as though you regard it as a well-stocked ATM that dispenses cash without consequences.

What has changed, Jessica?

Have you felt the heat of Thomas's flame?

That possibility causes a fierce rigidity in the body.

It takes several minutes of slow, sustained breathing to recover.

Focus is returned to the issue at hand: What will it cost to buy your loyalty back?

Your file is brought from the study upstairs into the library and set down on the coffee table. Across from it, Thomas's paper-white narcissi rest atop the piano, near the photograph of us on our wedding day. A subtle fragrance perfumes the air.

The file is opened. The first page contains the photocopied driver's license you provided on the day you joined the study, as well as other biographical data.

The second page consists of printed photographs Ben was asked to gather from Instagram.

You and your sister look like siblings, but whereas your features are finely drawn and your eyes sharp, Becky's still hold on to the softness of childhood, as if a smear of Vaseline has coated the portion of the camera's lens that focused on her.

Caring for Becky can't be easy.

Your mother wears a cheap-looking blouse and she squints into the sunlight; your father rests his hands in his pockets as though they can help support him to remain upright.

Your parents look tired, Jessica.

Perhaps a vacation is in order.

CHAPTER
FORTY-FIVE

Wednesday, December 19

THOMAS TOLD ME to behave normally; to proceed as I have been all along so Dr. Shields won't suspect anything.

"We'll figure out a way to get you out of this safely," he said as we left the park. When we exited the gardens, he climbed onto a motorcycle, strapped on his helmet, and roared off.

But in the twenty-four hours since we parted, the uneasy feeling that crept over me in the Conservatory has ebbed.

When I got home last night, I couldn't stop wondering about Subject 5. I took a long, hot shower and shared some leftover spaghetti and meatballs with Leo. But the more I thought about it, the less sense it made. Was I really supposed to believe an esteemed psychiatrist and NYU professor pushed someone to suicide, and that she could do the same to me?

Probably that girl had issues all along, like Thomas said. Her death had nothing to do with Dr. Shields and the study.

Hearing from Noah also helped. He texted: *Free for dinner Friday night? A friend of mine has a great restaurant called Peachtree Grill if you like Southern food.* I replied immediately: *I'm in!*

It doesn't matter if Dr. Shields needs me that night. I'll tell her I'm busy.

By the time I put on my coziest pajamas, my conversation with Thomas has begun to grow faint and distant, almost like a dream. My anxiety is being replaced by something more solid and welcome: anger.

Before I crawl into bed, I restock my beauty kit in preparation for a busy day tomorrow. I hesitate when my hand closes around the half-empty bottle of burgundy nail polish. Then I pitch it into my trash can.

As I draw my comforter up to my neck, feeling Leo nestle by my side, I listen to the jangle of my across-the-hall neighbor's keys and think about how Dr. Shields suggested she might help find a job for my dad. But it seems as if she's forgotten all about that. And while the money has been good, the turbulence Dr. Shields has injected into my life isn't worth a few thousand dollars.

I sleep hard for seven hours.

When I wake up, I realize how simple the solution is: I'm done.

Before I leave for work, I dial her number. For the first time, I'm the one who is reaching out to request a meeting.

"Could I stop by tonight?" I ask. "I was hoping to get my most recent check . . . I could use the money."

I'm sitting on the edge of my bed, but the instant I hear her modulated voice, I stand up.

"How nice to hear from you, Jessica," Dr. Shields says. "I can see you at six."

Can it possibly be this simple? I think.

I feel a twinge of déjà vu. I had the exact same thought when I successfully snuck into the study.

The clouds are thick and heavy in the sky when I leave my apartment a few minutes later and head to the first of my half dozen clients. In nine hours, this will be finished, I tell myself.

I spend the day working on a businesswoman who needs a head shot for her company website, an author who is being interviewed on New York One, and a trio of friends going to a holiday party at Cipriani. I also duck home in the early afternoon to take Leo for a walk. I feel like I am easing back into my old life, anchored by the comforting weight of predictability.

I arrive at Dr. Shields's town house a few minutes early, but I wait until six on the dot to press the buzzer. I know exactly what I'm going to say. I'm not even going to take off my coat.

Dr. Shields comes to the door quickly, but instead of greeting me, she holds up an index finger. Her cell phone is pressed to her ear.

"Mmm-hmm," she says into it as she gestures for me to come inside.

She leads me into the library. What can I do but follow?

I look around the room while she continues listening to whoever is on the other end of the line. Atop a Steinway piano is a bouquet of white flowers. One petal has fallen onto the glossy black lid. Dr. Shields follows my gaze and walks over to pluck it off.

She smooths it between her fingertips, her other hand still holding the phone.

Then I see the bronze sculpture of a motorcycle. I jerk my eyes away before Dr. Shields notices me staring at it.

"Thank you for your assistance," Dr. Shields says as she briefly exits the room. I glance around, looking for more clues, but there are only a few paintings, a built-in bookshelf lined with hardbacks, and a glass bowl filled with bright oranges on the coffee table.

When she returns, Dr. Shields isn't holding the petal or her phone.

"I have your check, Jessica," she says. But she doesn't give it to me. Instead, she stretches out her arms. For a frozen moment I think she's trying to hug me. Then she says, "Let me take your coat."

"Oh, I can't stay long," I say. I clear my throat. "I know this is sort of abrupt and it wasn't an easy decision, but with all that is going on with my family I think I need to go home. I'm heading there on Friday and I'm going to stay through the holidays."

Dr. Shields doesn't react.

I keep babbling: "You know, they're not even going to Florida this year. Things are really hard for them. I've given it a lot of thought and I may even need to move back for a bit. I wanted to thank you in person for everything."

"I see." Dr. Shields sits down on the sofa and gestures to the seat next to her. "That is a big decision. I know how hard you're trying to build a life here."

It's a struggle to remain standing.

"I'm sorry, I'm meeting someone, so . . ."

"Oh," Dr. Shields says. The silver in her voice hardens into steel: "A date?"

"No, no." I shake my head. "Just Lizzie."

Why am I telling her this? It's like I can't break the pattern of revealing myself to her.

My phone rings, startling me.

I don't reach into my pocket to answer; I'll be out of here in two minutes and can call whoever it is back. Then the thought strikes me that it could be Thomas.

It rings again, the shrill peal cutting through the silence.

"Answer it," Dr. Shields says easily.

My stomach clenches. If I pull it out, will she be able to see the screen or hear the conversation?

It rings a third time.

"We don't have any secrets, Jessica. Do we?"

It's like I'm mesmerized by her; I'm unable to summon the will to disobey. My hand is shaking when I pull it out of my jacket pocket.

I see the little picture of my mother on the screen and I can't help it; I sink into the chair opposite Dr. Shields.

"Mom," I say, my voice almost a croak.

It feels like I'm being pinned down by Dr. Shields's stare. My limbs are leaden.

"I can't believe it!" my mother cries.

In the background, I hear Becky yell: "Florida! We're going to the ocean!"

"What?" I gasp.

The corners of Dr. Shields's lips curve into a smile.

"A messenger just delivered the package from the travel agency a few minutes ago! Oh, Jess, your boss is so wonderful to do this! What a surprise!"

I can't form the words to answer. My mind feels too sluggish to keep up with the events whirling around me.

"I didn't know about it. What was in the package?" I finally ask.

"Three airplane tickets to Florida and a brochure for the resort where we'll be staying," my mom gushes. "It looks so beautiful!"

Three tickets. Not four.

Dr. Shields reaches out and picks an orange from the bowl on the coffee table between us. She inhales the scent.

I can't stop staring at her.

"I'm so sorry you won't be joining us," my mom says. "Your boss wrote us such a nice note explaining that you need to work, but that she'll make sure you won't be alone on Christmas Day, that you'll be going to her home to celebrate."

My throat tightens. It's difficult to breathe.

"She's obviously so fond of you," my mom says over the sound of Becky's happy laughter. "I'm really proud you've found such a great new job."

"It's a pity you'll be needed here over the holidays," Dr. Shields says softly.

I can barely choke out the words. "I've got to run, Mom. But I love you."

Dr. Shields sets down the orange. She reaches into her pocket.

I lower my phone and stare at her.

"Their flight leaves tomorrow night," Dr. Shields says. Her voice is so precise; each word is like a musical chime. "I guess you won't be going home on Friday after all."

You can't just leave someone like her, Thomas had said in the frozen park.

"Jessica?" Dr. Shields pulls her hand out of her pocket. "Your check."

Without thinking, I take it.

I pull my eyes away from her probing gaze. They land on the bowl of bright fruit.

Then I realize the oranges are the same kind I used to sell every December for our high school's annual fund-raiser: Navel oranges. From Florida.

CHAPTER
FORTY-SIX

Wednesday, December 19

YOU REMINDED ME of April again tonight.

On that June evening just six months ago, she perched on a stool, swinging the top leg that was crossed over her bottom one, sipping wine. She held a frenetic energy, as usual, but her initial affect was buoyant.

This in itself wasn't cause for concern.

Her mood often shifted rapidly, like a sudden rainstorm interrupting a sunny day, like a cold morning swiftly yielding to afternoon heat.

It was as if her internal barometer reflected the month for which she was named.

But on that evening, her precipitous emotional turn was more abrupt than in the past.

Harsh words were spoken; she cried so hard she gulped for air.

Later that night, she took her own life.

Every lifetime is marked by transformative moments, as unique to each individual as strands of DNA.

Thomas's materialization in the darkened hallway during the black-out was one of these seismic experiences.

April's vanishing was another.

Her death, and the words we exchanged just prior to it, set into motion a downward trajectory, a descent into emotional quicksand. There was a second casualty: My marriage to Thomas.

Every lifetime contains these pivot points—sometimes flukes of destiny, sometimes seemingly preordained—that shape and eventually cement one's path.

You are the most recent one, Jessica.

You cannot vanish now. You are needed more than ever before.

There are two likely possibilities the facts point to thus far. Either you are lying, and you and Thomas have met or intend to meet, or you told the truth, which means Thomas is vacillating. His hesitation in replying to your text, and his conflicting responses, all indicate he may be on the brink of temptation.

In either case, more evidence is required. The hypothesis—Thomas is an unrepentant adulterer—has not been adequately tested.

You will be granted one evening to revert back to the compliant, eager young woman who entered my study as Subject 52.

You revealed that you had intended to leave town. This means you have cleared your work schedule.

Your friend Lizzie will be ensconced with her family, a thousand miles away for the holidays.

Your family will be blissfully eating from a seafood buffet and splashing in a warm saltwater pool.

You will be all mine.

CHAPTER
FORTY-SEVEN

Wednesday, December 19

"YOUR WIFE REALLY IS CRAZY!" I hiss into the phone.

I'm four blocks away from Dr. Shields's town house, but this time I've made sure she isn't following me. I'm huddled in the shelter of the entryway to a clothing store that has a GOING OUT OF BUSINESS sign plastered across the window. By now the clouds have cleared, but the winter sky is a shade between purple and black. The few people who hurry past are huddled in their coats, heads down and chins tucked into their collars.

"I know." Thomas sighs. "What happened?"

I'm trembling, but not from the cold. Dr. Shields is tangling me up; it's like a Chinese finger trap—the harder I struggle to escape, the more tightly I'm imprisoned.

"I just need to get away from her. You said you'd help me figure out a way. We need to meet again."

He hesitates. "I can't get away tonight."

"I'll come to you," I say. "Where are you?"

"I'm— Actually, I'm on my way to meet her."

My eyes widen. I feel my back stiffen.

"What? You were just at her place two nights ago. How am I supposed to believe you're separated when you're together all the time?"

"It's not like that. We have an appointment with our divorce lawyer," Thomas says. His voice is soothing now. "How about we talk tomorrow?"

I'm coiled so tight I can't even continue the conversation. "Fine!" I say before I hang up.

I stand there for a moment.

Then I do the only thing I can think of to regain a bit of control over my splintered life.

I walk out of the store's entryway and retrace my steps. When I am thirty yards away from Dr. Shields's town house, I cross the street and conceal myself in the shadows.

She steps outside fifteen minutes later, just when I'd begun to worry I'd missed her.

I trail her, making sure I stay as far back as possible, as she strides down two blocks, turns a corner, and continues on for another three.

I never worry I'll lose her, even as we approach a commercial area and the crowds grow thick. She wears a long, winter-white coat and her red-gold hair hangs loose around her shoulders.

She looks like the porcelain angel atop a Christmas tree.

In the distance, I can see Thomas waiting under an awning.

I'm confident he doesn't spot me; my hood is up and I duck behind an MTA bus stop.

But he catches sight of Dr. Shields.

A wide smile breaks across his face. His expression is a mix of anticipation and delight.

He doesn't look like a man who wants to divorce the woman approaching him; on the contrary, he is eager to see her.

The two of them don't realize I'm watching. I'm not sure how long I'll have before they disappear into the building for their meeting with their lawyer. But maybe I can learn something.

He steps toward her, stretching out his hand.

She takes it.

And in that instant, with him in his black tailored jacket and her in white, it is as though I am spying on them in a different moment, one I've only seen in a photograph: their wedding.

Thomas bends his head, cups the back of her neck, and kisses her.

It isn't the kind of kiss a man gives a woman he wants to be rid of.

I know this, because Thomas kissed me the same way only five days ago, when we met at the bar.

As I walk home now, I think about all the lies that link the three of us together.

Because I know now that Thomas is trying to deceive me, too.

After I watched him and Dr. Shields end their lingering kiss under the red awning, he wrapped an arm around her shoulders, pulling her close again. Then he opened the tall wooden door—not to an attorney's office, but to a romantic-looking Italian restaurant—and stepped aside so that she could enter first.

At least I've finally learned something concrete: Neither of them can be trusted.

I have no idea why. But I can't worry about that now.

The only question I need answered is which one of them is more dangerous.

PART
THREE

Often the person we judge most harshly is ourself. Every day, we criticize our decisions, our actions, even our private thoughts. We worry the tone of an e-mail we sent to a colleague might be misconstrued. We lambaste our lack of self-control as we throw away the empty ice-cream container. We regret rushing a friend off the phone instead of listening patiently to their troubles. We wish we had told a family member what they meant to us before they died.

We all carry the weight of secret regrets—the strangers we see on the street, our neighbors, our colleagues, our friends, even our loved ones. And we are all forced to constantly make moral choices. Some of these decisions are small. Others are life-altering.

These judgments seem easy to form on paper: You check a box and move on. In a real-life scenario, it's never as simple.

The options haunt you. Days, weeks, even years later you think about the people affected by your actions. You question your choices.

And you wonder when, not if, the repercussions will come.

CHAPTER
FORTY-EIGHT

Wednesday, December 19

DR. SHIELDS'S LATEST GIFT feels more dangerous to me than flirting with a married man or revealing painful secrets or being trapped in a drug addict's apartment.

It was bad enough when my own life was tangled up with Dr. Shields and her experiments. But now she's linking herself to my family. They probably feel like they've won the lottery with this trip. I keep hearing Becky squeal: "We're going to the ocean!"

As Ricky said when he grabbed my phone and stood over me in his kitchen, *Nothing's ever free in life.*

I'm unable to stop seeing the image of Dr. Shields and Thomas kissing outside the restaurant as I walk home after following her. I imagine them at a romantic table for two while the sommelier uncorks a bottle of red wine. I picture Thomas nodding his approval as he tastes it. Then perhaps he cups both of her hands in his to warm them. I would give anything to know what they are saying to each other.

Am I the topic of their conversation? I wonder. Do they lie to each other, just as they are lying to me?

When I reach my apartment building, I yank the security door closed so hard behind me that it jars my shoulder in the socket. I wince and rub it, then continue to the stairs.

I wind my way around to the fourth-floor landing, then step into the hallway. Halfway down, about three doors from my apartment, something small and soft-looking rests on the carpet. For a second I think it's a mouse. Then I realize it's a woman's gray glove.

Hers, I think as I freeze. The color, the fabric; I recognize her style instantly.

I swear I can smell her distinctive perfume. Why is she back at my apartment?

But as I draw closer, I realize I'm wrong. The leather is thick and cheap; it's the kind of glove someone would buy from a street vendor. It must belong to one of my neighbors. I leave it for them to retrieve.

When I reach my apartment and open the door, I hesitate in the entryway. I look around. Everything appears exactly as I left it, and Leo runs to greet me as usual. Still, I engage both of my locks instead of waiting until bedtime, like I usually do.

My nightstand lamp is always on for Leo when I know I'll be home after dark. Now I also flick on the brighter overhead light, then I turn on the one in the bathroom. I hesitate, then jerk back the shower curtain. I'd just feel better being able to see into every corner of my studio.

As I walk toward the kitchen, I brush by the chair where I drape clothes when I'm feeling too lazy to hang them in the closet.

Dr. Shields's wrap is there, peeking out from beneath the sweater I wore yesterday. I avert my eyes and continue on to the cabinet, where I grab a glass and fill it with water. I drink it down in three thirsty gulps, then I dig out a legal pad from the bottom of my junk drawer.

I take it to my bed and sit cross-legged on top of my comforter. The notes written on the page are a series of numbers that I briefly recall as an attempt to figure out a budget. I can't believe that merely six weeks ago, I was worrying about how to pay Antonia for Becky's occupational therapy, and hoping my BeautyBuzz appointments would align so I wouldn't have to lug my makeup case too far. In hindsight, my life was so quiet; my problems, so ordinary. Then came that impulsive moment when I grabbed Taylor's phone off her chair and replayed Ben's message. Those ten seconds changed my life.

I need to be the opposite of impulsive now.

I tear off the top sheet and draw a line straight down the middle of the new page with Dr. Shields's name atop one column and Thomas's name atop the other. Then I sit cross-legged on my bed and write down everything I know about both of them.

Dr. Lydia Shields: 37, West Village town house, NYU adjunct professor. Psychiatrist, with an office in Midtown. Researcher, published author. Designer clothes, expensive tastes. Former assistant named Ben Quick. Married to Thomas. I underline that last detail four times.

I add question marks after other possibilities. *Influential father? Client folders? Story behind Subject 5?*

I stare at the scant cluster of information on the page. Is that truly everything I know about the woman who holds so many of my secrets?

I move on to Thomas. I grab my laptop and try googling him, but although I get several hits for Thomas Shields, they are all the wrong men.

Perhaps Dr. Shields kept her maiden name.

I remember a few things from our encounter at the bar: *Rides a motorcycle. Knows all the words to the Beatles song "Come Together." Drinks draft IPA beer.* And then some details from our time in my apartment: *Likes dogs. In good shape. Scar on shoulder from surgery to repair a torn rotator cuff.*

I think for a moment, then add: *Reads The New York Times at Ted's Diner. Goes to the gym. Wears glasses. Married to Dr. Shields.* I underline that last detail four times, too.

I continue: *Late thirties? Occupation? Where does he live?*

I know even less about Thomas than I do about Dr. Shields.

There are only two other people I've heard about who are connected to them. The first, Ben, doesn't want to talk to me any more than he already has.

The second can't talk to me.

Subject 5. Who was she?

I peel myself off my bed and begin to pace the ten steps back and forth across my studio, trying to remember everything Thomas said in the Conservatory.

She was young and lonely. Lydia gave her gifts. She wasn't close to her father. This is where she killed herself.

I hurry back to my bed and reach for my laptop again. The two-paragraph article in the *New York Post* I find by googling "West Village

Conservatory" and "suicide" and "June" reveals that Thomas told the truth about one thing at least: A young woman died in the Conservatory. Her body was found later that same night by a couple out for a stroll in the moonlight. At first they thought she was sleeping.

The article also gives me her full name: Katherine April Voss.

I close my eyes and silently repeat it to myself.

She was only twenty-three, and she went by her middle name. The article holds few other details, aside from listing the lineage of her parents and much older step-siblings.

But it has given me enough to begin tracing the trajectory of her life, and where and how it intersected with Dr. Shields's.

I rub my forehead as I contemplate my next step. A dull throbbing has formed between my temples, maybe because I haven't eaten much today, but my stomach is too knotted to tolerate food now.

As desperate as I am for information, I don't want to reach out to April's grieving parents yet. But there are other threads I can pursue. Like most twenty-somethings, April established an active social media presence.

Within a minute, I find her Instagram account. It's open for anyone to follow.

I pause before viewing the images, just as I did when I first began to investigate Dr. Shields online.

I have no idea what I'll see. I feel as if I'm crossing a threshold from which I won't be able to return.

I tap on her name. Tiny square photos fill my screen.

I enlarge the most recent one, the last photograph April ever posted, as I make the decision to work backward in time.

It is dated June 2. Six days before she died.

The sight of her smiling face makes me flinch, even though it looks like the kind of picture I might take with Lizzie, two girlfriends clinking margarita glasses and having a good time. It seems so ordinary, given what happened less than a week later. The caption April wrote reads: *With @Fab24—BFFs!* A dozen people commented, stuff like *luv this* and *sooo pretty.*

I stare at April's features. This is the girl behind the number assigned by Dr. Shields. She had long, straight dark hair and pale skin. She was thin; very thin. Her brown eyes appear too large and round for her narrow face.

I write down *Fab24/best friend* on a fresh sheet of the notepad under April's name.

I scroll through the photos one by one, scrutinizing each for clues to record: A background location. The name of a restaurant on a printed napkin. The people who make repeated appearances.

By the time I've reviewed the fifteenth picture, I know that April also wore silver hoop earrings and owned a black leather jacket. She loved cookies and dogs, just like I do.

I return to the photo of April and Fab24. I know it's not my imagination. April looks happy, genuinely happy. And then I spot it—the fringe of a taupe wrap on the chair behind her.

My head jerks up at the sound of footsteps in the hallway.

They seem to be heading toward my apartment.

I wait for a knock, but it doesn't come.

Instead, there's a rustling sound.

I unfold my legs and ease off my bed. I creep across the floor, hoping the whisper of my socks against the wood isn't audible.

My door contains a peephole. As I move to position my eye behind it, I'm gripped by the fear that all I'll see is Dr. Shields's piercing blue eye filling the other side of the thin glass.

I can't do it. My breathing sounds so ragged I'm certain she can hear it through the door.

My adrenaline surges as I press my ear to the door. Nothing.

If she's there, I know she won't leave until I do what she wants. I imagine she can see straight through into my apartment, just like she was able to watch me through the computer all those months ago. I have to look. I force myself to turn my head and bring my eye nearer to the peephole. My chest tightens as I gaze through it.

No one is there.

The absence of anyone feels almost as jarring as a presence would be. I step back, gasping. Am I losing my mind? Dr. Shields and Thomas are at dinner together. I saw them. That much is true.

Leo's high, staccato bark pulls me out of my thoughts. He's staring at me with a quizzical expression.

"Shh," I whisper to him.

I tiptoe over to the window. I pull down the slat of a blind with my fingertips and peek out. My eyes scan the street: There are a few women getting into a taxi, and a man out walking his dog. Nothing appears amiss.

I ease out my fingers and scoop up Leo, bringing him to bed with me.

He'll need a walk soon. I've never been afraid of taking him out at night. But now I don't like the thought of descending the stairs, with blind turns at every corner, and making my way down a street that, by then, may or may not be empty.

Dr. Shields knows exactly where I live. She's been here before. She knew how to get to my family. Maybe she knows even more about me than I ever imagined.

Ben is right. I need to get my file.

I continue looking through April's photos, enlarging one so I can make out the lettering on a street name. Then I come to a picture taken in early May, of a guy asleep in bed with a floral comforter rumpled around his bare torso. A boyfriend? I wonder.

His face is mostly obscured because of the angle of the photo; I can just see a sliver of it.

My gaze roams over the nightstand next to him. It holds a few books—I jot down their titles—a bracelet, and a half-full water glass.

And one other thing. A pair of glasses.

My body is collapsing; it's as though I've stepped off the precipice into thin air and now I can't stop my plummet.

My hand trembles as I enlarge the photo.

The glasses are tortoiseshell.

I zoom in on the sleeping man, the one April presumably photographed in her bed.

It's not possible. I want to grab Leo and run, but to where? My parents would never understand. Lizzie already left town for the holidays. And Noah . . . I barely know him. I can't involve him in this.

I thrust away my computer, but I can't stop seeing the straight line of his nose, and the hair falling over his forehead.

The man in the photo is Thomas.

CHAPTER
FORTY-NINE

Wednesday, December 19

YOU LOOKED SO SCARED when you left my town house tonight, Jessica. Don't you know no harm will befall you?

You are needed too much.

The scheduled dinner with my husband reveals no new information. Thomas easily parries when faced with questions about his day and his plans for the rest of the week. He responds with queries of his own, filling any potential silences with remarks about his delicious pasta Bolognese, and the roasted brussels sprouts he ordered for us to share.

Thomas is an excellent squash player. He is adept at anticipating the angles of his opponent's serve; he quickly maneuvers around the court.

But even the most accomplished athletes tire under sustained pressure. That's when mistakes occur.

After the plates are cleared and a delicious apple tarte tatin served for dessert, Thomas playfully inquires whether there is anything special Santa should place under the tree this year.

"It's always hard to know what to get the woman who has everything," he says.

Thomas has proven to be a nimble opponent, but now an unexpected opportunity presents itself.

"There is something," he is told. "What about those delicate silver stacking rings?"

The sudden rigidity in Thomas's body is palpable.

Another pause.

"Have you seen the ones I'm talking about?"

He casts his eyes down at his plate, feigning a sudden interest in the crumbs of his dessert.

"Oh, maybe, I think I know what you mean," he says.

"What do you think of them?" he is asked. "Do you think they're . . . pretty?"

Thomas raises his eyes. He reaches out to touch my hand, lifting it in the air, as if considering how it would appear so adorned.

He shakes his head. His gaze is intent. "They're not special enough."

The check is delivered and Thomas glides past the moment.

He is rebuffed at the door of the town house. This is a bit personal to admit, Jessica, but you have to agree we've moved beyond the acquaintance stage by now. Physical intimacies with Thomas have not been reestablished since the betrayal of last September. Our marriage is still on shaky ground; they will not be resumed tonight.

Thomas accepts the gentle rejection gracefully. Too gracefully?

His sexual appetite has always been strong. The current enforced marital abstinence will stoke his libido, increasing his urge to succumb to temptation again.

After the door is closed behind Thomas, and the newly installed deadbolt secured behind him, the town house is returned to its usual order. Normally, these chores would have been completed after your departure, but time didn't allow on this busy day.

The newspaper is gathered from the coffee table and tucked in the recycling bin. The dishwasher is emptied. Then the study is surveyed. The faintest scent of oranges perfumes the room. The bowl containing them is picked up and brought to the kitchen. The oranges are dropped into the trash can.

Citrus fruits have never held much appeal.

After the lights are extinguished on the main level and the stairs climbed, a lilac-colored silk nightgown and matching robe are selected. Night serum is dotted around the eyes with the gentle touch of my ring finger, then a rich moisturizing cream is applied. Aging, though inevitable, can be managed gracefully with the proper arsenal.

When the evening's rituals are complete and a glass of water brought to the nightstand, one task remains. The ecru file containing the name JESSICA FARRIS on the tab is lifted from the center of the desk in the small study adjoining the bedroom. It is opened.

The photographs of your parents and Becky are scanned again. In less than twenty-four hours, they will be aboard a plane heading hundreds of miles away. Will their absence feel more pronounced as the gulf between you grows?

Then, a Montblanc fountain pen, a cherished gift from my father, is lifted to a fresh page of the yellow legal pad containing meticulous notes. The new entry is dated Wednesday, December 19, and details of my dinner with Thomas are recorded. Special attention is paid to capturing his reaction to the suggestion that silver stacking rings would be a welcome gift.

Your folder is closed and centered on the desk once again, atop a second folder belonging to another subject. They are no longer being kept with the others. They were brought home a few days ago, after the new lock was installed on the front door.

The name on the tab of the folder beneath yours is KATHERINE APRIL VOSS.

CHAPTER
FIFTY

Thursday, December 20

I NEED TO STICK as close to the truth as possible when I see Dr. Shields.

Not just because I'm not aware of how much she knows. I also don't know what she's capable of.

I barely slept last night; every time the building's old floorboards creaked, or someone climbed the stairs and walked past my apartment, I froze, listening for the scrape of a key in my lock.

It isn't possible that Dr. Shields or Thomas could have obtained a key to my place, I tried to reassure myself. Still, at around two A.M., I dragged my nightstand over to block the door and took my can of Mace out of my purse and tucked it under my pillow, within easy reach.

When Dr. Shields sent a text at seven this morning summoning me to her town house after work, I immediately responded *Okay*. It was pointless to resist, and more important, I didn't want to agitate her.

If I can't get out of this trap by pulling away, maybe I need to lean into it, I thought.

I came up with my plan in the shower this morning as I stood under the spray of hot water that couldn't seem to warm me. I have no idea how she will react to what I'm going to tell her. But I can't continue like this.

I arrive at her town house at seven-thirty, following a busy day of work. All of my clients were festive, prepping for holiday parties and, in the case of my last appointment of the day, a young woman anticipating a proposal from her boyfriend.

I barely saw their faces as I did their makeup. Instead, visions of Thomas in April's bed collided in my mind with my thoughts of what I would say to Dr. Shields after she closed the door of her town house behind us.

She lets me in instantly, almost as if she were hovering in the hall-way, waiting for the sound of the doorbell. Or maybe she watched me approach from an upstairs window.

"Jessica," she says by way of greeting.

Just that. Just my name.

Then she locks the door behind me and takes my coat.

I stand beside her while she hangs it in the closet. She steps back and nearly bumps into me.

"Sorry," I say. She needs to remember this moment. I'm planting a seed for my cover story.

"Would you care for a Perrier?" Dr. Shields asks, leading the way toward the kitchen. "Or perhaps a glass of wine?"

I hesitate, then say, "Whatever you're having would be lovely." I make sure my tone carries gratitude.

"I just opened a bottle of Chablis," Dr. Shields says. "Or would you prefer Sancerre?"

As if I'd know the difference between varieties of grapes.

"Chablis is fine," I say, but I'm not going to have more than a few sips. My mind needs to be sharp.

She fills two crystal glasses with slim stems and hands me one. My eyes dart around the room. I haven't seen any evidence that Thomas is on the premises, but after the way they acted last night, I need to be sure he isn't within earshot.

I take a small swallow of wine and then plunge right in, keeping my voice low. "I have to tell you something."

She turns to regard me. I know she can sense my nervousness; it feels like it's radiating off me. At least I don't have to pretend to manufacture it.

She gestures to a stool and takes the one next to me. We're swiveled to face each other and we're sitting much closer than we usually do. I twist my body an extra few inches so that I have a clear view of the room. Now no one can sneak up on me.

The faintest blue-violet shadows form crescent shapes under Dr. Shields's eyes. She probably hasn't been sleeping well, either.

"What is it, Jessica? I hope by now you know you can tell me anything."

She picks up her wineglass and then I see it: *Her* hand is shaking almost imperceptibly. It is the first time I've witnessed a vulnerability.

"I haven't been completely honest with you," I say.

I see her throat move as she swallows. But she doesn't rush in. She waits me out.

"The man from the diner . . ." I say. Something changes in her eyes; they narrow the slightest bit. I'm very careful with my words as I continue. "When he wrote back to my text, he actually said he wanted to meet me. He asked me to give him a day and time."

Dr. Shields's gaze remains fixed on me. She isn't moving.

I have the fleeting thought that she's turned to glass, sculpted from the same Murano material as the falcon she said was a gift for her husband. For Thomas.

"But I haven't replied," I continue.

This time I wait her out. I drag my eyes away from hers under the pretext of needing a sip of wine.

"Why is that?" Dr. Shields finally asks.

"I think Thomas is your husband," I whisper. My heart is clattering so loudly I'm sure she can hear it.

She draws in a sharp inhalation of breath.

"Hmmm," she murmurs. "What led you to this assumption?"

I have no idea if I'm traveling down the right path now. I'm hop-scotching through a minefield, but I don't know how much she knows, so I have to give her a piece of the truth.

"When I showed up at Ted's Diner, I realized I'd seen the man before," I say. This is the tricky part; I fight back a feeling of light-headedness. "I recalled passing him on my way into the museum, when the crowd was gathered around the woman who was hit by the taxi. I only noticed him because I was looking at everyone there to try to figure out if they were part of the test. I'm sure he didn't see me, though."

Dr. Shields doesn't respond. She's expressionless. I have no idea how she feels about what I'm saying.

"When I told you about the man I spoke to in front of the photographs, it confused me that you thought he had sandy hair. I didn't even connect your question to the guy in front of the museum. But then I saw him—Thomas—again at the diner."

Dr. Shields finally opens her mouth to speak. "And those simple things led you to this conclusion?"

I shake my head. The next part sounded good when I rehearsed it earlier today. But now I have no idea if it will convince her. "The jackets in your coat closet . . . . They're all so big. They clearly belong to a man who's tall and broad, not like the guy in the photo in your dining room. I noticed them last time I was here and I double-checked again tonight."

"You are quite the detective, aren't you, Jessica?" Her fingers caress the stem of her wineglass. She raises it to her lips and takes a sip. Then: "Did you figure this all out on your own?"

"Sort of," I say. I can't tell if she believes me, so I continue with the story I'd planned: "Lizzie was just talking about how she had to order an extra costume for an understudy in a play who was much bigger than the original actor. That's what made me think of it."

Dr. Shields abruptly leans forward and I flinch. I make sure I hold her gaze.

After a moment, she gets up off her stool without a word. She reaches for the wine bottle on the counter and walks back to the refrigerator. When she opens the door, I glimpse only a row of Perrier water and a carton of eggs. I've never seen a fridge so bare.

"Speaking of Lizzie, I'm going to meet her right after this for a drink," I continue. "Do you know any place nearby that's good? I told her I'd text her when we finish."

That's another of my safeguards, along with the Mace I've put in my purse and my clear view of my surroundings.

Dr. Shields closes the refrigerator door. But she doesn't come back around the counter to sit with me.

"Oh, is Lizzie still in town?" Dr. Shields asks.

I almost gasp. Lizzie left yesterday, but how can Dr. Shields know that? If she got to my parents, maybe she got to Lizzie, too.

I can't even remember if I've told her anything about Lizzie's holiday plans. Dr. Shields took notes of all of our conversations. I never did.

I start to babble: "Yeah, she was thinking about going earlier but some stuff came up, so she's here for another couple days."

I force myself to stop speaking. Dr. Shields remains across the counter from me. She's studying me. It's like she's pinning me down with her gaze.

There are four other rooms behind me, including the powder room. Because Dr. Shields has repositioned herself across the kitchen, I can no longer look at her and keep watch on the doorways.

Instead, all I can see are the hard, gleaming surfaces of her kitchen: gray marble counters, stainless-steel appliances, and the metal spiral of the corkscrew she has left by the sink.

"I am glad you were honest with me, Jessica," Dr. Shields says. "And now I am going to do the same. You are right: Thomas is my husband. The man in the photograph was my mentor when I was in graduate school."

I exhale the breath I didn't realize I was holding. At last there's one piece of information that aligns with what Thomas and Dr. Shields have both told me, and with my instincts.

"We've been married for seven years," she continues. "We used to work in the same building. That's how we met. He's also a psychiatrist."

"Oh," I say, hoping that one word will encourage Dr. Shields.

"You must be wondering why I've been pushing you toward him," she says.

Now I'm the one to remain silent. I don't want to say anything that could set her off.

"He cheated on me," Dr. Shields says. I think I catch the sheen of tears in her eyes, but then the glimmer is gone, and I don't know if it was just a trick of the light. "Only once. But the details of that betrayal made it particularly painful. And he promised he would never do it again. I want to believe him."

Dr. Shields is so precise and careful with her words; it feels like she's finally telling me the truth.

I wonder if she saw that intimate photo of Thomas in April's bed, with the floral comforter exposing his bare shoulders. How painful that must have been.

How much worse things would be for her if she knew what I'd done.

I'm desperate to hear more. Still, I know I can't let down my guard around her even for a second.

"Of all the questions I've asked you, we never covered this one," Dr. Shields continues. "Have you ever truly been in love, Jessica?"

I don't know if there's a right answer. "I don't think so," I finally say.

"You would know," she responds. "The joy—the sense of completeness it can offer a person—is directly proportional to the amount of anguish one experiences when that love is withdrawn."

It's the first time she has ever appeared soft and swept up in emotion.

I need to make her believe I'm on her side. I had no idea Thomas was her husband when I took him back to my apartment. Still, if she learns about it, well, I have no idea what she'd do to me.

My mind flashes back again to Subject 5, splayed out on a bench in the gardens on the last night of her life. Surely the police investigated her death before it was ruled a suicide. But was she truly alone when she died?

"I'm so sorry," I say. My voice trembles a little, but I hope she thinks it's from compassion instead of fear. "What can I do to help?"

Dr. Shields's lips curve up in an empty smile. "That is why I picked you," she says. "You remind me a bit of . . . well, of *her*."

I can't help it; I whip my head around to check behind me. The front door is maybe twenty yards away, but the lock appears complicated.

"What is wrong, Jessica?"

I reluctantly twist my body back around. "Nothing, I just thought I heard a noise." I pick up my wineglass. Instead of taking a drink, I simply hold it. It may be heavy enough to use as a weapon.

"We are completely alone," she says. "Do not worry."

She finally comes back from behind the counter and reclaims her seat next to me. Her knee brushes mine as she arranges herself on the stool. I suppress a flinch.

"The young woman Thomas cheated with . . ." The words want

to remain locked away, but I have to ask. "You said she reminded you of me?"

Dr. Shields reaches out and touches my arm with her thin fingers. The blue veins on the tops of her hands stand out sharply against her skin.

"There was a similar essence," she says. When she smiles, I see it: A few more tiny, sharp lines around her eyes appear, like the cracks in the glass are spreading. "She had dark hair, and she was full of life."

Her hand is still holding my forearm. Her grip feels imperceptibly tighter. Full of life, I think. What a strange way to describe a young woman who took her own.

I wait for her next words and wonder if she's going to say April's name, or if she'll refer to her as a study subject.

She looks at me. Her eyes sharpen again. And it's as if the woman I saw just moments ago—the softer one, who was clearly yearning for her husband—has slipped behind a mask. Her words are devoid of emotion again now. She sounds like a professor, lecturing on an abstract subject.

"Although the woman Thomas betrayed me with wasn't as young as you, she was about ten years older. Closer to my age."

Ten years older.

I know Dr. Shields sees the shock in my face, because her own expression tightens.

There is no way April, the young woman in all of those Instagram photos, was in her thirties; besides, the obituary reported that she was twenty-three. Dr. Shields isn't talking about April.

If Dr. Shields is telling me the truth, there's a second woman Thomas was with during his marriage. There are three, counting me. How many were there, in total?

"I just can't imagine anyone would do that to you," I say, taking another tiny sip of wine to cover my surprise.

Her head dips in a nod. "The important thing is to ensure that he won't do it again. You understand, right?"

She pauses. "That is why I need you to reply to him right now."

I go to put my wineglass on the counter, but misjudge the distance. It teeters on the edge of the marble, and I catch it just before it falls to the floor and shatters.

I see Dr. Shields catalog the incident, but she doesn't remark on it.

My plan has gone drastically awry. The confession that I had thought would liberate me feels like a noose.

I pull my phone out of my bag and type out the text as Dr. Shields dictates: *Can we meet tomorrow night? Deco Bar at 8?*

She watches as I hit *Send*. Less than twenty seconds later, a reply arrives.

Panic floods my body. What if he wrote something incriminating?

I'm so dizzy I want to put my head between my knees. But I can't. Dr. Shields is staring at me like she can read my thoughts.

I swallow hard against the nausea rising in my throat as I look down at my phone.

"Jessica?" she prompts.

Her voice sounds tinny and distant, as if it is coming from far away.

My hand is shaking as I turn my phone so Dr. Shields can see Thomas's response: *I'll be there.*

CHAPTER
FIFTY-ONE

Friday, December 21

EVERY THERAPIST KNOWS the truth shape-shifts; it is as elusive and wispy as a cloud. It morphs into different incarnations, resisting attempts to define it, molding itself to the viewpoint of whoever claims to possess it.

At 7:36 P.M. you text: *I'm leaving in a few minutes to meet T. Should I offer to buy him a drink, since I'm the one who asked him out?*

The response: *No, he is traditional. Let him take the lead.*

At 8:02 P.M., Thomas approaches Deco Bar, where you await. He disappears from view as he enters through the doorway. He never looks around at the neighboring restaurants and cafés, including the one directly across the street.

At 8:24 P.M., Thomas leaves the bar. Alone.

When he reaches the curb, his hand dips into his pocket and pulls out his cell phone. He gestures with his other arm for a taxi.

"Are you sure you wouldn't like anything else, ma'am?"

The waiter's intrusion blocks the view out the large, plate-glass window. By the time the server leaves, Thomas is also gone. A yellow cab pulls away from the spot where he stood only a moment ago.

A second later, my phone rings. But the person calling is not Thomas. It is you.

"He just left," you say breathlessly. "It wasn't at all what I was expecting."

Before you can continue, the call-waiting signal beeps. Thomas is on the other line.

After twenty-two glacial minutes—a stretch of time that housed emotions ranging from rage to despair to thin threads of hope—everything is converging too quickly now.

"Hold for one moment, Jessica. Gather your thoughts."

All traces of authority are removed from the tone as Thomas is greeted: "Hello there!"

"Where are you, sweetheart?" he asks.

Ambient noises, such as the clatter of dishes or the conversation of nearby diners, may be available to him. It is vital that the response is consistent in both the manner and word of a woman who, while not entirely carefree, is enjoying a spontaneous outing after a long day.

"Near the office. I just stopped for a bite since I haven't had a chance to grocery shop this week."

Across the street, the door of Deco Bar opens and you emerge holding your cell phone to your ear. You stand on the sidewalk, looking around.

"How long until you'll be home?" Thomas asks. His voice is gentle, his words unhurried. "I miss you and I'd really love to see you tonight."

The amassed clues—the brevity of the meeting combined with Thomas's unexpected request—allow hope to buoy to the surface.

Deco Bar and the café across the street are less than twenty minutes from the town house. But a debriefing is required from you before Thomas can be faced.

"I am just finishing up," Thomas is told. "I'll phone you when I am in a taxi."

Meanwhile, you remain on the sidewalk, hugging your arms around yourself against the cold. Your expression cannot be deciphered from so far away, but your body language conveys uncertainty.

"Perfect," Thomas replies, and the call is terminated.

You are still holding on the other line.

"Apologies for the delay," you are told. "Please, continue."

"He didn't come there for a date," you say. Your cadence is slower now; you have had time to shape your response. This is unfortunate.

"Thomas wanted to see me because he was suspicious. He caught sight of me at the museum after all. He knew it wasn't an accident that I showed up at the diner. He asked me why I was following him."

"What did you say?" The question comes out sharply.

"I flubbed it," you say meekly. "I insisted it was just a coincidence. I don't think he believes me. But Dr. Shields, he's clearly a hundred percent devoted to you."

Your job is not to form conclusions, yet this is too compelling to ignore. "Why do you presume this?"

"I know I told you I'd never been in love before, but I've seen it in other people. And Thomas said he was married to a wonderful woman, and that I should stop bothering him."

Is it possible? All the worrisome signs—the late-night phone calls, the unscheduled visit by the woman with the swinging coat to Thomas's office, the suspicious lunch at the Cuban restaurant—were simply a mirage.

My husband passed the test. He is true.

Thomas is mine again.

"Thank you, Jessica."

The view from the window displays a winter landscape: you walking down the sidewalk in your black leather coat, the tails of your red scarf a splash of color against the night.

"And that is all you two talked about?"

"Yeah, that was the essence of it," you say.

"Enjoy your evening," you are told. "I will speak with you soon."

Three twenties are put on the table—an enormous tip, inspired by the happiness that feels too big to contain.

As a cab is hailed outside the café, my cell phone rings.

Thomas, again.

"Have you left the restaurant?" he asks.

Instinct shapes my response: "Not yet."

"I just wanted to let you know I've run into a little traffic," he says. "So there's no need to rush."

Something in his tone triggers an alarm, but he is told: "Thanks for letting me know."

Data is swiftly considered: Twenty-two minutes at Deco Bar. Too brief for a romantic interlude. Yet it seems unlikely that the contents of the conversation you reported with Thomas would require so much time.

You are barely visible two blocks ahead. But you are traveling in the opposite direction of your apartment. Your stride grows swifter, as if you are eager for what awaits.

You are in a rush, Jessica. Where are you going?

Thomas's delay affords the opportunity to gather more information. And a brisk walk in the cool air helps to clear the mind.

You proceed another block. Then you rapidly spin around. Your head swivels from side to side as you survey your surroundings.

Only the dark cloak of nightfall and the distance separating us, combined with the fortuitous location of a cordoned-off building, which provides a shield, prevents you from noticing your pursuer.

You turn and continue.

Several minutes later, you arrive at another small restaurant called Peachtree Grill.

A man waits inside the glass doors to greet you. He is approximately your age, with dark hair, and he wears a navy puffy coat accented with red zippers. You lean into his open arms. He hugs you tightly for a moment.

Then you both disappear deeper into the restaurant.

You profess to be honest, yet you've never mentioned this man before.

Who is he? How important is he to you? And what have you told him?

How many other secrets are you holding, Jessica?

CHAPTER
FIFTY-TWO

Friday, December 21

MY CONVERSATION WITH THOMAS at Deco Bar was exactly as I described it to Dr. Shields.

He found me there at a few minutes past eight P.M. at a table in the back area. I was nursing a Sam Adams, but he didn't even order a drink. The bar was crowded, but no one seemed to be paying much attention to us.

Still, we stuck to the script.

"Why have you been following me?" Thomas asked as my eyes widened in surprise.

I protested that it was a coincidence. He looked skeptical and told me that he was married to a wonderful woman and that I should leave him alone.

We repeated variations of this dialogue until the two women at the next table turned to stare. I didn't have to pretend to be embarrassed.

This was all good; we had witnesses. And although I hadn't seen Dr. Shields when I'd surreptitiously looked around the bar, I wasn't going to rule out the possibility that she had engineered a way to track our conversation, or at least watch our interaction.

That meeting with Thomas didn't last long. But it was actually our second encounter of the day.

At four o'clock, several hours before we met at Deco Bar, Thomas and I had convened at O'Malley's Pub, the same place where we'd met exactly one week ago before I brought him to my apartment. Back when I had no idea he was Dr. Shields's husband.

Thomas had to cancel a client appointment to create a gap for the late-afternoon meeting; our conversation was too important to have over the phone. And we needed to talk before the date Dr. Shields had orchestrated.

I arrived first at O'Malley's. Since it wasn't even happy hour yet, only a couple other people were there. I made sure to take the table farthest from them. I positioned myself with my back to the wall so I could have a full view of the room.

When Thomas walked in, he nodded at me, then ordered a Scotch from the bar. He took a big gulp even before he sat down and removed his coat.

"I told you my wife was crazy," he said. He ran a hand over his forehead. "Now, why did she have you ask me out on a date?"

We both wanted the same thing from each other: information.

"She told me you cheated on her," I said. "She manipulated me into seeing if you'd do it again."

He muttered something under his breath and finished his Scotch, then signaled to the bartender for another. "Well, I guess we have an answer for that already," he said. "You haven't told her anything about us, have you?"

"Whoa, you want to slow down there?" I suggested, pointing to his drink. "We're meeting again in a few hours and we need to be sharp."

"I get it," he said. But he still stood up and retrieved his second drink.

"I didn't tell her we slept together," I said when he returned to the table. "I'm not planning to ever tell her about that."

He closed his eyes and sighed.

"I don't get it. You say she's crazy and you want to leave her," I said, "but when you're around her, you act like you're in love with her. It's like she's got this weird hold on you."

His eyes snapped open.

"I can't explain it," he finally said. "But you're right about one thing: It is an act when I'm with her."

"You've been unfaithful before." I already knew the answer, but I had to smoke him out.

He frowned. "Why is that any of your business?"

"It's my business because I've gotten sucked into the middle of your twisted relationship!"

He glanced behind him, then leaned closer to me and lowered his voice. "Look, it's complicated, okay? I had a little fling."

One fling? He was only being partly honest.

"Does your wife know who she was?" I asked.

"What? Yeah, but she was a nobody," he said.

I felt myself bristle. I wanted to throw the Scotch in Thomas's face.

A nobody who was a subject in Dr. Shields's study, just like me. A nobody who was now dead.

He saw the expression on my face and backtracked: "I didn't mean— It was just some woman who owns a clothing boutique a block over from my office. A one-night thing."

I looked down at my bottle of Sam Adams. By then I'd almost peeled off the entire label.

So he wasn't referring to April. At least his story aligned with Dr. Shields's about this affair.

"How did she find out about it?" I asked. "Did you confess?"

He shook his head. "I sent Lydia a text that was meant for the other woman. Their names started with the same letter; it was just a dumb mistake."

This was interesting, but it wasn't the affair I wanted to know about. What about Subject 5?

So I asked him, straight out. "What about your relationship with April Voss?"

He gasped, which was an answer in itself.

When he spoke again, his face was pale. "How do you know about her?"

"You're the one who first told me about April," I said. "Only that night in the Conservatory Gardens, you referred to her as Subject 5."

His eyes widened. "Lydia doesn't know, does she?"

I shook my head and checked the time on my phone. We still had several hours before Dr. Shields believed we were meeting.

He took another healthy swig of his drink. Then he looked me directly in the eyes. I could read genuine fear in his. "She can never, ever find out about April."

That was almost exactly what he'd said about us a few seconds ago, too.

The door to the pub swung open so hard it banged against the wall.

I flinched as Thomas whipped around.

"Sorry!" A portly guy with a red beard stood in the doorway.

Thomas mumbled something and shook his head, then turned back to me. His expression was grim.

"So you're not going to tell Lydia about April?" he asked. "You have no idea what you would destroy if you did."

I finally had something on Thomas. It was the opportunity I needed.

"I won't tell her," I said.

He started to thank me, but I cut him off. "As long as you tell me everything you know."

"About what?" Thomas asked.

"About April," I said.

He didn't give me much. I thought about what Thomas had revealed while I walked to meet Noah for a late dinner at Peachtree Grill following my second drink of the day with Dr. Shields's husband, the one in which we'd read our lines like actors onstage.

Thomas had said he'd been with April only once, last spring. He'd gone to meet a friend at a hotel bar. After the friend left and Thomas lingered to pay the bill, April slid into the seat across from him and introduced herself.

It's the scene Dr. Shields had me re-create at the bar at the Sussex Hotel with Scott, I think, and suppress a shudder. But I don't reveal that to Thomas; I might need to hold information over him again.

Did Dr. Shields set up April to test Thomas, and did April lie about it—just like I did?

Or is the truth even more depraved than that?

According to Thomas, he went to April's apartment later that same night and left a little after midnight. Aside from the way they met, it sounds eerily like our date.

Thomas insisted he had no idea until after April died that she was connected to his wife. But given that April was a subject in Dr. Shields's study, too, there was no way it was a random encounter.

The cover story Thomas and I created for Dr. Shields tonight might buy us a little time, I think as I approach Peachtree Grill. I heard relief in her voice when she thanked me after I told her Thomas was devoted to her.

But something tells me it won't last.

Dr. Shields has a way of pulling the truth out of people, especially when it comes to things they want to bury. I've learned that firsthand.

Tell me.

It's like I can hear her voice in my head again. I spin around and search the sidewalk. But I don't see her anywhere.

I resume walking, even faster now, eager to get to Noah and the normality he represents.

A secret is only safe if one person holds it, I think. But when two share a confidence, and both have self-preservation as their main motive, one of them is going to give. I deleted the text chain in which I asked Thomas on a date before I knew he was married to Dr. Shields. But I doubt he did.

Thomas is a cheater and a liar; strange traits for someone married to a woman who is obsessed with morality.

He says he wants out of the marriage. Who's to say he won't sacrifice me to do it?

I know three things happened last spring: April served as Subject 5 in Dr. Shields's study. April slept with Thomas. April died.

What I need to do now is find out which one of them, Dr. Shields or Thomas, first drew April into their warped triangle.

Because I'm not entirely convinced her death was a suicide.

CHAPTER
FIFTY-THREE

Friday, December 21

THOMAS IS WAITING on the steps of the town house.

His first words defuse the suspicion that formed when no traffic was encountered between Deco Bar and my home.

"My plan was foiled," he says wryly as he wraps me in an embrace. It's not dissimilar to the physical greeting you just received from your friend in the navy coat, Jessica.

"Oh?"

"I was hoping to get here first so I could run you a bath and open some champagne," he says. "But my key didn't work. Did you have the locks changed?"

It's a stroke of luck that the new security measure coincides with the story created for Thomas during the cab ride back to the town house.

"I completely forgot to tell you! Here, come inside."

He hangs his coat in the closet, alongside the lighter ones you so cunningly noticed, before he is led into the study.

Instead of champagne, two snifters of brandy are poured from the bottle on the sidebar. A story like this calls for a bracing drink.

"You look distressed," he says, taking a seat on the couch and patting the cushion beside him. "What is it, sweetheart?"

A soft sigh hints that it isn't easy to begin. "There's this young woman who entered my study," he is told. "It's probably nothing . . ."

It's better if he coaxes out the story; Thomas will believe he has a stake in it.

"What did she do?" he asks.

"Nothing yet. But last week, when I stepped out of the office for lunch, I saw her. She was standing across the street from my office. She just . . . watched me."

A sip of brandy. Thomas's hand closing protectively over mine. The next few sentences are delivered with a slightly halting quality.

"There have been a few hang-ups on my phone as well. And then last Sunday, I saw her outside the town house. I have no idea how she obtained our home address."

Thomas's expression is attentive. Perhaps gears are beginning to spin in his head as he is led toward a conclusion to a vexing puzzle. But he needs to hear more.

"For confidentiality, I can't reveal much about her. But even during those initial survey questions, it was clear she had . . . issues."

Thomas grimaces. "Issues? Like the other girl in your study?"

A nod provides the answer to his questions.

"That explains it," he says. "I don't want to alarm you, but I may have seen her, too. Does she have dark curly hair?"

Now your appearances at the museum and diner have an explanation.

Downcast eyes camouflage the expression they contain: triumph.

Thomas likely imagines a swirl of other, troubling emotions that cannot be voiced due to professional rules of discretion. Actions always speak louder than words: Thomas's sensible wife would not install a new lock without good reason.

Thomas's embrace feels like his voice did in the darkness on the first night we met. Finally, it feels like safety again.

"I'm going to keep her away from you," Thomas says firmly.

"From us, don't you mean? If she has followed you as well . . ."

"I think I should sleep here tonight. In fact, I insist. I can stay in the guest room if you'd prefer."

His eyes contain hope. My hand touches his cheek. Thomas's skin is always so warm.

This moment feels suspended, infused with a crystalline quality.

My response is whispered. "No, I want you with me."

You were the one who shaped tonight. *He's a hundred percent devoted to you.*

Jessica, everything is riding on your words.

CHAPTER
FIFTY-FOUR

Saturday, December 22

IS IT ETHICAL TO PRETEND to have been friends with a dead girl in order to get information that could save you?

I sit across from Mrs. Voss in April's childhood bedroom, which still has posters featuring inspirational sayings and collages of photos on the wall. A bookshelf is lined with novels, and there's a dried corsage from a long-ago dance hanging from a closet door handle. It's almost as though the space has been preserved for April to walk in at any moment.

Mrs. Voss wears brown leather leggings and a winter-white sweater. The Voss family—Jodi is April's mother and Mr. Voss's much younger, second wife—lives in the penthouse of an apartment overlooking Central Park. April's bedroom is bigger than my entire studio.

Mrs. Voss perches on the edge of April's queen-size bed while I sit in the tufted light green chair by the desk across from her. As we talk, Mrs. Voss's fingers never stop moving. She smooths imaginary creases in the comforter, straightens an old teddy bear, and rearranges throw pillows.

When I'd phoned this morning, I'd told her that I'd known April from when we'd both studied abroad in London during our junior year of college. Mrs. Voss was eager to see me. To camouflage the fact that I was five years older than April, I'd turned to my makeup kit: a smooth, clear complexion, pink lips, and brown mascara on curled lashes helped peel a few years off my age. A high ponytail and jeans and my Converse sneakers completed the costume.

"It was so nice of you to come by," Mrs. Voss says for the second time while I sneak another look around the bedroom. I'm desperate to gather more clues about the girl I have so much in common with in some ways but couldn't be more different from in others.

Then Mrs. Voss asks me a question: "Would you share a memory with me?"

"Let's see, a memory . . ." I say. I feel perspiration prickle my forehead.

"Something I wouldn't have known about April?" she prompts.

Although I've never been to London, I remember April's photos from that semester in her Instagram photos.

The lie slips off my tongue as smoothly as if it had been waiting there all along. Dr. Shields's tests have taught me how to play a role, but that doesn't erase the sick feeling in the pit of my stomach. "She kept trying to make the guards at Buckingham Palace laugh."

"She did? What did she do?" Mrs. Voss is nakedly eager for hidden details about her daughter. I guess because there will be no memories of April formed in the future, she wants to collect as many as she can from the past.

I glance at a framed poster in the corner of April's room that has the following quote in a flowing cursive: *Sing like no one is listening . . . Love like you've never been hurt . . . Dance like nobody's watching.*

I want to pick a detail that will make Mrs. Voss feel good. I rationalize that maybe if she can imagine her daughter in a happy moment, it'll offset some of the immorality of what I'm doing.

"Oh, she did the funniest dance," I say. "The guards didn't even smile, but April swore she saw the corner of one of their mouth's twitch. That's why it's such a great memory . . . I couldn't stop cracking up."

"Really?" Mrs. Voss leans forward. "But she hated to dance! I wonder what got into her?"

"It was a dare." I need to derail this avenue of conversation. I didn't come here to share phony stories with a grieving mother.

"I'm sorry I couldn't make it to the funeral," I say. "I've been living in California and I just got back to town."

"Here," Mrs. Voss says. She gets off the bed and walks over to the desk behind me. "Would you like a program from the service? There are photos in it of April through the years. There are even some from her semester in London."

I stare at the pale pink cover. There's an embossed drawing of a dove over the name *Katherine April Voss* and then a quote written in italics: *And in the end, the love you take is equal to the love you make.* At the bottom are the dates of April's birth and death.

"What a beautiful quote," I murmur, not knowing if that's the right thing to say.

But Mrs. Voss nods eagerly. "April came over a few months before she died and asked me if I'd ever heard it before." Mrs. Voss eyes grow faraway and she smiles. "I told her, of course, that it was from a Beatles song called 'The End'—not that she'd know because they were well before her time. So we downloaded the song on her iPhone and played it together. We each put in an earbud to listen."

Mrs. Voss wipes away a tear. "After she— Well, I remembered that day, and the quote seemed perfect."

The Beatles, I think, remembering how Thomas had sung along to "Come Together" in the bar on the night we were together. He's obviously a big fan, so he must have sung "The End" to April on the night they met and slept together. I can't suppress a shudder; it's another eerie similarity between me and Subject 5.

I tuck the program in my purse. How awful it would be for Mrs. Voss to know that the quote is intricately connected to the whole sinister web that ended in her daughter's death.

"Were you in touch with April much over the spring?" Mrs. Voss asks me. She's back on the bed now; her thin fingers keep worrying the silky tassel on a throw pillow.

I shake my head. "Not really. I was in a bad relationship with this guy and I sort of lost touch with my friends."

Take the bait, I think.

"Oh, you girls." Mrs. Voss shakes her head. "April didn't have a lot of luck with men, either. She was so sensitive. She was always getting hurt."

I nod.

"I actually didn't even know she was interested in anyone," Mrs. Voss says. "But after . . . well, one of her friends told me she was . . ."

I hold my breath, hoping she'll continue. But she just stares into space.

I furrow my brow, like something has just occurred to me.

"Actually, April did mention a guy she liked," I say. "Wasn't he a little older?"

Mrs. Voss nods. "I think so . . ." Her voice trails off. "The worst part is not knowing. I wake up every morning thinking: *Why?*"

I have to look away from her shattered eyes.

"She was always so emotional," Mrs. Voss said. She picks up the teddy bear and hugs it to her chest. "It's no secret she'd been in and out of therapy."

She glances at me questioningly and I nod again, like April had shared this information with me.

"But she hadn't tried to hurt herself in years. Not since high school. It seemed like she was getting better. She was looking for a new job . . . She must have been planning this, though, because the police said she had taken all that Vicodin. I don't even know how she got the pills." Mrs. Voss drops her head into her hands and releases a small sob.

So the police did investigate, I think. Given that April had tried to hurt herself in the past, it probably was a suicide. It should make me feel safe, but something still isn't adding up.

Mrs. Voss lifts her head. Her eyes are red-rimmed. "I know you hadn't seen her in a while, but didn't she sound happy to you?" she asks, sounding desperate. I wonder if she has anyone else to talk to about April. Thomas had said April wasn't close to her father, and probably April's real friends have moved on with their lives.

"Yes, she did seem happy," I whisper. The only way I can keep from bursting into tears and running out of the room is by telling myself that maybe the information I'll get could help Mrs. Voss in her search for answers, too.

"That's why it surprised me that April was seeing a psychiatrist," Mrs. Voss says. "She showed up at the funeral and introduced herself to us. She was stunningly beautiful, and so kind."

My heart skips a beat.

There's only one person this could be.

"Have you talked with her recently?" I ask. I make sure my voice remains soft and uniform.

Mrs. Voss nods. "I reached out to her in the fall. It was April's birthday, October 2. It was such a hard day. She would have been twenty-four."

She sets the teddy bear back down. "We'd always do a mother-daughter spa day on her birthday. Last year she picked this awful light-blue nail polish shade that I told her looked like an Easter egg." She shakes her head. "I can't believe we actually had a little argument about that."

"So did you see the psychiatrist that day?" I ask.

"We met in her office," Mrs. Voss says. "Before, when April had gone to therapy, we always knew about it. We paid for it. So why was it different this time? I wanted to know what she and April talked about."

"Did Dr. Shields tell you?" I ask.

I immediately realize my mistake in giving the therapist's name. I flinch, waiting for Mrs. Voss to notice.

How can I explain it? I can't say April mentioned the name of her psychiatrist to me months ago and I've remembered all this time. Mrs. Voss will never believe it; minutes ago I told her I'd lost touch with April.

Mrs. Voss is going to know I'm an impostor. She'll be furious, as she'll have every right to be. What kind of sick person fakes a friendship with a dead girl?

But Mrs. Voss doesn't seem to catch my slip.

She shakes her head slowly. "I asked if I could see her notes from April's sessions. I thought there could be something in there, something I didn't know about that could help explain why April did it."

I'm holding my breath. Dr. Shields is so scrupulous, her notes would detail the date when she first saw April. They could reveal whether Thomas or Dr. Shields was the one who drew April in. If Dr. Shields initiated the contact, she's probably even more dangerous than I thought.

"Did she share the notes?" I ask.

I'm pushing too hard; Mrs. Voss looks at me curiously. But she continues.

"No, she reached for my hand and told me again how sorry she was

for my loss. She said my questions were natural, but that part of the healing process was needing to accept that I might never have an answer.
No matter how hard I pressed, she refused to let me see them. She said
it would violate confidentiality mandates."

I exhale a little too loudly. Of course Dr. Shields would safeguard
her notes. But was it because she was protecting April's secrets, or was
she protecting herself—or her husband?

Mrs. Voss stands up and smooths down her sweater. She's looking me
directly in the eye now, and all traces of her tears are gone. "Remind me
again, were you and April in the same study-abroad program? I'm sorry,
I don't remember her mentioning your name."

I lower my head. I don't have to fake my shame.

"I wish I'd been a better friend to her," I say. "Even though I was so
far away, I should have stayed in touch."

She walks over and pats my shoulder, as if absolving me.

"I haven't given up, you know," she says. I have to tilt back my head
to see the expression on her face. Her sorrow is still there, but now it's
mingled with determination.

"Dr. Shields seemed like a good therapist, but she must not be a
mother. Otherwise, she would know that when you lose a child, there
is no healing," she says. "That's why I'm still looking for an answer."

Her voice grows stronger as she stands up straighter. "That's why
I'll *never* stop looking for an answer."

CHAPTER
FIFTY-FIVE

Saturday, December 22

FINALLY, THERE IS AN ANSWER: Thomas is true.

The pillowcase on the left side of the bed holds the scent of his shampoo again.

Sunlight's warm glow fills the room. It is almost eight A.M. Remarkable. Relief manifests physiologically in myriad ways: Insomnia is banished. The body feels rejuvenated. The appetite returns.

Thomas's renewed display of fidelity is healing more than just our wounded marriage.

Nearly twenty years ago, another seismic betrayal—this one involving my sister, Danielle—left me with a jagged emotional scar.

Today that scar feels less prominent.

A note folded into a little tent waits on the nightstand. A smile forms even before it is read: *Sweetheart, there's fresh coffee downstairs. I'll be back in twenty with bagels and smoked salmon. Love, T.*

The words are so ordinary, yet so magical.

After a leisurely breakfast, Thomas departs for the gym. He will return later to pick me up for a scheduled dinner with another couple. My errands are routine, but my stop at the new boutique a few doors down from my hair appointment at the salon is not. The mannequin in the window wears a pink teddy with a V in the front. It's more subtle than the sort of lingerie you would probably choose, Jessica, but the soft silk and high-cut legs are flattering.

On impulse, the teddy is purchased.

After a lavender-scented bubble bath, a dress is selected that covers the lingerie. Thomas will discover it later tonight.

Before the dress can be slipped on, a text pings.

The message is from you: *Hi, just checking to see if you'll be needing me to do anything more in regard to the last assignment. If not, Lizzie invited me to go home with her for Christmas, so I thought I'd book a flight.*

How interesting.

Could you ever truly believe details concerning your whereabouts would be carelessly overlooked, Jessica? Lizzie and her family are celebrating the holidays at a luxury condo in Aspen.

Before a reply is crafted, your folder is retrieved from the desk in the study. Dates are double-checked. Indeed, Lizzie departed yesterday to meet her family in Colorado.

The doorbell rings.

Your folder is replaced atop April's, in the center of the desk near the fountain pen that was a gift from my father.

"Thomas! You're early!" He is given a lingering kiss.

He glances at his watch. "Do you need another few minutes?"

"Just one."

Upstairs, perfume is dabbed behind my ears and Thomas's favorite high heels are chosen.

Thomas is still waiting by the door. "Warren said they were running a little late, so I told him not to worry, that we'd be there right on time to hold the table."

"Hopefully dinner doesn't take too long," he is told. "I was thinking we could make it an early night. I've planned a surprise for you."

CHAPTER

FIFTY-SIX

Saturday, December 22

THE KEY GLIDES into the lock.

My hand shakes as I twist it. Then I push the door open.

A soft beeping sound erupts as I step into Dr. Shields's town house. I close the door behind me, sealing off the light from the two outside sconces. Now the hallway is so shadowy I can barely make out the alarm keypad on the left side of the entranceway.

I slip off my shoes so I don't track any mud or dirt inside, but I keep my coat on, in case I need to leave fast.

Thomas gave me the security code when he called today. He told me he'd leave the keys he'd copied under the doormat.

Use the silver one for the bottom lock and the square one for the top, he'd said. *I'll try to keep Lydia out until eleven.*

He also told me I'd have thirty seconds to deactivate the alarm.

I walk over to the keypad and punch in the four digits: 0-9-1-5. But in my haste, I mistake the 6 for a 5 in the dim light.

I realize my error a split second later.

There's a long, shrill noise, then the beeping resumes. It's faster now, sounding almost frantic, blurring with the thudding of my heart.

How many seconds have elapsed? Fifteen? I have to get it right or the security company will summon the police.

I press in each number carefully.

The alarm makes a final, high-pitched sound. Then it falls silent.

I withdraw my gloved hand from the numbered pad and exhale. I wasn't sure until now if Thomas had given me the right four digits.

My legs are so weak I have to lean against the wall to steady myself.

I stand there for a full minute. Then another. I can't dislodge the fear that Thomas and Dr. Shields are just a floor above me, hiding in her study.

I could still leave; I could put on my shoes, arm the alarm, and replace the keys. But then I'll never know what Dr. Shields might be holding over me.

I saw your file upstairs on her desk this morning, Thomas had said. *It was resting on top of April's.*

Finally, I know where the elusive manila folder is—the one I'd seen on Dr. Shields's office desk during our early sessions. The one Ben had told me I needed to find.

Did you look inside? I'd asked Thomas.

I didn't have time. She was asleep, but she could've woken up at any second.

I'd squeezed my eyes shut in frustration at his words. What did it matter if I knew where Dr. Shields kept my file when I'd never be able to get it?

Then Thomas had said: *I can get you into the house.*

His tone told me there was a catch even before he continued.

But only if you agree to photograph all of Lydia's notes on April for me. I need that file, Jess.

It didn't hit me until after we'd hung up that maybe this was why Thomas pretended to still be in love with Dr. Shields: He was staying close to get April's file.

Just a few minutes have elapsed since I entered Dr. Shields's home, but it feels like I've been frozen in the hallway for much longer. I finally take ten steps forward. Now I'm next to the staircase landing. Still I can't bring myself to begin to climb: Even if this isn't a trap, with every progressive movement, I'm going deeper into this morass.

Other than the soft hiss of a nearby radiator, it is completely quiet.

I have to do something, so I put my foot on the first step. It groans.

I wince, then continue to slowly make my way up. Though my eyes have adjusted to the murky light, I place each foot down carefully to make sure I don't slip.

I finally reach the top and stand there, unsure of which way to turn. The hallway stretches to the left and right. Thomas only told me Dr. Shields's office was on the second floor.

There's a light coming from the left. I start to head that way.

Then my phone rings, shattering the oppressive silence.

My heart leaps into my throat.

I fumble in my coat pocket, but my gloves slip against the smooth surface of the phone and I can't get a firm grip on it.

It rings again.

Something's gone wrong, I frantically think. Thomas is calling to tell me they're coming home early.

But when I finally pull out the phone, instead of Thomas's code name—Sam, the last three letters of his name reversed—I see my mother's smiling face in the little circle on the screen.

I try to hit *Decline Call* but with my glove on, the touchscreen doesn't work.

I use my teeth to grip the fingertips of the glove and try to pull it off as my phone rings again. My hand is so clammy the leather sticks to my skin. I tug harder. If anyone is upstairs, they certainly know I'm in the house now.

Finally, I manage to switch my phone to vibrate.

I remain immobile, listening intently, but there's no indication anyone else is nearby. I take three deep breaths before I can force my shaking legs to move again.

I continue walking toward the dim glow of the light and arrive at its source: the nightstand by Dr. Shields's bed. Thomas and Dr. Shields's bed, I correct myself as I stand in the doorway, staring at the steel-blue quilted headboard and creaseless comforter. Next to the small lamp is a single book, *Middlemarch*, and a tiny bouquet of anemones.

This is the second time today I've violated such an intimate space. First April's old bedroom, and now this one.

I'd give anything to be able to scour it for more clues about who Dr. Shields is, like a diary, old photos or letters. But I keep walking, toward an adjoining room.

It's the study.

The folders are right where Thomas said he'd seen them this morning.

I hurry to the desk and carefully remove the top one, the one with my name on the tab. I open it and see a photocopy of my driver's license and the biographical information I gave to Ben back on that first day, when I blithely walked into the study, hoping to make some easy money.

I pull out my phone and photograph the first page.

Then I flip it over and gasp.

The faces of my parents and Becky smile up at me from the second page. I recognize the photo that Dr. Shields has printed out: It's from my Instagram feed, last December. The image is slightly blurred, but I can still see the edge of the Christmas tree that was in my parents' living room.

Questions fire in my brain: Why does Dr. Shields have this? How soon after she met me did she copy it? And how did she get access to my private Instagram account?

But I don't have time to stop and think. Dr. Shields always seems to be a step ahead of me; I can't shake the fear that she'll sense I'm here. That she could come home at any minute.

I continue snapping pictures, making sure I keep the pages in order. I see my two computer-survey questionnaires printed out. The prompts flash by:

Could you tell a lie without feeling guilt?

Describe a time in your life when you cheated.

Have you ever deeply hurt someone you care about?

And those final two questions before Dr. Shields asked me to expand my participation in her study:

Should a punishment always fit the crime?

Do victims have the right to take retribution into their own hands?

Next come notes and notes from a yellow legal pad filled with neat, graceful handwriting.

Surrender to it . . . You belong to me. . . . You look as lovely as ever.

I feel nauseated, but I keep flipping the papers like I'm on autopilot as I document each one. I can't let myself take in the significance of what I'm seeing.

Through the slight gaps in the slatted wooden blinds covering a window, I see the sweep of headlights. I freeze.

A vehicle is traveling down the street slowly. I wonder if the flash from my iPhone's camera was visible from the driver's vantage point.

I press my phone against my leg to block the glow of the screen and remain completely motionless until the car passes by.

It could have been a neighbor, I think, as my anxiety swells. Maybe even one who saw Thomas and Lydia leave together an hour ago. If they noticed anything strange, they could be dialing the police right now.

But I can't leave yet. Not until I finish photographing the pages. I flip them as fast as possible, alert for any noise that could indicate someone is approaching the town house. After I've turned the last page, with several underlines beneath my words *He's a hundred percent devoted to you,* I straighten them all, tapping the edges against the desk to make sure they are aligned. I slip them back into the manila folder.

Then I pick up April's file.

It seems a little thinner than mine.

I dread opening it; it feels like lifting aside a rock, knowing a tarantula might lurk beneath it. But I'm not photographing it just because Thomas wants the information. I need to know what it contains, too.

The very first page looks identical to the one in my folder. April's grainy photograph stares out at me from her driver's license, her too-big eyes making her appear startled. Beneath the photocopy are her biographical details: full name, date of birth, and address.

I snap a picture, then turn to the next piece of paper.

There, in Dr. Shields's flowing blue script, is the answer I desperately need. April entered Dr. Shields's study and became Subject 5 on May 19.

Fifteen days before that, on May 4, April posted the photograph of Thomas in her bed on Instagram.

Even if she'd taken the picture of Thomas days or weeks before and waited to post it, her encounter with him came before she entered Dr. Shields's study.

Thomas is the one who drew in April.

I suck in a sharp breath. My gut was wrong; he is the more dangerous of the two.

I stare at the date again to make sure I'm getting the facts correct. The one thing that's now clear is that my story no longer mirrors April's. Dr. Shields couldn't have used April to test Thomas, like she did me.

It's also apparent that April didn't remain one of Dr. Shields's subjects for long. She'd only answered a few survey questions and didn't even go back for the second session. Why did she stop?

Thomas is the only person who knows I'm in the town house. And if he's the one who orchestrated the events that led to April's death, then I'm not safe.

I need to get out of here. I finish going through the file, snapping photos of the notes as quickly as I can. The second-to-last page is titled *Conversation with Jodi Voss, October 2*. And then there is only one piece of paper left.

It's a certified letter dated only a week after Dr. Shields met with Mrs. Voss on April's birthday. It's addressed to Dr. Shields.

A few lines sear themselves into my vision as I wait for my phone camera to focus: *Investigating the death . . . Katherine April Voss . . . family requests voluntary release of notes . . . Possible subpoena . . .*

This is what Mrs. Voss must have been alluding to when she told me she'd never stop looking for answers. She'd hired a private investigator to help her find them.

I close the file and center it directly beneath mine, just the way Dr. Shields left it. I have everything I need. Though I still want to look around for more clues since I know I'll never have this opportunity again, I have to leave now.

I retrace my steps back to the staircase, moving much faster than I did on the way up. In the entranceway I slip on my shoes, reset the alarm, and ease open the door. I tuck the key beneath the mat and stand up. No neighbors are within sight. Even if they glimpsed me, all they'd see is someone in a dark coat and hat casually walking down the front steps.

I don't breathe easily until I've rounded the corner.

Then I collapse against the cold metal of a street lamp, my hand still clutching my phone in my pocket. I can't believe I got away with it. I didn't leave any evidence behind—no lights switched on, no dirt tracked on the pristine carpets, not even a single traceable fingerprint. There's no way Dr. Shields can ever know I broke into her house.

But I find myself examining my movements in my mind again and again, just to make sure.

After I am safely home, with my own door locked behind me and the nightstand wedged against it, I start thinking about Mrs. Voss. She believes the file on April holds the truth about why her daughter killed herself. She's so desperate to get it that she hired a private investigator.

But Thomas, who claims he only slept with April once, seems just as eager to see the file.

A part of me wonders if I should anonymously send the photos to the investigator, and let the chips fall. But that might not solve anything, and Thomas would know who gave up the file.

When it comes down to it, I've only got myself to rely on.

I wrote that line in Dr. Shields's survey on my first session. It has never seemed more true than right now.

So before I e-mail Thomas the photographs of April's file, I'm going to study them.

I have to figure out why hiding his connection to Subject 5 is so important to him.

CHAPTER
FIFTY-SEVEN

Saturday, December 22

How are you spending this evening, Jessica? Are you with the handsome man in the navy coat with red zippers that you embraced in front of the restaurant last night?

Perhaps he will be the one who will finally enable you to experience true love. Not the storybook version. The real kind, which sustains through phases of dark, until the return to light.

You may already know what it feels like to sit beside him at a booth, across from another couple, and bask in utter contentment. Perhaps he is highly attentive to your well-being, as Thomas is to mine. He might signal the waiter for a refill of your beverage the moment before your glass is emptied. His hand may find reasons to touch you.

Those are external actions; easily witnessed. But it is not until you have been with a man for many years that you can know him well enough to recognize his hidden, internal intricacies.

They emerge over the course of the evening meal, blotting out the newly established equanimity like a slow-moving eclipse.

When Thomas is distracted—when another gear of his mind is occupied—he overcompensates.

He laughs a bit too robustly. He asks many questions—about the other couple's upcoming vacation plans, and the private school they're considering for their twins—which gives the appearance of engagement, but actually frees him from having to fill conversational lapses. He works his way, methodically, through his meal: Tonight the order is his medium-rare steak first, then the potatoes, and finally the green beans.

When an individual is so deeply familiar, their habits and mannerisms become easy to decode.

Thomas's thoughts are elsewhere tonight.

Midway through his black onyx chocolate cake, Thomas pulls out his vibrating phone. He glances at the screen and frowns.

"I'm so sorry," he says. "A patient of mine has just been admitted to Bellevue. I hate to cut this short, but I have to go consult with the attending doctors."

Everyone at the table expresses understanding; this sort of interruption is a natural consequence of his line of work.

"I'll be home as soon as I can," he says as he lays a credit card down on the table. "But you know how these things go, so please don't wait up."

The brush of his lips; the bittersweet taste of chocolate.

Then my husband is gone.

His absence feels like a theft.

The town house is dark and still. The bottom step groans softly under my step, as it has for years. In the past, that noise was comforting; it often signaled that Thomas had finished locking up and was coming to bed.

Upstairs, a light shines softly on the nightstand in the empty bedroom.

This moment was supposed to be very different. Candles would be lit; music would softly play. My dress would slowly slip down, revealing the hint of enticing pink silk.

Instead, my shoes are returned to the closet. Then my earrings and necklace are replaced in their velvet compartments in the top drawer of the bureau. Thomas's note from this morning rests alongside the gems, like another precious item.

His words, so comfortingly ordinary, have been committed to memory.

Still, the note is opened and read again.

Three tiny beads of ink mar the sentences.

These smudges bring forth a sudden clarity.

They were made with a specific fountain pen that leaves blots on the page when the nub rests against the paper for too long.

This fountain pen is always kept in the same place: the desk in my study.

Twelve swift steps are taken across the bedroom and past the threshold into the study.

When Thomas reached for the pen before going out for bagels, he would have seen two files—yours and April's, with the names clearly visible on the tabs—only inches away on the surface of the desk.

The instinct to grab the folders and check their contents is almost uncontrollable; however, it must be suppressed. Panic begets errors.

There are five items on the desk: the pen, a beverage coaster, a Tiffany clock, and the folders.

At first glance, everything appears intact.

But something almost imperceptible is amiss.

Each item is scrutinized in turn, as a rising wave of anxiety is battled.

The pen is exactly where it should be, on the top left-hand corner of the desk. The clock is opposite it, at the top right-hand corner. The coaster is beneath the clock, because beverages are always held in my right hand, which frees my left hand to write notes.

The alteration is spotted within a minute. It would be invisible to ninety percent of the population, however.

Individuals who fall into the vast majority, the right-handers, rarely recognize the inconveniences those of us in the minority are acutely attuned to. Simple household items—scissors, ice-cream scoops, can openers—are all designed for the right-handed. Water fountain buttons. Car cup holders. ATMs. The list continues.

People with right-hand dominance naturally orient the page to the right side of the body when they take notes. People who use their left hands to write orient the page to the left. The practice is automatic; it requires no conscious thought.

The folders have been moved several inches to the right of their usual resting spot on the desk. They are now in the space where the brain of a right-handed person would decree they belong.

The file folders briefly blur as my vision swims. Then reason reasserts itself.

Perhaps Thomas simply brushed the folders a few inches aside when he replaced the pen, and then attempted to recenter them.

Even if Thomas had picked them up out of curiosity, or in a search to find a sheet of paper for his note before he discovered a blank pad in the top desk drawer, he would have realized they were client folders. Therapists are bound by rules of confidentiality; Thomas abides by this professional mandate. Even in our private discussions about clients, they are never mentioned by name. Even special clients, like Subject 5.

Thomas was told about my first encounter with Subject 5, how she fled the NYU classroom in tears midway through her initial computerized survey session. When Subject 5 revealed to my assistant, Ben, that the questions had triggered an intense emotional reaction for her, Thomas agreed that the moral course of action was to provide her with some expert guidance. He listened supportively as our subsequent interactions were described—the conversations in my office, the gifts, and finally the invitation for cheese and wine at the town house on a night when Thomas was occupied at a business event.

He understood that she became . . . special.

But her name has never been spoken between us.

Not once. Not even after her death.

Especially not after her death.

However, Thomas did see the e-mail sent to me by the private investigator hired by the Voss family. If he hadn't made the connection by then that Subject 5's name was Katherine April Voss, it certainly became crystal clear to him in that moment.

The tension stored in my muscles eases slightly as my thought process continues along a reassuring path.

If Thomas had seen everything in your file, Jessica—the pages of notes detailing *our* conversations, the specifics of your assignments, and your accounts of your interactions with him—his behavior surely would have been altered. At breakfast, his affect seemed unremarkable. It remained so when he arrived at the town house this evening.

And yet . . . at dinner tonight, his tenor changed. He grew increasingly distracted. His departure was abrupt; his farewell kiss, perfunctory rather than regretful.

It is difficult to think clearly; the two glasses of Pinot Noir consumed this evening hamper my ability to draw a firm conclusion.

Other considerations swim through my mind: Despite the rules of confidentiality, you and April are unlike all of the others who have entered my office. Neither of you were technically clients. And Thomas thinks you both hold one other distinction: that each of you has caused his wife great distress.

April is fading away. She can cause no fresh pain.

But Thomas believes that you, Jessica, have demonstrated potential menace, enough to inspire me to install a new lock on the front door of the town house. He could have reasoned that an ethical breach was preferable to ignoring information that would protect his wife.

The probability must be acknowledged: Thomas looked at your file.

The impact of the realization feels like a physical blow. The edge of my desk is grasped until equilibrium is reestablished.

If he chose to pretend otherwise, what would be his motivation?

No clear answer is forthcoming.

Communication is a vital component of a healthy partnership. It is a necessary foundational aspect of a romantic relationship, as well as a therapeutic one.

Yet self-preservation must trump the blind trust of one's spouse. Particularly when one's spouse has proved untrustworthy in the past.

The twenty-four-hour reprieve has ended. All conclusions have been upended. Thomas must be watched more closely than ever.

The folders are placed in a locked filing cabinet. The door to my study is firmly closed.

Then a text is sent to him: *I'm going to call it an early night. Let's talk tomorrow?*

My phone is turned off before he can reply. In the bedroom, the usual nightly rituals are performed: My dress is hung in the closet, serum is applied, and pajamas are selected.

Then the new lingerie is crumpled into a ball and shoved into the back of a drawer.

CHAPTER
FIFTY-EIGHT

Sunday, December 23

I WAS UP MOST OF LAST NIGHT studying my file and April's.

As best as I can tell, Thomas's affair with the boutique owner is the one Dr. Shields was referring to that night in her kitchen, when her hand trembled and her eyes filled with tears. It's the reason why she decided to use me as a real-life test for her husband, to make sure it wouldn't happen again.

I briefly flash back to the memory of Thomas's mouth trailing its way down my stomach as he pushed aside my lacy black thong and I flinch.

I can't think about that now; I need to focus on figuring out why Thomas was so transparent about his relationship with the boutique owner and so fearful of anyone learning he'd been with April.

What made one affair so different from the other?

It's why I'm walking into the Blink boutique this morning, looking for the store's owner: Lauren, the woman Thomas slept with.

It wasn't hard to pinpoint who she was and where she worked. I had clues. Her name began with an *L*, the same initial as Lydia. And she owned a clothing boutique located a block away from Thomas's office.

There were three possible stores. I identified the right one by checking out the websites. Blink's featured a photo of Lauren and the backstory of how she started the boutique.

I can kind of see why I remind Dr. Shields of Lauren, I think as I step into the bright, funky store. When I saw her picture on the website, it was hard to tell, but in person I acknowledge that she does look a bit like me, with her dark hair and light eyes, even though, as Dr. Shields stated, she's probably a decade older.

She's busy with a customer, so I inspect a rack of blouses organized by color.

"Looking for anything special?" a saleswoman greets me.

"Just browsing," I say. I flip over a price tag and wince: The long-sleeve, sheer top is $425.

"Let me know if you want to try anything on," she says.

I nod and continue pretending to consider the blouses, while I keep an eye on Lauren. But the customer she's with is buying multiple items for last-minute Christmas gifts, and she occupies Lauren by asking for her opinion.

Finally, after I've made a slow lap around the tiny store, the customer heads to the cash register. Lauren starts to ring her up.

I grab a scarf off an accessory table, figuring it will be one of the less expensive items. By the time Lauren hands the customer a glossy white bag with the store's logo—an oversize sketch of a pair of closed eyes with long, thick lashes—I am at the register waiting.

"Would you like this gift-wrapped?" she asks.

"Please," I say. It'll buy me a few more minutes of her time, so I can gather my courage.

She slips the scarf into tissue paper and ties a pretty bow around it while I swipe my credit card to cover the $195 charge. If I can get the information I need, it's a small price to pay.

Lauren hands me the signature bag and I notice she's wearing a wedding band.

I clear my throat.

"I know this sounds kind of weird, but is it possible to talk in private for a minute?" I ask. I feel the cold metal of my rings and realize I'm running my thumb over them. According to Dr. Shields's file on me, that's one of my tells when I'm anxious.

Lauren's smile disappears. "Sure." She draws out the word, almost like it's a question.

Lauren leads me to the back of the shop. "What can I help you with?" she asks.

I need her first, instinctual response. I learned from Dr. Shields that's usually the most honest one. So instead of saying anything, I pull out my phone and turn it around so Lauren can see the photo of Thomas I've cropped out from the wedding picture he texted me. It was taken seven years ago, but the picture is clear and he basically looks the same.

I keep my eyes on her. If she refuses to talk to me or just tells me to leave, her initial reaction is all I'll have. I have to be able to read her expression, to decipher any signs of guilt or sorrow or love.

It isn't what I expect.

There's no strong emotion in her face. Her brow furrows slightly. Her eyes are quizzical.

It's as if she recognizes Thomas but can't quite place him.

"He looks vaguely familiar . . ." she finally says.

She meets my gaze. She's waiting for me to fill in the blanks.

"You had an affair with him," I blurt. "Just a couple of months ago!"

"What?"

Her cry of surprise is so loud that her coworker turns around: "Everything okay, Lauren?"

"I'm sorry," I sputter. "He told me, he said——"

"It's fine," Lauren calls back to her colleague, but her voice has an edge, like she's angry now.

I try to gather myself; she'll probably throw me out in a minute. "You said he looks familiar. Do you even know him at all?"

My voice cracks and I force back tears.

Instead of recoiling like I'm crazy, Lauren's face softens. "Are you okay?"

I nod and wipe my eyes with the back of my hand.

"Why in the world would you think I had an affair with that man?" she says.

I can't come up with anything to say other than the truth. "Someone told me you had . . ." I hesitate, then force myself to continue. "I met him a few weeks ago and . . . I'm worried he might be dangerous," I whisper.

Lauren rears back. "Look, I don't know who you are, but this is nuts. Someone told you I had an affair with him? I'm married. *Happily* married. Who told you that lie?"

"Maybe I got it wrong," I say. There's no way I can go into all of this with her. "I apologize, I didn't mean to insult you . . . Could you just look again and see if you can remember if you've ever seen him before?"

Now Lauren is the one studying me. I wipe my eyes again and make myself meet her gaze.

She finally stretches out her hand. "Let me see your phone."

As she gazes at the photo, her face clears. "I remember him now. He was a customer."

She looks up at the ceiling and bites her lower lip. "Okay, it's coming back to me. He walked in a few months ago. I was just putting out some items from the fall line and he was looking for some special outfits for his wife. He spent quite a lot of money."

The chime over the door announces the arrival of a new customer. Lauren glances her way and I know my time here is limited.

"Was that all?" I ask.

Lauren raises her eyebrows. "Well, he returned everything the next day. That's probably why I even remember him at all. He was very apologetic but said they weren't his wife's style."

She looks toward the front of the shop again. "I never saw him again," she says. "I didn't get the feeling that he was dangerous at all. In fact, he seemed really sweet. But I barely spent any time with him. And I certainly didn't have an affair with him."

"Thank you," I say. "I'm so sorry I bothered you."

She turns to go, then looks back at me. "Honey, if you're that scared of him, you really should go to the police."

CHAPTER
FIFTY-NINE

Sunday, December 23

IN A PSYCHOLOGICAL ASSESSMENT known as the Invisible Gorilla experiment, subjects believed they were supposed to count passes between players on a basketball team. In actuality, they were being evaluated on something else entirely. What most subjects did not notice while tallying the tosses of the ball was that a man in a gorilla suit had walked onto the court. Focusing so strongly on one component blinded the subjects to the big picture.

My hyperfocus on Thomas's fidelity, or lack thereof, may have obscured an unexpectedly shocking aspect of my case study: that you have an agenda of your own.

You have been solely responsible for reporting what occurred during all of your encounters with my husband—from the museum, to Ted's Diner, to the most recent rendezvous at Deco Bar. Your interactions with Thomas could not be witnessed because of the danger that he would notice my presence.

But you have proven to be an accomplished liar.

In fact, you snuck into my survey in a move that appeared entrepreneurial but was actually duplicitous.

All of your revelations are reviewed again, this time through a new lens: You lied to your parents about the circumstances of Becky's accident. You sleep with men you barely know. You claim that a respected theater director crossed unwanted sexual lines with you.

You hold so many disturbing secrets, Jessica.

Your life could be destroyed if they were released.

Despite your promises of honesty, you continued to lie to me after you became Subject 52. You confessed that Thomas *did* quickly respond to your initial text suggesting a date right after you encountered him at Ted's Diner, but that you withheld this information from me. And the twenty-two-minute meeting between you and my husband at Deco Bar, for what should have been a five-minute conversation, remains a loose thread, Jessica.

What did you leave out? And why?

Your desire to go home for the holidays and remain there seemed quite abrupt. After that attempt was thwarted, you suggested that you might join Lizzie's family for Christmas. But you lied about that, too, when you falsely claimed that Lizzie had invited you to the family farm in Iowa for the holidays.

Something is deeply amiss, Jessica.

Your motives for wanting to flee must be scrutinized.

You wrote something quite telling during your very first session. The words form in the mind, one by one, just as they appeared on the screen as you typed, unaware that you were being watched via the laptop's camera: *When it comes down to it, I've only got myself to rely on.*

Self-preservation is a powerful motivator, more reliably so than money or empathy or love.

A hypothesis forms.

It *is* possible that the tenor of your meetings with my husband was markedly different from what you described.

Perhaps Thomas covets you.

You know the truth about your role in this experiment.

Why would you contaminate the results?

You understood that significantly more would be asked of you if you continued in my morality study. Maybe you feel as if it is too much.

You clearly want to be released from our entanglement. Did you reason that the best way to escape would be by creating a false narrative, one that would provide the resolution you think I want? One that would free you from any future involvement?

You could be congratulating yourself right now on having scored so much—gifts, money, even a luxurious Florida vacation for your family—before cunningly devising a way to move on with your life.

You might be so focused on your own self-interest that you are ignoring the wreckage you are leaving in your wake.

How dare you, Jessica?

Twenty years ago, my younger sister, Danielle, was faced with moral temptation. More recently, so was Katherine April Voss. These two young women chose poorly.

Both of their deaths can be attributed to direct results of those ethical breakdowns.

You were brought in to serve as a morality test for my husband, Jessica.

But perhaps it is you who failed it.

CHAPTER
SIXTY

Sunday, December 23

I KEEP COMING BACK to this one question. My gut tells me I have to unravel it until I expose the secret buried at its core: Why did Thomas fabricate an affair with Lauren, the boutique owner, when he's so desperate to hide the real one he had with April?

I can't walk away from this, even though I have my file. Dr. Shields isn't going to let me go until she's through with me. All I can do to protect myself is try to figure out what happened to April, so I can keep it from happening to me.

Lauren told me to call the police if I was frightened of Thomas. But what could I say?

I pursued a married man. I even slept with him. Oh, and his wife hired me; she kind of knew about it. And by the way, I think one or both of them might be involved with this other girl's suicide.

It sounds preposterous; they'd think I was nuts.

So instead of phoning the police, I make a few other calls.

First I dial Thomas's cell. I barrel in without preamble: "Why are you pretending you slept with Lauren when all you did was buy clothes at her boutique?"

I hear his sharp intake of breath.

"You know what, Jess? I've got Lydia's notes on April, and you have

Lydia's notes on you. So we're even. I don't need to answer your questions. Good luck."

Then he hangs up.

I immediately hit *Redial*.

"Actually, you only have the first thirteen pages from April's file. I never sent you the last five. So you do need to answer me. But in person." I need to be able to read his face, too.

The line is so quiet that I worry he's hung up on me again.

Then he says, "I'm in my office. Meet me here in an hour."

After he gives me the address, I press *End Call* and pace, thinking hard. His tone was impossible to decipher. He didn't sound angry; there wasn't even any strong emotion in his voice. But maybe he's one of those guys who is most dangerous when he seems calm, the way it's always quiet just before a thunderclap erupts.

An office seems like a safe enough place. If Thomas wants to hurt me, wouldn't he pick another location, one that isn't linked to him? But it's Sunday, and I don't know if the building will be empty.

Lauren said she thought Thomas seemed like a nice guy. That was my impression of him, too, both at the museum and on the night we hooked up. But I can't ever shake the memory of what happened the last time I was alone in an office with a man who seemed nice.

So I make a second call, this one to Noah, and ask him to meet me outside Thomas's building in ninety minutes.

"Everything okay?" he asks.

"I'm not sure," I say honestly. "I have an appointment with someone I don't know that well and I'd just feel better if you were there to pick me up after."

"Who is it?"

"His name is Dr. Cooper. It's kind of a work thing. I'll explain it all when I see you, okay?"

Noah sounds a little dubious, but he agrees. I think of all the things I've done—given him a fake name, told him several times I've had weird or stressful days, expressed concerns about trusting others—and I promise myself I really will tell him as much as I can. It's not just because he deserves it. I'd feel safer having someone else know what's going on.

As I feared, the hallway is empty as I approach Thomas's office at 1:30 P.M.

At the end of the corridor, I find Suite 114. There's a plaque on the side of the entrance listing his full name, Thomas Cooper, and those of a few other therapists.

I lift my hand. Before I can knock, the door swings open.

I instinctively take a step back.

I'd forgotten how big he is. His frame fills most of the entryway, blotting out the weak winter sunlight streaming in from the window behind him.

"This way," Thomas says, stepping aside and jerking his head toward what must be his private office.

I wait for him to go first; I don't want him behind me. But he isn't moving.

After a few seconds, he seems to comprehend my concern and he abruptly turns and strides through the waiting area.

As soon as I'm inside his office, he closes the door.

The space seems to shrink, hemming me in. My body clenches up as panic tears through me. No one can help me if Thomas is truly dangerous. There are three doors between me and the outside world.

I'm trapped, just like I was with Gene.

So many times I've fantasized about what I would do if I could relive that night in the quiet theater, after everyone else had left: I've beaten myself up for just standing there, frozen, while Gene got off on my vulnerability and fear.

Now I'm in a situation that feels eerily similar.

And I'm paralyzed again.

But Thomas merely walks around his desk and sits in the leather rolling chair.

He looks surprised when I remain standing.

"Have a seat," he says, gesturing to a chair facing him. I sink into it, trying to steady my breathing.

"My boyfriend is waiting outside," I choke out.

Thomas raises an eyebrow. "Okay," he says, sounding so nonplussed that I know he isn't planning to do anything harmful to me.

My terror continues to ebb away as I take in Thomas's appearance: He looks exhausted. He's wearing an untucked flannel shirt, and he's unshaven. When he takes off his glasses to rub his eyes, I notice they're red-rimmed, the way mine always get when I haven't slept enough.

He puts his glasses back on and steeples his hands. His next words come as a surprise.

"Look, I can't make you trust me," he says. "But I swear, I'm trying to protect you from Lydia. You're already in so deep."

I break eye contact with him and glance around the room, trying to get clues about who Thomas is. I've been in Dr. Shields's office and the town house, and both of those places reflect her cool, remote elegance.

Thomas's office is so different. Beneath my feet is a soft-looking rug, and the wooden shelves are overflowing with books of all shapes and sizes. On his desk is a clear jar filled with butterscotch candy in yellow wrappers. Beside it is one of those coffee mugs with an inspirational quote wrapped around its perimeter. I stare at the two words in the middle of the quote: *love you.*

It sparks a question. "Do you even love your wife?" I ask.

He dips his head. "I thought I did. I wanted to. I tried to . . ." His voice sounds a little ragged. "But I couldn't."

I believe him; I was entranced by Dr. Shields, too, when I first met her.

In my pocket, I feel my phone vibrate. I ignore it, but I imagine Dr. Shields holding her sleek, silver phone to her ear, waiting for me to answer. The tiny lines in her exquisite face, the face that appears carved from flawless white marble, are deepening.

"People get divorced all the time. Why didn't you simply end it?" I ask.

Then I remember what he told me: *You can't just leave someone like her.*

"I tried that. But to her, our marriage was perfect, and she refused to see that we had any problems," Thomas says. "So you're right, I did make up the affair with that woman from the boutique—Lauren. I picked her almost on a whim. She seemed believable, like someone I'd want to sleep with. I deliberately texted Lydia and pretended it was meant for Lauren."

"You sent your wife a fake text?" How desperate he must have been, I think.

Thomas looks down at his hands. "I thought for sure Lydia would leave me if I cheated on her. It seemed like an easy way out. She wrote a whole book titled *The Morality of Marriage*. I never believed she'd insist on trying to repair our relationship."

He still hasn't answered a basic question: Why didn't he just admit he had the affair with April?

So I ask him.

He picks up his mug and takes a sip, his fingers covering up most of the words in the quote. Maybe he's trying to buy time.

Then he puts it down. But the words facing me are different because he twisted the position of the mug when he moved it: *take is equal.*

Like a jigsaw puzzle coming together, the entire line blooms in my mind: *And in the end, the love you take is equal to the love you make.*

I was right: Thomas must have sung that line by the Beatles to April on the night when they were together. That's how she discovered the song she listened to with her mother.

"April was so young," Thomas finally says. "I thought it might be hard for Lydia to know I'd chosen a twenty-three-year-old." He appears even sadder now than he did when I first came in; I swear I can see him fighting back tears. "I didn't know at first how damaged April was. I figured we both wanted a one-night thing . . ."

He looks at me meaningfully, and I know what he isn't saying: *Like you and I did.*

I feel my cheeks grow warm. Inside my pocket, my phone vibrates again. Somehow it feels more insistent now.

"How did April become Subject 5?" I ask, trying to ignore the buzzing against my leg. My skin feels prickly, like the vibration is spreading out across my entire body. Like it's trying to consume me.

I glance to my left, at the closed door to Thomas's office. I didn't see him lock it. I don't recall him bolting the main door to the suite after he let me in, either.

Thomas no longer feels like a threat to me. But I can sense danger lurking nearby, like the curl of smoke from an approaching fire.

"April got really attached to me, for some reason," Thomas continues. "She called and texted a bunch of times. I tried to let her down gently . . . She knew from the beginning I was married. A couple weeks later, it stopped as abruptly as it all started. I figured she'd moved on, met somebody new."

He pinches his forehead between his thumb and index finger, like he has a headache.

Hurry, I think to myself urgently. I can't identify why, but my instincts are telling me to get out of this office quickly.

Thomas takes another sip from his mug before he continues. "Then Lydia came home and told me about this new subject in her study, a young woman who'd had a traumatic reaction to the experience. We talked about how the survey must have triggered something, perhaps a repressed memory. *I* was the one who encouraged Lydia to talk to her in person, to help her. I didn't know it was April. Lydia only ever called her Subject 5." Thomas lets out a harsh laugh that seems to encapsulate all the snarled, complicated feelings he must hold. "I didn't realize April and Subject 5 were the same person until a private investigator contacted Lydia about her file."

I'm barely breathing. I don't want to interrupt him; I'm desperate to hear what else he knows. But I'm also acutely aware of the phone against my leg. I'm waiting for the buzzing to start up again.

"I've had some time to piece it together," Thomas finally says. "And my best guess is that April figured out who my wife was. Then she signed up for the study because it was a link to me. Or maybe she felt like Lydia was her competition and she wanted to learn more about her."

My head jerks to the right, toward the window. What was it that commanded my attention? Maybe a muffled noise, or a movement on the sidewalk or street outside. The blinds are angled, so I can only catch shards of the view. I can't tell if Noah is there.

Whatever danger I'm sensing does not appear to be emanating from Thomas. I believe his story: He wasn't in contact with April in the weeks before her death.

It isn't just blind faith or my instincts that tells me this, however. I've read April's file a half dozen times by now. And I've learned a key piece of information about the relationship between Dr. Shields and April: I know some of what happened between them on the night that April died.

Dr. Shields wrote about it in script that looks more jagged than her usual graceful handwriting. Their final encounter is documented on a page in the file right before April's obituary, the one I looked up online. And I captured it all in photographs on the phone in my pocket, the one that feels unusually warm right now. The one I keep expecting to erupt again at any moment.

You disappointed me deeply, Katherine April Voss, Dr. Shields wrote. *I thought I knew you. You were treated with such warmth and care, and you were given so much—intense attention to your mental well-being, carefully selected gifts, even encounters like the one tonight when you came to my home and perched on a kitchen stool, sipping a glass of wine while the slim gold bangle I'd taken off my arm and given to you slid down your wrist.*

You were invited in.

Then you made the revelation that shattered everything, that put you in a completely different light: I made a mistake. I slept with a married man, just some guy I met at a bar. It only happened once.

Your big eyes filled with tears. Your lower lip quivered. As though you deserved sympathy for this transgression.

You were seeking absolution, but it was not granted. How could it be? There is a barricade that separates moral individuals from immoral ones. These rules are very clear. You were told you crossed that barrier, and that you would never be welcomed into the town house again.

You had revealed your true, flawed self. You weren't the guileless young woman you initially presented yourself to be.

The conversation continued. At the conclusion of it, you were given a farewell hug.

Twenty minutes later, all traces of you were gone. Your wineglass was washed and dried and replaced in a cabinet. The remnants of the Brie and grapes were tipped into the trash can. Your stool was realigned into its proper position.

It was as if you'd never been here at all. As if you no longer existed.

I hadn't even skimmed Dr. Shields's written words the first time I'd seen them. I was too worried about getting out of her town house before she arrived home. But later, in the safety of my apartment, I'd read them again and again.

Dr. Shields's notes don't indicate that she knows the married man April confessed to sleeping with was Thomas. She seems to believe that

April entered her study with no ulterior motives, when it's obvious to me now that April was obsessed with Thomas, obsessed enough to find a way into Dr. Shields's research project. Then she seemed to grow attached to Dr. Shields. April was a lost girl; she seemed to be searching for someone or something to hold on to.

It seems strange that April revealed she had an affair with an unnamed married man to Dr. Shields, that she tiptoed up to the brink of an explosive disclosure. But I kind of get it, given the magnetic pull Dr. Shields exudes.

Maybe April was seeking absolution, the same way I sought it from Dr. Shields when I told her my secrets. Perhaps April also thought that if the woman who spent her career studying moral choices offered her a pardon, then April wasn't so flawed after all.

"I'll text you the missing pages," I say to Thomas. "Can you answer one more question, though?"

He nods.

I think about the night I watched them under the restaurant awning. "I saw you with Dr. Shields one evening. You seemed so in love. Why did you act like that?"

"Her file on April," he says. "I wanted to get in the house so I could see it. If there was something April said that could link her to me, I was worried Lydia might realize it later and it could send her over the edge. But I could never find it, not until I saw it on her desk."

"There's nothing in there that ties you to April," I say.

"Thank you," he whispers.

But that may not be true, I realize. There's one tiny detail, floating just beyond the edge of my consciousness. It's like a helium-filled balloon dancing on a high ceiling. I can't grasp it no matter how hard I try. It has something to do with April; it's an image or memory or detail.

I glance at the window again as I pull my phone out of my pocket. I'll go back and study her file afresh once I leave here, I think. Now I just need to get out.

I look down at my phone to pull up the final five photographs of April's file. That's when I see the missed calls are from BeautyBuzz. There are four, including two voice mail messages.

Did I forget about a job? I wonder. But I'm certain I'm not scheduled to work until five P.M.

Why would the company be so frantic to get ahold of me?

I quickly tap on the missing photos and text them to Thomas. "Now
you have everything," I say as I stand up. He's already bent over his
phone, intently studying them.

I play the message from BeautyBuzz. My eye is drawn back to the
window. I think I can see the shadows of people passing by again, but
I'm not sure.

The voice mail isn't from the program coordinator, like I thought.
It's from the owner of the company, a woman I've never spoken to before.

"Jessica, please call me at once."

Her voice is clipped. Angry.

I press *Play* to listen to the second one.

"Jessica, you are being terminated, effective immediately. You need
to return this message as soon as possible. We've learned you have
violated the noncompete clause you signed when you joined our company. We have the names of two women you recently solicited as freelance clients while using the BeautyBuzz name. Our lawyers will file a
cease and desist if you continue."

I look up at Thomas.

"She got me fired," I whisper.

Dr. Shields must have called BeautyBuzz and told them about Reyna
and Tiffani.

I think about my rent that's due in a week, Antonia's bills, my father's
job loss. I imagine Becky's sweet, trusting face as she learns the only
home she has ever had is about to disappear.

The walls are closing in on me again.

Is Dr. Shields going to get me sued if I don't do what she wants?

I think about what she wrote in her notes on me: *You belong to me.*

My throat is tight, and my eyes are burning. A scream is trapped in
my throat.

"What happened?" Thomas asks as he rises from behind his desk.

But I can't answer him. I burst through the office door and then into
the empty waiting room, and I tear down the hallway. I need to call the

owner of BeautyBuzz and try to explain. I need to talk to my parents and make sure they're still safe. Could Dr. Shields do something to them? Maybe she isn't planning to pay for their trip after all; she could have found out my credit-card number and used it for the deposit.

If she so much as *touches* Becky, I'll kill her, I think frantically.

I'm gasping and crying by the time I throw open the main door of the building and run outside. The icy winter air feels like a slap against my face.

I spin around on the sidewalk, frantically looking around for Noah. Inside my pocket, my phone starts to vibrate again. I want to rip it out and throw it against the sidewalk.

I don't see Noah anywhere. My tears stream down harder. I was beginning to think I could depend on him.

But now I realize I can't.

I'm about to turn around when I glimpse a puffy blue coat a block away. My heart soars. It's him. I recognize the back of his head; I already know his walk.

I start to run, weaving past people.

"Noah!" I call out.

He doesn't turn around, so I keep running. I'm panting and it's hard to pull enough oxygen into my lungs, but I force my legs to go faster.

"Noah!" I cry again when I'm closer. I want to collapse into his strong arms and tell him everything. He'll help me; I know he will.

He whips around.

The expression on his face stops me as abruptly as if I've slammed into a brick wall.

"I was starting to fall for you," he says, biting off every word. "But now I know who you really are."

I take a step toward him, but he holds up a hand. His mouth is a grim line. His soft brown eyes are hard.

"Don't," he says. "I don't ever want to see you again."

"What?" I gasp.

But he just turns around and keeps walking, moving farther and farther away from me.

CHAPTER
SIXTY-ONE

Sunday, December 23

MY PREMATURE RETREAT TO BED allowed for a particularly early rising time this morning.

It will be a busy day.

When my phone is turned on, it reveals a new text from Thomas. At 11:06 P.M. last night, he reported that his patient was stable at Bellevue and he apologized again for the truncated evening.

A reply was sent at 8:02 A.M.: *I understand. What are your plans for today?*

He wrote that he was en route to his squash game and breakfast at Ted's Diner. *I'll catch up on paperwork this afternoon*, he wrote. *Movie tonight?*

The response he received: *Perfect.*

His morning activities are just as he described: He exits the gym, dines at Ted's, and heads directly to his office.

Everything changes at precisely 1:34 P.M.

That is when you are spotted striding down the sidewalk, a shopping bag in hand.

You also disappear into Thomas's office building.

Oh, Jessica. You have made a grave mistake.

Do victims have the right to take retribution into their own hands?

In your second computer session, you sat in the NYU classroom and answered this query in the affirmative, Jessica. You barely hesitated. You didn't fiddle with your rings or look up at the ceiling while you thought; you quickly brought your fingertips to the keyboard and formulated your response.

How do you feel about this question now?

Finally, there is concrete evidence of your staggering betrayal.

What are you doing in there with my husband, Jessica?

Whether you are enmeshed in a physical affair is almost immaterial at this point. You two are colluding behind my back. The treachery you have consistently exhibited should have been a warning sign.

By now you have created so many degrees of deception, such layered deceit, that you are enmeshed in a salacious subterfuge from which there can be no return.

"Lady, are you okay?"

A passerby holds out a paper napkin. It is regarded with confusion.

"Looks like you cut your lip," he says.

After a moment, the napkin is pulled away. The metallic taste of blood lingers in my mouth. Later, ice will be applied to reduce the swelling. But for now, lip balm is located in my makeup bag.

It is an exact replica of the lip balm you left in my town house last week, the one that infuses your lips with a rosy, beguiling shade.

The tube bears the logo BeautyBuzz. It is manufactured by your employer, Jessica.

The phone number of the company is quite easy to obtain.

While you are conspiring with my husband, a phone call is placed.

When one speaks with authority, people listen. The receptionist who answers transfers my call to a manager, who in turn promises to reach the company owner to convey the information immediately.

Apparently, BeautyBuzz takes its noncompete clause quite seriously.

You keep mentioning the desire to escape town for the holidays.

You are not going anywhere, Jessica.

But it seems that you will be able to enjoy some unexpected time off from work after all.

Should a punishment always fit the crime?

The loss of your job is not a severe enough punishment.

But a more fitting one presents itself shortly, while you are still ensconced in my husband's office.

A young man in a puffy blue coat accented with red zippers approaches and pauses on the corner next to Thomas's building. He looks around, as if he is waiting for someone.

He is instantly familiar; he is the one you embraced so warmly the other night. The one you kept hidden from me.

While you conduct your assignation with my husband, a spontaneous, parallel tête-à-tête occurs on the sidewalk just outside Thomas's office.

Wouldn't you agree that it seems just?

"I'm Dr. Lydia Shields," he is greeted.

It is vital that my tone and facial expression appear somber. Professional. A tinge regretful that it has come to this. "Are you here for the intervention for Jessica Farris?"

Jessica, your paramour seems quite startled at first. "What?" he says.

Once he confirms that he has come to this destination to meet you, credentials are established. A business card is offered. Still, he requires convincing.

It is explained to him that the other participants have already departed, and that Dr. Thomas Cooper, your longtime therapist, is still in his office trying to reason with you.

"Her paranoia and anxiety typically respond to treatment," he is told. "Unfortunately, her destructive behavior is so pervasive and persistent that the typical patient confidentiality must be compromised in order to protect those who might be harmed."

It is evidence of how smitten Noah is with you that it takes three detailed examples of your deceitful nature to even get him to begin to consider that the woman being described is, in fact, you.

Your behavior of late is detailed: Your recent job termination due to your ethical violations. Your dangerous visit to a drug dealer's apartment. Your habitual one-night stands, often with married men and using a different persona.

Noah winces at your last misdeed, so that dictates the necessary direction for the remainder of the conversation.

Noah is wounded.

It is time to home in for the kill.

Concrete evidence is more persuasive than anecdotal testimony, which could be dismissed as heresy.

The text you sent earlier this month is retrieved on my phone and shown to Noah.

Dr. Shields, I flirted but he said he was happily married. He went up to his room and I'm in the hotel lobby.

"Why would she send you that?" Noah asks.

He appears stunned. He is cycling through denial. His next stage will be anger.

"I specialize in compulsions, including those of a sexual nature," he is told. "I have been consulting with Dr. Cooper on this aspect of Jessica's personality."

Noah is still teetering on the edge of disbelief. So another text is pulled up and displayed. You sent it merely two nights ago, just before you left to see Thomas at Deco Bar. The same evening you met Noah at Peachtree Grill.

I'm leaving in a few minutes to meet T. Should I offer to buy him a drink, since I'm the one who asked him out?

The day of the text transmission is clearly visible: Friday. A thumb covers the rest of the text exchange as the phone is held out for Noah's perusal.

Noah grows pale. "But I saw her that night," he says. "*We* had a date."

Now surprise is feigned. "Oh, are you the one she met at Peachtree Grill? She told me about that, too. She actually felt a little guilty that she had seen another man right before she went out with you."

His anger comes on swiftly, Jessica.

"She is a very self-destructive young woman," Noah is told as his face transforms. "And unfortunately, her narcissistic personality—while enchanting at first—renders her sadly unredeemable."

Noah walks away, shaking his head.

Not two minutes later, you burst out of Thomas's building and chase after Noah.

After he rebuffs you, you stand on the sidewalk, staring forlornly after him.

The shopping bag is still in your hand.

Now the logo of the closed eyelids is visible. It is strikingly familiar.

Ah, Jessica, how industrious of you. So you have visited Blink, too.

You must think you are so cunning. Perhaps you have even learned the truth about Lauren, not the story Thomas concocted.

Were you surprised to learn that my husband never had an affair with Lauren?

You can't possibly believe the person who knows Thomas best, his loving wife of seven years, accepted that pathetic fabrication, can you?

His affair with the boutique store owner was determined to be an invention barely a week after his "accidental" text arrived on my phone: When Lauren was sought out and asked for assistance in selecting my outfits for a weekend getaway, she recommended several items, including the unstructured dresses she'd picked up on her recent buying trip to Indonesia.

A brief conversation ensued concerning her travels.

She revealed that she had just spent a week in Bali and another in Jakarta, arriving back in the States only three days prior to my visit to her boutique.

It is impossible that my husband could have had plans to meet her, both on the date when he texted *See you tonight, gorgeous,* and on the night he claimed their affair had begun, when he said she'd slid into a seat across from him at a hotel bar.

His lie was never challenged, however. It needed to remain standing.

Thomas had an excellent reason for trying to camouflage his one-night stand with April by layering the story of another, made-up dalliance over it.

And of course, his wife had an even better reason for hiding her own knowledge of both the counterfeit affair and the real one with April.

Would it come as a surprise to you that I've known the truth about my husband and Subject 5 all along?

Jessica, you may think you have figured everything out. But if you have learned only one thing since becoming Subject 52, it is that you must suspend your assumptions.

It is a pity that you are so distraught. But you brought this on yourself.

Right now you feel all alone.

Not to worry, though. You will be in my company soon enough.

CHAPTER
SIXTY-TWO

Sunday, December 23

HAVE YOU SPOKEN with your family recently, Jessica? Are they enjoying their vacation in Florida?

I stare at the text, feeling the questions sear me.

Dr. Shields took away my job. She took away my boyfriend. What has she done to my parents and Becky?

I'm in bed, my knees pulled up to my chest, Leo beside me. After Noah left me on the corner, I tried calling and texting him, but he didn't respond. Then I did the only thing I could think of: I came home and cried gut-wrenching tears. They've slowed to quieter sobs by the time the message from Dr. Shields comes in.

I never responded to my mother's call last night when I was creeping through Dr. Shields's town house, I think as I sit bolt upright. And she didn't leave a message.

I dial my mom's cell immediately, fighting back panic. The automated voice mail message comes on.

"Mom, please call me right away," I blurt.

I try my dad's cell next. Same thing.

I start to hyperventilate.

Dr. Shields never even told me the name of the resort. My mom phoned right after they arrived, telling me all about their waterfront room and saltwater swimming pool, but she didn't specify where they were staying and I was so thrown by everything going on in my life that I never asked.

How could I have been so careless?

I call my parents again, each in turn.

Then I grab my coat and push my feet into my boots and tear through the door. I run down the stairs, pushing past a neighbor who is carrying a bag of groceries. She gives me a startled glance. I know my mascara is probably smeared and my hair is wild, but I no longer care how I look for Dr. Shields.

I sprint down the street, frantically waving for a cab. One pulls over and I jump into the back. "Hurry, please," I say, giving the driver Dr. Shields's home address.

I still don't have a plan fifteen minutes later when I arrive. I just pound on the door until my hand throbs.

Dr. Shields opens it and looks at me with no surprise, as if she has been expecting me.

"What did you do to them?" I shriek.

"Excuse me?" Dr. Shields responds.

She is flawless, as usual, in her dove-gray top and tailored black slacks. I want to grab her shoulders and shake her.

"I know you did something! I can't reach my parents!"

She steps back. "Jessica, take a deep breath and calm down. We cannot have a conversation like this."

Her tone is a rebuke; it's as if she's dealing with an irrational child.

I'm not going to get anywhere by screaming at her. The only way she'll give me answers is if she thinks it's on her own terms, if she's in control.

So I shove back my anger and fear.

"Can I please come inside so we can talk?" I ask.

She opens the door wider and I follow her inside.

There's classical music playing, and her home is as immaculate as ever. Fresh petunias adorn the glossy wooden table in the entryway, beneath the panel for the alarm system.

I avoid looking at it as I pass.

Dr. Shields leads me to the kitchen and gestures to a stool.

As I slide onto it, I see a platter on the granite counter holds a cluster of violet grapes and a wedge of creamy cheese, as if she has been expecting company. Beside it is a single crystal goblet filled with pale gold liquid.

It's all so proper and precise and insane.

"Where is my family?" I ask, fighting to keep my tone level.

Instead of answering immediately, Dr. Shields walks unhurriedly to a cabinet and withdraws a matching crystal glass. For the first time, she doesn't ask if I want any. Instead, she goes to the refrigerator, takes out a bottle of Chardonnay, and fills the goblet.

She sets it down in front of me as if we're two friends about to share confidences.

I want to scream but I know if I try to rush her, she'll prove her dominance by making me wait even longer.

"Your family is in Florida having a wonderful time, Jessica," she finally says. "Why would you think anything else?"

"Because you sent me that text!" I blurt.

Dr. Shields arches an eyebrow. "All I did was inquire about their vacation," she says. "There is nothing untoward about that, is there?"

She sounds so sincere, but I can see through her act.

"I want to call the resort," I say. My voice is shaking.

"Certainly," Dr. Shields says. "Don't you have the number?"

"You never gave it to me," I shoot back.

She frowns. "The resort name has never been a secret, Jessica. Your family has been there for three days."

"Please," I beg. "Just let me talk to them."

Without a word, Dr. Shields rises and retrieves her phone from the counter. "I have the resort confirmation information here," she says as she scrolls through her e-mails. It seems to take an inordinately long time. Then she recites a number.

I dial it immediately.

"Happy holidays, Winstead Resort and Spa, this is Tina," a woman answers in a singsong voice.

"I need to reach the Farris family," I say urgently.

"Of course, I'll be happy to connect you. May I have a room number?"

"I don't know it," I whisper.

"Just a moment, please."

I stare at Dr. Shields, who meets my gaze with her ice-blue eyes as, incredibly, cheerful Christmas music plays while I'm on hold: *Santa Claus is coming to town.*

Then Dr. Shields edges my glass of wine closer to me.

I can't bring myself to take a sip. I fight back an acute feeling of déjà vu. I was just here a few days ago, confessing that I know Thomas is her husband, but that's not what is prompting the unsettling sensation roiling through me right now.

The music abruptly cuts off.

"I have no record of any guests by that name," the resort operator says.

My body buckles.

My vision swims and I dry heave.

"They're not there?" I cry.

Dr. Shields picks up her glass and takes another delicate sip, and her unconcerned gesture is what unleashes my anger again.

"Where is my family?" I demand again, locking eyes with her. I push back my stool, nearly knocking it over, as I stand up.

She sets her glass down on the counter.

"Oh," Dr. Shields says. "Perhaps the reservation is under my name."

"Shields," I say into the phone urgently. "Try that, please."

Silence stretches across the phone line.

I can feel my pulse throbbing between my ears.

"Ah," says the clerk. "Here it is. I'll connect you now."

My mother answers on the second ring, her voice so familiar and safe that I almost burst into tears again.

"Mom! Are you okay?" I ask.

"Oh my goodness, sweetheart, we are having the best time," she says. "We just got in from the beach. Becky got to pet dolphins—they have a whole program here. Your dad took so many pictures!"

They're safe. She didn't do anything to them. At least not yet.

"You're sure you're all right?"

"Of course! Why wouldn't we be? We do miss you, though. But what a wonderful boss you have to do this for us! You must be very special to her."

I'm so disoriented by now that I can barely manage to end the call and hang up, promising to phone again tomorrow. I can't reconcile my mother's happy chatter with the terrible worry my mind had created.

I put my phone down.

Dr. Shields smiles.

"See?" she says calmly. "They're perfectly fine. Better than fine."

I splay my hands on the hard, cold granite countertop and lean forward, trying to concentrate.

Dr. Shields wants me to think it's all me, that I'm unstable. But I didn't conjure losing my job or losing Noah. Those are absolute facts; I still have the voice mails from BeautyBuzz on my phone. And Noah hasn't responded to me. I'm positive it isn't a coincidence that both things happened while I was in Thomas's office. I can't prove it, but Dr. Shields knows I was with him. Maybe she could have even found out I slept with him; Thomas could have told her to save himself.

She's punishing me.

I feel her hand gently pat my back and I whip around.

"Don't!" I say. "You got me fired. You told BeautyBuzz I was freelancing when I went to Reyna and Tiffani!"

"Slow down, Jessica," Dr. Shields instructs.

She returns to her stool and crosses one long, slender leg over the other. I know what I'm supposed to do, the part she wants me to play, so I sit down on the stool next to her.

"You didn't tell me you lost your job," she says. To an observer, it would look like she's truly concerned: Her brow is furrowed, and her tone is gentle.

"Yeah, someone turned me in for violating my noncompete clause," I say accusingly.

"Hmmm . . ." Dr. Shields taps an index finger against her lips, and then I see the lower one looks slightly swollen, as if it was recently injured. "Didn't you tell me that the boyfriend who was on drugs was so suspicious of you? Is it possible he might have reported you?"

She gives me a slight, Cheshire-cat smile. She has an answer for everything.

But I know she did it. Maybe she didn't give them Reyna and Tiffani's names, but she could have made an anonymous call pretending *she* was a client I'd solicited. I can see her saying something in that fake-concerned voice, like, *Oh, Jessica seemed like such a nice young woman, I hope I don't get her into trouble.*

But then I remember Ricky's insistent questions before I pushed those free cosmetics into Tiffani's hand and fled. I'm certain the tubes had the BeautyBuzz logo on them; all my lip glosses and balms do. It would be easy to track down my employer.

"Jessica, I'm very sorry you lost your job," Dr. Shields says. "However, I certainly did not cause it."

I rub my temples; everything was so clear just a few minutes ago. But now I don't know what to believe.

"I hope you don't mind me saying so, but you look unwell," Dr. Shields remarks. She nudges the platter closer to me. "Have you been eating?"

I haven't, I realize. When I saw Noah on Friday night at Peachtree Grill, he kept trying to tempt me with fried chicken and biscuits, but I only managed a few bites. I don't think I've had anything but coffee and a LUNA bar or two since then.

"But what about Noah?" I say, almost to myself. My voice breaks on his name.

He was happy to hear from me this morning, though he might have thought my request was strange. I keep picturing his hand held up like a barrier, stopping me from getting close.

"Who?"

"The guy I was seeing," I say. "How did you find him?"

Dr. Shields cuts a piece of cheese and puts it on a thin round cracker before handing it to me. I stare down at it and shake my head.

"You never even told me you were dating anyone," Dr. Shields says. "How could I engage in a conversation with somebody I didn't know existed?"

She lets silence hang there for a moment, like she's punctuating her point.

"I have to tell you, Jessica, I am beginning to resent your accusations," she says. "You completed your assignments, for which I paid you. You assured me that Thomas was faithful. So why would I be interfering in your life now?"

Is it possible? I put my head in my hands and try to replay the past few days, but everything is jumbled. Maybe Thomas is the one who has been lying to me. Maybe my own instincts were wrong. They've been off before; I trusted Gene French when I shouldn't have. Maybe I've done the opposite now.

"Have you been sleeping, you poor thing?"

I lift my head. My eyes feel gritty and heavy. She knows I haven't been, like she knew I haven't been eating; she didn't even need to ask.

"I'll be right back," Dr. Shields says. She slips off the stool and disappears. Her footsteps are so light I can't tell where she is in the house.

I'm completely depleted, but it's the kind of tired where I know I won't be able to sleep well tonight. My brain feels thick and sludgy, but my body is jittery.

When Dr. Shields returns she is holding something, but I can't tell what it is. She walks into the kitchen again and pulls out a drawer. I hear a faint rattle, then I see she is transferring a small, oval white pill from a bottle into a Ziploc bag.

She seals the bag, then walks over to me.

"There is no doubt I'm to blame for your state," she says softly. "Clearly, I've pushed you too hard with all of our intense conversations, and then the experiments. I shouldn't have gotten you involved in my personal life. That was unprofessional."

Her words wind around me like one of her cashmere wraps: soft, comforting, and warm.

"You're so strong, Jessica, but you've been under tremendous pressure. Your father's layoff, the post-traumatic stress you've been feeling ever since that night with the theater director, all your financial worries . . . And of course, the guilt over your sister. It must be exhausting."

She presses the bag into my hand. "The holidays can be such a lonely time. This will help you sleep tonight. I shouldn't give you a pill without a prescription, but consider it a last gift."

I look down at it and without even thinking, I say, "Thank you."

It's like she is writing my script, and I'm just reciting the lines now.

Dr. Shields reaches for my mostly full wineglass and dumps the contents in the sink. Then she scrapes the cheese and grapes into the trash can, even though the platter has barely been touched.

The emptied glass. The rind of cheese.

I stare at her as a bolt of energy races through my body.

She isn't looking at me. She's totally absorbed in tidying up, but if she saw my face she'd know something was terribly wrong.

The notes she wrote in April's file swim through my mind: *All traces of you were gone . . . Your wineglass was washed . . . Brie and grapes were tipped into the trash can . . .*

It was as if you'd never been here at all. As if you no longer existed.

I look down at the clear Ziploc bag with the tiny pill in my hand.

An icy fear suffuses my body.

What did you do to her? I think.

I need to get out, now, before she realizes what I know.

"Jessica?"

Dr. Shields is looking directly at me. I hope she mistakes the emotion in my face for despair.

Her voice is low and soothing. "I just want you to know there is no shame in admitting when you can use a little help. Everyone needs an escape sometimes."

I nod. My voice wavers when I speak. "You know, it might be nice to finally get some rest."

I tuck the pill in my purse. Then I push my body off the stool and pick up my coat, forcing myself to move slowly so I don't reveal my panic. Dr. Shields doesn't seem to want to escort me out; she remains in the kitchen, running a sponge over the pristine granite. So I turn and walk toward the front hallway.

With every step, I feel a pricking sensation between my shoulder blades. I finally reach the door and pull it open, then step through and close it gently behind me.

The minute I get home, I pull out the plastic bag and look more closely at the small, oval pill. A number code is easily decipherable on the tablet, so I check it out on a pill identifier website. It's Vicodin, the same prescription drug Mrs. Voss told me April overdosed on in the park.

I now have a pretty clear idea of who gave them to April, and why.

Dr. Shields must know that Thomas slept with April, otherwise she wouldn't have put the pills in April's hand. What I need to figure out is how Dr. Shields got April to swallow them.

I have to go back to the West Village Conservatory Gardens and find the bench near the frozen fountain. The spot April chose for her death must have some significance.

Does Dr. Shields also know that Thomas made up the affair with Lauren from the boutique? If I figured this out, then Dr. Shields, with her falconlike attention to detail, surely has.

How much longer until she discovers my unauthorized encounter with Thomas and all the lies I've told her?

And when she learns I've slept with her husband, what will she do to me?

CHAPTER
SIXTY-THREE

Monday, December 24

ARE YOU GETTING THE DEEP, dreamless rest you so desperately need, Jessica?

There won't be any interruptions. You are utterly alone.

You no longer have work to distract you. And Lizzie is away. Perhaps you had intended to spend Christmas Eve with Noah, but he has retreated to Westchester to be with his family.

As for your family, they are unreachable. This morning the hotel concierge phoned and surprised them with a day-long trip on a sailboat. It is so difficult to get cell phone reception out on the ocean.

Even your new friend Thomas will be occupied.

But those who are surrounded by family and festive activities can feel isolated, too.

Cue the scene: Christmas Eve at the Shields family estate in Litchfield, Connecticut, ninety minutes outside of New York City.

In the grand living room, a fire blazes in the hearth. The delicate Limoges nativity figurines are arranged on the mantel. This year the mother's decorator has chosen white lights and perfect pinecones to accent the tree.

It all looks so beautiful, doesn't it?

The father has uncorked a bottle of Dom Pérignon. Smoked salmon with caviar on crostini are passed.

Stockings lay below the tree. Although there are only four people in the room, there are five stockings.

The extra one has been filled for Danielle, as it has been every year. The custom is to donate to a meaningful charity in her name and place the envelope bearing the check in the stocking. Usually the recipient is Mothers Against Drunk Driving, although Safe Ride and Students Against Destructive Decisions have also been chosen in the past.

Next week will mark the twentieth anniversary of Danielle's death, so the check is a particularly large one.

She would have been thirty-six years old.

She died less than a mile away from this living room.

As the level of champagne in the mother's second glass grows lower, her stories about the younger daughter, her favorite, grow more hyperbolic.

This is another holiday custom.

She winds up a rambling tale about Danielle's summer as a counselor at the country club's day camp.

"She was such a natural with children," the mother ruminates pointlessly. "She would have been the most wonderful mother."

The mother has conveniently forgotten that Danielle reluctantly took the job at the father's insistence and was only hired because the father played golf with the country club director.

Typically, the mother is indulged.

But today a rebuttal is impossible to withhold: "Oh, I'm not sure how much Danielle actually liked those kids. Didn't she call in sick so often that she almost got fired?"

Although an affectionate tone is sought, the words cause the mother to stiffen.

"She *loved* those children," the mother counters. Her cheeks redden.

"More champagne, Cynthia?" Thomas offers. It's an attempt to break the tension that has suddenly infused the room.

The mother is allowed to win the point by having the last word, although she is wrong.

Here is what the mother refuses to accept: Danielle was thoroughly selfish. She took things: A favorite cashmere sweater that was then stretched out, because Danielle wore a size larger. An A-plus paper for my junior-year English class that was stored on a shared home computer and resubmitted under her name the following fall.

And a boyfriend who had pledged to be true to the older sister.

Danielle never suffered consequences for those first two transgressions or so many before them; the father was preoccupied with work and the mother, predictably, excused her.

Perhaps if she had been held responsible for her misdeeds all along, she would still be alive.

Thomas has crossed the room to refill the mother's glass.

"How it is possible that you look younger every year, Cynthia?" he asks, patting her on the arm.

Usually Thomas's attempts at peacemaking feel loving.

Tonight's is perceived as another betrayal.

"I need a glass of water." What is actually needed is an excuse to leave the room. The kitchen feels like a place of refuge.

Over the past twenty years, items in this kitchen have been altered: The new refrigerator contains a built-in dispenser for ice water. The hardwood floor has been replaced by an Italian tile. The dinner plates behind the glass-fronted cabinets are now white with blue trim.

But the side door is exactly the same.

The deadbolt still requires a key to unlock it from the outside. From inside the kitchen, a simple twist of the small oval knob disengages the lock or engages it, depending on which way the knob is turned.

You have never heard this story, Jessica.

No one has. Not even Thomas.

But you must have known you were special to me. That we are inexorably linked. It is one of the reasons why your actions have cut so deeply.

If only *you* had behaved, we might have had a very different relationship.

Because despite all of our superficial differences—in age, socio-economics, educational levels—the most important pivot points in our lifetimes eerily echo. It is as if we were destined to come together. As if our two stories are mirror images.

You locked your younger sister Becky in on that tragic day in August.

I locked my younger sister Danielle out on that tragic night in December.

Danielle often snuck away to meet boys. Her favorite trick was to leave the kitchen door open by disengaging the deadbolt so that she could reenter the house undetected.

Her subterfuge was no concern of mine. Until she went after my boyfriend.

Danielle coveted my things. Ryan was no exception.

Boys fell over Danielle all the time; she was pretty, she was lively, and her sexual boundaries were nearly nonexistent.

But Ryan was different. He was tender and appreciated conversation and quieter nights. He was my first in so many ways.

He broke my heart twice. Initially, when he left me. Then again, a week later, when he started dating my younger sister.

It's remarkable how the simplest of decisions can create a butterfly effect; how a seemingly inconsequential action can cause a tsunami.

An ordinary glass of water, like the one being filled in this kitchen right now, is what began it all on that December night almost exactly twenty years ago.

Danielle was out with Ryan, unbeknownst to our parents. She had disengaged the deadbolt to disguise her late return home.

Danielle never suffered consequences. She was long overdue for one.

A quick, spontaneous twist of the lock meant she would be forced to ring the bell and awaken my parents. My father would be apoplectic; his temper has always been short.

It was impossible to fall asleep that night; the anticipation was too delicious.

From an upstairs window at 1:15 A.M., the headlights of Ryan's Jeep were observed being extinguished halfway up our long, winding driveway. Danielle was spotted slipping across the lawn, toward the direction of the kitchen door.

A thrill suffused my body: How did she feel when the knob refused to yield?

Surely the doorbell would soon sound.

Instead, a minute later, Danielle scurried back to Ryan's car.

Then the Jeep reversed its path down the driveway, with Danielle in the passenger's seat.

How was Danielle going to get out of this? Maybe she'd appear in the morning with some ludicrous excuse, like she'd been sleepwalking. Even my mother wouldn't be able to ignore Danielle's deceit this time.

Unaware that their youngest daughter had stuffed pillows beneath her comforter as a decoy, my parents slept on.

Until a police officer appeared at the door a few hours later.

Ryan had been drinking, which he never did when we were together. His Jeep crashed into a tree at the bottom of our long windy road. They both died in the accident; her instantly, him at the hospital from massive internal trauma.

Danielle had made so many wrong choices that created the circumstances of the accident: Stealing my boyfriend. Drinking vodka five years before she was legally allowed to do so. Sneaking out of the house. Not owning up to her transgression by ringing the doorbell and facing our parents.

The final result of the kitchen door being locked was not anticipated.

But it was merely one in a string of factors that led to her death. Had she altered any of her choices, she could be in the living room right now, perhaps with the grandchildren our mother so desperately wants.

Like your parents, Jessica, mine are only privy to part of the story.

If you knew how tightly we are bound by these dual tragedies, would you have lied to me about Thomas?

There are still questions about your involvement with my husband. But they will be answered tomorrow.

Your parents have been told that you will be spending the holiday with me, and that they should enjoy themselves and not worry if they don't hear from you.

After all, we will be very busy with plans of our own.

CHAPTER

SIXTY-FOUR

Monday, December 24

I DIDN'T NOTICE the narrow silver plaque affixed to the bench when I met Thomas here less than a week ago; it was too dark.

But now, as the midafternoon sun hits it, I see the gleam of the reflective memorial.

Her full name and dates of birth and death are engraved in a graceful font, followed by one line. Dr. Shields's silvery voice reads the inscription in my mind: *Katherine April Voss, Who surrendered too soon.*

Dr. Shields installed the plaque here. I know it.

It bears her trademark: Understated. Elegant. Menacing.

This quiet spot deep within the West Village Conservatory Gardens is composed of concentric circles: the frozen fountain is in the middle. Ringing it are a half dozen wooden benches. And surrounding the benches is a walking path.

I stand with my arms encircling myself, too, as I stare at the bench where April died.

Since I left Dr. Shields's town house last night, I've pored over my file, and April's, again and again. I remember the line Dr. Shields wrote about me, *This process can set you free. Surrender to it,* in a script that looks not unlike the message adorning the plaque.

I shiver, even though in the daytime, these frozen gardens aren't so spooky. I've passed several people out for strolls, and the laughter of children not too far away carries through the crisp air. In the distance, an elderly woman in a bright green knitted hat pushes a small shopping cart. She's heading my way but moving slowly.

Still, I feel unnerved, and utterly alone.

I was so certain answers would be contained in Dr. Shields's notes.

But the missing piece of the jigsaw puzzle, the one I was sure I'd seen in April's file but couldn't pinpoint, remains elusive.

The elderly woman is closer now, her slow, heavy footsteps bringing her to the edge of the sitting area.

I rub my eyes, and yield to the temptation of a bench. I don't choose April's, though. I sit on the one next to it.

I'm more tired than I've ever been.

I slept for only a few hours last night, and my uneasy rest was jarred by nightmares: Ricky lunging at me. Becky falling into a swimming pool in Florida and drowning. Noah walking away.

Taking Dr. Shields's pill was never an option, though. I'm through accepting her gifts.

I massage my temples, trying to ease the pounding in my head.

The woman in the green hat takes a seat on the bench one over from mine. April's bench. She digs into her cart and pulls out a loaf of Wonder bread with bright polka-dot packaging. She begins tearing a slice into little pieces and tossing them onto the ground. Instantly, as if they've been waiting for her, a dozen or so birds descend.

I pull my eyes away from them as they flutter around the food.

If the clue isn't in the notes, maybe I can find it by retracing April's footsteps. Immediately before she came to this Conservatory, April sat on a stool and conversed with Dr. Shields in her kitchen, just as I did last night.

I visualize other locations where our paths have intersected: April and I both hovered over keyboards in the NYU classroom, letting Dr. Shields probe our innermost thoughts. We probably even sat at the same desk.

The two of us were then invited into Dr. Shields's office, where we perched on the love seat, allowing our secrets to be teased out of us.

And of course, April and I each met Thomas at a bar, and felt his heated gaze, before bringing him to our homes.

The old lady continues tossing bread out for the birds.

"Mourning doves," she says. "They mate for life, you know."

She must be talking to me, because there's nobody else around.

I nod.

"Want to feed them?" she offers, walking over and extending a fresh slice of bread toward me.

"Sure," I say absently, taking it and tearing off a few bits to scatter.

Other places April and I have both been: Her bedroom at her parent's apartment, the one with the ragged teddy bear still atop her comforter. And there was a photograph of the Insomnia Cookies storefront near Amsterdam Avenue that I recognized in her Instagram feed. I've stopped in there before, too, for snickerdoodle or double chocolate mint cookies.

Obviously, we've also both visited this garden.

I wouldn't even have known of April's existence if Thomas hadn't invited me here to warn me about his wife.

Thomas.

I frown, thinking about how so much imploded—my job, my relationship with Noah—while I sat in a chair across from Thomas's desk and he talked about the fake affair he concocted with the woman from the boutique.

Thomas's office is one place I've been that April never frequented; Thomas said he only met with April on that night that ended in her apartment. Although, if she was really obsessed with him, she may have looked up the location of his workplace.

I toss out the last of my bread.

There's something tugging at the edges of my mind. Something that has to do with Thomas's office.

A mourning dove flutters past me, fracturing my thoughts. The small bird lands on April's bench, by the old lady, and perches above the silver plaque.

I stare.

Adrenaline surges through my body, wiping away my exhaustion.

April's name in that flowing script. The dates of her birth and death. The dove. I've seen it all before.

I lean forward, my breath quickening.

I realize where it was: on her funeral program, the one Mrs. Voss gave me.

I can almost feel my fingertips closing around the thing I've been hunting. My pulse hitches.

I grow very still as I reconsider a fact that has always seemed strange: Thomas faked an affair with some inconsequential woman to cover up his encounter with April. He was also desperate to get April's folder; desperate enough to find a way to sneak me into the town house while he distracted Dr. Shields.

The clue that has been dancing around the edges of my consciousness was never in the folder, though.

I reach into my purse and pull out the funeral program that Mrs. Voss gave me, the one bearing April's name and the sketch of the dove.

I slowly unfold it, smoothing out the paper.

There's one vital difference between it and the scene on the bench just a few feet away from me.

It's like when I was sent to the bar at the Sussex Hotel and I talked to two men: The detail that distinguished them, the wedding ring, was the one that really mattered.

The quote on the bench is different from the quote on the funeral program.

I read it on the program again, even though I know the line from the Beatles song by heart:

And in the end, the love you take is equal to the love you make.

If Thomas had sung those words on the night he and April had met, she wouldn't have asked her mother about the line's origin. She would have known they were lyrics from a song.

But if she had merely seen the quote on his coffee mug, as I had, her curiosity might have been piqued.

I close my eyes and try to remember the exact layout of Thomas's office. It contained a few chairs. But no matter which one a visitor claimed, they would have a clear view of his desk.

April *had* been in Thomas's office, the one just blocks away from Insomnia Cookies.

But she didn't go there to stalk him.

There's only one other reason that could explain it, and also answer the question of why Thomas went to such lengths to conceal their one-night stand. Why he's still so terrified of anyone finding out.

Mrs. Voss told me that April had been in and out of counseling.

April didn't meet Thomas for the first time at a bar.

April met Thomas when she went to see him for therapy, as a client.

CHAPTER
SIXTY-FIVE

Monday, December 24

ON THE NINETY-MINUTE car ride back to Manhattan, sleep is feigned to avoid conversation with Thomas.

Perhaps he welcomes this: Instead of turning on the radio, he drives in silence, his stare fixed straight ahead. His hands grip the steering wheel. Thomas's rigid posture is atypical, too. During long rides, he usually sings along to the music and taps out the beat on his thigh.

When he pulls up in front of the town house, my awakening is simulated; a blinking of the eyes, a quiet yawn.

There is no discussion about the sleeping arrangements for tonight. By mutual, unspoken agreement, Thomas will stay at his rental apartment.

Brief good-byes are exchanged, along with a perfunctory kiss.

The hum of his engine fades as his car moves farther and farther away.

Then there is only a deep, desolate silence in the town house.

The new deadbolt requires a key to unlock the door from the outside.

But from the inside, a turn of the oval knob is all that is required to engage the lock.

———

One year ago, Christmas Eve unfolded so differently: After our return from Litchfield, Thomas built a fire in the hearth and insisted that we each open a gift. He was like a young boy, his eyes shining, as he selected the perfect package to place in my hands.

His wrapping was elaborate but messy, with too much Scotch tape and ribbons.

His presents were always heartfelt.

This one was a first edition of my favorite Edith Wharton book.

Three nights ago, after you reported that Thomas had rebuffed your advances at Deco Bar, hope swelled; it seemed this sweet ritual could continue. An original photograph of the Beatles by Ron Galella had been purchased, framed, and carefully encased in layers of tissues and bright paper for Thomas.

Now it sits by the white poinsettia in the living room.

The holidays are the most wrenching time to be alone.

A wife regards the flat, rectangular present that will not be unwrapped tonight after all.

A mother stares at the stocking bearing the name Danielle that will never be opened by her daughter.

And a different mother experiences her first Christmas without her only child, the daughter who took her life six months ago.

Regret feels more pronounced in the stillness.

All it takes is a few taps of my fingertips against the computer's keyboard. Then, a text is sent to Mrs. Voss:

In honor of April's memory, a holiday donation has been made to the American Foundation for Suicide Prevention. Thinking of you. Sincerely, Dr. Shields.

The gift isn't meant to appease Mrs. Voss, who is desperate to see the file labeled KATHERINE APRIL VOSS. The contribution is merely a spontaneous gesture.

April's mother is not alone in craving the story of what happened in April's final hours: An investigator has formally requested my records, and threatened the possibility of a subpoena. Thomas, too, exhibited excessive curiosity about April's file after he was informed that the Voss family had hired a private detective.

Because the absence of notes from our last encounter would be suspicious, a truncated version of them was created. They held the truth; this was critical, given the slim possibility that April might have called or texted a friend just before her death, but the accounting of our interaction was much softer, and less detailed:

You disappointed me deeply, Katherine April Voss. You were invited in . . . Then you made the revelation that shattered everything, that put you in a completely different light: I made a mistake. I slept with a married man . . . *You were told you would never be welcomed into the town house again . . . The conversation continued. At the conclusion of it, you were given a farewell hug . . .*

The substitute notes were created immediately after Subject 5's funeral service.

It is understandable that her mother covets them.

But no one will ever be able to view the true recording of what happened that evening.

Just like April, those notes no longer exist.

A single, lit match devoured those pages from my yellow legal pad. Flames greedily consumed my words, lapping at the blue-inked cursive.

Before those notes turned to ash, here is what they contained:

SUBJECT 5/ *June 8, 7:36 P.M.*

April knocks on the door of the town house six minutes after the appointed time.

This is not uncharacteristic; she has a relaxed approach to punctuality.

Chablis, a cluster of purple grapes, and a wedge of Brie are offered in the kitchen.

April perches on a stool, eager to discuss her upcoming interview at a small public relations firm. She gives me a printout of her résumé and requests advice about how to explain her somewhat checkered job history.

After a few minutes of encouraging conversation, my slim gold bangle, the one April has repeatedly admired, is slid onto her wrist. "For confidence," she is told. "Keep it."

The tenor of the evening abruptly changes.

April breaks eye contact. She stares down at her lap.

At first it seems she is overcome with positive emotion.

But her voice wobbles: "I feel like this job will give me a fresh start."

"You deserve one," she is told. Her wineglass is topped off.

She slides the bangle up and down on her forearm. "You're so good to me." But her tone doesn't contain gratitude; instead something more nuanced infuses it.

Something not immediately identifiable.

Before it can be discerned, April drops her face into her hands and begins to sob.

"I'm sorry," she says through her tears. "It's that guy I told you about . . ."

She is obviously referring to the older man she brought home from a bar weeks ago, and grew obsessed with. April's unhealthy fixation has already been managed through hours of informal counseling; her regression is disappointing.

My impatience has to be hidden: "I thought you were through with all of that."

"I was," April says, her tear-streaked face still lowered.

There must be some unresolved detail that is keeping her from moving on; it is time to unearth it. "Let's go back to the beginning and get you over this man once and for all. You walked into a bar and saw him sitting there, right?" she is prompted. "What happened next?"

April's foot begins to twirl like a propeller. "The thing is . . . I didn't tell you everything," she begins haltingly. She takes a long sip of wine. "I actually met him for the first time when I went to his office for a consult. He's a therapist. I didn't end up seeing him again for counseling, though, it was just that one session."

This is utterly shocking.

A therapist who sleeps with a client, however briefly April was under his care, should lose his license. Clearly, this morally bereft man took advantage of an emotionally fragile young woman who came to him for help.

April looks at my hands, which are clenched into fists. "It was partly my fault," she says quickly. "I pursued him."

April's arm is touched. "No, it was not your fault," she is emphatically told.

She will need more help to recover from her belief that she is to blame. There was an imbalance of power; she was sexually exploited.

But for now she is allowed to continue with the story that weighs so heavily on her.

"And I didn't just bump into him at a bar like I said," she admits. "I had a big crush on him after that initial session. So I . . . I followed him one night after he left his office."

The rest of her description of her encounter with the therapist matches her original telling: She saw him sitting alone at a table for two in a hotel bar; she approached. They ended the evening in bed at her apartment. She phoned and texted him the next day, but he didn't reply for twenty-four hours. When he finally did, it was clear he was no longer interested. She persisted with more phone calls, texts, and invitations to meet. He was polite but never wavered.

April recounts her story choppily, with pauses in between her sentences, as if she is choosing each word with great care.

"He is an abhorrent person," April is told. "It doesn't matter who initiated things. He took advantage of you and violated your trust. What he did bordered on criminal."

April shakes her head. "No," she whispers. "I also messed up."

She can barely choke out her words. "Please don't be mad at me. I never admitted this to you. I was too ashamed. But . . . he's actually married."

A sharp intake of breath accompanies the terrible revelation: *She's a liar.*

The very first thing April did, before we even met in person, was promise to be honest. She signed an agreement to that effect when she became Subject 5.

"You should have revealed this to me much earlier, April."

The counseling April received was predicated on the assumption that the man who spurned her after she brought him home to her bed was single. So many hours, wasted. Had she been forthcoming about the origin of their relationship, and his marital status, the situation would have been handled very differently.

April isn't the victim, as was believed only moments ago. She shares culpability.

"I didn't exactly lie to you, I just left that part out," she protests. Incredibly, April sounds defensive now. She is shunning responsibility for her actions.

There are crumbs beneath April's stool; she must have been aware that when she bit into a cracker, she scattered them. But she just left them, another one of her messes, for someone else to clean up.

My finger is placed beneath April's chin and gentle pressure is applied so that her head is lifted and eye contact established. "That was a serious omission," she is told. "I am deeply disappointed."

"I'm sorry, I'm sorry," April blurts. She begins crying again and wipes her nose on her sleeve. "I've wanted to tell you for so long . . . I didn't know how much I'd like you."

A frisson of alarm sends a jolt through my body.

Her words are not logical.

Her anticipated feelings for me should not have dictated what she revealed about the man she slept with. There should have been no connection at all.

The nickname Thomas gave me years ago, the falcon, is significant now.

You can pick up on a seemingly throwaway comment by a client and trace it all the way back to the source of why they came in for therapy, even if they don't realize it themselves, he said once, admiration ringing through his voice. *It's like you have X-ray vision. You see through people.*

A falcon homes in on the slightest undulation in a field of grass; that is the signal it is time to swoop in.

April's discordant words are the slight ripple in a verdant landscape.

She is considered more closely. What is she hiding?

If she is frightened, she will shut down. She must be coaxed into the illusion of safety.

My tone is gentle now; my utterance deliberately echoes hers: "I didn't know how much I'd like you, either."

Her wineglass is topped off again. "I'm sorry if I sounded harsh. This information just came as a surprise. Now, tell me more about him," she is encouraged.

"He was really kind and handsome," she begins. Her shoulders rise as she takes in a breath. "He had, um, red hair . . ."

The first clue emerges: She is lying about his appearance.

A common misconception, perpetuated in movies and television shows, is that individuals engaged in a falsehood reliably exhibit certain tics: They look up and to the left as they try to conjure a story. When they speak, they either avoid eye contact, or engage in it excessively. They bite their nails, or literally cover their mouths as a subconscious symptom of their unease. But these tells are not universal.

April's giveaways are more subtle. They begin with a change in her respiration. Her shoulders visibly rise, signaling that she is taking deeper inhalations, and her voice grows slightly shallow. This is because her heart rate and blood flow change; she is literally out of breath due to these physiological alterations. She has exhibited these signs before: once, when she tried to pretend her father's frequent travel and general absence from her life wasn't painful, and again when she claimed that it no longer bothered her that she had been shunned by the popular girls in high school, even though she was so traumatized by her ostracization that she swallowed pills in a suicide attempt during her junior year.

But in those cases, she was lying to herself.

Lying to me is very different.

That is what she is doing now.

Why would April fabricate details about the man's appearance after admitting so many other difficult truths?

April continues describing the man, reporting that he is of average height, and slender. She is encouraged with a gentle nod and a touch on her wrist, which has the dual purpose of confirming her pulse rate is elevated—another sign of deceit.

"I asked him to stay the night, but he couldn't, he needed to get home to his wife," April continues. She sniffs and wipes her tears with a napkin.

A terrible suspicion begins to form. The man was a therapist. He was married. April appears to need to confess this because it has been weighing on her.

But she is trying to hide his identity from me by camouflaging his appearance.

Who is he?

Then April gives a little flip of her hand, as if what she is about to say next is nothing but a simple, throwaway line: "Right before he left, he hugged me and said that I shouldn't fall for him. He told me I deserved better, and that someone I'd find the person who would be my true light."

Five seconds can change a life.

Wedding vows can be sealed with a kiss. A lottery ticket can be scratched to reveal a winning number. A Jeep can slam head-on into a tree.

A wife can discover her husband's infidelity with a disturbed young woman.

You are my true light.

That is the inscription on my wedding band, and on Thomas's. We chose it together.

Five seconds ago, those words belonged only to us. Knowing they were always pressed against my ring finger provided me with such contentment. Now they feel as if they are searing my skin, as if they could melt the white gold of my ring.

April and Thomas slept together; *he* is the mysterious married therapist.

It seems as if such a shattering revelation should create a sound. But the town house is silent.

April takes another sip of wine. She appears calmer since she has released a partial confession, an attempt to alleviate her guilt as well as serve as a secret apology for sleeping with my husband.

But she didn't just sleep with him. She grew obsessed with Thomas.

Is this why she entered my study? To learn more about Thomas's wife?

The state of deep shock can cause a person to feel numb. That is what is occurring now.

April continues chattering, seemingly unaware that everything has changed.

April knew from the moment we met that she'd slept with my husband.

Now we both do.

April and Thomas betrayed me deeply. But only one of them can be dealt with right now.

Perhaps April thinks she can just stroll out of the town house tonight and carry on with her life, leaving me with another mess—this one impossible to simply sweep up.

My husband's lips were on hers. His hands roamed over her body.

No.

"Let's take a walk," April is told. "There's a special place I want to show you." A pause, then a decision is made: "Finish your wine. I just need to run upstairs and get something first."

We arrive at the fountain in the West Village Conservatory Gardens fifteen minutes later, and sit side by side on a bench. It's a quiet place, perfect for a conversation. And that's all that occurs: a heartfelt talk.

My last words to April: "You should leave before it gets too dark."

She was still alive then; she did not ingest a single pill in my presence. She must have done so after my departure, during the two-hour window before the discovery of her body by a couple out for a moonlit stroll.

CHAPTER
SIXTY-SIX

Tuesday, December 25

WE'RE ALL FEARFUL of Dr. Shields—me, Ben, and Thomas. I'm sure April was, too.

But there's only one person who seems to unnerve Dr. Shields: Lee Carey, the private investigator. The one Mrs. Voss told me about. The one who sent a certified letter to Dr. Shields requesting April's file.

I've decided I have to tell him everything. Maybe if Dr. Shields gets tangled up in his investigation she'll stop trying to destroy my life. As bad as things are for me right now, I know they can get a lot worse if I don't find a way out.

I pull up the photograph I took of Mr. Carey's certified letter when I snuck into Dr. Shields's town house, and find his contact information.

I make myself wait until nine A.M. to call, because it's Christmas.

His phone rings four times, then the automated voice mail message plays. I feel my body sag, although I should have anticipated that he might not answer.

"This is Jessica Farris," I say. "I have some information on Katherine April Voss that I think you should know."

I hesitate. "It's urgent," I add, leaving my cell phone number.

Then I open my laptop and begin searching for a flight to Florida so

I can join my family. Not only am I desperate to see them, but I want to be out of the city when Dr. Shields and Thomas learn I've told the investigator about April being Thomas's client as well as Dr. Shields's research subject. And about the Vicodin that was likely pressed into her hand, just as it was into mine.

The earliest flight I can find to Naples leaves at six A.M. tomorrow.

I book it immediately, even though it costs over a thousand dollars.

The e-mail confirmation from Delta brings me some relief. I'll take Leo along in his carrier, and enough clothes so that I can go home to Allentown instead of returning to New York if that seems like the safer course.

I'm not even going to tell my parents I'm meeting them at the resort. I can't risk having Dr. Shields find out.

When I feel comfortable returning to New York, I'll re-create my life, like I've had to do before. The money I've earned from Dr. Shields will tide me over for a little while. And I know I can find another job; I've been working since I was a teenager.

Noah won't be as easily replaced, though.

He won't reply to my texts and phone calls, so I have to find another way to reach him. I think for a minute, then pull out my legal pad.

Our relationship began with a lie, when I gave him a fake name.

Now I need to be completely honest with him.

I don't know how Dr. Shields got to him, or what she said. So I start with the moment I picked up Taylor's phone off the chair in her apartment, and end with my realization in the Conservatory Gardens that April was Thomas's client.

I even write about how I slept with Thomas. *I know you and I had only gone out twice by then, and we weren't in a committed relationship . . . but I regret it, not only because of who Thomas turned out to be, but because of what you have come to mean to me.*

My letter ends up being six pages.

I tuck it in an envelope, then put on my coat and grab Leo's leash.

As I walk down my hallway, I notice how quiet it is. The majority of the rentals here are studios or one-bedrooms; it's not a building that draws in families. Most of my neighbors are probably away visiting relatives for the holidays.

I pause as I step out the front door, feeling disoriented.

Something is off.

The streets are completely still. The cacophony of noises has been silenced. It's as though all of New York is suspended for an intermission, waiting until the curtain is lifted and the next act can begin.

Surely I'm not the only person left in the city. But it feels that way.

I'm walking home from Noah's apartment, where I dropped off the letter with his doorman, when my cell phone rings.

It could be anyone. I don't have designated ringtones for different contacts.

But I know who it is even before I look at the screen.

Decline.

Dr. Shields's name disappears from the surface of my phone.

What can she possibly want from me on Christmas?

Ten minutes later, when I'm almost back to my apartment, it rings again.

My plan for the rest of the day is to stay inside, with my door double-locked, and pack for my trip. I'll order an Uber early tomorrow and head straight for the airport.

I'm not going to answer her calls.

I'm prepared to hit *Decline* again. But when I look at the screen this time, I see an unfamiliar number.

The private investigator, I think.

"Hello, this is Jessica Farris," I say eagerly.

In the almost imperceptible pause that follows, my heart stutters.

"Merry Christmas, Jessica."

I instinctively look around, but I don't see a soul.

I'm a block away from home. I could scoop up Leo and run, I think. I could make it.

"Dinner is at six o'clock," Dr. Shields says. "Would you like me to send a car for you?"

"*What?*" I say.

My mind is spinning, trying to keep up with her: She must have used a burner phone, maybe even the one she had me use to call Reyna and Tiffani. That's why I didn't recognize the number.

"You do recall I told your parents that you and I would celebrate the holiday together," she continues.

"I'm not coming over!" I shout. "Not tonight, and not ever again!"

I'm about to hang up when she says in her silvery voice, "But I have a gift for you, Jessica."

It's the way she says it that makes my blood freeze. I've heard this tone before. It signals that she's at her most dangerous.

"I don't want it," I say. My throat tightens. I've almost arrived at my building.

But the security door is open.

Did I remember to pull it shut tightly when I left? The sudden stillness of the city distracted me; I could have forgotten.

Is it safer inside, or out here on the street?

"Mmm, that's a shame," Dr. Shields says. She's enjoying this; she's like a cat playing with an injured mouse. "I guess if you won't come over and accept my gift, I'll have to turn it over to the police."

"What are you talking about?" I whisper.

"The digital recording," she says. "The one of you breaking into my town house."

Her words hammer into me.

Thomas must have set me up. He's the only one who knew I snuck in there.

"I just noticed my diamond necklace is missing," Dr. Shields says lightly. "Luckily, I thought to check the security camera I recently installed. I know how desperate you are for money, Jessica, but I never thought you'd resort to this."

I didn't take anything, but if she turns in that recording, I'll be arrested. No one will ever believe Thomas, her husband, gave me the key. Dr. Shields could say I watched her enter the alarm code when I was over there. She'll have the perfect cover story.

I can't afford a lawyer, and what good would it do? She'll outmaneuver me at every turn.

I was wrong; things could get worse for me. Much worse.

I know what I need to say to appease her.

I close my eyes. "What do you want me to do?" I ask hoarsely.

"Just show up for dinner at six," she says. "No need to bring anything. See you then."

I spin around, staring at the empty streets.

I'm hyperventilating.

If I'm arrested, it will not only destroy my life but my family's, too.

A gust of wind forces the security door to swing open a few inches. I jerk back instinctively.

Dr. Shields isn't here, I tell myself. She knows I'll show up at her house for dinner.

Still, I grab Leo and burst through the entryway before sprinting up the stairs.

I have my keys out long before I reach my floor. I can see my hallway is clear, but I don't stop running until I reach my apartment.

Once I'm inside, I search my entire studio before I put Leo down.

Then I collapse onto my bed, gasping.

It's a little after eleven o'clock. I have seven hours to figure out how to save myself.

But I have to acknowledge I might not be able to.

I close my eyes and imagine the faces of my parents and Becky, conjuring memories I've amassed through the years: I see my mother rushing into my elementary school nurse's office in her good blue suit, the one she wore to her secretarial job, because the nurse had called to report I was running a fever. I see my father standing in the backyard, bending his arm as he teaches me how to throw a football with a perfect spiral. I see Becky tickling the bottoms of my feet as we lay head to toe on opposite ends of the couch.

I hold on to the visions of the only people I love in this world until my breathing has finally slowed. By then, I know what I have to do.

I stand up and reach for my cell phone. My family called earlier this morning and left a message wishing me a Merry Christmas. I couldn't answer; I knew they'd hear the strain in my voice.

But now I can't put off revealing any longer what I've kept hidden for fifteen years. I might not ever get another chance to tell my parents what they deserve to know.

I dial my mother with trembling fingers.

She answers immediately: "Honey! Merry Christmas!"

My throat is so tight it's hard to speak. There's no easy way to do this—I have to plunge right in. "Can you put Dad on, too? But not Becky. I need to talk to you two alone."

I'm gripping the phone so hard my fingers hurt.

"Hold on, sweetie, he's right here." I can tell from my mother's tone that she knows something is very wrong.

Whenever I'd imagined this conversation before, I could never get past the opening sentence: *I have to tell you the truth about what happened to Becky.*

Now I hear my dad's deep, gravelly voice: "Jessie? Mom and I are both on." And I can't even say that one line.

My throat is so tight; it's like the nightmare where you can't make a single sound. I'm so dizzy I feel like I'm going to pass out.

"Jess? What is it?"

The fear in my mom's voice finally releases my words.

"I wasn't there when Becky fell. I left her alone in the house," I choke out. "I locked her in the bedroom."

There's utter silence.

It feels as if I am being broken apart; as if my secret has kept me glued together all these years and now it's shattering.

I wonder if they are picturing Becky's limp body being loaded onto the ambulance stretcher, like I am.

"I'm sorry," I say through sobs that wrack my body. "I shouldn't—"

"Jessie," my father says firmly. "No. It was *my* fault."

My head jerks up in surprise. His words don't make sense; he must have misunderstood me.

But he continues: "That window screen, it had been broken for months. I kept meaning to replace it. If I had, Becky wouldn't have been able to unlock it."

I collapse onto my bed, my head swimming. Everything has been turned upside down.

My father blamed himself, too?

"But I was supposed to watch her!" I cry out. "You trusted me!"

"Oh, Jess," my mother says. Her voice sounds oddly broken. "It was too much to leave you alone with Becky all summer. I should have found another way."

I expected their anger, or worse. Never did I imagine my parents were carrying around as much pain and guilt as me.

My mom continues: "Honey, it wasn't any one thing that caused Becky to get hurt. It wasn't anyone's fault. It was just a terrible accident."

I listen to her gentle words wash over me. I wish more than anything I could be there to squeeze in between them, like I did when I was a little girl, so they could envelop me in a hug. I feel closer to my parents than I have in years.

And yet there's an emptiness inside of me in the space that once held my secret.

I may have found my family only in time to lose them again.

"I should have told you sooner," I say. My cheeks are damp, but my tears are coming more slowly now.

"I wish you had, Jessie girl," my dad says.

Then I hear the low rumble of Leo's growl. He's staring at my door.

I'm on my feet again instantly, my senses on high alert. Even after I hear the familiar voices of the couple who live at the end of the hall, my posture remains rigid.

My mother is still talking about the need to forgive ourselves. I can picture my dad nodding and rubbing her back. There's so much more to say to them. And yet no matter how desperately I want to, I can't stay on the phone even a minute longer. Dr. Shields is expecting me soon, and I still don't know how I'm going to protect myself.

I ease off the phone after telling them again that I love them.

"Can you give Becky a big hug from me?" I say. "I promise I'll call you guys later." I hesitate before I press *End Call,* hoping it's the truth.

After I hang up, I want to curl up under the covers and absorb everything that has just happened. So much of my life has been constructed around a fallacy; my own assumptions imprisoned me.

But I can't dwell on any of that now.

Instead, I brew a cup of strong coffee and start to pace, forcing myself to focus. Maybe I should leave the city tonight. There must be a rental car place that's open on Christmas; I could start driving to Florida.

Or I could stay and try to fight Dr. Shields.

Those are the only two choices I can see.

I try to think like Dr. Shields would: logically and methodically.

Step one: I need to see the recording, because how do I even know it exists? And if it does, I'm not sure I believe that I'm identifiable on it. I wore dark clothing, and I didn't turn on any lights in the town house.

Still, it may not be safe to go to her house. I have no idea what she's planning.

Step two: I need to put safeguards into effect. I actually have a few already, I realize. Noah will know the whole story when he reads my letter. And I've called the investigator; if I get cornered, I can show Dr. Shields the number on my cell phone to prove it. I can't picture her being physically violent, but I want to be prepared just in case.

But most important, I'm finally holding some of Dr. Shields's secrets. Is that enough?

CHAPTER
SIXTY-SEVEN

Tuesday, December 25

YOU ARE PRECISELY ON TIME, Jessica.

Still, you are made to wait for a full ninety seconds after you press the town house buzzer.

When the door is opened, your appearance comes as a surprise, and not a welcome one.

By now you should be floundering, on the verge of a breakdown.

Instead, you stride into the town house looking more confident and appealing than ever.

You wear all black: Your coat hangs open to reveal a high-neck dress that hugs your curves, and leather boots that hit above your knee. They give you an extra three inches of height, so that we are eye to eye.

You take in my appearance as well: a pure white wool knit dress, with diamonds at my ears and neck.

Do you notice the symbolism? The colors we chose are yin and yang. They represent beginnings—including Christenings and weddings— and endings, such as funerals. Black and white also are opponents in a chess game. Fitting, given what will occur shortly.

Rather than wait for my signal on how to proceed, you lean forward and kiss my cheek. "Thank you for having me, Lydia," you say. "I brought you a little present."

Aren't you full of surprises? You are clearly up to something. Using my first name is a transparent attempt at a power move.

If you are trying to throw me off balance, it is going to take a lot more than this.

Your lips are curved into a smile, but they quiver ever so slightly. You are not as tough as you pretend.

It is almost disappointing how easy it is to parry with you. "Come inside."

You shrug out of your coat and hand it to me. As if you expect me to wait on you.

You are still holding the silver package tied with a red bow.

It's unclear what is going on, but you will need to be put in your place quickly.

"Let's go to the library," you are told. "Drinks and hors d'oeuvres are waiting."

"Sure," you say lightly. "You can open my gift there."

Someone who does not know you well would not see through your bluster.

You are allowed to lead the way. This will give you the illusion of control, and make what comes next that much more satisfying.

As you step over the threshold into the library, you gasp.

You are not the only one delivering surprises today, Jessica.

You stand there, blinking, as if you cannot quite believe what you see.

The man on the love seat stares back at you in stunned silence.

Did you truly expect me to celebrate the holiday without my husband, the one you claim is a hundred percent devoted to me?

"Why is *she* here?" Thomas finally blurts. He rises as his head swivels from you to me.

"Darling, didn't I mention that my subject Jessica would be joining us? The poor thing had no one to spend Christmas with. Her family left her all alone for the holiday."

His eyes are wide and round behind his glasses.

"Thomas, you know how attached I get to these young girls."

He flinches. "But you said she was harassing you!"

You recover from your shock admirably quickly, much faster than Thomas. By now you are visibly bristling, Jessica.

"Did I say that?" A pause. "Wait, is she the girl you said was follow-ing *you*?"

Thomas blanches. It is time to redirect this line of conversation.

"There must be some misunderstanding. Shall we sit?"

The small love seat and two straight-back chairs form a semicircle. The coffee table is parallel to the love seat.

Where you choose to position yourself will be informative, Jessica, just as it was on the first day you entered my office.

But you don't move; you remain just inside the room, as if you might break for the front door at any time. You jut out your chin and say, "I don't believe you."

"I beg your pardon?"

"There's no recording of me in this house."

You can be so predictable, Jessica.

The room is crossed and the slim silver laptop resting on the piano is opened. With a touch of a button, the digital recording plays.

The camera, which was purchased and hidden in the foyer at the same time the new deadbolt was installed, captured you entering the house and bending down to remove your shoes. The images are shadowy, but your distinctive hair is immediately recognizable.

The laptop is abruptly closed.

"Satisfied?"

You shoot an accusing look at Thomas, who shakes his head almost imperceptibly.

You hesitate a moment, no doubt running through mental calcula-tions before accepting that there is no other option available to you, then your shoulders slump. You skirt the coffee table and choose the chair farthest away from my husband. You place the gift on the floor by your feet.

There could be many reasons for your seat selection. One is that if you ever saw Thomas as an ally, you do not now.

Thomas already has a Scotch on the coffee table in front of him, and the bottle of white Burgundy rests in an ice bucket. It is retrieved and two glasses poured.

The wine is crisp and refreshing, and the heavy crystal glass feels satisfying in my hand.

"What do you want from me?" This is a question that could be asked in many different ways, from belligerence to obsequiousness. Your tone contains pure resignation.

Your body language is protective now; your arms are folded across your lap.

"I want to know the truth," you are told. "What is the true nature of your relationship with my husband?"

Your eyes flit to the laptop again. "You know everything. He cheated on you and you set me up to see if he'd do it again."

Thomas recoils and glares at you.

If you and Thomas were a couple seeking marital therapy in my office on Sixty-second Street, establishing harmony would be the goal. Accusations would be discouraged; confrontation expertly diffused.

Here the opposite is sought. Your division is necessary to offset any collusion on your parts.

The fire crackles in the hearth. You and Thomas both flinch at the sharp, sudden sound.

"Mini-quiche?" The hors d'oeuvres platter is offered to you, but you shake your head without even looking at it.

"Thomas?" He reaches over and pops one in his mouth so quickly the gesture seems automatic. A napkin is passed to him.

He takes a big sip of Scotch. You abstain from drinking anything. Perhaps you want to keep your wits about you.

Now that the opening tone has been set, it is time for the evening to truly begin.

And just as in the survey that brought us together, it starts with a morality query.

"Let's backtrack. I have a question for the two of you."

Your head jerks up, as does Thomas's. You are both on high alert, wary of what might come next.

"Imagine you are a security guard stationed at a podium in the lobby of a small professional building. A woman you recognize because her husband has leased an office there asks you to hail a cab because she is feeling ill. Would you leave your post in violation of your duties to help her?"

You look utterly bewildered, Jessica. As you should; what could this possibly have to do with you? But the faintest hint of frown appears on Thomas's brow.

"I guess so," you finally say.

"Well?" Thomas is prompted.

"I suppose . . . I would also leave and help her," he says.

"How interesting! That's exactly what the security guard in *your* building did."

He inches closer to the armrest. Farther away from me.

He wipes his palms on his khakis as he follows my gaze to the piece of paper tucked partially beneath the laptop.

Two days after April's death, this particular sheet of paper was removed from the visitor's log in the lobby of Thomas's office, the one the security guard maintains.

This was done, of course, without Thomas's knowledge.

Thomas's professional reputation would be destroyed if news got out that he had slept with a young woman who had come to him for a psychological consult. He might lose his license.

It was expected that after Thomas's one-night stand with April, he would swiftly expunge evidence revealing the origin of their connection. Any electronic records, such as the appointment in his iCalendar and notes on his computer from the session, would be deleted.

But attending to every last detail is not one of Thomas's strengths.

He is so accustomed to passing by the security guard's station that he might have forgotten all guests must sign in to gain admittance to the building. April's full name and the time of her visit would be recorded in the thick, leather-bound log.

The general time frame of April's consult could be pinpointed: She met Thomas shortly before she joined my study.

The sheet containing her neat, rounded signature was torn out and tucked into my purse long before a cab could be hailed by the guard— but then, 5:30 P.M. on a rainy weekday is always a tricky time to find a taxi.

Now that piece of paper is retrieved from beneath the laptop and passed to Thomas.

"Here's the page from the visitor's log on the day Katherine April

Voss had her consult with you," Thomas is told. "A few weeks before you slept together at her apartment."

He stares at it for a long moment. It's as though he can't quite process what he is seeing.

Then he bends over and dry heaves into his napkin.

Thomas is not always effective at managing his stress.

His eyes shoot up to find mine. "Oh my God, Lydia, no, it's not what you think—"

"I know exactly what it is, Thomas."

When Thomas raises a shaking hand to lift his glass of Scotch, the gauntlet is laid down.

"I have something each of you desperately needs," you and Thomas are told. "The digital tape and the visitor's log. If those items fell into the hands of authorities, well, it would be difficult to explain. But there's no reason for that to happen. You can both have what you desire. All you have to do is tell me the truth. Shall we begin?"

CHAPTER
SIXTY-EIGHT

Tuesday, December 25

THE INSTANT I SEE THOMAS in Dr. Shields's library, I know my plan won't work.

She is a step ahead of me, again.

After she called, I thought about going to the police, but I worried the information I could give them wouldn't be enough. She'd probably concoct some compelling story about me being a disturbed girl who'd stolen her jewelry; she'd find a way to flip things so that *I* was the one who got arrested. So in the hours before I responded to her summons, I found an electronics store that was open on Christmas Day and bought a slim black watch that could record conversations.

"Last-minute present?" the clerk asked.

"Sort of," I answered as I hurried out the door.

I was bringing Dr. Shields a gift, but not this one. The present I was assembling was far more personal and consequential.

The watch was intended to record her words when she opened her gift. I had Dr. Shields to thank for the idea: She was the one who illustrated the strategy of having a secret witness to a conversation when she had me visit Reyna and Tiffani.

I envisioned her staring down at her present, stunned, as I hit her with the second part of my one-two punch: *I know you gave April the Vicodin she overdosed on.*

She would be dangerously mad. But she wouldn't be able to touch me, because I'd also tell her about how I'd set up e-mails on my computer addressed to Thomas, Mrs. Voss, Ben Quick—*and* the private investigator—with the evidence I've compiled, including a photograph of the pill Dr. Shields gave me. *I wrote that I was on my way to see you. The e-mails are scheduled to be automatically sent tonight unless I get home and delete them,* I'd planned to say. *But if you don't hand over what you have on me, then I won't hand over what I have on you.*

That last part would be a lie because I still intended to find a way to turn in Dr. Shields. But if I could shock her into saying something incriminating on my secret recording, I'd at least have evidence to offset whatever story she concocted.

Now, as I sit in the library watching Thomas wipe his mouth with a napkin, I know I need to figure out a new strategy—fast.

I can't believe Dr. Shields just told Thomas she knows he slept with April and that April was his client.

Thomas suddenly looks like a completely different man than the confident, take-charge guy who pulled off his jacket and covered the elderly woman who was hit by a taxi outside the museum.

My mind swirls as I try to reframe everything I thought I knew. I was right; April went to Thomas for therapy. But Dr. Shields doesn't realize I'm aware of this, or that I already knew Thomas slept with April. It's an explosive secret, one that could cost them everything. Why was she so cavalier about stating that information in front of me?

All of Dr. Shields's moves are premeditated. So this wasn't a slip. It was deliberate.

My stomach clenches like a fist as I realize she must already be certain that I'm not going to tell anyone.

A secret is only a secret if one person holds it.

What is she going to do to ensure I won't reveal it?

My mind flashes to a vision of April, slumped on the park bench.

I shrink back against my seat as my entire body begins to tremble. My mouth is so dry I can't swallow.

Dr. Shields tucks back a stray tendril of hair and I see the vein on her temple throb, a blue-green blemish on an otherwise-perfect sheet of marble.

The tasteful platter of hors d'oeuvres, the crackling fire, the elegant library with leather-bound volumes lining a shelf—how could I ever have thought bad things couldn't happen in such an enviable setting?

Focus, I instruct myself.

Dr. Shields isn't a physically violent person, I tell myself again. Her sharpest weapon is her mind. She wields it mercilessly. If I succumb to panic, I'll lose.

I force myself to stare at her as Thomas gasps, "Lydia, I'm sorry. I shouldn't have—"

She interrupts him: "I'm sorry, too, Thomas."

Then I hear it: the disconnect between her words and her tone.

She doesn't sound furious or cuttingly sarcastic, as a wife should in this moment.

Compassion fills her voice instead. It's as though she believes she and Thomas are aligned together against the adulterous affair; as though they are both innocent parties.

As my gaze seesaws between them, it hits me why Dr. Shields hasn't simply left Thomas: She can't.

Because she's desperately in love with him.

She didn't give April the pills only because she was jealous and furious. She also did it to protect Thomas, so that April could never reveal she'd been his client. I told Dr. Shields that I'd seen what love looks like in other people. And now I realize it's true: I see it on her face whenever she talks about or gazes at her husband. Even now.

But her love for Thomas is as twisted as everything else about her: It's all-consuming and toxic and dangerous.

Dr. Shields replaces the visitor's log under the laptop. Then she takes a seat on the chair opposite me. "Shall we begin?"

She appears completely composed, like a professor in front of an audience, conducting a lecture.

She spreads out her hands. "Now, I'll ask my question again, this time to both of you: Do either of you have anything to confess about the true nature of your relationship?"

Thomas starts to say something, but Dr. Shields cuts him off immediately: "Hold on. Think very carefully before you reply. So that you don't influence one another, I'll speak to each of you privately. You have two minutes to decide how you are going to answer." She glances down at her watch and I push up my sleeve to check mine.

"Your time starts now," Dr. Shields says.

I look at Thomas, trying to read what he's going to say, but his eyes are tightly shut. He looks so awful I wonder if he's going to get sick again.

I feel nauseated, too, but my mind is leaping through all the scenarios and the possible repercussions.

We could both confess the truth: We did sleep together.

We could both lie: We could stick to our script.

I could lie and Thomas could divulge the truth: He might sell me out to get the visitor's log.

Thomas could lie and I could disclose the truth: I could blame it on him, say he pursued me. If I do this, Dr. Shields claims she'll give me the digital recording. But will it really end then?

No, I realize. There is no right move.

Dr. Shields takes a sip of wine, her eyes staring at me from over the rim of the glass.

The Prisoner's Dilemma, I think. That's what she's re-creating. I read about it once in an article someone posted on Facebook. It's a common tactic in which suspects are placed in solitary confinement and given incentives to see if they'll rat each other out.

Dr. Shields sets down her wineglass, the crystal making a delicate chime as it touches the coaster.

There can't be much time left.

Images collide in my brain: Dr. Shields alone in the French restaurant at a table for two. I see her stroking the crest of the falcon, and feel the warm press of cashmere around my shoulders as I sobbed in her office. A line from her notes in her precise, graceful script: *You could become a pioneer in the field of psychological research.*

I tried to use the lessons she taught me to trap her tonight. She out-maneuvered me even before I began.

But now I realize it isn't over, because I've finally pinpointed her weak spot: Thomas. He's the key to undoing her.

My breathing is shallow; a rushing noise fills my head.

I need to think several steps ahead, like she always does. I know that no matter how we answer, Dr. Shields is never going to turn him in; she needs to find a way to blame this on me. Just like she probably did with April to justify giving her the Vicodin.

I was the one under scrutiny by Dr. Shields from the moment I entered her study, but I've been scrutinizing her all along, too. I know so much more about her than I realized—everything from the way she walks down a street to what she keeps in her refrigerator and, more important, how her mind operates.

Will it be enough?

"Time's up," Dr. Shields announces. "Thomas, would you join me in the dining room?"

I watch the two of them disappear from view and my mind flashes through all of the variables again from Thomas's perspective. I think about what's at stake for him: The tabloids would pounce on a story about a handsome therapist and his affair with a wealthy, damaged young woman who committed suicide. He'd probably lose his license, and the Voss family might sue him.

I know quite a bit about Thomas, too. I think back to our encounters, from the museum to the bars to my apartment to the Conservatory Gardens. And the final one, in his office.

With a sudden, swift certainty, I know how he is going to answer.

Dr. Shields comes back into the room less than a minute later, alone. I can't read what might have just transpired from her expression; it's as if she is wearing a mask.

She sits down on the end of the love seat closest to my chair. She reaches out and lightly touches my bare leg where there's a gap between my boots and the hem of my dress. I force myself to remain still, even though I want to recoil.

"Jessica, do you have anything to confess about the true nature of your relationship with my husband?"

I look directly at her. "You're right. I wasn't completely honest before. We slept together." I was worried my voice would waver, but it doesn't; it sounds assured. "It happened before I knew he was your husband."

Something changes in her eyes. The light blue of her irises appears to darken. She remains perfectly still for a moment. Then she nods crisply, as if this has confirmed something she already knows. She rises and smooths her dress before heading back toward the dining room.

"Thomas, can you join us?" she calls.

He walks into the room slowly.

"Will you please share with Jessica what you just told me?" she prompts him.

I clasp my hands firmly on my lap and try to smile, but my jaw is clenched too tightly. I can still feel the icy touch of her fingers on my leg.

Thomas drags his eyes to mine. In them I see pure defeat.

"I told her nothing happened between us," Thomas says dully.

He lied.

I guessed correctly.

He didn't do it to protect himself, he did it to protect me. He is giving up the opportunity to obtain the visitor's log.

Dr. Shields is obsessed with morality, with telling the truth. But Thomas understands the nuances of ethical choices; he lied because he thought it would save me, even if it meant sacrificing himself. For all his failings, there is a core of goodness in him. Perhaps that's one of the reasons why she loves him so desperately.

I can feel Dr. Shields's anger; it's like a swelling, red force in the room, pressing in on me, stealing away my breath.

The silence hangs heavily for a moment, then Dr. Shields says, "Jessica, can you repeat what you told me?"

I swallow hard. "I said we slept together."

Thomas cringes.

"Now, one of you is clearly lying," Dr. Shields says. She folds her arms across her chest. "And it seems pretty obvious it's you, Thomas, since Jessica has nothing to gain from a false confession."

I nod, because she's right.

What she does next is going to reveal if the risk I took paid off.

Dr. Shields walks over to the piano and pats the laptop. "Jessica, I'll be happy to give you the recording. All you need to do is return what you took from me first." Her gaze flits to Thomas and I know exactly what she means. She isn't talking about a necklace.

She's re-creating what happened with Gene French in her own warped way; she's using my secrets to inflict maximum pain.

"I can't," I say. "I never took any of your jewelry and you know that."

"Jessica, I'm disappointed in you," she says.

Thomas takes a step deeper into the room. Closer to me.

"Lydia, let the poor girl go. She told you the truth; I was the one who lied. Now this is between the two of us."

Dr. Shields shakes her head sorrowfully. "That necklace is irreplaceable."

"Lydia, I'm sure she didn't take it," Thomas says.

This is what I gambled on by telling the truth. I need him to see that despite the fact that I've followed her rules, she's going to find an excuse to destroy me.

She gives me a gentle smile. "I will wait until tomorrow morning to alert the authorities, since it is Christmas." She pauses. "This will also give you some time to talk to your parents first. After all, once they know the truth about Becky, they'll understand why you were so desperate for money. Because of your guilt."

This is exactly how she did it to April, I think as I drop my head into my hands and feel my shoulders shake. She coaxed out April's secrets and used them like knives against her. She made April feel completely hopeless, as though everything she loved had been taken away. As though life was no longer worth living. Then she gave her the pills.

Dr. Shields believes she has stripped away everything from me, too: My job. Noah. My freedom. My family.

She's giving me the night alone because she wants me to follow April's path.

I wait a bit longer.

Then I lift my head.

Nothing in the room has changed: Dr. Shields stands by the piano, Thomas hovers behind the chair opposite me, and the platter of food rests on the table.

I look at Dr. Shields.

"Okay," I say, making sure my voice sounds meek. "But before I go, can I ask you a question?"

She nods.

"Is it ethical for a psychiatrist to dispense Vicodin to a client without giving her a prescription?" I ask.

Dr. Shields smiles. I know she's thinking about the pill she gave me.

"If a friend is going through a difficult time, it isn't unheard of to offer a single dose," she says. "Of course, I would never officially condone it."

I lean back and cross my legs. Thomas is staring at me quizzically, probably wondering why I seem so composed all of a sudden.

"Yes, well, you gave Subject 5 far more than a single dose," I say, locking eyes with her. "You gave April enough to kill her."

Thomas inhales sharply. He moves another step closer to me; he's still trying to protect me.

Dr. Shields is frozen; she doesn't even appear to be breathing. But I can sense her brain whirling, composing a new narrative to offset my accusation.

Finally, she walks across the room to take the chair opposite mine.

"Jessica, I have no idea what you are talking about," she says. "You think I wrote April a prescription for Vicodin?"

"You're a psychiatrist—you're allowed to prescribe medicine," I challenge.

"True, but there would be a record if I ever wrote her a prescription," she says, spreading out her hands. "And I didn't."

"I can ask Mrs. Voss," I say.

"Go right ahead," Dr. Shields responds.

"I know you gave her the pills," I say. But I'm losing ground; she's blocking everything I throw at her.

Thomas reaches up and touches his left shoulder. The gesture appears reflexive.

"How could I give Vicodin to someone else, when I've never even taken it myself?" Dr. Shields asks in a reasonable tone, the one that tried to convince me she hadn't gotten to Noah or made me lose my job.

My watch is recording everything, but Dr. Shields hasn't incriminated herself. Worse, I've enraged her. I can see it in the glint in her narrowed eyes; I can hear it in her steely tone.

I'm losing.

"You've never taken it," Thomas says. He's speaking in an odd-sounding monotone.

We both turn to look at him. His hand is still on his left shoulder— the one with the recent scar from his rotator cuff surgery. "But I have."

The slight smile drops from her face.

"Thomas," Dr. Shields whispers.

"I didn't need more than a few," he says slowly. "But I never threw out the rest of the bottle. April was in this house the night she died, Lydia. You told me she came to see you and that she was upset. Did you give her my old pills?"

He turns, as if he is going upstairs to check.

"Wait," Dr. Shields says.

She remains perfectly still for a moment, then her face crumbles. "I did it for you!" she cries.

Thomas staggers, then collapses onto the love seat. "You killed her? Because I slept with her?"

"Thomas, I didn't do anything wrong. April made her own choice to swallow those pills!"

"Is it murder if you only provide the weapon?" I ask.

They both whip around to face me. For once, Dr. Shields doesn't have a response.

"But you did more than that," I continue. "What did you say to April to drive her to the edge? You must have known she was suicidal in high school."

"What did you say to her?" Thomas echoes hoarsely.

"I told her that my husband had a one-night stand and he regretted it!" The words burst out of Dr. Shields in a torrent. "I said he called her a nothing. He said it was the biggest mistake of his life and he would give anything to undo it."

Thomas shakes his head, looking dazed.

"Don't you see?" Dr. Shields pleads. "She was such a foolish girl! She would have told somebody about you!"

"You knew how fragile she was," Thomas says. "How could you?"

Dr. Shields's face tightens. "She was disposable. Even her own father didn't want to be around her." Dr. Shields reaches out for Thomas, but he roughly pulls his hand away. "We can say April took those pills from our medicine cabinet; we knew nothing about it."

"I don't think the police will see it that way," I say.

Dr. Shields doesn't even look at me; she's staring at Thomas beseechingly.

"The authorities won't believe Jessica. She broke in here, she stalked you, she was obsessed with me," she says. "Did you know she was accused of stealing before? There's a respected director who fired her because of it. She sleeps around and she lies to her family. Jessica is a very disturbed young woman. I have all her survey answers to prove it."

He briefly slides down his glasses and rubs the bridge of his nose.

When he speaks, his voice booms through the room: "No."

Thomas finally has the courage to confront Dr. Shields directly. He is no longer trying to escape from her with fake texts and fabricated stories.

"If our stories match, we'll be okay," she says desperately. "It's two respected professionals against one unstable girl."

He looks at her for a long moment.

"Thomas, I love you so much," she whispers. "Please."

Her eyes are glassy with tears.

He shakes his head and stands up. "Jess, I'm going to make sure you get safely home," he says.

"Lydia, I'll come back tomorrow morning. We can call the police together then." He pauses. "If you bring up the video, I'll tell them I gave Jess the key to our house and she was picking up something for me."

I stand, leaving the present by my chair, at the precise moment Dr. Shields crumples to the floor.

She is splayed on the carpet, looking up at Thomas, the white fabric of her dress bunched around her legs. Tears stained black by mascara run down her cheeks.

"Good-bye, Lydia," I say.

Then I turn and walk out of the room.

CHAPTER
SIXTY-NINE

Tuesday, December 25

OF ALL THE LOSSES incurred tonight, the only one that matters is Thomas.

Your job was to test him so that he could be returned to me. Instead, you took him away forever.

Everything is gone now.

Except for the present you left behind.

It is the size of a book, but too thin and light to contain one. The shiny silver wrapping paper is like a carnival mirror, contorting my reflection before tossing it back at me.

A single tug unfurls the red bow. The paper yields to reveal a flat white box.

Inside is a framed photograph.

Even when pain seems to have crescendoed, there can be yet another peak. Seeing this picture pushes me onto that jagged edge.

Thomas is asleep on his stomach, a floral comforter rumpled around his bare torso. But the setting is unfamiliar; he is not in the bed we shared.

Was he in yours, Jessica? Or April's? Or yet another woman's?

It no longer matters.

Whenever insomnia gripped me throughout our marriage, his

presence always provided comfort. His solid warmth and steady exhalations were a balm to the ceaseless churning of my mind. He never knew how many times I whispered, "I love you," as he slept on peacefully.

A final question: *If you truly loved someone, would you sacrifice your life for theirs?*

The answer is simple.

A last note is recorded in the legal pad: a full, detailed, and accurate confession. All of the questions Mrs. Voss sought will finally be answered. Thomas's involvement with April is left out of the note. It may be enough to save him.

The sheets from the legal pad are left on the table in the foyer, where they will be easily found.

Not too many blocks away from here is a pharmacy that remains open twenty-four hours a day. Even on Christmas.

Thomas's prescription pad is retrieved from his top dresser drawer; he kept one at home in case of an after-hours patient emergency.

It is completely dark out now; the endless sky is devoid of a single star.

Without Thomas, there will be no light tomorrow.

I write myself a prescription for thirty Vicodin pills, more than enough.

EPILOGUE

Friday, March 30

IT SEEMS AS THOUGH the young woman staring back at me in the reflective glass should look different.

But my curly hair, black leather jacket, and heavy makeup case haven't changed over the course of the last few months.

Dr. Shields would probably say you can't judge someone's internal state by their external attributes, and I know she's right.

True change isn't always visible, even when it happens to you.

I shift my makeup case into my left hand, even though my arm doesn't ache like it used to when I worked for BeautyBuzz. Now that I've been hired as a makeup artist for an off-off-Broadway show, I only have to lug it to and from the theater on West Forty-third Street. Lizzie was the one who got me the interview for it; she's the assistant costume designer.

It isn't a Gene French production. His career is over. I was never forced to make the moral choice of whether to tell his wife that he was a predator. Katrina and two other women went to the media with their own stories of how he'd abused them. His downfall was swift; behavior like his is no longer allowed to slide by without repercussions.

I think on some level I knew why Katrina was reaching out to me, but I wasn't ready to stand up to Gene then. There's not much I'm grateful to Dr. Shields for, but at least because of her, I'll never be anyone's prey again.

I lean closer to the glass, pressing my forehead against the cool window, so I can see inside.

Breakfast All Day is crowded, with nearly every red-leather upholstered booth and counter stool claimed, even though it's nearly midnight. Turns out Noah was right; a lot of people crave French toast and eggs Benedict after a Friday evening out.

I don't see Noah, but I picture him in the kitchen, measuring almond extract into a mixing bowl, a dish towel tucked into his waistband.

I close my eyes and silently wish him well, then keep walking.

He called me the day after Christmas, when I was in Florida with my family. I hadn't learned about Dr. Shields's suicide yet; Thomas didn't give me the news until later that night.

We talked for nearly two hours. Noah confirmed that Dr. Shields had gotten to him outside of Thomas's office. I answered all of his questions, too. Although Noah believed me, I knew even before we hung up that I wouldn't hear from him again. Who could blame him? It wasn't just that I'd slept with Thomas; too much had happened for us to have a fresh start.

Still, I find myself thinking about Noah more than I'd expected.

Guys like him don't come around all that often, but maybe I'll get lucky again someday.

In the meantime, I'm making my own luck.

I glance down at the time on my phone. It's 11:58 P.M. on the last Friday of the month, which means the payment should have landed in my checking account by now.

Money is vitally important to you. It appears to be an underpinning of your ethical code, Dr. Shields wrote about me during my first computerized session. *When money and morality intersect, the results can illuminate intriguing truths about human character.*

It was easy for Dr. Shields to sit back and form judgments and assumptions about my relationship with money. She had more than enough; she lived in a multimillion-dollar town house and wore expensive designer clothes and grew up on an estate in Litchfield. I saw a picture of her on a horse in her library; she drank fine wine and described her father as "influential," which is code for wealthy.

The academic exercise she engaged in was completely removed from the reality of an existence spent living from paycheck to paycheck, where a veterinarian's bill or an unexpected rent hike can cause a financial domino effect, threatening to demolish the life you've built.

People are motivated to break their moral compasses for a variety of primal reasons—survival, hate, love, envy, passion, Dr. Shields wrote in her notes. *And money.*

Her study has been terminated. There will be no more experiments. The file on Subject 52 is complete.

Yet I still feel linked to Dr. Shields.

She seemed omniscient; as if she could see inside of me. She appeared to know things before I told her, and she drew thoughts and feelings out of me that I didn't realize I possessed. Maybe that's why I keep trying to envision how she would record my final encounter with Thomas, the one that occurred several weeks after her fatal overdose.

Sometimes at night, when my eyes are closed and Leo is snuggled up next to me, I can almost picture her graceful cursive, forming the sentences on her yellow legal pad, as her silvery voice floods my head, flowing along with the arcs and loops of the words.

If she had been alive to create a record of that meeting, here's what I imagine her notes might contain:

Wednesday, January 17

You call Thomas at 4:55 P.M.

"Can we meet for a drink?" you ask.

He agrees swiftly. Perhaps he is eager to talk about all that transpired with the only other person who knows the real story.

He arrives at O'Malley's Pub in jeans and a blazer and orders a Scotch. You are already seated at a small wooden table with a Sam Adams in front of you.

"How are you holding up?" you ask as he eases into his chair.

He exhales and shakes his head. He looks as if he has lost weight, and his glasses don't hide the dark crescents under his eyes. "I don't know, Jess. It's still hard to believe all of it."

He was the one to summon the police to the town house after finding the written confession in the foyer.

"Yeah, for me, too," you say. *You take a sip of beer and let the silence stretch out.* "Since I lost my job, I've got all this time to think."

Thomas frowns. Perhaps he is remembering sitting across from you in his office, hearing you whisper, She got me fired.

"I'm really sorry about that," *he finally says.*

You reach into your purse for a pale pink document and put it on the table, covering it with your palm as you flatten out the creases.

His eyes land on it. He hasn't seen it before; there is no reason he would have.

"I'm not so worried about a job for myself," *you say.* "I'll find one. The thing is, Dr. Shields promised to help my father get one, too. My family has a lot of medical expenses."

You smooth the paper again, and slide your hand down so the sketch of the dove at the top is visible.

Thomas glances at it once more and fiddles with the thin cocktail straw bobbing in his Scotch.

He seems to be catching on that this isn't simply a social encounter.

"Is there anything I can do to help?" *he asks.*

"I'd appreciate any suggestions you have," *you reply as you move your hand down another few inches. Now Katherine April Voss's name is visible in a pretty font.*

Thomas flinches and rears back in his seat.

He lifts his eyes to meet yours, then he takes a big sip of his drink.

Your hand moves again. Now the quote is revealed: And in the end, the love you take is equal to the love you make.

"April was asking her mother about this line shortly before she died," *you say. You let that sink in.* "I guess she'd seen it somewhere. Maybe it's the kind of thing she'd read on a coffee mug."

His face is now pale. "I thought we could trust each other, Jess," *he whispers.* "Can't we?"

You shrug. "A friend once told me that if you have to ask if you can trust someone, you already know the answer."

"What does that mean?" *he asks. His voice is wary.*

"I just want what's due to me," *you say.* "After everything I went through."

He drains his Scotch, the ice clinking in the glass.

"How about I help you with your rent, until you're back on your feet?" He looks at you hopefully.

You smile and shake your head slightly.

"I appreciate your offer, but I had something more substantial in mind," you say. "I'm sure Dr. Shields would agree that I deserve it."

You turn over the funeral program. There is a dollar sign with a number written next to it on the back.

Thomas gasps. "Are you kidding?"

Thomas, of course, is the sole recipient of his wife's estate, including the multimillion-dollar town house. He has his job, his license, and his reputation intact. It would be surprising if you, with your inquisitive and industrious nature, had not already confirmed this. And you believe it is a small price for him to pay for your family's well-being.

"I'm happy to receive it in monthly installments," you say, pushing the program toward him.

Thomas is slumped in his chair. He has already conceded defeat.

You lean forward until only a few inches separate your faces. "After all, trust can be bought."

You leave almost immediately, pushing through the door and striding onto the sidewalk. Within moments, you are enveloped by the crowd, just another anonymous girl in the city.

Perhaps you are confident in your decision.

Or maybe an insistent question will haunt you:

Was it all worth it, Jessica?

ACKNOWLEDGMENTS

From Greer and Sarah:

Our thanks go first to Jen Enderlin (also known as "Saint Jenderlin"), our brilliant, kind, and all-around superb editor and publisher at St. Martin's Press. Her vision, support, and enthusiasm for us and this novel makes us so grateful every day.

Katie Bassel, our publicist, works tirelessly on behalf of our books—and does so with good humor and good fashion!

The dream team beside these two amazing women nurture our novels through the publication process with great care, energy, and boundless creativity. We are so lucky to have them working on behalf of our books. Thank you to Rachel Diebel, Marta Fleming, Olga Grlic, Tracey Guest, Jordan Hanley, Brant Janeway (a special shout-out to you for coming up with the book's title!), Kim Ludlam, Erica Martirano, Kerry Nordling, Gisela Ramos, Sally Richardson, Lisa Senz, Michael Storrings, Dori Weintraub, and Laura Wilson.

Thanks also to our wildly generous and supportive Mama-bear agent, Victoria Sanders, as well as her wonderful crew: Bernadette Baker-Baughman, Jessica Spivey, and Diane Dickensheid at Victoria Sanders and Associates.

To Benee Knauer: Your encouragement, calm manner, and story smarts once again helped us find the right path as we set out to write this novel.

Our gratitude to all of our foreign publishers who have shared our work around the globe, including Wayne Brookes at Pan Macmillan UK, whose e-mails always make us laugh—and make us feel like we are supermodels instead of writers!

Our deepest appreciation to Shari Smiley and Ellen Goldsmith-Vein at the Gotham Group for their passionate work to bring our novels to the screen. And to Holly Bario at Amblin Entertainment and Carolyn Newman at eOne Entertainment for making our experiences in Hollywood so exciting.

And last but never least, to our readers: We love connecting with you, so please find us on Facebook, Twitter, and Instagram. And to sign up for our very occasional newsletters, please visit our websites: www.greerhendricks.com and www.sarahpekkanen.com We'd love to stay in touch with you.

From Greer:

For someone who spends her days writing, I find it almost impossible to put into words how much a part of my life Sarah Pekkanen has become. Co-author, business partner, beloved friend, cheerleader, counselor—the list could go on and on. You truly have become the sister I never had. Thank you for everything.

I am deeply grateful to my friends both in and outside the publishing industry (you know who you are!), especially my early readers, Marla Goodman, Vicki Foley, and Alison Stong. And my running partners, Karen Gordon and Gillian Blake, who listen to it all as we track our mileage.

Much appreciation to this very special support team: Katharina Anger, Melissa Goldstein, Danny Thompson, and Ellen Katz Westrich.

Extra-special thanks to my family: the Hendricks, Alloccas, and Kessels, especially those who commented on early drafts: Julie and Robert (best brother ever!).

Elaine and Mark Kessel, aka Mom and Dad, this one belongs to you. Thank you for encouraging my love of reading, writing, and psychology—and for always telling me I deserve it.

Rocky and Cooper, for keeping me company (although sometimes a bit too much company).

Paige, you have taught me so much about courage and self-awareness. You impress and inspire me every day.

Alex, the joy you provide me is boundless. You have the biggest heart and no one makes me laugh more.

And finally to John, who not only listened to me brainstorm ideas over boozy brunches and long dog walks, but also provided fantastic notes. You make everything possible and make it all worthwhile. Twenty years and counting . . .

From Sarah:

I can't imagine sharing this publishing journey with anyone other than Greer Hendricks. Your deep and constant support is a layer of bedrock in my life. Your funny texts always make me laugh. Your emotional intelligence and tireless drive to make every page we write the best it can be inspires me. G, we are truly better together!

Thanks to Kathy Nolan for her creative help on my website; to the Street Team and my Facebook friends and readers for their support; and to the booksellers, librarians, and book bloggers who have helped our novels find their way into the hands of readers.

I'm always grateful to Sharon Sellers for helping me clear my mind in the gym, and to my fantastic hometown Gaithersburg Book Festival crew (with a special shout-out to Jud Ashman). My thanks also to Glenn Reynolds for being a wonderful co-parent.

Bella, one of the great dogs, sat patiently by my side as I wrote.

Love always to my parents, John and Lynn Pekkanen. Dad, you taught me how to write, and Mom, you taught me how to dream big. You two are the best. And to the rest of the strong, funny Pekkanen crew: Robert, Saadia, Sophia, Ben, Tammi, and little Billy. Thank you for always being there.

Roger Aarons lived through every part of this book with me, from reading early drafts (and catching even the most minuscule of typos), to cooking for me like Noah did for Jess, to being the best plus-one a girl could ask for at publishing events. Roger, I'm so grateful you came into this chapter of my life.

And to my three amazing sons: Jackson, Will, and Dylan. You fill me with so much love and pride every single day.

OUT NOW

The Wife Between Us

By Greer Hendricks and Sarah Pekkanen

When you read this book, you will make many assumptions.
It's about a jealous wife, obsessed with her replacement.
It's about a younger woman set to marry the man she loves.
The first wife seems like a disaster; her replacement is the perfect woman.
You will assume you know the motives, the history, the
anatomy of the relationships.

You will be wrong.

★

'Fans of *Gone Girl* and *The Girl on the Train* will adore this
classy domestic noir set in New York' *Daily Express*

'With shocking twists, this intricate thriller proves all is not
what it seems for the discarded first wife and the woman about
to marry her ex. Addictive' *Woman & Home*